Praise for *The End of Vandalism*

'A major figure in American literature, author of a string of novels without a dud in the bunch ... Drury gives us the wondrous and engaging stuff of real storytelling'
DANIEL HANDLER, NEW YORK TIMES

'Brilliant, wonderfully funny ... It's hard to think of any novel – let alone a first novel – in which you can hear the people so well. This is indeed deadpan humor, and Tom Drury is its master.'
ANNIE DILLARD

'What excellent champagne Tom Drury is. He makes you feel smarter and funnier than you have any real right to. Under his spell you can appreciate both the scary emptiness and the scary fullness of your life, and when you've finished the bottle you wish you'd had more. Drury is a big-time American talent.'
JONATHAN FRANZEN

'Some writers are good at drawing a literary curtain over reality, and splashing upon the curtain all the colours of their fancies. And then there are the writers who raise the veil and lead us to see for the first time. Tom Drury belongs to the latter, and is a rare master at the art of seeing.'
YIYUN LI

'Here's an author who sees and hears what others either miss or fail to note the significance of.'
RICHARD RUSSO

'The always fresh perspective of this one-of-a-kind writer will have you responding like his character who "laughed with surprise in her heart".'
KIRKUS REVIEWS

'Although Drury has been compared to Garrison Keillor and Raymond Carver, he's really in a class of one.'
LOS ANGELES TIMES

'Drury's fiction is chockablock with ... tiny epics unfurling and resolving in quick, universally funny vignette'
BOSTON GLOBE

'Extraordinary ... This is a quiet book that grows in emotional resonance.'
PUBLISHERS WEEKLY on *The End of Vandalism* (A Best Book of the Year)

'An endlessly entertaining tapestry of human comedy and small-town living.'
BOOKLIST on *The End of Vandalism*

'Miraculous ... reads like life itself ... Drury builds a world in rural Iowa where we move in and settle and it feels so real, so plain, yet so absorbing it might be a memory of home.'
MEN'S JOURNAL on *The End of Vandalism*

'Remarkable ... Every so often a debut novel appears that simply stuns you with the elegance and beauty of its writing ... A+'
ENTERTAINMENT WEEKLY on *The End of Vandalism*

'Breathtaking ... A remarkable achievement ... At once funny, sad, and touching ... Drury's alchemy draws on the best of Keillor and Carver to produce a new alloy.'
NEW YORK NEWSDAY on *The End of Vandalism*

The End of
Vandalism

The End of Vandalism

Tom Drury

This paperback edition pubished in Great Britain in 2015 by:

Old Street Publishing Ltd
Yowlestone House, Devon EX16 8LN
www.oldstreetpublishing.co.uk

ISBN 978-1-910400-29-6

10 9 8 7 6 5 4 3

A CIP catalogue record for this title is available from the British Library.

Printed and bound by CPI Group (UK) Ltd, Croydon, CR0 4YY

Portions of this book previously appeared in *The New Yorker.*

Map by Christian Potter Drury

The author is grateful for permission to quote from the following:

Alfred E. Brumley, arr., "This World Is Not My Home." Copyright 1946 Stamps-Baxter Music/
BMI. All rights reserved. Used by permission of Benson Music Group, Inc.

John Miles Chamberlain and Thomas D. Nicholson, *Planets, Stars and Space.* Copyright © 1957
by Creative Education, Inc. Reprinted by permission of the publisher.

Harry Emerson Fosdick, *The Assurance of Immortality.* Copyright 1913 by the Macmillan Company. Reprinted by permission of the author's estate.

Wing-Tsit Chan, *A Source Book in Chinese Philosophy.* Copyright © 1969 by Princeton University Press. Reprinted by permission of Princeton University Press.

Han-shan, tr. Burton Watson, *Cold Mountain.* Copyright © 1970 Columbia University Press,
New York. Reprinted with the permission of the publisher.

Matthew Moore, Lyrics and Music, "Space Captain." Copyright © 1970 Irving Music, Inc. (BMI).
All rights reserved. International copyright secured.

TO CHRISTIAN

I would like to thank Robert Gottlieb, Sam Lawrence, Sarah Chalfant, Hilary Liftin, Deb Garrison, and Dusty Mortimer-Maddox. Special thanks to Veronica Geng, for advice, encouragement, and brilliance from the start.

COUNTY *of* GROUSE

ROMYLA   HWY 41   STONE CITY

RTE 29   RTE 33   JACK WHITE ROAD   MIXERTON   HWY 18

LUNENBERG

RUST RIVER

LAPOINT SLOUGH   WALLEYE LAKE   CHESLEY

MARGO   HWY 8

LAKE MARGO   WHITE FARM   KLAR FARM

GRAFTON

ROBESHAW FARM   HAMILTON FARM

PINVILLE   KESSLER FARM   BORIS

NORTH PIN R.

PIN RIVER

WYLIE

HWY 56

SOUTH PIN RIVER   MORRISVILLE   PRINGMAR

▬▬▬ BLACKTOP
:::::: GRAVEL
～～～ RIVER

CONTENTS

I HAVE LOST THINGS:
An Introduction to Tom Drury's
The End of Vandalism

by Jon McGregor

First, a warning.

If you read *The End of Vandalism* you will become one of those people who try and foist it upon other people, your eyes shining with the unsettling delight of having lived through it. You will become one of those people who quote the best sentences, flicking through the pages to where you have them underlined. Listen to this description of the vet, you'll say: 'His face was narrow, his hair thick, his eyes widely spaced. He'd been working with horses a long time.' Or this account of someone working on a broken-down car: 'She had got down on her hands and knees and looked, but this hadn't fixed it.' Or the scene with Sheriff Dan Norman painting his own election signs late at night: 'The signs were nothing fancy. They said things like DAN NORMAN IS ALL RIGHT.' I could go on. You probably will. But be careful. It's not enough to tell people that this book is funny. There's more to it than that.

1

The advocates of Tom Drury's work have a problem: his novels look very similar to many other quietly-spoken realist novels of the rural American mid-west, and there's no easy way of explaining why this one is so different. Grouse County, the setting for *The End of Vandalism* and the follow-up novels *Hunts in Dreams* and *Pacific*, is a fictional location, but one we think we recognise: a flat land, with gravel roads, scattered farmhouses, and the occasional lake. Water-towers. Ditches. Barns. This is unremarkable territory, which has been well-mapped in American fiction of the last 150 years. And yet. There is something a little off-kilter. Drury has talked in interviews of drawing on his own childhood memories – he grew up in Iowa – while setting these stories in the present day. So there is a kind of dislocation; an often 1950s or 1960s sensibility dropped into a 1990s social landscape. 'Family agriculture seemed to be over,' the narrator notes at one point, 'and had not been replaced by any other compelling idea.' These people seem adrift, uncertain of their place in the world while at the same time all too certain of their own identity. This is realism, then, but a realism jolted just that little bit sideways.

And it's those sideways jolts – a retiree who takes LSD to ease his aching neck, a man who dies in his attic 'surrounded by the jars of his jar collection', the time Dave Green flew to Hawaii by accident – that give *The End of Vandalism* the vivid come-aliveness which distinguishes it from the other quietly-spoken realist rural novels for which it could easily be mistaken. There is a steady accumulation of unexpected detail, as, page by page, we meet new characters, and are given new information about them, and learn new and more complicated ways in which their lives intersect. There is no resorting to archetype, no easy use of shorthand; these people are, in very particular ways, downright odd. As all of us are. In the stories of our own lives things happen moment by moment, and we keep getting stranger, and this is the truth Tom Drury is leading us to here.

The characters in this novel are in love with storytelling. They launch into wildly tangential stories with little prompting, usually knowing that they will be patiently heard or at the least not interrupted. The stories are often not being told for the first time, and have the air of being honed in the retelling. (As does, of course, Drury's careful prose.) We learn, in passing, of Lester Ward, who ran the hatchery in Pinville and always wore a hat; we learn why the sheriff's department has no more than a barbershop's worth of space (it goes back to 1947, 'when the sheriff was a popular fellow called Darwin Whaley'); we hear, very briefly, about the failed Mixer cult of Mixerton; and we are reminded of Helene Plum, who 'reacted to almost any kind of stressful news by making casseroles, and had once, in Fairibault, Minnesota, attended the scene of a burned-out eighteen-wheeler with a pan of scalloped potatoes and ham.' (Notice the geographical detail, there; an essential part of the story, to those hearing it told in Grouse County. Notice, too, the deliciously impeccable punctuation.)

These stories are both the novel's subject and its method. We move through the book, from scene to scene, character to character, location to location, by way of story: stories told, stories lived, stories hinted at. It's been said, by people I wish could know better, that *The End of Vandalism* lacks a plot. And it's true that if you're the kind of reader who can get to the end of a novel where sixty characters muddle their way through a great variety of incident and tangled

3

interaction, and still complain that 'there wasn't much of a plot', this may not be the book for you. But if you live in the real world, where life stalls and lurches forward with little real pattern and where the textures of our relationships accumulate moment by moment, then this is a novel you will recognise as being crammed with narrative. These are not just quirky rural anecdotes Drury is spinning out for us. These are intricate, interconnected stories of the big things that happen in people's lives; the failures and successes of relationships, businesses and families, the making and thwarting of plans.

I don't think it would be too much of a spoiler – this is a book about real life, after all – to say that while everyone talks about how outrageously, laugh-out-loud funny this book is, they do sometimes forget to mention that there is a great sadness at its heart. When it comes, after much patient accumulation of quiet detail and story and straight-faced laughter, it hits with the shock of a bird striking a window; a great blue heron, say, gliding into the picture window of a newly-renovated frame house overlooking a peaceful and unruffled lake. There is tranquility, and gentle good humour, and then there is a crash and a bloody mess, and then there is tranquility again and things are changed. It's a particular, lasting sadness, one from which there is no easy recovery or resolution; one which is in fact still vivid seventeen years later, when we meet these same characters again in Tom Drury's fifth novel, *Pacific*. Forget all that stuff about the healing power of time, Drury tells us, quietly. Time won't heal a thing. This book will hurt you, if you read it properly, and it will make you feel complicit, the way two happy home-owners feel complicit when they step outside to look at the still-warm body of a broken bird and think that if only the house hadn't been built just there the bird would still be alive.

(I'm wondering, here, if it's any coincidence that the image I've chosen for a sudden shock is that of a bird striking a window, when just such an incident occurs in the book a few pages earlier. I suspect it's a mark of Tom Drury's carefully worked sophistication that it is not.)

Complicit? Well, yes. If you read this book properly, with something approaching the same patience and empathy and open-heartedness which Drury has offered his characters, you will become invested in these lives. And this investment will be something you have created, as a reader, in collaboration with Drury. You will have given life to these people, only to let them experience pain. You will have allowed yourself to feel something like love for a group of complicated characters who do messy and regrettable and sometimes unlikeable things. Charles 'Tiny' Darling, to take one example, spends most of the book slouching towards trouble for what are often, in his telling, perfectly reasonable motives. And he does these things with such a good-natured acceptance of his own failures that we find ourselves rooting for his future well-being. 'I don't consider myself a loser,' he says, in what I take to be one of his and therefore the entire novel's defining moments; 'and yet, I have lost things.' How can you not love someone with such saint-like humility and self-knowledge?

This is the love that the best fiction teaches.

The best fiction teaches us to be better readers, and to be less tolerant of weaker or softer writing, and *The End of Vandalism* does that. But the best fictions also make us better readers of the world, and of the people around us: more

5

attuned to the stories lying about the place, more aware of particularities, more likely to see the humour which insists on arising, and the sadness. *The End of Vandalism* does all of that as well. Brace yourself. Don't say I didn't warn you.

JON MCGREGOR
NOVEMBER 2014

If you do not attain happiness, always remember that you are on a good path, and try not to leave it.
—*the elder Zosima, The Brothers Karamazovv*

PART I

WORLD OF TROUBLE

ONE

ONE FALL they held the blood drive in the fire barn at Grafton. Sheriff Dan Norman was there mainly as a gesture of good will, but one of the nurses didn't make it, so Dan agreed to place the gauze in the crook of everyone's arm. "And I thank you," he would say.

It was early afternoon when Louise Darling came in. Dan knew her somewhat. Tiny Darling was along too—her husband. Dan thought Tiny had done some break-ins at Westey's Farm Home on Highway 18. There was no real proof.

Louise had a red scarf over her hair. She removed her CPO coat so they could draw her blood. She wore a dark green T-shirt with a pocket. Dan admired her long white wrists and pressed the square of gauze to her pulse.

"I thank you, Mrs. Darling," he said.

Then came Tiny. He had red hair, and a tattoo of an owl on the back of his hand. "You ought to be sending this blood to Port Gaspar," he said.

"Where?" said Dan.

"Port Gaspar," Tiny repeated. "The Navy sold the Eskimos a load of frozen salmon that turned out to be poisoned. So now they're sick. They've got blood poisoning. And guess what the Navy does. Of course, they send in some lawyers to threaten the Eskimo community."

"Where is Port Gaspar?" said Dan.

"In the South Pole," said Louise. She had large green eyes and faded freckles. "We heard the report on the radio. It might not have been the Navy, but they came on Navy boats."

"As observers," said Tiny. "They rode on the decks in their own little section, cordoned off with cords. Now the Eskimos need to have their blood flushed out."

Sheriff Dan Norman released Tiny's arm and spoke to Nurse Barbara Jones. "Where does this blood go, anyway? All to Mercy?"

"That's right," she said, "but I'll tell you what. One time my second cousin got blood-poisoned. You can't mess with it. Dan, you know her—my cousin Mary."

"Mary Ross," said Dan.

"Mary Jewell," said the nurse. "Now, her mother was a Ross—Viola Ross. She was first cousins with Kenny Ross, who went to Korea. She couldn't even walk across the room."

Louise Darling straightened her coat and tilted her head to the side. "I'm not sure if these were actual Eskimos," she said.

"It was cold enough to be Eskimos," said Tiny. "Those lawyers said, Any more complaints, we're taking down this whole town with a snowplow."

"Their houses were made of snow," said Dan.

"Evidently," said Tiny.

Dan Norman next ran into Tiny Darling at a fight that happened one Sunday night at the Lime Bucket tavern. Dan had especially disliked bar fights ever since the time he got stabbed in the back with a pool cue and ended up going to a chiropractor instead of being outdoors all that summer. The chiropractor kept a bottle of vodka on a big safe behind his desk and insisted on being called Dr. Young Jim because, he said, his deceased father had been known as Dr. Old Jim. This time Tiny had Bob Becker by the hood of a red sweatshirt and was knocking his head against the handles of a foosball machine.

Dan collared Tiny and pulled him outside. The first snow of the year had begun and they could see it falling at a slant all up and down the empty street. Tiny was alert but quite drunk. From what Dan had been able to find out, the fight had been over whether Tanya Tucker was washed up in her career, with Tiny taking the position that she was not.

In the sheriff's cruiser Dan and Tiny headed southwest on the Pinville blacktop, toward the lockup at Morrisville. About halfway there Tiny took a swing at Dan, and Dan had to pull over, get Tiny out, put the handcuffs on him, and stuff him in the back of the cruiser.

"I always thought you were smart," said Dan through the cage. "Come to find out I'm sadly mistaken."

"My arms are going out of their sockets," said Tiny.

"Just as well be smacking your own head on the handles," said Dan.

A long silence followed. "You have snow on your hat," said Tiny.

Dan slowed for a raccoon groping its way across the road. "We know it was you that broke in at Westey's," said Dan. "Pretty clumsy on that door, by the way. But it's beside the fact, since we're not going to prosecute, so I don't really know why I bring it up."

Tiny laughed. "How tall is this cruiser?" he said. "A foot and a half?"

The lights were low at the jail in Morrisville, and inside, the two deputies and some of their friends were projecting slides of nudes onto a map of the county. "I wish I lived on Floyd Coffee's farm tonight," said Deputy Earl Kellogg, Jr. Dan told them to cut it out and take Tiny Darling and put him in a cell. Then he sat down to do the paperwork.

"Dopers are out there pushing dope," said Tiny. "People stabbing that guy in the alley behind the bank. On the other hand is me, who gave blood."

"What's your real name, Tiny?" said Dan.

"Charles," said Tiny. "I'm in the plumbing supply."

"What a lie," said Earl Kellogg. "Dan, Ted Jewell's daughter called. I forget her name."

"There's Shea and there's Antonia," said Ed Aiken, the other deputy.

"All right," said Earl. "The junior class there at Morrisville-Wylie is having a dance against vandalism, and this Shea Jewell said they want you to be a chaperon. They had Rollie Wilson from the EMTs, but you know Wilson's had that fire."

"We'll see," said Dan.

"It's semi-formal," said Earl.

Dan unplugged the projector, took the slides, and left. It was still snowing. He took a roundabout way back to Grafton and found himself coming up on Tiny and Louise's place. Their yard light blinked through the trees. Tiny and Louise rented the white farmhouse that used to be the Harvey and Iris Klar place and was still owned by the Klars' daughter Jean, who lived thirty miles away, in Reinbeck, and had a job that had something to do with the brick and tile company there.

Dan pulled in the driveway and got out. A white square-headed dog bolted from the toolshed and came leaping over

14

the fine blue snow. The dog hardly made a sound, and Dan talked him into going back to the shed. Meanwhile, Louise Darling had opened the front door. Dan walked over to the house. Someone had lined the foundation with hay bales—that was good. Louise wore jeans and a white sweatshirt. Dan stepped inside, closed the door, and noticed that Louise had no shoes or socks on. The living room was dark except for the violet TV light.

Louise turned on a table lamp. "Where's Tiny?" she said. She had long full brown hair parted on the side. Over in the corner a black camera stood on a tripod—Louise worked for Kleeborg's Portraits in Stone City.

"Tiny got in a fight with Bob Becker at the Lime Bucket," said Dan. "Tiny's fine, but he's drunk, so I took him to the Morrisville jail for overnight."

"He's not hurt," said Louise.

"No," said Dan. "As I say, he won the fight."

"What's he charged with?" said Louise.

"I'm not bringing anything," said Dan. "I wash my hands of it. What are you watching?"

"What does that mean," said Louise, "if you wash your hands?"

Dan stared at the TV. "He'll be let go in the morning," he said. "At eight o'clock in the morning they'll let him go when they go off their shift."

Louise went and drank something amber from a small glass. "God damn it," she said. "Why can't people leave Tiny alone?"

Dan sat down on the arm of a chair. "Louise," he said, "in all fairness, people might ask the same of Tiny. He can be pretty obnoxious."

Louise picked up a pack of cigarettes and sat down on the couch. "This is true," she said.

"What *is* this?" said Dan, gesturing toward the TV.

"KROX *Comix Classix*," said Louise. "There's this tired priest, see, and this moth is driving him crazy in his room. The priest had to ride a bicycle over rocks all day." Louise lit a cigarette.

"Huh," said Dan.

"It's a comedy set in Italy," Louise said.

They watched that for a minute. Dan took off his hat and hung it on his knee.

"My face aches," said Louise.

Dan went home in his cruiser. He had a fried-egg sandwich and a bottle of Miller beer. He lived in a turquoise and white mobile home outside of Grafton. He looked at the nude slides, but they were too small.

Louise painted her toenails—Dan had noticed that. She painted her toenails dark red. He imagined her dabbing away in some empty room of that drafty farmhouse.

An unusual series of thefts began in February. There were still waves of snow on the ground. The stolen items were huge—combines, feed trucks, even a yellow road grader from the county shed outside Wylie—and seemed to up and vanish. Soon the rumor started that a gang was involved, a possible gang that people called the Freight Haulers. There was much discussion but no consensus.

In the midst of this, old Henry Hamilton had a tractor stolen from his machine shed. When Dan arrived to take the report, Louise Darling was there as well. It was Sunday morning. Louise had blue earmuffs on. Henry kept chickens, and Louise nestled a gray egg carton in the crook of her arm.

They all three went into the machine shed, trailed by Mike, Henry's part-shepherd. The shed had tin sides and a corrugated ceiling of translucent green plastic. There was a blue Chevy pick-up, an ancient silver corn picker, and a place where the tractor had been. It was quiet. Henry brought up the Freight Haulers.

"They're supposed to take everything to Texas in secret railroad cars," he said. "This was an Allis-Chalmers, orange in color, with a radio. I put an umbrella on for shade in the summer. Of course, that's put away now."

"Did you lock the shed?" said Dan.

"I never have locked," said Henry. "I have all my keys confused in a drawer."

"Might want to rethink that," said Dan.

"I wonder if it was these freight guys," said Louise.

Dan walked around scuffing the dirt floor with his boot. "The whole idea is three-quarters myth," he said.

"What?" said Louise, lifting the blue fur off one ear.

"My opinion, it's overblown," said Dan.

"Not according to the fellow from the extension office," said Henry. "He said there are some things you can let go by, but not when they throw it in your face. He wouldn't go beyond that. Now, what a guy ought to do, is slip over to the railroad yard and do some asking around with them."

"I thought they just wanted great big items," said Dan.

Henry lit his pipe and fanned out the match. "That was a good-sized tractor," he said.

Mike slowly raised his head and barked once at the lime-colored light through the ceiling.

"Mike's trying to say it was guys from space," said Louise.

"No, Mike sees that swallow poking out his head," said Henry.

17

Louise and Dan left the shed and walked over by the hog pen in front of Henry's barn. It was cold. Louise's cheeks were red. She slipped the toe of her boot through the rail, and some pigs came over to chew on it.

"You're not missing anything, I hope," said Dan.

Louise pulled her earmuffs from her head, the blue pads coiling together. "There were lights going by last night," she said. "That's all. I thought it could be Tiny—these lights going up and down the wallpaper. Tiny and I got separated, and it occurred to me he might be mad about that."

"You and Tiny?" said Dan. "No kidding."

Louise wiped her nose with the back of her glove. "We weren't getting along," she said. "We would talk but it wouldn't be about anything."

"What makes you say he might be mad?" said Dan.

"Who wouldn't be?" said Louise. "It was seven years, practically. You begin to wonder what you had in mind the whole time."

"Did he ever threaten to or actually hit you?" said Dan.

"No," said Louise. "He might have taken a swing but it never would hurt."

"Because there's no reason you have to sit around living in fear," said Dan. "That isn't written anywhere."

"Not mad like that," said Louise. "Tiny would never hurt the individual person. More frustrated kind of mad."

"But you're still on the farm," said Dan.

"I still am," said Louise. "Tiny went to live with his brother Jerry Tate in Pringmar. It's good in the sense that Jerry racked up his snowmobile on New Year's Eve. He was wearing a scarf that got caught in the belt thing."

"God damn," said Dan.

Louise opened and closed the egg box. "Jerry is lucky to be alive," she said. "It's a trial separation."

"We can give you what we call special attention," said Dan. "We can come by your place on our patrols. It's not really the height of security, but it's still something."

"All I have is the rusty Vega," said Louise. "The whole bottom is about to shear off. They could haul that freight right now—it'd be O.K. with me."

"You know, though," said Dan, "sometimes you drive by a pickup and it might be parked on the shoulder with the flashers on. Now, say there's baled straw all over the road, maybe there's a man, there's a woman, picking up the bales. Well, it's easy to see what happened. But it's too late to tie them tighter, obviously."

"O.K., I'm lost," said Louise, and she blinked. Dan was quiet for a moment. He could almost hear her eyelids going *poink, poink.*

"When the bales fall off," he said.

Henry came around the corner of the barn with a bucket in his hand. "That's right, you needed eggs," he said. He led them into the low red chicken house. The room was warm and hazy and full of straw. The chickens beat their wings and ran like mad in every direction.

Dan got the crop duster Paul Francis of Chesley to take him up to look for the stolen machinery. They got off from the Stone City airport and headed south. The county had its winter colors—gray and bark brown shot through with strips of pale white. After a while, Paul, like all small-plane pilots in Dan's experience, wanted Dan to try the wheel.

"Look left," said Paul. "Look right. Look up. You even have to look up."

The sun came out. "Where would you put a road grader?" said Dan.

"Keep your eyes moving," said Paul. "Where could you bring her down if an emergency happened?"

"Back to you, in that case," said Dan.

The small plane droned into the blue air. The engine roared and the heater blasted, but the cold was like a brilliant curtain all around them. When Dan tested the responsiveness of the wheel, the wing tilted and the plane headed into the watery space above.

"Level, level," said Paul. Dan scanned a row of black instruments leading to a red and gold medallion that said, "The Sky Is Thine, O Lord."

"You're not looking," said Paul. "Disregard the panel at this stage. I'll tape them gauges up with masking tape."

"I hate this," said Dan. "I don't want to be the pilot. That's what you're for, and how about taking me over Martins Woods? I mean it. Lesson over, king's ex."

"All right," said Paul.

They said nothing for a while. Dan watched the snowy fields, the shimmering creeks, the cars on slick blacktop.

"Have you given any thought to joining our Methodist prayer group?" said Paul.

"No," said Dan.

They flew for another hour. When Paul came in to land at Stone City he didn't like the set of his wings, so he pulled up and went around again. They flew right into the sun, and Dan put his hand over his eyes. Paul still wasn't overly pleased with the setup, but he brought the plane bouncing down on the runway. Dan banged his ear against the door of the plane.

Dan met Louise at Kleeborg's Portraits at the end of the day. They took the cruiser out to a tuxedo shop on Old Highway 18. There was one green car in the parking lot.

"It looks pretty closed," said Dan.

"No, because it's Thursday, and all the retail stores are open until nine on Thursday," said Louise. "Is this like a date?"

"Is what like a date?"

"This right now."

"I don't know. More or less."

Dan got out of the car, and Louise joined him on the sidewalk, where they stood looking at the rows of shiny jackets. "You can't tell me this place isn't closed," said Dan.

But he pushed the door, and it opened. A small barrel-chested man in jeans and pointy sideburns and tiny cowboy boots stood looking at a cummerbund. "The lady left," he said. "There was a lady here a while ago, but now she's left."

"Are those flares?" said Louise, pointing to the cuffs of the man's jeans.

"They're boot cut," he said, and then he was out the door.

Louise watched him drive away in the green car. "Boot cut, my ass," she said.

Dan looked into a little room in back. "Hello?" he said. A woman lay on a green vinyl davenport with her eyes closed.

"Is she dead?" said Louise.

Dan shook his head. "Her stomach's moving," he said. "I think she's asleep."

"Well, what should we do?" said Louise.

"I have a black coat," said Dan. "And I have black pants. So all I need, pretty much, is a tie." He picked out a narrow bow of red plaid, held it under his chin, and cleared his throat.

"Wait," said Louise. She found a white shirt in cellophane

21

and pressed it to his chest. "I don't think you're supposed to wear plaid unless it's the actual tartan of your clan."

"Keep in mind this is only semi-formal," said Dan.

"It was on *National Geographic*," said Louise. "They had a special about Scotland."

"I forget which tartan my clan does favor," said Dan.

"Get the shirt, too," said Louise. She went over and tried on a powder-blue jacket with winged lapels. Her fingertips barely cleared the cuffs as she turned before a three-way mirror. "Check out this ugly son of a bitch," she said.

Dan slipped the tie in his pocket and came over. Louise looked into the planes of the mirror, her hair tucked into the jacket collar. Dan lifted Louise's hair and laid it like cloth on her shoulders. He saw a row of her in the mirror. She pressed the back of her neck against his hands. Her eyes closed, then opened: *poink*.

"You hurt your ear," she said. They began to kiss.

At the End of Vandalism Dance, held in the Grafton gym, Dan stationed himself near the punch table to watch out for spikers. He spoke with Mrs. Thorsen, the small, strangely high-waisted science teacher. A band called Brian Davis and Slagheap played their own songs plus covers they had customized to reflect the theme. Every now and then Dan would go to the lobby doors and look out, to chase away the drinker kids hanging around the street lamp in their cars.

The gym was dark except for stage light, and the music rattled through it like sheets of tin. When the dancing was fast it reminded Dan of the Pony, and when it was slow it reminded him of people wandering in the cold. In the center of the floor the shop class had built a mysterious display. It was a row of tall, pointed wooden slats with a double-hung window built in and a flashing yellow light bolted to one side.

"It's a collage of the different vandalism things," said Mrs. Thorsen. She wore a yellow dress and her eyes were exaggerated by mascara. "You have the fence, the glass, the construction light. They were going to make another one and go ahead and break the glass and paint on the fence, and show the before and the after. I'm not sure why they didn't, because probably it would have been better."

"Probably," said Dan.

"But I'm not going to say anything," said Mrs. Thorsen, "because the shop class always takes such intense shit. Every dance is the same. You should have seen their Stairway to Heaven."

After the intermission, Brian Davis came back with Slagheap and played "Rikki Don't Throw That Lumber." Mrs. Thorsen started telling Dan about the chinchillas she was raising with her husband. She practically had to shout. Something was wrong with the chinchillas, Dan couldn't quite understand what. About this time Tiny entered the gym with a blue wrecking bar. Later everyone would say it had been like a music video, with dancers parting as if by hypnosis and the band playing "China Grove." Dan had his back turned, but Mrs. Thorsen in her yellow dress was watching as Tiny moved past the punch area. He glided to the vandalism collage and swung the head of the crowbar through the window, spraying glass toward the stage. He exploded the orange light and splintered the planks of the fence. Then Dan got to him and tried to enclose him in his arms. "Whoa, whoa, China Grove," sang the band. Tiny set his shoulders and shrugged out of Dan's hold. Somehow Dan caught the head of the crowbar on the temple. It was probably not intentional, just a little whack on the temple. Dan fell back against the fence, and Tiny ran out.

By the time the glass and the other mess had been swept up and Dan had convinced Mrs. Thorsen to go on with the dance, Tiny was gone and the drinker kids had strategically moved their cars to the ball diamond across the street. Dan slipped on his suit coat and got into the cruiser carefully. He knew he had been hit on the head but thought it was not bad. He tried to radio in about what had happened, but when he turned the knob to tune the frequency, the light went out behind the dial.

He drove east on the gravel road to Louise's house, where he found her sitting at the kitchen table, with a camera taken apart and neatly laid out in front of her.

"I must be psychic," she said. "I saw a show about police to-night, and here you are in my kitchen."

"Has Tiny been here?" he said.

"A couple days ago," said Louise. "It was funny what he wanted. He wanted this old shot glass he got one time at the Sands Hotel in Las Vegas. 'Where's my little Sands glass?' he said. 'Where's my little Sands glass?' I had no idea what he was talking about. I'm going, 'Which glass, Tiny? A glass with sand in it?' But he had to have that glass."

"What did he want it for?" said Dan.

She shrugged, examining a small red-handled screwdriver in her hand. "I guess to drink out of," she said. "He wanted some other glasses, too. I guess his brother Jerry doesn't have much for the kitchen."

"Are you all right?" said Dan.

Louise nodded. "Except for this camera," she said.

Dan looked at the camera parts on the checkered tablecloth—springs and mirrors and pins.

"Give me your hand," he said. She did. Her fingers were strong and warm. "Thanks," he said. They held hands across the table.

"You're welcome," said Louise.

Dan called Deputy Ed Aiken on Louise's telephone and arranged to meet him at Tiny's brother's place in Pringmar. Jerry Tate lived in a gray bungalow on land that sloped down from the road. Heavy bushes surrounded the house, and Christmas lights still burned in the windows. Jerry Tate invited them in to sit but said he could not make coffee because he wasn't supposed to move around after nine o'clock.

"I had a run-in with a snowmobile," said Jerry. "Seven little plates have gone out of kilter. I might not come back one hundred percent. But the doctor says it shouldn't interfere with my plans."

"What plans are those?" said Dan.

"It's a figure of speech," said Jerry.

So Ed Aiken made coffee, and they drank it, and after a while Jerry said it wasn't his business but it seemed to him that Tiny might keep going if he saw the cruisers out front. Dan and Ed went to move the cars and talk things over, and when they came back Jerry had locked the house up and turned off the lights.

TWO

LOUISE DIVORCED Tiny that spring and found herself unable to watch television in a satisfying way. She could not settle into a show but had to keep drifting from station to station. On *Jeopardy*, as soon as there was a question that she could not answer, she would guess blindly—"Fiji? What is the island of Fiji?"—and change the channel to one of those phony crime shows, which she wouldn't watch for long either.

One Sunday afternoon, after watching parts of a basketball game, *Fishing with André*, and *How Steel Is Made*, Louise drove the five miles into Grafton to see her mother. A sack of groceries occupied the seat beside her, the road was blank and empty, and the radio station played three Evelyn "Champagne" King songs in a row.

Mary Montrose lived on the west side of town in an L-shaped green house with white shutters. Louise pulled into the driveway and noticed an orange plastic bucket on the ground by the willow tree. She walked up the sidewalk, singing, "Get loose, get funky tonight."

Louise went in the front door and down the hall, and just as she entered the living room the sun filled it with green light through the green curtains. Louise shifted the groceries from one arm to the other. "I'm going to make you spaghetti bake," she said.

Mary Montrose lay reading a book on the davenport. She marked her place and sat up, a tall woman with silver-gray hair held back by a network of barrettes. "I thought I heard somebody in the driveway," she said.

"What are you reading?" said Louise.

"Oh, some mystery," said Mary. "I got it from the bookmobile. I don't know whether I like it or not. There's an awful lot of killing. They just killed some people at a picnic."

"That's no good," said Louise. She carried the groceries into the kitchen and put them away. There was vodka in the freezer, and she made herself a vodka and cranberry juice, and returned to the living room.

"Pretty drink," said Mary.

"It's called a Twister," said Louise. "Would you like one?"

"You know," said Mary, "I wish I had a dress of that shade."

Louise took a drink. "You know what I wish?" she said. "That I was a rock singer. I really mean it. I wish that."

"You can carry a tune," said Mary.

"Maybe I should go on a concert tour," said Louise. "Say, why is there a bucket in your yard?"

"There shouldn't be," said Mary. She got up and walked to the window. "Oh, look at that," she said. Then she checked the thermostat and came back to the davenport.

Louise sat down in the chair facing her mother. It was a recliner, and Louise reclined. She picked at the dark, star-shaped leaves growing along the arm of the chair. "Have you given any thought to cutting this back?" she said. "Look what it's doing to the arm of this chair. Look what it's doing to the davenport. I'm not saying to get rid of it. I'm saying get rid of some of it. Look at this. The arm of this chair is returning to the soil."

Mary looked sadly at the magnificent ivy plant, which began on the coffee table and coiled its way around the room. "It would be too hard," she said.

"Oh, Christ," said Louise. "It would not, Mom. It would not. Do you want spaghetti bake or what?"

"Well, before they all died, they were grilling hamburgers at this picnic in my book," said Mary, "and it made me hungry for a hamburger on the grill. Why don't we run up to the lake and get a hamburger from the Lighthouse?"

"I can put hamburger in the spaghetti," Louise suggested.

"I never get out of here," said Mary. "I wouldn't think it would be the end of the world if we ran up to the lake. Your problem is you sit out at that farm and you get isolated. You do, you get isolated."

"I don't get isolated," said Louise.

"I don't know what else you'd call it," said Mary.

"Don't call it anything," said Louise.

"Besides," said Mary, "wouldn't you guess that sooner or later Jean Klar is going to get married and want to come back and live in that house? Sweetie, you're a renter. You rent."

"I know I rent," said Louise. "I'm very aware of that."

"They have Jimmy Coates's house up for sale," said Mary. "They want eighty-five hundred dollars, and I'll bet you could get it for six thousand."

"The problem with Jimmy Coates's house is it would smell like Jimmy Coates," said Louise. "And I don't have six thousand dollars."

Mary sighed. She went to the front hall and retrieved a brightly shellacked walking stick. Louise brought her chair

29

upright and finished the Twister. "Where'd you get that?" she said.

Mary handed the stick to Louise; it had a snake's features wood-burned into the handle. "Hans Cook," she said. She put on a maroon jacket and zipped it up to her chin. "He was bringing his truck back from Ohio and he stopped to see some caves. They had a museum and little huts showing panoramas of Indian life."

Louise examined the stick. "What are you going to do with a cane? You run across the room when the phone rings."

"The phone doesn't ring."

In fact Mary's phone rang often. She held the so-called widow's seat on the Grafton town council. The seat, of course, was not strictly for widows. But Mary had been preceded on the council by Dorothy Frails, whose husband had been electrocuted while doing what he thought was going to be simple wiring on their back porch. And before Dorothy Frails there had been another widow, but not many people remembered who that was or how she lost her husband. (It was Susan Jewell, whose husband, Howard, took a nap in the attic, surrounded by the jars of his jar collection, and never woke up, on October 4, 1962.) Mary had been on the council nine years. She considered dog issues her specialty, and once, at a convention in Moline, had given a slide presentation on the history of the muzzle.

Louise and her mother walked outside. Mary headed for the willow, speared the orange bucket with the walking stick, and tossed it over the hedge into Heinz and Ranae Miller's yard.

"I thought that was your bucket," said Louise.

"No, I believe it's Heinz's," said Mary.

They went up to Walleye Lake on Route 33. Louise's Vega made a huge racket. It had a piece of metal sticking out of the muffler. Louise knew this because she had got down on her hands and knees and looked, but that did not fix it. Summer was more than a month away, and the sky had an anxious pale color. Mary rode with one hand on the dashboard and the other on the edge of the seat. Louise stubbed out a cigarette in the ashtray.

"How is Hans Cook?" she said.

"Oh, Hans Cook is all right," said her mother. "But I'll tell you, we went to a movie in Stone City, what, two, three weeks ago, and the way he laughed really embarrassed me. The movie was supposed to be funny. I know that. But you have to draw the line somewhere."

"What movie was this?" said Louise.

"Oh, with Carol Burnett," said Mary. *"Annie.* I was about to crawl down the aisle and out the door. There again, I know he takes drugs."

"Oh, right," said Louise.

"Well, he takes LSD," said Mary.

Louise stared at her. "Hans Cook takes the drug LSD?" she said. "Big fat Hans?"

Mary pointed at the windshield. "You never mind. Keep your eyes on the highway."

"I see it," said Louise. "Are you kidding me about Hans Cook?"

"His neck gives him trouble," said Mary. "He's always driving someplace, and he says his head kind of pushes down on his neck. He's not built right. He has an extra vertebra. He has something extra, anyway. Well, this is what he says. He claims the LSD makes his neck feel better."

"What does he take for a headache, crack?"

Mary took off her glasses and cleaned them with a tissue. The glasses had square lenses and dramatic arms, and Mary's eyes looked small and tired without them. "No, I don't think he takes crack," she said.

"Maybe he's been spiking your wine cooler," said Louise, and Mary didn't say anything, so Louise said, "Jesus Christ, you're not taking it, too."

Mary glanced at a windmill going by outside the window. "I don't doubt that Hans would give me some," she said. "But I wouldn't take any, and Hans knows this. The drug is paper. It would be like chewing a receipt from the store."

They drove into the town of Walleye Lake. A woman in an oncoming station wagon began to turn in front of them but slammed on the brake when Louise leaned on her horn.

"That's right, honey," said Louise. "I'm coming straight."

The Lighthouse was across the street from the Moonview Inn in town. It was a drive-in restaurant built around a bleached-orange tower. A green neon tube circled the top of the tower, and the light was on although it was not yet dark. In full season, waitresses in white sailor hats would circulate among the cars, but in the spring customers had to line up at the counter under the tower, and on this evening the line was long. Directly in front of Louise and Mary were a father and a little girl carrying a stuffed horse. The little girl had light blue eyes and long brown hair. Mary said hello to her and asked the name of the horse.

"Can't touch this," said the girl. "Hammer time."

"Hammer, how ferocious," said Mary. "I used to have a horse, her name was Velvet. That's right, a big old lady like

32

me. I was chosen from all the girls in all the riding clubs to bring my horse Velvet to opening day of the Iowa State Fair. I had white leather gloves that rode high on my arms, and who do you think was on the horse by my side? Well, it was Tim Thompson. He was the best barrel racer in the nation, and he was from California."

The father had turned to listen. He wore a cardigan sweater with a bowling pin on it, and had the same spooky eyes as his daughter. Together they reminded Louise of the kind of peaceful, doomed space aliens you might see on *Outer Limits*. The girl chewed on the neck of the stuffed horse, then raised her head. "What's a barrel racer?" she said.

"That's someone who rides around barrels like they did in Western times," said Mary, leaning thoughtfully on her walking stick. "Anyway, this Tim Thompson—"

"Why did they ride around barrels?" said the girl.

"Sweetie, I guess they were in their way," said Mary. "But you can disregard the barrels. They really don't have much importance to the story. Anyway, everyone knew Tim Thompson. So we rode up the midway and onto the racetrack, and when we got to the grandstand Tim Thompson turned to me and said, 'Mary, you ride better than the women do in California. You ride much better than they do.' See, he was tickled by my riding, and he said he was going to give me a present. But then the fair got going, and there was a rodeo that he had to be in, and he forgot about the present. Well, I didn't forget, but I rode home in a dream anyway. The only other thing I'd ever done was walk beans. It was a long time later when a delivery boy brought a package to my dad's farm. This boy worked for Supersweet in Grafton, and his name was Leon Felly, and he had freckles over every bit of his face.

He gave me a cardboard box, and I opened it, and it was an ivy plant from Tim Thompson."

"Did you hear that?" said the father. "The lady got her present finally." He rubbed his forearm absently, and soon he turned his daughter and himself away from Mary.

"She has a crutch," the girl said.

Louise looked sideways at Mary. "That ivy is from your mother," she said.

Mary scowled. "What ivy?" she said. "You always just assume you know what I'm talking about. There's a big world of ivy out there, Louise. You've never seen the plant from Tim Thompson. It died that winter—the winter following the fall when I rode in the fair. It was one of the worst winters we ever had, and a big frost came and tore up all the hollyhocks and all the ivy, including the ivy that Tim Thompson gave me."

"He never gave you no kind of ivy," said Louise.

Mary laughed bitterly. "We walked out the windows onto snowdrifts that year," she said.

"You never walked out the windows," said Louise.

Meanwhile, a commotion had developed at the head of the line. The father picked up his daughter, and Mary and Louise stepped away from everyone to see. A customer wearing a red letter-jacket that said "Geoff Lollard School of Self-Defense" in white flannel letters was shouting at the man behind the counter. The customer was a big guy with a butch haircut and kept smacking the counter with his hand. The counterman was young and heavy, with a green apron, and a fearful smile plastered on his face.

"You're in a world of trouble, you smiling son of a bitch," said the customer. "I know where you live! I know when closing time is! I know where you work! You work here! Stop smiling, god damn it! I'll cut you. So help me I will."

"Oh, Pete," said the counterman. He had a hollow, sad, sing-song voice that seemed to rasp a nerve in the man in the red self-defense jacket. "Oh, now, Pete, settle down."

Pete kept cursing the counterman. He seized a gleaming napkin dispenser and began stalking him down the length of the counter.

"You don't want to do this, Pete," said the counterman, and Pete threw the dispenser viciously. The counterman dived and the dispenser knocked a deep-fat-fryer basket off its peg on the back wall.

The counterman got up. "Well, great, Pete, you cracked it," he said. "I hope you're pleased with yourself, because you really have cracked it."

But Pete had already left the counter, and now he stormed past the line of customers, tilting his head, swearing at the sky. His features were delicately arranged in the center of his big face, and he had a Band-Aid above one eye. As he passed Louise and Mary, he veered close, and his boot struck the butt of Mary's walking stick. The stick was pulled from Mary's hand, and as she stepped backward into the blue-eyed father and daughter, Pete and the stick seemed to wrestle briefly before falling over on the asphalt. It was apparent that Pete had scraped the heels of his hands, and the people in the line gasped and touched the heels of their own hands protectively. Pete scrambled to his feet and began to run, as if the stick were after him. He made it to an orange Volkswagen bus that was parked under a herbicide billboard, and he got in and drove away.

"Do you want help?" the man with blue eyes asked Mary. His voice was constricted by his daughter's arms around his

35

neck. "I guess he tried to steal some candy. My understanding is, he put a roll of candy in his pocket."

"Him and the other guy must know each other," said Louise.

"Oh, yeah!" said the man. "I'm sure they go way back. I guess this Pete guy thought the other one would just play dumb while he made off with the candy."

Mary took out her barrettes, brushed her hair, and put the barrettes back. "So you think the guy in the red," she said, gesturing at the herbicide sign, "knew the cook beforehand?"

Louise took her cigarette case, unsnapped it, and bent to light a cigarette. "He just said he did, Ma," she said.

"Oh, yeah!" said the man. "No question but what they know each other. Ease up, honey. You're strangling Dad. I would definitely call 911 if I was that guy. I don't know why he isn't calling them right now. I would be. You bet I would."

"You know what, though," said Mary. "I'll bet that guy got away with the candy anyway."

The man nodded. "Pete did," he said.

"Well, wait," said Mary. "Pete, or the one in the red coat?"

"Pete *is* the one in the red coat," said the man.

"Pete got in the van," said Louise.

The man nodded. "That's right," he said. "Pete got in the van."

"Be quiet about Pete!" said the little girl. She touched a hand to her forehead. "I'm sick."

"You're fine," said the father.

"Put a Band-Aid on my eye," said the girl.

Louise and Mary ordered the California hamburgers, and French fries, and mugs of root beer. Louise gave the counterman a cigarette and reached across to light it for him. His fingers trembled as he formed a shield around Louise's

36

lighter. Then he set out two red and white cardboard baskets for their fries. Louise and Mary ate in the car, returned the heavy glass mugs to the counter, and drove home to Mary's house. They watched a television show about murder; Louise discovered a large flaw in the plot, and Mary had a glass of milk and sat on the davenport. During a commercial, Louise looked at the clock on the wall and turned to Mary.

"Do you really think I'm that isolated?" she said.

Mary looked at her blankly, touched by something profound. She walked out to the hallway, speaking to Louise from the dark.

"I didn't get home with my stick," she said.

The next day Louise helped the portrait photographer Kleeborg with high school graduation photos. She applied makeup, tilted and adjusted lights, put film holders in Kleeborg's old hands. The day went normally except for one girl who did not look very promising from the start. She had short, straight blond hair, but her eyes were red and her clothes crooked. She was supposed to have her portrait taken in the outdoor setting. This was in the corner of the studio and amounted to a section of rail fence with plastic leaves and an evergreen backdrop. While Louise was trying to get some Murine drops in the girl's eyes, however, the girl just hunkered down with her back to the fence and moaned.

"I don't want to go away to school," she said. A drop of Murine spilled from the corner of her eye and rolled down her cheek. "I don't want to go away to school. And I'm so hung over. I will never pick up another glass of wine in my life."

"Why is she on the floor?" shouted Kleeborg. He lifted the cloth from his head and stood beside the camera. "Your whole life is in front of you!" he said. He had been using this expression all week, but now it sounded like a threat. Louise helped the girl up, took her into the bathroom, and got her some Alka-Seltzer. The girl's name was Maren Staley, and it turned out that she had been accepted at the University of Oregon but didn't want to go there and leave her boyfriend, Loren. But her mother, who hated Loren with a passion, had her mind set on Oregon and had gone as far as forging enthusiastic letters to the college and signing Maren's name.

Maren threw her head back and drank the water with the Alka-Seltzer. She set the glass on the toilet tank and, panting softly, said, "It's just that I don't want to go away to school."

Louise put an arm around her shoulder. "Maybe it wouldn't be so bad," she said.

They went out in the hallway. There was a brass bed that had been used in advertisements for Brown's department store, and Maren lay down on it. Then she got up, went in the bathroom, and threw up. She came back drying her face with a towel and lay down again. "Whatever made me think I could drink," she said. "Whatever, ever made me think I could drink." Louise knew the kind of hangover the girl had—it helped to say things more than once. Soon Maren fell asleep, and she did not wake up for about two and a half hours, when she went out and bicycled slowly away.

On Wednesday night after work, Louise drove over to Walleye Lake to pick up her mother's walking stick, which someone at the Lighthouse had leaned against the counter near the lost-and-found shelf. The stick was ugly to Louise, and she dropped it in the back of the car and buried it with old newspapers. She decided to drive by the lake on her way out of town. The street to the water was narrow and flanked by bars, a barbershop, a small park, and a consignment store with a broken window. Some old men in fishing caps looked up, and one of them waved at the sound of Louise's car, and Louise got the impression that he was toothless, although she did not get that good a look.

She parked and walked down Town Beach. The water was choppy and gray, and Louise's hair swirled around her face. She stopped at the edge of the water to wet her hands. The lake was sparse and wild, like a place where TV scientists would go to find blind fish from the beginning of time. The sand was covered with black weeds and tiny gray rocks. Up the beach, someone called her name and waved from the corner of the stone picnic shelter. It was Johnny White, who had graduated with Louise from Grafton High School in 1974.

Louise had seen him a few times since then. Once she saw him at a car wash, wrestling a towel from a coin machine. Once she saw him sitting on a bench in Grafton with a large black Afghan dog. She and Johnny had dated in high school. She remembered watching from the bleachers as he performed in the class play, a musical about labor conflict in California. He sang a ballad called "Peaches (Find Me a Girl)." He flung his strong arms wide. "Peaches! Peaches! These two arms grow weary of peaches." Louise had had some Wild Irish Rose before the play, and she remembered thinking that she didn't know anyone else with the sheer guts to get up and sing that song. Johnny sang in a smooth tenor voice that sounded very false to Louise, but somehow that did not take away from the accomplishment. Now Johnny worked for the county, and he was wearing a knee-length denim coat over a green shirt and tan pair of pants. When he was in high school his face had had a boyish appeal, but now he looked heavy, and on his head he wore one of those puffy leather caps that rock stars wear when they go bald. But his eyes were still sort of handsome.

Louise and Johnny sat under the wooden rafters of the picnic shelter. It turned out that these days Johnny lived in the former First Baptist Church in Pinville. (Pinville was a very small town on a back road between Grafton and Morrisville.) The church had been purchased from the Baptists several years before by Johnny's father, a wheeler-dealer farmer who was often said to be "rich on paper."

"Dad was going to make it a supper club," said Johnny. "It could still happen. Probably not, though. He just bought a quonset full of auger parts from a guy in Sioux City. He thought he could turn them over fast. But there's something wrong with them. I'm not sure what. I think they might be impounded."

"Is that right," said Louise.

"It's like when I went to Cleveland," said Johnny. "This was after Lisa and I had been married one year. We rented her uncle's house in Cleveland, and we started a restaurant on East Superior. We took a Sinclair station and converted it into a restaurant. But they put out the word on us. They said our hot dogs tasted like gasoline."

"Did I hear something about this?" said Louise. "Was there an explosion or something?"

"No, there wasn't any explosion," said Johnny. "There wasn't even any gasoline by that time. We had emptied out the tanks, and the man from the county came down and *watched* us empty out the tanks. But we were ruined by this gas rumor, because hot dogs were the mainstay of the restaurant, hot dogs and franks."

40

"I'm sorry," said Louise.

"If we hadn't gone bankrupt, I bet Lisa and me would still be married," said Johnny. "Once I accidentally put my hand on the grill, and she just watched. You can't really see the scar in this light. Wait. Here it is. It's sort of like the whole hand is a scar. I don't know. We have two kids, Megan and Stefan, and I will say I miss those goddamned kids."

"They stayed in Cleveland?" said Louise.

"Well, Parma," said Johnny. "Same thing."

Louise and Johnny talked for a while longer, and then Louise left him sitting under the picnic shelter and walked to her car. Leaving Walleye Lake, Louise turned on the radio. Johnny Cash was singing about an auto worker who built himself a car out of parts he had smuggled out of the factory over a period of many years.

The lighter popped out, and Louise put a cigarette in her mouth. She looked at the orange ring of the lighter. "Give me that car," she said.

The town council met in the lunchroom of the former Grafton School, which had been built out of brick in 1916 and left mostly vacant since 1979, when the Grafton School merged with Morrisville-Wylie. The official name of the resulting school district had been Morrisville-Wylie-Grafton, but that was too long, and although people suggested taking some of the first several letters from each town and calling the district Mo-Wy-Gra, this was plainly foolish, and so the district went on being Morrisville-Wylie, as if Grafton had floated off the map. Louise, who had stopped by the meeting in order to return her mother's walking stick, came in just as four firemen were finishing a request for new axes. They had brought some

41

of the old ones along to show their decrepit condition, but the council said to wait until the state money came in, to which Chief Howard LaMott said, "What state money? There is no state money. I've been chief four years now, and guess how much state money there has been in that time. None," and the four firemen picked up their axes and left, looking dismayed enough to go out and chop something down.

Louise watched them go, and noticed Hans Cook sitting two rows back. The chairs were small, especially in relation to Hans. He wore a red Tyrolean hat and smoked a Tiparillo, the ash of which he deposited in the cuff of his gray pants. He seemed to be rocking slightly in his chair. Next up was the issue of Alvin Getty's dog biting Nan Jewell. Nan Jewell was a good eighty years old and made her way to the front of the room wearing a dark blue dress with a white lace collar—a beautiful old dress, a dress a Jewell *would* wear. Alvin Getty stood among the chairs with his German shepherd, King, on a leash. King wore a red bandanna, kept his head down, and moved a chair around with his tail.

"King is not a bad dog," said Alvin Getty. "He bit you the one time—O.K., that's true. But you were in his garden. That makes no difference to me, but this is a dog. Wrong, yes, it was wrong. This is why I'm willing to do what I've been saying all night, since six-thirty and it's now nine-thirty, and that is, I will build a great big cage and stick him in it."

"That's no garden," said Nan Jewell. "It's an empty lot strewn with tires. I hardly think I would be walking in such a mess. I walk down the middle of the sidewalk, because if I don't, I could get dizzy and fall. And this is well known."

"You show me a tire on that property and I will swallow it whole," said Alvin Getty.

Hans Cook laughed heartily. Louise's mother stood. She wore a black turtleneck and a green jumper with large pockets. "Thank you," she said. "There's only one thing you can do with a German shepherd who bites, and I don't think it's any great secret. The idea of a cage does not impress me. Jaspersons' dog was supposedly kept in a cage, and we know how that turned out. Looking at King here tonight with his pretty scarf, naturally we all want to scratch his head. But I say put him to sleep. Who's with me?"

"Wait," said Alvin. "I have a witness. Mrs. Spees owns the pet store in Stone City. And that store has a good selection, too. Go ahead, Mrs. Spees."

But before Mrs. Spees could begin, Louise stood and raised her hand.

"What is it, honey?" said Mary.

"The floor yields to Louise Montrose," said Alvin Getty.

"Darling," said Louise. "It's Louise Darling. Mom, I got your stick back from the lake."

"Oh, thank you," said Mary. "Just leave it by the door. That's my walking stick, everybody."

"I also have something to say about the topic," said Louise. "I think you should give the cage a try. I don't think Jaspersons' dog is a fair comparison, because they never made a sincere effort."

"Thank you for your opinion," said Mary. "Nobody wishes a cage would work more than I do."

Louise went home and had spaghetti and asparagus for supper. She took a bath, turned on the TV that was perched on her dresser, and got in bed. The wind came up and seemed to lift the windows in their frames. Louise fell asleep and dreamed that ivy was growing over the top of her. When she awoke, it was that late hour in which they play the strangest commercials. Here was one for a 900 number you could dial in order to talk to people with serious illnesses. On the screen a beautiful young woman sat wrapped in a blanket with a telephone in her lap. Louise got up and turned off the TV. She got back in bed. The wind blew, the house made one of its mysterious cracking sounds, and the phone rang.

"I've been trying to sleep," said her mother. "I can't sleep, and it's your fault. I know I've made mistakes, but please tell me what compels you to stand up in front of people and say I'm wrong."

"Well," said Louise, "you were being so mean to that dog."

"You care more about a dog than you do about your own mother," said Mary. "Why can't you be on my side? I stand up there all alone, and all you're concerned about is a dog."

"The topic was a dog," said Louise.

"You leave me stranded among strangers," said Mary.

"I'm on your side, Mom," said Louise. "I'm on your side. What did happen with King?"

"This is what I mean," said Mary. "King, King, King, King, King."

"Why don't you make a drink and calm down," said Louise.

"What happened to the almighty King," said Mary.

"Why don't you fix yourself a drink," said Louise.

Mary sighed. Then she was quiet for so long that Louise began to wonder whether she had put the phone down and walked away.

"That pet shop woman talked for one solid hour," said Mary. "They had to table my motion and adjourn just to get rid of her."

THREE

ONE SATURDAY, Sheriff Dan Norman was kneeling on top of his trailer house, trying to patch a rusty spot that was beginning to leak, when a religious woman came by. She had yellow hair pulled into a thick braid. Her Bible was white, and she held it in both hands, like a big white sandwich.

"Does Jesus live in this home?" she said.

"Pardon?" said Dan. He stood up. In his hands were a trowel and a can of orange sealant, called Mendo, that he had got at Big Bear.

"Did you know that Jesus could live in this trailer?" said the woman. "Because he can. You accept him as your personal savior, he's here tomorrow."

"I'm comfortable with my beliefs," said Dan.

"Well—what are they?" said the woman.

"Let's just say I have some," said Dan, "leave it there."

"Fine with me," said the woman. She tucked the Bible under her arm and climbed the aluminum ladder leaning against the side of the trailer. She stepped onto the roof and held out her hand. "My name is Joan Gower," she said. "I'm from Chicago originally, but I've lived in this area seven years."

The sky had the blue depth of a lake. Joan Gower took the

45

trowel from Dan Norman's hand. He thought for a minute that she was going to pitch in, but it was a brief thought, because she hurled the trowel to the ground.

She sighed. "Wouldn't it be a miracle if we could throw away our sins that easy?" she said. "God, what a miracle that would be." She stared sadly downward, and it seemed to Dan that she had in mind particular sins, occurring on such and such a day.

"Look at that," said Dan: the trowel had stuck in the ground, like a sign. He climbed down to retrieve it, but the phone rang and he went inside, leaving Joan Gower standing up on the roof of the trailer.

The man on the telephone told Dan to go look in a shopping cart at the Hy-Vee. He did not say which Hy-Vee. He did not say what was in the cart. He said he was calling Dan at home so the call could not be traced. Dan's approach to mystery callers was to treat them casually, get them talking, so he said, "You know, we don't, as a rule, trace calls at the office either. Call tracing is tricky, and the phone company doesn't like to do it. They will do it, I'm not saying they'll never do it, but they won't do it if they don't have to. Sometimes you can get what is called a pen register, but that takes a warrant, and warrants are hard to get, too. I know in this county they are. It seems like the judges are all afraid of being overturned down the line, know what I mean?"

"Goodbye," said the man.

"Now just wait a minute," said Dan. "Which Hy-Vee?" But it was too late.

Dan hung up the phone, put on his sheriff's jacket, and went back outside. Joan Gower had come down from the roof and was leaning on a sawhorse, smoking a reedlike cigarette.

46

Dan brought the ladder down, returned it to the shed out back, and explained to the woman that he had to go.

"May I share a verse with you?" said Joan Gower.

"O.K., one verse," said Dan.

She stood, rested her cigarette on the spine of the sawhorse, and opened the Bible to a place marked by a thin red ribbon.

"Set me as a seal upon thine heart," she read, "as a seal upon thine arm: for love is strong as death; jealousy is cruel as the grave: the coals thereof are coals of fire, which hath a most vehement flame. Many waters cannot quench love, neither can the floods drown it: if a man would give all the substance of his house for love, it would utterly be contemned."

Joan Gower retrieved her cigarette and took a drag. "Song of Solomon, eight: six and seven," she said. "What does that say to you?"

"I don't know," said Dan. "Love is powerful."

Joan nodded. "Good," she said. "Solomon is grappling with the idea of love."

On the highway Dan turned on the reds, and he got to the Hy-Vee in Chesley pretty fast, but he found nothing unusual in any of the shopping carts. He saw Lenore Wells in the dairy section—she was on antidepressants, as always, and smiled her small, lonely smile. Her father had hanged himself in the vault of the Morrisville bank, and her brother was serving fifteen years in Anamosa for stealing a mail truck. Sad, sad family. Lenore told Dan about two cranes that had flown over her house early that morning, and Dan thought she was going to weep, but instead she shook her head and reached down to get some string cheese.

There were two more Hy-Vee stores in the county, in Morrisville and in Margo. At the Hy-Vee in Morrisville the

47

boys brought the groceries out to your car, and so there was always a line of cars at the curb, but there were no carts in the parking lot.

The store was at one end of a little shopping center, and Dan entered through a wide corridor in which about one hundred 4-H girls were involved in a confusing demonstration of soil erosion. On a long narrow table they had set up a miniature landscape covered with sand and were now attacking the sand with fans, and squirt guns, and even their hands, although their hands corresponded to none of the erosive forces they had studied, and using them was against the rules. The girls wore white jumpsuits with green sashes, and these outfits were splattered with sand and water, and all around the table was chaos, except for one end, where the older girls presided calmly over the area designated Contour Plowing. Dan was glad to get into the Hy-Vee store, but when he looked at the idle grocery carts, he saw nothing in them except broken lettuce leaves. He left the Morrisville Hy-Vee and drove to the one in Margo.

There he found a shopping cart with a cardboard box in it. The cart was in the northwest corner of the parking lot next to a yellow Goodwill bin. Dan looked at the box, which had once held a case of Hamm's beer. The top was closed, each flap overlapping the next. Dan heard crying. Lifting the flaps, he found a baby wrapped in a blue flannel shirt. A note was taped on: "My name is 'Quinn.' Please look out for me." The baby had dark eyes, much dark hair, and a loud, deep cry. Dan picked up the Hamm's box and put it in the front seat of the cruiser. He fastened the seat belt and shoulder harness as well as he could around the box. The baby howled powerfully, but once the car was in motion he looked around, burped, and fell asleep.

Dan headed for Mercy Hospital in Stone City, but three miles out of Margo he picked up a radio call from the deputy Ed Aiken. Some kids were on top of the water tower in Pinville, and Ed Aiken could not get them to come down.

"Try the bullhorn," said Dan.

"Did that," said Ed.

"Say you're calling their folks," said Dan.

"Did that."

"I guess you'll have to go up after them."

"No, sir," said Ed, who had found it almost impossible to climb since an incident in his teens when he had come very close to falling off the roof of a barn.

"Jesus, Ed," said Dan, "get over it.

"I'm not going up that ladder," said Ed.

"O.K., but I have a baby with me," said Dan. "I found a baby at the grocery store in Margo."

"Maybe it belongs to somebody," said Ed.

"Well, I suppose it does," said Dan.

The water tower was by the tracks in Pinville. It was the old silver kind with a red bonnet, a ladder, and an encircling walkway that provided a good platform to stand on while writing graffiti. A small crowd had gathered in the grass around the base. Someone had come by with a box of tomatoes, and many of the people were chewing on tomatoes and staring up at the water tower. Ed Aiken came over to the passenger side of the cruiser when Dan pulled up. Ed was a thin man, and the one thing you would say about him day to day was that he rarely seemed to get a decent shave. Right now, for instance, he had a little flag of toilet paper flying under his chin as he opened the cruiser door. The baby started to cry again.

49

"Aw," said Ed, "let me hold the little darling."

He lifted the baby from its box, the blue shirt trailing like a blanket. "Do you like your Uncle Ed?" he said. "Say, sure you do."

Dan took a turn at the bullhorn without any luck, and then he climbed the water tower. A cage made of hoops protected the ladder, but it seemed that if you slipped and fell the main function of the hoops would be to shear off your head on the way down, and Dan felt a vacuum in his lower parts as he climbed. He watched the people eating tomatoes, and when he could no longer make out the individual tomatoes, he stopped looking down. The culprits were three boys in sleeveless black T-shirts and jeans with the knees torn out. Their setup was professional, with hats, rags, a bucket of red paint, a tray, some turpentine, and a roller screwed onto a stick. In jagged, running letters they had written "Armageddon" and "Tina Rules."

"Who's Tina?" said Dan.

"Tina of Talking Heads," said Errol Thomas.

"What are you thinking of, coming up here in daylight on a Saturday afternoon?" said Dan. "Did you imagine for a second that you wouldn't get caught?"

"We want people to know," said Albert Robeshaw.

"We want people to wake up," said Dane Marquardt. He cupped his hands and yelled "Wake up!" at the people on the ground. "Look at them, they're so insignificant."

"We're in a band," said Errol Thomas.

"I would've guessed that," said Dan.

The boys packed all their stuff into a gunnysack, and they and Dan headed down the ladder. On the ground, Ed Aiken was holding Quinn over his shoulder, patting him, pivoting slowly.

"How is he?" said Dan.

Ed raised his eyebrows and whispered, "Just dropping off."

It rained most of the time for the next two weeks. This was the long, gray rain known to every fall, when the people of Grouse County begin to wonder whether their lives will acquire any meaning in time for winter. Water filled ditches, flooded basements, and kept farmers from their fields, but it did not stop anyone from visiting the sheriff's office in Morrisville with supplies for the baby left at the Hy-Vee. Of course, the baby had never been to the sheriff's office, but the sheriff had found him, and so the people turned up, craning their necks and looking into the hall behind the desk as if expecting to spy the abandoned Quinn in one of the cells or maybe lying on the floor. The visitors were farm women, for the most part, and they came shaking the water out of their scarves, and carrying bundles of diapers, cases of formula, and bales of bleached-out clothing that in at least one case had not been worn since World War II. Helene Plum even brought a beef-macaroni casserole in Corning Ware, although it was not clear who was supposed to eat it. But then, Helene Plum reacted to almost any kind of stressful news by making casseroles, and had once, in Faribault, Minnesota, attended the scene of a burned-out eighteen-wheeler with a pan of scalloped potatoes and ham. True story, told by her daughter-in-law.

At first Dan and the deputies tried a policy of accepting nothing at the station and directing all supplies over to the Children's Farm in Stone City. That was where Quinn was. But it seemed you couldn't tell people they had come to the wrong place—they wouldn't hear it. This was partly out of dignity and partly because Stone City was a good half hour

51

from Morrisville. So when Dan would say, "The baby is out of our hands," or Earl Kellogg, Jr., would say, "They got the baby over in Stone City," the women would leave their offerings on the bench against the wall, or on the floor, and say, "Well, hope he can use this busy box," or "Well, see that he gets these sleepers worn by our Ted," and then they would turn and go back out to their El Caminos in the rain. The sheriff and his deputies must have made six or eight trips to the Children's Farm. There was stuff enough for ten babies, and sometimes the sheriff's department looked more like a Similac warehouse than an agency of the law.

Claude Robeshaw and his son Albert came in on the ninth or tenth day of rain, but they didn't have anything for Quinn. Claude's concern was his son's share—about seven hundred and fifty dollars—of what it would cost to restore the paint job on the Pinville water tower. Claude Robeshaw was tall, with plowlike features. He was seventy-one years old to Albert's fifteen. When Dan himself was a teenager he had baled straw for Claude Robeshaw, and he remembered one August Sunday when Claude was driving the tractor and Dan, Willard Schlurholtz, and the Reverend Walt Carr were working the hayrack. The temperature was ninety-seven degrees, and Claude decided that after every round they'd better have a beer so nobody would get dehydrated, and after five rounds young Dan fell off the rack.

"I'll climb that tower and paint it myself," said Claude. "That kind of money, I'll silver-plate the bastard. I'm serious. I'm dead serious. Why, Jesus Christ, some outfit comes down from out of state and they are playing this county like a piano."

"Claude," said Dan, "your quarrel really is with the board of supervisors. But as it was told to me, they've got to have

52

somebody who is bonded. Now, what is bonded? Well, you go to the state and the state bonds you, and to find out any more about it, I guess you'd have to go to the state. But this is what it costs, apparently, to get somebody who is bonded."

Claude turned grimly to his son, who was almost as tall, with short brown hair, jean jacket, eyeglasses. "Do you understand what the sheriff is saying?" he said.

"No," said Albert.

"It's bullshit, that's why," said Claude.

"They went out and got three bids," said Dan. "I'll grant you this was not the lowest. There was one bid that was lower, but that was by a company, their crew got drunk over in De Witt and ran their truck into the river, and it was a big production to get it out. Yes, it's a lot of money. But those words went up, and they have to come down. People are mad in Pinville, Claude. They had a fine water tower, and now you drive into town, you think the place is called Armageddon."

Albert laughed, and this angered Claude. "So help me God," he said, "I will knock you through the wall of this station."

"Then I'd be dead," said Albert. "That's like saying, 'So help me God, I'll cut your throat.' Or, 'So help me God, I'll poison your food.'"

Claude made room on the bench by moving aside a yellow quilt that had come in that day for Quinn. He sat down, removed a cigar from its glass tube, pared the end away with a jackknife, and lit up. "I believe I had you too late in life," said Claude. "I already had two daughters and three sons, and maybe I should have stopped right there. I know it's been one sorry situation after another. Maybe I should tell the sheriff about when you decided to run away and live in a tree."

"Do," said Albert. "I want you to."

So then he didn't. But it was not a long story, and he had told it so many times, to prove so many different points about Albert's character, that most anyone around Grafton knew the gist of it. When Albert was five or six years old, he got mad at Claude and Marietta and decided to move out to the woods behind the Robeshaw farm. He took a can of beans, a can opener, a fork, and *The Five Chinese Brothers*. Well, he sat down under an evergreen to read, and he wondered if he hadn't brought the wrong book, because it always gave him a chill to see the picture of the first brother's huge face as he held in the sea. But he read the whole thing and then he was hungry, and he managed to open the can and begin eating the beans. But when he came upon the little cube of pork in the beans, he didn't know what it was, and it scared him, and he ran crying for home.

Dan waited for Earl Kellogg to come on shift, and when he did Dan left the office for the day. But it was cold, raining, and getting dark, and this made Dan think that winter was coming, so he decided to go over to the Children's Farm with the yellow quilt, which had been brought in that day by Marian Hamilton and wouldn't do anyone any good folded up there on the bench.

The Children's Farm was a dark brick castle on a hill. It had narrow windows and lightning rods and stone figures that lined the roof, representing the virtues of Hygiene, Obedience, Courtesy, Restraint, and Silence. The structure was built in 1899, and rebuilt after a fire nine years later, and seemed specially designed to remind the children passing through that their circumstances were tragic. There was a farm—seventy acres and two barns, one big, one small, which were slowly falling down—and it used to be, going way back, that the hands and the children would raise their own food and even make their own shoes. Now the fields were leased to other farmers, the kids wore navy tennis shoes from Kresge's, and the barns had not held animals for twenty-five, thirty years. Still, cows had been there once, and it was raining, so the place smelled like wet cows as Dan stepped from his cruiser, tucked the quilt under his coat, and headed across the gravel to the front door. There was a white Ford Torino in the driveway with the parking lights on and the motor running, and Dan looked in, as was his habit, and sitting behind the steering wheel was the woman, Joan Gower, who had thrown his trowel off the roof of the trailer.

She rolled down the window. A lime paisley scarf covered her hair. "Is something wrong?" she said. "Oh, Sheriff, how are you?"

"I'm fine," said Dan. "Do work here?"

"I volunteer," said Joan. "Well, I'm volunteering to read to Quinn. I know the community has really poured its heart out, but it occurred to me that the one thing he probably doesn't have is someone to read him stories. That's why I brought these books. See this? Jesus is riding a burro on Palm Sunday. Isn't that a beautiful illustration? And here he is, making fish for the multitude. Isn't that the greatest?"

Rain dripped from the visor of Dan's hat. "I have to tell you something, Joan," he said. "This is an infant. Bible stories might be a little bit over his head."

"Well, that's what they said, but the age doesn't matter. I saw a story in a magazine about a child whose parents read him the multiplication tables every night before he was born, and now Princeton University is running tests on him. But these people say Quinn doesn't have time to hear a story. Does that make any sense to you? What is it that he's supposed to be doing? I don't see what would occupy a baby's time to the point where he couldn't listen to a Bible story. This evades me completely. Plus, somebody has to provide him with a religious instinct—otherwise, when he's christened it won't take, and he runs the risk of going to Hell. And I told them this. Well, they have to run it by their supervisor."

"You talked to them just now?" said Dan.

"Well, no," said Joan. "It's been a while, but they said they couldn't predict when the supervisor would be in. It seemed like they were giving me a song and a dance, but then I thought, Why don't I wait and see if he shows up. But I suppose it's getting late now."

Dan coughed. "Yeah, it is," he said. "Maybe you ought to go on home and call them tomorrow. Where do you live?"

"I don't mind waiting," said Joan. "But I guess you have a point. Maybe I'm a little keyed up about this baby. I don't know why. It's been raining so hard. I think I need to see him with my own eyes. I would feel better if I could just see him. I mean, look at this place. It's like the Munsters' house."

"Joan, that baby is fine," said Dan. "He's strong, he's healthy, he's got more blankets than anyone I've ever known."

"Maybe you could put in a good word for me," said Joan. "Maybe if you suggested it, they would let me read to him. Tell them my church might do a benefit for him. Which is true, we might."

"I'll talk to them," said Dan, "see what I can do." He watched Joan Gower drive up to the highway, and then he went into the lobby, which was heavy with the smell of musty furniture. He gave the quilt to Nancy McLaughlin, the night administrator. She had her arm in a cast and explained that she had been knocked down by a rainy gust while trying to get from her car to her house. She took him to see Quinn. They had him on the second floor, which was painted yellow and gray. In a low room with bright lights, Dan's second cousin, the nurse Leslie Hartke, was giving Quinn a bottle.

"Hi, Dan," she said. "Want to feed him?"

Dan shook his head. "Just brought another quilt over," he said.

"This has been a bonanza for us," said Nancy McLaughlin, rubbing her cast with her hand.

"Oh, come on," said Leslie Hartke. "Feed the baby." So Dan washed his hands and sat down, and Leslie gave him the baby, and the baby's blankets, and the bottle. The baby took the bottle for a moment, looked at Dan with wide eyes, and began to cry.

"I remind him of Hy-Vee," said Dan.

On his way out, Dan paused with Nancy McLaughlin to watch some boys playing checkers in the common room. The boys wore pajamas and sat at a card table in the corner by the stairs. The common room had high plaster walls, and the only sound was the melancholy click of the checkers.

"King me," said one of the boys.

The other stared at the board. "Fuck," he said.

"Checker time's over," said Nancy McLaughlin. "Good night now." After the boys had disappeared up the stairs, Dan asked Nancy about Joan Gower.

"Not a happy woman," said Nancy. "She read me a verse, what was it, something about being shut up in the hands of my enemies."

Dan tried all the way home to decide whether Joan Gower was trouble or just overly dedicated to whatever it was she believed in. When you got down to it, Dan did not know what anyone believed in. He had told her he was comfortable with his own beliefs, but that was just to keep her moving. He didn't have any beliefs to speak of. A world that would deposit a child in a beer carton in the middle of nowhere seemed capable of you-name-it, but Dan did not think that you-name-it qualified as a belief. The trailer was dark in the rain. Dan had left a Folgers can under the drip in the corner of the bedroom, and he emptied the can in the sink and put it back in place.

In order to see the records of the Mixerton Clinic, Dan had to talk to Beth Pickett. She was a spindly older doctor who stamped around with her chin in the air. She had begun her career in 1944, as an intern with Tom Lansford, a famous general practitioner in Chesley. Dr. Pickett had seen Grouse County medicine through its youth and would not let go. She was insufferable, and the public loved her dearly.

Dan waited in Dr. Pickett's office, where the walls were crowded with homemade images of Dr. Pickett. She had been needlepointed, watercolored, and macraméd, although the last made her look like the trunk of a tree. She had been sketched and caricatured many, many times. Soon the doctor marched into the room and sat down behind the desk.

"We don't think the baby was born in a hospital," said Dan. "We thought we'd take a list of the people who came in pregnant, and a list of the people who gave birth in the hospitals, and compare the two lists. It's a pretty simple idea."

"Well, it's not as simple as you think," said Dr. Pickett, "because when a woman comes into this clinic, nobody sees the records. They're protected by legislation I went to Des

Moines and got passed in the summer of 1966. A man named Clay drove me down. He was a big drinker. All the time I was talking to the legislature, he was down at the Hotel Leroi. Drank and drank and never got drunk."

"All I need is the names," said Dan. "Maybe I could just look at the names."

"No," said Dr. Pickett. "The names are in the records, and the records cannot be seen."

They went back and forth like this for a while, but however Dan could think to phrase it, Dr. Pickett said no, and finally Dan said he could come back with a warrant if that's what it took.

Dr. Pickett pretended not to hear. "That's right," she said, "you come back anytime."

"Help me find this woman," said Dan. "Come on."

Dr. Pickett brought out some brandy and poured it into jam glasses. "I don't see what good that would do," she said, pushing a glass across the desk, steering it around a plaster bust of herself. "When I went to medical school, I lived in Grand Forks, North Dakota, with Aunt Marilyn Beloit. This was many years ago. Every house on her street was a bungalow, and they were all small and nicely taken care of. Aunt Marilyn was a singer who went by the name of Bonnie Boone, and she must have done all right, because she had all her suits tailored in Fargo. Anyway, also living in this neighborhood was a young woman, not married, who had given birth to a child and left it on the doorstep of a family named Price. The Prices lived up the hill, and they didn't lack for money. Well, this was the way it was done in those days. Babies were left on doorsteps all the time, and it was not unusual to open your door in the morning and find that three or four had

59

been deposited overnight. I'm exaggerating, of course, but it worked very smoothly, as I recall, and you didn't talk about it, but you didn't throw up your hands in horror, either. Anyway, one evening I took the bus home, and as I was walking by this woman's place—her name was Nora, and she rented the back of a house—she asked me to come over and visit after supper. She was older than I was, but we were not that far apart in age, so I said yes. Well, it turned out that Nora was a bohemian. She had a piano and a pregnant cat and a big bottle of red wine, and her bed was a mat in the middle of the living room floor, which I thought was an unusual arrangement. We had two or three glasses of wine, and the next thing we knew that big black and white cat had crawled onto the bed and broke her water. Nora dragged out a suitcase, opened it, and lined it with towels. She put the cat in the suitcase, and that cat began to purr so loudly it sounded like singing. I was spellbound, but with the wine I could not keep my eyes open past three kittens. When I awoke there were five, suckling in the suitcase, and Nora was playing the piano."

Dan waited for her to conclude the story, but that seemed to be it, so he said, "Did it ever bother Nora that she gave her baby away?"

Dr. Pickett shook out a handkerchief and blew her nose. "It bothered her a great deal," she said, "and I believe she tried to get it back. But Jack Price was a judge, so you can imagine how that went over."

Claude Robeshaw did not give up on the water-tower issue, and the county board of supervisors eventually agreed to a deal in which he would put up four hundred dollars toward the restoration, and his son would pay off the rest by working after school for the sheriff's office. Dan did not have to go along with this arrangement, but it seemed like the punishment would mean more to young Albert if he had to put in time; also, let's face it, sheriff was and remains an elected position in Grouse County, and Claude Robeshaw was a faithful Democrat, who once had Hubert and Muriel Humphrey to his house for supper.

The first thing Dan had Albert do was clean up the basement of the sheriff's substation in Stone City. This was a tiny storefront on Ninth Avenue that once had been a barbershop called Jack's. The reason the sheriff's department got no more than a barbershop's worth of space in the county seat goes back to 1947, when the sheriff was a popular fellow called Darwin Whaley. He was handsome and young and just back from the South Pacific, and the board of supervisors hated him. The supervisors got their own way about everything, and wanted to keep getting their way, and decided that the thing to do with Darwin Whaley was stick him far from the rest of the government, where he would have a hard time finding out what was going on. So they built the sheriff's building off in Morrisville—where it is to this day—and for years the sheriff had no place whatsoever in Stone City, although the courthouse was there, and appearing in court and consulting court records were common things for the sheriff to do. It was in 1972 that the county made a deal with the dying barber, Jack Henry, to buy his shop and rent it back to him for one dollar a year until his demise. But Jack Henry surprised his doctors by holding on until 1979, at which time the sheriff (this would have been Otto Nicolette) finally got his barbershop.

The basement was still full of everything a careless barber with one foot in the grave might care to throw down there:

newspapers, hamburger crusts, magazines, sun-faded comb displays, pop bottles, torn seat cushions, burned-out clippers with tangled cords, radios with cracked faces, moldy calendars featuring bland farm scenes or naked women with scissors and comb. The worst was the hair tonic, which would take Albert several days to find but which he could hear dripping everywhere, like underground springs. He went to work with a shovel and an aluminum basket. On the second day he uncovered two barrels full of mannequin heads—many more heads than one barber would need, you would think, but it turned out that each one was printed with dotted lines suggesting a different cut or style. This would have seemed touching to anyone who had been around when Jack was barbering, because he was known for having exactly one haircut in his repertoire and applying it equally to all customers. Albert carried the heads up the narrow stairs in the aluminum basket. They had the feel of an important archaeological find, and Albert kept three for a use he had not yet determined, but the rest went into a dump truck parked in the alley.

The cleanup took place during a week when Dan was testifying before a grand jury in a drug case involving a restaurant called Rack-O's on Highway 41. Once, returning to the office, he found Albert dangling his legs over the side of the desk, smoking a cigarette.

"I just used the phone," said Albert. "I hope that's all right. I was calling Lu Chiang. She's the exchange student from Taiwan. They put her out on Kessler's farm."

"Long way from home," said Dan.

"You wouldn't believe how hard they make her work," said Albert. "She has to take care of these chickens all by herself.

If it wasn't for her, the chickens would all be dead. Candy Kessler stays in town every night, but Chiang has to go home to feed the chickens. She has to get up at six in the morning to feed the chickens. One of the chickens stayed out in the rain and got sick, and none of the Kesslers would speak to her until it got better."

"I never knew anyone with chickens where they weren't always getting sick," said Dan.

"There's a foreign-exchange guy named Marty in Kansas City, but he just kisses the host family's ass," said Albert. "He says she knew this was a farm area when she left Taiwan, so too bad."

"Something came up about Taiwan the other day," said Dan. "Oh, yeah, that's where they make our radar guns. One of them went on the blink, and we had to mail it back. Forty-three dollars postage."

"Chiang says she's not getting a very favorable impression of America," said Albert. "I said, 'Just wait.'"

The rain let up gradually, day by day, and the weather warmed into a wave of Indian summer. Farmers got back to work, and the combines were going around the clock. You could see the headlights through the stalks at night, dust plumes during the day. On the highway, every other vehicle seemed to be a tractor pulling a green wagon full of corn. The sunlight was golden. Lu Chiang's chores became less burdensome, and she got to go up to Pizza Hut with Albert Robeshaw.

Meanwhile, Quinn had not been forgotten, and various towns and clubs and churches struggled, not in an undignified way, over the right to carry his banner. It was felt that something should be done, no question, and that one large thing would be preferable to a lot of small things. So it was decided that a Big Day would be held for Quinn on Sunday, October 14, in the town of Romyla. A Big Day was what you called it when a town held a street event for any purpose other than to celebrate a conventional holiday. You could have a Big Day for sending a sick child to the Mayo Clinic, for new axes and boots for the fire department, or just for everyone to drink and dance on Main Street. Romyla was chosen because it had never had a Big Day, although it had conducted an Irish Fair for several years in the seventies and was considered capable of holding a well-run event—unlike, say, Boris, which was regarded as something of a joke town, barely able to keep a tavern in business.

They asked Dan to bring out the sheriff's department cruisers for the parade, and they also asked him to take his turn in the dunking booth. Dan agreed to the cruisers, and bought some hard candy for himself and the deputies to throw to the spectators. Ed Aiken was lukewarm to this idea, and Earl Kellogg said flat-out that it was sissified for anyone in a cruiser to acknowledge the crowd in any way, and that this was doubly true when it came to throwing candy, to which Dan said, "And we wonder why people hate the sheriff's department. And I don't mean not like, I mean hate."

"Well," said Earl, "if you want to do something people would get a charge out of, they already asked you to sit in that cage where they dump you in the water."

"Lester Ward broke his collarbone that way," said Dan. "You want to try it, you be my guest."

"Lester Ward," said Ed. "Isn't he the guy with all the decoys in his yard? Why would anybody want to dunk him?"

"No," said Dan, "but I know who you're thinking of. That's

Lyle Ward. Lester Ward's dead. He ran the hatchery in Pinville. You remember him—he always wore a hat."

"Oh, *Lester* Ward," said Ed.

Dan met Earl Kellogg and Ed Aiken in Romyla at ten-thirty on the Sunday morning of the benefit. They were all in their reflective sunglasses, and they stood in front of the Cotter Pin Tap watching the Methodist women unloading a van full of cakes for the cakewalk. The sun was bright, and it seemed that all the grass in town had just been mowed. Romyla had a hostile kind of pride that you didn't find anywhere else in the county, Dan thought. Earl Kellogg sneezed eleven times in rapid succession, and Ed pounded him on the back to help him stop.

A new red pickup pulled alongside them, with Claude Robeshaw, Lu Chiang, and Albert inside. Claude said good morning and went into the Cotter Pin, and Albert introduced Lu Chiang to Dan, Ed, and Earl. Lu Chiang had brown eyes and long black hair. She was one of those foreign students whose fresh clothing and generous expressions make the local kids seem edgy and strange. She, Albert, and Dan walked down the midway, which was in this case Main Street between the old telephone office and the tracks.

"Albert tells me you have a basement with heads in it," said Chiang.

"That's right," said Dan.

"It must be very comical," said Chiang.

"They're gone now," said Albert. "I threw them out."

"Now, Lu Chiang," said Dan, "how long does it take a person to get here from Taiwan?"

"The flight from Taipei to Tokyo was three and a half hours," said Chiang. "At Narita there was a long delay, and I fell asleep in my chair. Then I awoke and boarded a flight to Chicago, which lasted twelve hours. From Chicago there was a flight in a small, barren aircraft to Stone City, where Ron and Delia Kessler were waiting for me. I believe it was twenty-one hours from the beginning to the end."

Dan whistled. "Was this the longest you'd ever flown?" he said.

"Yes," said Chiang. "Seven hours from Tokyo, the flight attendants appeared with facecloths for everyone."

"I can't even picture Tokyo," said Dan.

The parade was late because the Morrisville-Wylie marching band was late, but the band members finally arrived, in a yellow bus, and led the way playing "On Wisconsin," "Quinn the Eskimo," and "The Girl from Ipanema." They were followed by blue-ribbon rider Jocelyn Jewell on Pogo, by a group of Korean War veterans pulling a cannon, and by floats representing the discovery of the infant in the grocery cart, the marriage of Julien Dubuque and Princess Petosa, and the complete line of Arctic Cat snowmobiles sold by Wiegart Implement in Wylie. The sheriff's cruisers ended the procession, and no candy came from their windows.

After the parade, Albert and Lu Chiang went down the line of musty blue tents, trying to win a prize. They threw baseballs at a row of stuffed cats that seemed to be nailed down, lost eight dollars at blackjack, and had their weights guessed almost to the pound in an unsuccessful attempt to win a plaster cow. Then they examined a red tractor that had been modified to run on LP gas, but it looked to their eyes like any other red tractor, and they wandered by the table of the Little Church of the Redeemer, where Joan Gower and a thin boy named Russ were giving away coin banks in the shape of a church to anyone who could recite a Bible verse from memory. Albert responded with the one about Caesar Augustus's decree that all the world should be taxed, and Joan said very good and handed him a church bank. Then she turned to Chiang, and when she learned that Chiang was a Buddhist, she picked up a stack of pamphlets, thumbed off five or six, and pressed them into the girl's hands.

"I want you to have this literature," said Joan. "I want you to take these home to your family. This part is about the death on the Cross, and this shaded area has to do with the Resurrection. This is a beautiful message for people of all nations. And I'll bet when you get down to it you will find that Jesus and Buddha have a lot in common."

"I think the Buddha is much heavier," said Chiang.

"You just take these home," said Joan.

Albert and Chiang headed for the Cotter Pin in search of old Claude. Along the way, Chiang let the pamphlets drop into a green barrel, and Albert gave her the church bank he had won.

The Big Day in Romyla raised more than two thousand dollars for Quinn, but it turned out that he did not need it. A rich couple came down from Minneapolis one weekend and made him their foster child. Because of the privacy laws, not even Nancy McLaughlin of the Children's Farm could give out the identity of the couple, but it was Mark and Linda Miles, who, with some foresight, had made their fortune selling soy-based eye makeup in northern Europe. Quinn was renamed Nigel Bergman Miles and given a bedroom about the size of Dan's trailer, overlooking one of Minnesota's ten thousand lakes.

Meanwhile, Dan kept looking for Quinn's mother. He never got to see the clinic records, and had to make do with rumors, anonymous tips, and crank phone calls. He ended up with a list of thirteen names, and during the month of October he was able to clear eleven of them. One had given birth in St. Louis and put the child up for adoption, five had miscarried without providing adequate explanation to their neighbors, two were men with female-sounding names, and three were elderly nuns at Sacred Heart Academy in Morrisville.

That left two possibilities: a woman who would not discuss the case over the phone, and a woman who had no phone.

Dan ruled out the first woman when, in the middle of their interview, she excused herself to turn up the radio to hear the theme song from *Cats*. This was at the laundromat where she worked, in Walleye Lake. Also, her story made sense and was verifiable. (It had to do with a troubled young man who once had a crush on her and now waged a relentless telephone campaign against her. Since the establishment of the Crimebusters Hot Line in Brier County, for instance, he had called up to link her name to well-publicized instances of arson, hit-and-run driving, and window-peeking.)

The woman with no phone was Quinn's mother, although she never admitted it. She lived in a house on a woody hill across from the county shed on the outskirts of Wylie. It was a house that had been moved to the site years ago, but it still looked out of kilter and always would. The doors would not close; winter wind would sweep through the cracks in the foundation. The house needed paint, and for some reason there was a rusted barbecue grill on the roof of the porch. There was no sign of children, no sign of animals, no sign of anyone except this woman, who was a little older than Dan had expected, wore a cotton dress, and had her hair tied up with a frayed green ribbon. She and Dan sat on the steps of the porch.

"I went to the doctor the one time," she said. "It wasn't for the baby. There was no pregnancy. That's where the confusion lies. It turned out to be a false alarm. I wrote it on my calendar."

"Who's your doctor?" said Dan.

"He's on my calendar," she said.

She got up, went inside, and came back with a wall calendar from the cooperative elevator in Wylie. It did have writing on it, lots of it, but it was unreadable, and had been scrawled across the days without regard for when one ended and the next began. Dan got up. The woman's eyes were still—she was watching the orange county trucks across the road. "Let's go for a ride," said Dan, and she said, "Where to?"

FOUR

IT WAS NOT long after this that Louise broke into Dan's trailer. She had broken into one other place in her life—the Grafton School, in 1972. Louise and her friend Cheryl Jewell had climbed a drainpipe, raised a window, and spray-painted thirty-one football helmets hanging on the wall of the gym.

Louise and Cheryl were sophomores, and they felt—and they were not alone—that too much importance was being placed on football at a time when the rest of the school was without money. Meanwhile, there were those helmets, like dinosaur eggs pegged up in a row, and the two girls took their spray paint and wrote the following, one letter per helmet: SEE THE LONELY BOYS OUT ON THE WEEKEND.

The words came from a Neil Young song, and were actually not about football but about buying a pickup and driving down to L.A. All Louise and Cheryl had to do was make it "boys," plural. Some football players protested in the school paper. "With the many activities available to us, such as pep rallies, snake dances, etc., we are far from lonely," they wrote.

No one ever found out who painted the helmets. The equipment managers were able to scrub the letters off using steel brushes dipped in turpentine, but there were those who felt the team played lightheaded all year due to the fumes. Louise was sixteen at the time. Now she was thirty-four, and the school was closed, and frost coated the windows of Louise's house. Also, the big white dog was in the living room. He sat on the couch, looking luminous and pleasantly surprised. Halloween was coming, and that seemed to be the extent of his message. Louise had a set of blue drinking glasses, and she was enjoying her third blue glass of red wine.

"You're supposed to be outside in the cold shed," said Louise to the dog, "but instead you're in the warm house. What are you doing on the warm davenport in the comfy house? You're not going to answer me, are you? I'll bet I could talk for a long time before I got an answer. Couldn't I talk a long time before getting an answer?"

Louise's mother then called her on the telephone. Hans Cook had acquired some venison, and it had ended up in Mary's deep freeze, and Mary wanted Louise to distribute it. Louise and Mary had been arguing recently, and this was clearly Mary's way of patching things up.

"The dog's in the house," said Louise. "He's sitting here watching TV."

"I don't think Les Larsen would like that," said Mary. Les Larsen rented the fields and outbuildings of the Klar place. "Isn't that dog supposed to be guarding the farm?"

"The farm is quiet as a mouse," said Louise. "How did Hans get this venison, anyway? Does he hunt?"

"I don't know," said Mary. "It was some trade he made. They were playing cards. I didn't get it all."

They talked a little more and said goodbye. Louise sipped wine and turned the television up.

"Now, watch," she said to the dog. "See what this lady's doing? Look at the TV. She's taking the real pearls and leaving the fake ones."

• • •

The next day was Saturday. Louise stood in front of her mother's deep freeze, down in the basement beside the stairs. Louise had a headache, and wore an ugly, shabby sweater. She kept bumping a coat rack bearing the little coats once worn by herself and her sister June.

"Why me?" said Louise. "Just curious."

"If I have you do it," said Mary, who was sitting on the basement steps drinking sherry, "it shows the importance I attach to it. Also, it gives you the chance to make some lasting friends."

"Can I have some of that sherry?" said Louise.

"It's all gone, sorry," said Mary.

"I have lots of friends," said Louise, who seemed to be drawn by the presence of the little wool coats into the tone of voice of an eight-year-old.

"Take some to Dan Norman," said Mary. "You like him."

Louise considered this remark. She and Dan had been brought together by the breakup of Louise's marriage, and now that it was good and broken up, they had not seen each other in a while. "He's never home," said Louise.

Mary nodded. "You think you hold office, when in fact the office holds you," she said.

Louise loaded her arms with white packages. "How many goddamned deer you got in here?" she said.

Mary stood. "I realize it's a lot," she said. "Don't feel compelled to take it all at once. Get that little Coleman and put some in there with some ice. That's what I got it out for. And don't forget to smile. It takes less muscle effort to smile than it does to frown."

"When my face is completely relaxed, people still think I'm frowning," said Louise.

"You have a beautiful face," said Mary. "An angel's face."

"Even you must admit my forehead is on the large side," said Louise.

"I've never believed that stuff about your forehead," said Mary.

• • •

Louise delivered venison to three people before bailing out of the task, and even those people—Nan Jewell, Jack White, and Henry Hamilton—lived more or less on her way home.

Nan Jewell had the southernmost of the Three Sisters, the big blue houses on Park Street in Grafton where the various members of the Jewell family lived. Nan was a rich and restless widow who held people to such a high standard that they usually fell short. When Louise arrived, the old lady was practicing the line of attack she would follow in church the next morning. She always thought people were taking negligent procedural shortcuts.

"They're not posting the hymns anymore and I would like to hear someone tell me why," she said. "They've always done it and now, lo and behold, they're not doing it. What about the people with arthritis? What about the people who need a little time to find the right page? Are they not welcome in our church? And another thing while I'm thinking about it. I don't know who's slicing the Communion bread lately, but they've got a lot to learn about what is meant by a wafer. I don't think a Jewell would cut Communion bread in this haphazard way. I don't think a Montrose would. Nor a Robeshaw, a Mason, a Kellson, a Carr."

"Boy, I know it," said Louise. But that was just what you said to Nan unless you wanted to be trapped with her all day. The fact was, Louise didn't know anyone named Kellson.

From Nan's house it was out in the country to Jack White's farm on the Margo-Chesley road. Jack White was the father of Johnny White.

Louise found Jack in his horse barn with the veterinarian Roman Baker. Jack had five Belgian horses, named Tony, Mack, Molly, Polly, and Pegasus. They were enormous animals with jaws like anvils. Louise started to tell Jack about the venison, but he said it would be a minute before he could concentrate on whatever it was she had to say. The problem was that some of his horses were walking backward.

"When did this start?" said Roman Baker. His face was narrow, his hair thick, his eyes widely spaced. He'd been working with horses a long time. "Change their diet recently? Might there be something spooking them?"

"Not that I know of," said Jack White. "But there again, I've been gone." He put his boot up on the rail and crossed his forearms on his knee, like someone in a fertilizer commercial. "Just yesterday got back from Reno. Spent five days in Tahoe and three days in Reno. That Tahoe is some of the prettiest country there is, and I saw Juliet Prowse in Reno. What a pair of legs on that lady. What a radiant complexion. Anyway, my son Johnny was watching the place for me while I was gone, and when I asked him, he said as far as he had noticed, the horses were not walking backward. I said, 'You mean to stand there and tell me if a horse was walking backward you

75

wouldn't notice it?' He said he might not. Well, the boy has personal problems, and that's no secret. As I always tell him, 'Johnny, you missed the boat.' I say, 'Johnny, see that little speck on the horizon? That right there is the boat.'"

"I saw him up at Walleye Lake last spring," said Louise. "We had a talk. He seemed very friendly."

Jack White dusted off the sleeve of his shirt. "He always liked you," he said. "And it's too bad he didn't marry somebody of your caliber, instead of that nut he did marry. Although it's certainly hard to put more than a tiny fraction of the blame on her."

Roman Baker took a silver penlight and examined Tony's ears. "You got anything unusual growing in the field?" he said.

Jack stood, adjusted his belt. "Boy, I sure don't think so," he said.

"Have you checked the fencerows?" said Roman.

"Sure," said Jack. "Well, no. Not really."

"It could be in the fencerows," said Roman.

"Let's do it right now," said Jack.

They took a pickup out in the bumpy pasture. Jack drove, following the fences, Roman Baker occupied the passenger seat, and Louise sat on the tailgate, weeds sweeping against her ankles. The southwest corner of the field was thick with dark green growth. The truck came to a stop. Roman got out and walked to the fence, where he crushed some spade-shaped leaves between his palms and raised his hands to his face.

"This has to go," he shouted. He filled his arms with weeds and pulled them from the ground. "All this," he said. "Everything from here on down."

Jack stepped out of the cab. "What's he saying?"

"He says it all has to go," said Louise.

Henry Hamilton's farm was just up the road from Louise's place. The milkweed that had once been properly confined to the ditches along the road had come up the driveway into the yard, and at this time of year the air was thick with flying seeds. The fences needed work, and pigs seemed to come and go as they pleased. Driving in, Louise saw one come out from behind a propane tank and tear through the long grass to the grove.

Henry's house was dimly lit and warm and smelled of boiled cabbage or boiled greens of some kind. But it wasn't as if he had just boiled the greens—it was as if they had been boiling for years. On the kitchen table he had spread the comics from the Sunday paper and was carving a jack-o'-lantern. Mossy seeds spilled over the newspaper.

"These kids from *The Family Circus* don't have any sense," he said.

"I agree," said Louise. "There is a pig out."

"I've been after that guy for two days," said Henry. He turned the pumpkin toward Louise. "Do you think this looks like Tiny?"

"Kind of," said Louise. "The mouth does."

"I haven't seen him in the longest time," said Henry.

"Well, you know we're divorced," said Louise.

Henry put down his knife. "I didn't know that," he said.

"Henry," said Louise. "You remember. You notarized my statement."

Henry thought for a moment. "O.K. That's right. So I did."

He resumed work on the pumpkin. "I try to get one of these out every year. Sometimes I see a fair amount of children. Other times, the night goes by and I don't see anyone. One year I made divinity and I'll be goddamned if one person showed up."

77

"It doesn't look like Tiny anymore," said Louise.

She was right. There had been something subtle that was now gone.

Henry shrugged. An old Moorman's Feed clock ticked like time itself. "How does divorce suit you?" he said.

"It's all right," said Louise. "I don't have to cook anything I don't want to eat. That's a plus."

"Hey, my new tractor came in," said Henry.

"Good for you," said Louise.

They went out to see it. It was a large red tractor, and the wheels were already caked with dried mud. Henry let Louise climb up and drive it around the yard.

"She's a beauty," said Louise. "You're going to love this cab."

"I had to sell my oil well to get it, but I think it's going to be worth it," said Henry.

"I didn't know you had an oil well," said Louise.

"I had an oil well in Oklahoma," said Henry.

Louise went out with the girls that night. This had been planned weeks ago. Perry Kleeborg had suggested it. He had accused her of moping around to the point where it was affecting her performance. He received a business magazine called *Means of Production* free in the mail, and evidently he'd been reading it.

"Oh, my performance," said Louise. "You must excuse my performance."

"You ought to go out with the girls," said Kleeborg. "Do something to relax your mind a little bit."

Louise pressed wet contact sheets to the wall. "I don't know any girls," she said.

"I have Five Hundred Club every Thursday," said Kleeborg. "I know it's helped me. Do you play five hundred?"

"I've never understood the concept of trump," said Louise. "I like slapjack."

"Not really a club-type game," said Kleeborg.

"No," said Louise.

"Do you bowl?" said Kleeborg.

"I have bowled," said Louise.

"Well, you ought to do something," said Kleeborg.

Not long after this, as it happened, the chairman of the county board of supervisors had his picture taken at the Kleeborg studio. His name was Russell Ford, and his skin was bad, and he seemed to think that if he got just the right pictures, it would somehow make his skin better. Removing scars and bumps from a photograph is not hard, but Russell was after something elusive, and Louise eventually had to take the photographs to Big Chief Printing in Morrisville to have them touched up. The airbrushers there were two women named Pansy Gansevoort and Diane Scheviss. They roomed together in an A-frame on the south shore of Walleye Lake, and were somewhere in the lost years between twenty-seven and thirty-two. The three women had some laughs over Russell's homely features, and decided to get together one Saturday night.

Louise found Pansy and Diane in the Hi-Hat Lounge on Route 29 in Morrisville. It seemed they had already been drinking hard among the Halloween decorations. Pansy's face was a high red, and Diane had broken a glass. If alcohol, for Louise, was like a slow train through hills and scenic lowlands, for Pansy and Diane it seemed more like an elevator after the cable had snapped.

Louise tried to impose some order. The table at which they sat was a video game pitting a giant bat against a humorous figure representing the player. Louise suggested they try this, and they did, but without success. The stream of quarters required was more or less continuous, and no sooner would they get the little person moving than the bat would sweep in, ending the game. Louise said, "I don't even get the object."

"I guess stay away from the bat," said Diane.

At this, Pansy drank off some vodka and began to talk. "My boyfriend used to slap me," she said. "No reason necessary. He would slap me for good things or bad things, in sickness and in health. He would slap me to improve his luck. Then he slapped me in front of my mother, and she pushed him down the stairs."

"All right, Pearl!" said Diane.

"So he stopped slapping me," said Pansy, "and started burning me with the cigarette. I missed the slapping at first, until I got used to the cigarette. Then he stopped smoking. They outlawed smoking at work, and he said if he couldn't smoke at work, it would be easier all around if he didn't smoke at home either. He tried a pipe for a while, but it wasn't like the cigarette. Finally he moved out. I miss him, I miss all the terrible shit he did."

Diane rocked the weeping Pansy. "I know you do, babe," she said.

"Why?" said Louise.

Pansy wiped her eyes with a cocktail napkin. "He's going through changes," she said. "He's deeply troubled. Are we ready for a round?"

Louise laid ten dollars on the table and got up to use the bathroom. She washed her hands and looked at herself in the mirror. She felt as if she had strayed far from the people she understood. On the other hand, she lived within twelve miles of where she was born.

Dan Norman was on the ten o'clock news. Shannon Key had interviewed him for Channel 4 out of Morrisville. She was asking about the baby who had turned up at the Hy-Vee in Margo.

"Are you interviewing suspects?" Shannon asked.

"No," said Dan. "We're not even sure there was a crime. So suspects, no, that would be overstating it."

"Are you interviewing anyone?"

Dan gave this consideration. He looked into the camera by mistake and became somewhat rattled. "Well, yeah," he said. "I mean, of course."

"Channel 4 has learned that forty yards of green corduroy were stolen from Not Just Fabric in Margo, on or about the same day the baby was found," said Shannon Key.

"We know all about that," said Dan. "We don't think there is any connection."

"When do you expect results?"

"I don't know if you've ever watched a spider making a web," said Dan. "But I have, Shannon, and it takes a long time and a lot of going back and forth. And even when this web is done, somebody might come along and destroy it just by their hat brushing against it. Know what I mean?"

Louise picked up the phone and dialed Dan's number. She did not expect him to be home, and the phone rang in that neutral way it does when no one is going to answer. But he did.

"A spider?" she said. "What the hell is that all about?"

"It's a metaphor," said Dan.

"Would you like to come over for a beer?" said Louise.

"I better not right now," said Dan. "Apparently there's been an accident up at the Sugar Beet. I'm picking up things on the radio."

"What kind of things?" said Louise.

"Things about an accident," said Dan. "Tell you what. How about you coming over here? I shouldn't have to go out, but I had better stick by the radio awhile."

"O.K."

"I don't have any wine and I don't have any vodka."

"I have those."

It should not have surprised Louise that Dan was gone by the time she got there. A manila envelope was stuck in the doorframe, and in the envelope was a note saying the key was under the rock. The path from the door to the driveway was lined with white-painted rocks, and Louise could not find any key. She checked under several rocks, and with the last one she broke a pane of glass above the doorknob.

Louise let herself in and put on some lights. She swept up the broken glass and dumped it in a wastebasket. Looking for a corkscrew, she found instead a letter from Dan's Aunt Mona, who was scheduled for exploratory surgery on the eighteenth of November but beyond that had little to say. Louise poured wine and carried a snack tray into the living room.

One of those bankers who had stolen all the depositors' money was on TV. This one had purchased a boat, a plane, and a cattle ranch in Kenya with a partner. He was speaking to a room crammed with Harvard University students. They were practically hanging from the rafters. It was a seminar on the educational channel.

"I did some things I'm not very proud of," said the man. "Basically they fall into two categories—financial errors and screwing people over. Whatever I wanted I could easily have by snapping my fingers. Oh, I was a bad character."

The students asked critical questions but seemed at the

same time to be taking notes so perhaps they could pull the same shit someday. And certain things about the banker reminded Louise of Tiny, such as the way he ran his hand over his face when asked a hard question, and the self-centeredness of him: I did this, I did that, always I. This was Tiny through and through. She changed the channel and watched the Saladmaster man bashing frying pans together.

Louise then went out and got her overnight case from the car. She showered, washed her hair, brushed her teeth, and put on a cotton nightgown. She pulled the blankets off Dan's bed and went out to sleep on the davenport. Later, when Dan came home, she sat up from a dream and said, "Just put her in a bucket."

"It's all right," said Dan. He was in the kitchen washing his hands.

Louise swept the hair from her eyes. "I was dreaming," she said.

"What about?"

"I was at the circus. They made me be a clown," said Louise. "It was awful. What time is it?"

Dan looked at his watch without pausing in the washing of his hands. Louise felt like a scientist, observing his habits. "Two-thirty," he said.

"I had to break the window," said Louise.

"Yeah, I was so careful to write a note, I forgot to leave the key," said Dan. He shut off the faucet and dried his hands slowly on a dishtowel.

"Well, was there an accident?" said Louise.

Dan came into the living room. "A guy hit a tree."

"How is he?" said Louise.

Dan sat down in a low chair with a bottle of beer. The chair was close. Louise could have touched Dan's forearm with her

83

foot, except her foot was under a blanket. "Well, not very good," he said.

Louise nodded and listened. Grafton can be very quiet in the middle of the night. "What's it doing outside?" she said.

"Raining," said Dan.

"They were predicting rain."

"They were right," said Dan.

"Here we are," said Louise.

"I'm glad to see you," said Dan.

"Come closer," said Louise. "What are you thinking about?"

"Your eyebrows."

"Yeah? What about them?"

"What they would be like to kiss," said Dan.

"You can find out," said Louise.

So he kissed her eyebrows, holding her face in his hands. They had kissed before, but not to this degree. Dan unbuttoned Louise's nightgown. Louise put her arm out and knocked over the beer bottle.

"You're wrecking the place," said Dan.

"It's my way," said Louise.

Later, they watched the streetlight shining on the trailer window. Louise asked Dan whether he had found the mother of the grocery store baby.

"Yes," he said. "She's not all there."

Louise had the house, but for those first times they mostly ended up at Dan's trailer. Part of the reason was Louise's farm-style bed. It came with the house and had contained generations of Klars. It was a tasteful bed, and Louise felt thrilled at not having to sleep in it anymore.

Dan had made his bed out of a mattress, three-quarter-inch plywood, and cement blocks. It provided a good, sturdy platform for ranging around and trying to anticipate the other person's desires. Dan surprised Louise with his sexual side, and she felt like a retired skier from the movies who learns everything over again and wins the big jump against the East Germans in a blur of sun on snow. There was a spell on the mobile home, and when they had to leave, they wanted only to come back. Three, four, five nights. She cried once, shook with tears, and there was nothing that could be done to make her stop. He tried to console her ("Don't cry. Don't, Louise. It's all right. Don't cry …"), but what could be done? It just had to come out.

Halloween fell on a Wednesday that year, and in the morning Louise sat up in Dan's bed, put on her socks, and looked out the little window just in time to see Hans Cook towing away her car.

She pulled jeans on under her nightgown and ran outside calling "Hans! Hans!" But the tow truck and the Vega chained to it were well down the road and moving at a fair clip. She could hear him shifting, up on the blacktop.

Louise turned in the grass; her feet were freezing. Dan's car was on ramps beside the trailer—it wasn't going anywhere—and the cruiser had some ungodly theft-foiling device that no one could get around except Dan. (This went back to 1982, when one of the sheriff's cars was stolen from the Lime Bucket, driven to the sand pits, and rolled down the bank into a hundred and ninety feet of water.) Back inside, Dan slept in orange light, and Louise called her mother.

"I wish I could help," said Mary, "but I don't know anything about it. Are you sure it was Hans? It doesn't sound like Hans."

"Where's he going, that's what I don't understand," said Louise. "Does he still work with Ronnie Lapoint at the station? Because if I remember right, sometimes that wrecker is at the station and sometimes it's at Hans's. They more or less divide it. Or do they? Maybe Ronnie Lapoint would know what's going on."

"Oh, no, Ronnie and Hans split up," said Mary. "They split up, oh, it's been a good two months anyway. See, Hans felt that Ronnie was giving work to Del Hetzler that should have rightfully gone to Hans. So Hans told him, you know, 'If I hear another word about Del Hetzler, I'm taking my truck, I'm taking my phone number, and I'm setting up on my own.' So Ronnie says, 'Well, go ahead, you so-and-so. I never liked you anyway.' Now, I had to laugh when I heard this, because you didn't know Doc Lapoint, Ronnie's dad, but this is word for word what Doc Lapoint was like."

"Fine, Ma, how do I get to work?" said Louise.

"Won't Dan give you a ride?" said Mary.

"I don't want to ask him," said Louise. "He was working late last night. And tonight is Halloween, another long shift."

"That's right," said Mary. "They've already got six or eight hog feeders overturned on Main Street. I can see them from my window. They take them from the hardware store. You know, you wonder why they don't chain them up or something. Maybe we need an ordinance to make people chain up their hog feeders around Halloween time."

"Can you give me a ride to work?" said Louise.

"Where are you?" said Mary.

"At Dan's," said Louise.

"Well, I don't want to come over there."

"Why not?"

"Why do you think not?" said Mary.

"I'll walk to your house," said Louise.

"Yeah, why don't you," said Mary.

Louise showered, and dried her hair. She put coffee on. A shower tended to fog Dan's bathroom mirror for the rest of the day, and Louise sat at the kitchen table in her underwear while putting on her makeup. There was a little round mirror on the table. She could see only part of her face at a time. The furnace came on, and Dan's coffeemaker made a sound that was just like a human sigh.

Louise dressed and went out. The sun was partly hidden by the grain elevator, but blinding anyway. She blinked. "Thanks a lot, Hans," she said to herself.

Mary was pouring her orange juice and listening to the radio by the kitchen window when Louise arrived. Bev Leventhaler, the county extension woman, was on the radio explaining how to put away a pumpkin bed for the season. "I got some new guidelines from the folks at Iowa State last week, and I want to pass them along to you," said Bev Leventhaler. "They are unusual, and I'm not going to pretend they're not. But I'm told that these methods have produced some very high yields when tried in an experimental situation. First, go down to your local hardware store and tell them you want a dowel rod two inches thick by eighteen inches long. Perhaps you may have a similar dowel rod at home. Look in your closet or garage or workshop. I know we have a lot of extra dowel rod at our house. Seems like every time I turn around I'm tripping over dowel rod."

Louise went to the radio to find some music, but Mary said, "Wait, I want to hear this."

"Next," Bev Leventhaler continued, "you will need a twelve-by-twelve sheet of black polypropylene, a handful of common twist ties, and six gallons of solution of calcium and lime. This is sold commercially as Calgro or Zing, and you should be able to find it in your town, but if not, Big Bear in Morrisville I know does carry Zing in powdered form. Just remember, if you do get the powder, you need enough powder to *make* six gallons, not six gallons of powder ..."

Mary drove Louise to work, leaving her on the shaded street beside Kleeborg's Portraits. "Call Hans," said Mary. "He has an answering service. The girl's name is Barb."

"I will," said Louise.

"And I meant to ask you," said Mary. "How's that venison going?"

"It's in my freezer," said Louise.

Louise called Hans, but he did not get back to her until the middle of the afternoon. She was taking prints from the fixer, and she looked at the prints (a stern girl on a horse) and cradled the phone with her shoulder.

"Well, I'm sorry, Louise," said Hans. "I don't really know what to tell you. About six o'clock this morning the phone rang and it was Nan Jewell. Actually, it would've been earlier than that, because *Se Habla Español* was on. So I said, 'Buenos días,' and Nan said, 'Hi, Hans. Louise Darling's car is broken down by the side of the road, and I want you to come get it and take it up to McLaughlin Chevy.' Now, in retrospect, it did sound kind of funny. I mean, it was your car, why weren't you doing the calling? So I said to Nan, I said, 'Well, who told you it wouldn't start?' And she said that you told her it wouldn't start, but that you didn't have the money to fix it. So she was going to have it towed and repaired, and this would be as a favor to you. So at that point I wasn't going to argue with her. But I'm sure sorry. I don't know what she was thinking of."

"I don't either."

"I'll tell you what, though," said Hans. "I'm going to bill her for that tow."

"Well, O.K., but I'm not paying for it," said Louise.

"Well, I don't think you should," said Hans. "You didn't call me, she called me."

"That's right."

"I know it is."

Louise called the Chevy place. The mechanics had worked up a long list of repairs they said were needed.

"The car runs O.K.," said Louise.

"I wouldn't say that," said the mechanic.

"Just don't touch it," said Louise.

Dan waited for Louise at the Strongheart at four-thirty that afternoon. This was a diner on Hague Street in Stone City, within walking distance of Kleeborg's. The restaurant was small and not clean but featured excellent tenderloin sandwiches.

"Hello, Daniel," said Louise.

They ordered food from an old man named Carl Peitz, who had been at the Strongheart forever. He smiled constantly, as if there were something wrong with him.

"Now, I had a key made for you," said Dan. He emptied his pockets on the table. There was a red comb, an Allen wrench, a ball of string, a tape measure, a dog biscuit, fingernail clippers, and a skeleton key. "Don't tell me I lost it already," he said.

"How did you get to be sheriff?" said Louise.

"I don't remember," said Dan.

"Man, I'm about hungry enough to eat this biscuit," said Louise.

"Don't," said Dan. "It's a knockout biscuit." He got up and went to look in the cruiser.

Smoke rose from the grill. Carl Peitz removed his apron, fanned the smoke.

"Is that ours?" said Louise.

She went home that night to the farm. It occurred to her that sometimes you need to stop and catch your breath. She went to Hy-Vee first, to get groceries and some candy for the trick-or-treaters who might or might not show up.

Some did. There were vampires, dinosaurs, a ballerina, a hobo with a sawdust beard. Louise stood in the doorway shoveling Red Hots into plastic pumpkins with black straps, giving while the giving was good. The parents stayed back, by pickups and station wagons, out of the light. The white dog knocked down a little girl dressed as Paula Abdul and, taking advantage of the confusion, sprinted into the house.

By nine o'clock or so, no one else seemed to be coming, and Louise poured some Canadian Club and turned on a movie featuring the Wolf Man and his wife. The wife was a prosecutor in Michigan, and she was looking into a string of murders, for which her husband was responsible. But the wife didn't even know the guy was a werewolf. He himself took his time facing the truth, and there were long, uninteresting scenes with him in a research library at Ann Arbor, looking at the ancient and horrific picture books that are always found in such movies. Then he tried to figure out some way to tell his wife, because she wanted to have children, and he had to keep putting her off, while his wolf side was all for killing her and getting it over with.

The prosecutor was crashing through the trees along Lake Huron, her husband at her heels, when a commercial came on. Louise stood and stretched, rubbed her stomach. The movie was falling apart, and she could sense thousands of people across the Midwest rising to rid themselves of it. She turned down the sound, heard a noise, and went to the window.

She cupped her hands around her eyes. Four or five people were coming up the driveway. At first she thought they were trick-or-treaters, because she could see the bobbing yellow features of a jack-o'-lantern. But the people were too tall to be children, and no one turned toward her door. Up the driveway they went, a group of shadows, traipsing into the farmyard. It was something to see. They had come to drag out a hayrack, or push over a shed, or let something loose from where it was supposed to be. A car would be up the road, waiting. Louise snapped her fingers, and the white dog trotted from the kitchen with a red plastic flower in his mouth. "Give Louise the flower," said Louise, and she took it from him. Then she opened the door and pushed the dog onto the steps. "Make us proud," she said.

FIVE

TINY DARLING was still living with his brother Jerry Tate down in Pringmar. This was going better than might have been expected. Jerry, who worked for the post office in Morrisville, liked having his brother's company. He liked Tiny's sense of humor and Tiny's conviction that everyone and everything was out to get him and his kind, although when you looked around it was hard to identify anyone of Tiny's kind. He was an advocate of the laboring class who would say things like "It's the working man who gets a ball-peen hammer between the eyes every morning of his life," but he hardly ever did lawful work. He could handle rudimentary plumbing, and when it came to getting a raccoon out of an attic, he was thought to excel. He was a steady drinker who sometimes seemed unusually intent on losing consciousness. One night not long after Louise divorced him, he wandered into Francine Minor's house and fell asleep on her kitchen counter, a loaf of bread for a pillow.

He would have preferred to stay married, because without Louise there was no one he respected to listen to him discuss his ideas. But he could handle being divorced. It was only when he heard that Louise and Dan had moved in together that he decided to leave the area. It just slowly dawned on him that this was more than he could bear to hang around and observe. Jerry thought this was an unproductive attitude. Grafton and Pringmar were thirteen miles apart, and the orbits of the two towns did not much overlap. But Tiny was stubborn, and Jerry's reasoning had no impact. "Stealing is like being a chef," said Tiny. "You can find work anywhere."

He left in November, when the weather in Pringmar was characterized by a combination of wind and freezing rain known locally as spitting. Tiny sat in his car with yellow box-elder leaves blanketing the windshield. Jerry, a heavyset man in a purple turtleneck and a down vest, brought out a broom and swept the leaves away.

"It's not too late to change your mind," he said. "There is no reason for you to run away. You're divorced? I'm sorry. A lot of people are divorced. The statistics are frightening. I don't know what you're worried about."

"Do you know that I am thirty-nine years old?" said Tiny. "I've never seen the Grand Canyon. I've never seen the Four Faces. The world is passing by me."

"You've been to Las Vegas," said Jerry.

"I'm talking about wonders of nature," said Tiny. "Look around, Jerry. Tell me what's here."

"Your car, and my car, and my house," said Jerry.

"Everything is plowed. Everything that isn't nailed down, they plow. What happened to the great wild country? This is where I would like to go."

"You're talking about something that never existed."

"Well, goodbye."

"And what about your indictment? You have a court date coming up."

"What a shame, I'll miss it," said Tiny.

"You can't run from your problems," said Jerry.

"I've never been able to follow that logic," said Tiny. "Assume the problems are at point A, and I get in the car and drive to point B. Are you with me? Problem here, me there. What have I just accomplished?"

Jerry took the broom over to the house and laid it on the steps. "What do I tell the police?" he said.

"Say I went to Owatonna. That's the last thing you know."

"So, lie."

"If it's the sheriff, tell him Louise likes her toast so light, most people wouldn't consider it toast."

"Laugh, clown, laugh," said Jerry.

"Well, I'm off."

"Isn't June Montrose in Colorado?" said Jerry.

Tiny had dated both Montrose sisters, taking up with Louise after June joined the Army and went to Germany.

"Maybe our paths will cross," he said.

"That would be a pleasant social event," said Jerry.

"Goodbye, then," said Tiny.

"Goodbye," said Jerry. "You should at least stop and see Mom before you go."

"Not hardly," said Tiny.

Their mother was Colette Sandover of Boris. She'd had three marriages, each of which resulted in the birth of a child and ended with the death of the husband. For this reason she was sometimes called Killem instead of Colette. She had been a redhead all her life and one day woke up with perfectly white hair. The children of Boris regarded her as a witch, an impression she encouraged by casting spells and walking in her garden calling, "O Lucifer, appear to me now. O Lucifer." She read *Consumer Reports* and *The New England*

Journal of Medicine and took cough syrup every day whether she was coughing or not. Her tax bills were so delinquent that even town officials skirted the issue. Tiny blamed her subconsciously for his failures. He had inherited her red hair, which, like a child's cap, made him seem foolish and insubstantial the nearer he got to middle age.

Jerry Tate was the oldest, and then Tiny Darling, and then Bebe Sandover. Bebe was the one who got away. She had graduated from hotel management school in St. Louis and now worked for a hotel in San Francisco. She almost never came home, and people took this as proof of her remarkable good sense.

Tiny had been indicted for knocking apart the vandalism display at the high school dance. Reading the court documents, you would have thought he had leveled the town of Grafton with his bare hands. But all indictments seem slightly out of proportion when you read them in black and white, and Tiny definitely did a number on that little shop project. People assumed that Dan and Tiny had been struggling for the affections of Louise. And that was part of it. On the other hand, smashing up a dance was something that Tiny might have done anyway, to make some philosophical point known only to him and that even he would be unclear about the next day. The public defender Bettina Sullivan considered a free-speech defense but decided to argue that Tiny's childhood had been tough on him. She asked him to think of some examples and write them down for her.

"My stepfather worked for Rugg Molasses in Morrisville," Tiny wrote. "This was when Rugg took up that whole lot to the south and actually manufactured molasses. Now I believe that there is just research left there, because the molasses smell has almost completely gone away. One day they called in my stepfather and fired him from his job. He had been a Rugg man eleven years and was therefore disappointed at this turn of events. He was not one to sit and think of his troubles so he hunted a lot after being fired. He would walk down the railroad tracks smoking a cigarette and in late afternoon he would come home. He always got something, whether it be rabbit, pheasant, possum, squirrel, etc. One winter afternoon my sister Bebe and I were sitting and watching television when my stepfather came home from his hunting and asked us to come outside. He had killed two squirrels and set them up on the hood of his car with their backs to the windshield and he had lit two cigarettes and put them in the squirrels' mouths. He asked us if we had ever seen animals smoking before and we replied that we had not. There was smoke coming from the cigarettes which is a mystery to this day. Then he approached the squirrels and pretended to carry on a conversation with them, arguing as to the reasons why he should not be fired from his job. I caught on to this but Bebe did not and she began crying. I told Bebe that he was playing a game. She still did not understand and continued crying and then ran into the house."

Bettina Sullivan may have read this, but she never mentioned the childhood defense again. She said she wanted to talk about a plea bargain. "What do I mean when I use this term 'plea bargain'? Think of a bargain in a store. It's similar but different …"

She probably would not care that Tiny had left town, and might even be relieved. She public-defended in three counties, and every time Tiny saw her, he had to refresh her memory of the charge against him, which seemed to emphasize his guilt in a gloomy way. She was very busy and also coached youth soccer, which Tiny knew because he had found the rules of soccer in her briefcase.

Tiny drove south and west, crossing seven counties, and by dark he was westbound on Interstate 80. His car was beat up but picturesque—a Pontiac Parisienne, metal-flake green, with mag wheels and lake pipes. The fan did not work, but at highway speeds air rushed in at the car's every seam. The windshield wipers worked, and sometimes they worked on their own, as if detecting a fine mist beyond Tiny's perception. A crack had climbed the left side of the windshield like a leafless tree.

It was cold in the speeding car, and Tiny thought back to the night, coming up on a year ago, when Louise had asked him to leave the old farmhouse. Her car had broken down, and she had walked home a mile and a half in eight-degree weather. When she came in, Tiny was trying to assemble a shiny kerosene heater he had stolen from the Stone City Cashway. It is beyond doubt that he failed to notice how cold her hands and feet were. She turned on the broiler of the stove and flopped down on the floor. She peeled off her boots and socks, opened the broiler door, rubbed her toes in the heat. She was crying softly. It turned out she had suffered the first phase of frostbite and this was the pain of reawakening tissue.

"Do you want some Kleenex?" said Tiny.

"I want a separation," she said.

Now on the radio Tiny picked up a preacher with his own translation of the Bible. Father Zene Hebert was his name, and he had a deep voice that issued great rolls of static when he pronounced the sounds *sss* or *ch*. Father Hebert thought we were witnessing the final minutes of our pleasant day on earth. Tiny sat forward, kneading the wheel. This kind of stuff always excited him. Father Hebert said the Roman Empire represented suppertime, and the eternal clock was now poised on midnight.

Tiny watched a televised hockey game in a dark tavern in Plain Park, Nebraska. He sat at the bar drinking shots and beers. The hockey was live from somewhere and, with last call looming, seemed like a miracle of light and motion. There were three other people in the bar: a bartender, a waitress, and a small man reading a paperback book by Robert Heinlein. The waitress had completed her chores and sat at an empty table eating spaghetti. She had brown hair. If you saw her across a wide street or highway, you might mistake her for Louise.

Tiny went over and sat down. "Would you like to ride around with me and listen to some cassette tapes?" he said. "I have Bad Company, Paul Simon, Ten Years After, and a lot more under the seat."

She displayed the back of her hand. "See this?" she said. "It's a pearl. It means engaged to be engaged. It's funny you should mention Paul Simon. My boyfriend is Ron Schultz, of the band Vodka River. I am pearled to Ron Schultz. Vodka River plays all around here, and one of their songs is 'The Boxer.'"

"I should know that," said Tiny.

"It's the one that goes 'lie-la-lie,'" said the woman.

"Oh, yeah," said Tiny, with no idea what she was talking about. He took out a small black comb and ran it through his hair. His free hand followed, smoothing. "I like a woman of your size," he said.

"That's too bad, because, as I say, I'm pearled," said the waitress. "But it is flattering, and one thing I can do is give you free passes to see Vodka River tomorrow night at the Club Car."

"I am here tonight," said Tiny. He took her hand.

She pulled her hand away. "That's too bad, because Vodka River was named one of the top ten bar bands in Eastern Nebraska. You could go to the Club Car now, but I'm afraid their set is probably winding down. Ron is the drummer. He sings lead on 'Please Come to Boston' and 'I Shot the Sheriff.' Now I'm sorry, but I have to go back to work. Being pearled is not the same as being engaged, but I'm not going to threaten what I have with Ron." She brushed her lips with a napkin and stood. "You can have my garlic bread if you want."

"Thanks," said Tiny.

The lights came up. The waitress took her dishes to the kitchen, and the man with the Heinlein book came over and sat down. He was pale and straw-haired, and wore a sweatshirt from Storybook Gardens in Wisconsin. His name was Mike, and he claimed to be the distributor in this area for a self-help program called Lunarhythm. Tiny wondered if Mike approached every stranger or just those who seemed to need self-help.

"I'll start a sentence and you finish it," said Mike. "'I don't mean to complain, but—'"

"I get headaches sometimes."

"Good. 'If there was one thing I could change about myself—'"

"I would go ahead and do it."

"'I wish I were an eagle, with—'—

"'With'? What do you mean?"

100

"There is no right or wrong answer. 'I wish I were an eagle, with—'"

"Deadly claws."

"Sure. 'Deadly claws' is fine. Why not… 'I don't consider myself a loser, and yet—'"

"I have lost things."

"There, that was pretty easy," said Mike. "Your answers suggest that you would in fact benefit from the Lunarhythm Plan. I mean, everyone does, but you would especially. You're what we call 'predisposed.' This is a program of self-hypnosis administered according to the thirteen-month calendar of the ancient Sumerians. Why thirteen months? Isn't that a needless complication? Well, not really, and I'll tell you why—"

"Give it up, Mike," said the waitress, while zipping a black and red Plain Park Trojans letter-jacket. "Did you tell him it costs six hundred dollars? It does, it costs six hundred dollars for these pathetic index cards."

"That's your opinion, Brenda," said Mike.

"I don't have six hundred dollars," said Tiny.

Mike's forehead dropped into his palms. "Oh, there's a payment plan," he said wearily. "But thank you, Brenda. Thank you for wrecking everything. I don't know what I did to deserve you for a sister. It must have been really bad."

"Well, the whole thing is *stupid*," said Brenda. She lit a cigarette and gave Mike one. "Come on, Michael. Those Lunarhythm people don't care about you. You're simply a pawn in their game. You've got to get a job. I told you that, Mama told you that, Daddy told you that. We've all told you until we're sick of talking."

Tiny called Louise on a phone in the corridor by the bathrooms. There was no answer, so he tried the sheriff's place. Dan Norman accepted the charges, which surprised him.

"Put Louise on."

"Louise is asleep," said Dan Norman. "You'd better call back at a decent hour. And let me give you a word of advice. Hold on. Here she is."

"Yeah? What, Tiny?"

"Put Louise on the line."

"This is Louise."

"Louise?"

"Yeah?"

"Don't forget the good side."

"I won't. Goodbye."

"The good side, the fun times."

"I'll try not. Goodbye now."

Tiny shifted the phone to his other ear. "Remember going across the lake in that paddleboat thing? Remember how you thought we were going over the dam? You really laughed. You have to admit that you laughed that time we were at the lake."

"I may have, Tiny. I don't remember every moment in my life and whether I laughed or not. If you say I did, it's possible."

"Then one of the pedals broke. What a disaster."

"Tiny, I have to get up in the morning."

"I'm going to see June."

"For what?"

"I'm already in Nebraska."

"Don't go to June's, for God's sakes. June is married. They don't want to see you."

"By the way, could you give me their phone number?"

"You'll just make a fool of yourself."

"Then at least you would be happy."

"I'm hanging up now."

"What's it like, fucking a robot? Does he take much oil?" But she had hung up.

The parking lot was as bright as any day. A man with a twitching eye sat in the back of a van with the doors open. "You look like someone who could use a cup of coffee for the road," he said. "Better yet, how about a hundred cups of coffee? Or a thousand?"

Tiny bought some speed from the man and glided the Parisienne back onto the highway. His anger left him, replaced by an expanding, chemical patience. Seeing in the rear-view mirror eighteen or twenty trucks bearing down on him, for instance, he showed no concern but only said, "Here come the semis."

The trucks passed the Parisienne like great ships on water. Many truckers who drive Interstate 80 take pride in their running lights. Strings of yellow and blue score the trailers as if square dances are taking place inside. And the cabs resemble ticket booths, strung with orange beads. Even some mud flaps are electric. Once, on a slight grade, the highway widened to add a slow lane, and trucks appeared on all sides of Tiny, and he seemed to be traveling through a canyon of light. This did not last. The illumination faded and disappeared, like a blinking code, and Tiny drove alone. Then a first-time caller on the radio said that Father Zene Hebert was a fraud. Hebert was not ordained and wouldn't know a biblical scroll if it hit him on the head. His real name was Herbert Bland or Herbert Grand. He was under indictment in Florida. A lamp by a bridge flared and darkened as Tiny passed. This kind of thing had been happening for years, and Tiny wondered if something in his body chemistry was putting out the lights.

103

His car broke down the next morning. It was fortunate in a way, because Tiny was falling asleep, suffering from road rapture. For miles, the things beyond his windshield—cars, bridges, culverts, farms, fences, mile markers—had been fusing into the image of a face. The stillness scared him. It meant his eyes were no longer seeing the movement of objects. It meant he was asleep.

He tried several ways to keep awake. He rolled down the window, smoked, and left the interstate, hoping that ditches, crossings, and two-way traffic would force him to be alert. But the state highway was empty, and the face came back. He tried to sing with the radio, but could not remember the words. Then the radio faded out. Tiny turned on the overhead light, and the car went into a stall. The problem was electrical.

Soon the Parisienne rolled to a stop, its alternator belt broken and gone. Tiny pulled the battery and began to walk. When a car came by, which was not often, he would turn and put out his thumb. He carried the battery under his arm and was reminded of happy times walking to school with a lunchbox, or taking the lunchboxes of other children. He looked at cattle, who looked at him. He mused about the possibility of retrieving a Camaro mounted on a pole to advertise a dealership in a place called Euclid. Nebraska seemed flat and intimate. He found one battered white ballet slipper on the shoulder and turned it over and over in his hands. Eventually an old pickup stopped. It was red, with a camper top, many dents, and decals on the back for the Everglades, the Keys, the Falls, and the Dells.

The driver of the truck was a sunburned, overweight woman named Marie Person. She was in her sixties and drove leaning forward, forearms curved to the wheel, shoulders gently rolling in a red-and-white-checked shirt. Marie was one of those eccentrics who travel the lonely highways of monotonous states and almost seem to have been hired by the tourism department to enliven the traveler's experience. These people have certain things in common. Often they hold a patent, or have applied for one but are being blocked by lawyers, or have some other reason to correspond frequently with Washington, D.C. Sometimes the stamped and addressed letters ride beside them, fanned out on the car seat, which is usually a bench and not a bucket. They travel at midday or late at night. They cross desolate stretches for vague and shifting reasons that often have to do with animals. They need a vaccine for Skip the pony or special food for Rufus the cat to get his urine flowing again. They are going to look at a calf in Elko named Dream Weaver or Son of Helen's Song. They know everyone in the low-roofed diners along the way, but no one seems to know them. This they account for by giving the details of some unpopular stand they have taken that made everyone furious but was after all the right thing to do. Their surnames are not traceable to other surnames you have heard.

Tiny felt comfortable with Marie Person. She was round and pleasant. Grapes rolled on the floor of her truck. Her story was colorful but did not demand much concentration. She had started out as a midwife in the Northwest Territory and had learned to fly. *Look* magazine sent a man to do a story on her, but he broke his leg on the ice and went back, and though she called a number of times, no one else came. Her husband, who'd taught her to fly, crashed his plane and died. Or maybe it was the man from *Look* magazine who died in the plane crash. Tiny wasn't listening that closely. Anyway,

Marie moved down here and had eleven children with a lawyer named Kenneth Strong. She lowered both visors to show the school pictures of her children. She gave their names but seemed to repeat herself. The pictures were old, the colors no longer right.

"Do you have any children, sir?" she said.

Tiny shook his head. "We went to the doctor a couple years back. It seems my sperm count wasn't up to par."

"Ohh," said Marie. "What will you build your life around?"

"We won't," said Tiny. "We're divorced."

"I'm sorry," said Marie Person, patting his hand.

"Talk to the county sheriff," said Tiny.

"Why?" said Marie.

"She lives with him."

"That must sting."

"I can tell you exactly when it fell apart," said Tiny. "One time I said to her that nine out of ten men become police because they're afraid they can't satisfy a woman in the bed. And she goes, 'Where'd you hear that?' It was very obvious. So I went out and got half in the bag, and when I came home she was asleep. 'Wake up,' I said. 'We have to talk.' See, because I wanted to talk to her. She was the one that didn't want to talk. I wanted to talk. So anyway, I gave a pull on the bedclothes, and evidently I was kind of worked up, because she fell out of bed. That I regret; that wasn't fair."

"No lady likes a violent man," said Marie.

She bought Tiny lunch at the Stuckey's outside Lesoka, Colorado. She handed him a napkin and said, "Here's your napkin." Afterward, she brought out a pack of Winstons.

"You want a child, here's what you do," she said. "Take two tomato plants to the Catholic church and sprinkle them with

106

holy water. Then plant them somewhere with rain and lots of sunshine. When one tomato has ripened from each plant, take both tomatoes to the one you love as a gift."

"I don't believe in that stuff," said Tiny.

Marie shrugged. "Yeah, it is kind of stupid. I'm going to the ladies' room."

Tiny finished his meal and had a cigarette. Then he had another cigarette. He savored the smoke, for there was no hurry. Marie was gone. He had seen her truck leaving. He wished that he had kept his battery with him.

Tiny walked on into Lesoka, which rhymes with Jessica, and took a room in a threadbare hotel near the railroad tracks. There was a candy machine in the lobby, featuring dusty and discontinued brands of licorice. Tiny lay down on a narrow bed with a thin white bedspread. He could not sleep. A train went by. Tiny counted the silhouettes of cats on Chessie boxcars. He turned the dial of the bedside radio until he found his friend Father Zene Hebert. The father was explaining that people will be allowed to bring clothing to Heaven. "The verse should read, 'In my Father's house are many mansions, each with a cabinet for thy garments.'" Tiny shut off the radio. He took a bath and went down to the street.

That evening he visited all the bars on Railroad Street in Lesoka—the Alley, the Lion's Tooth, the Golden Spike, Kato's Korner. He drank shots of Scotch whiskey until his eyes glowed, until his knees buckled, until his features blurred in the mirror. He stumbled from one bar to the next, pissing in doorways and on the Yosemite Sam mudflaps of a Silverado pickup. He got the impression that no one in Lesoka danced, and hauled likely couples before jukeboxes and forcibly manipulated their arms and legs to the songs of Suzanne Vega, Sly and the Family Stone, Carole King. His mighty finger crushed the buttons of his selections. He sprained the arm of a man named Jim. In turn, he was thrown into the alley behind the Alley.

There he talked to two criminals, or two kids claiming to be criminals, one car thief and one arsonist. Tiny told them about June and about Louise. The car thief thought he should just appear at June's and take his chances. He said June and her husband would be open to unexpected visitors because Colorado is an informal place where people like to party. The arsonist shook his head and said if it was him, he would play it safe and call ahead. This made sense to Tiny, but when he tried to use the telephone, the operator could not understand him, and said, in a musical and sympathetic voice, "Call it a night, sweetie. Go on home."

He walked the railroad tracks back to the hotel. Teenagers huddled around a burning barrel near an underpass. They looked at him with what might have been wonder. The encounter seemed to require some transaction or gesture. In his coat pocket Tiny found a piece of wood. He went to the barrel and dropped the wood into the flames. "Thanks, brother," said the teenagers. Tiny nodded solemnly, but something bothered him about the stick he had contributed to the fire. He did not realize until he was on the third floor of the hotel that it had been attached to his room key. He kicked in the door, fell face down on the bed, and said, "Thank you God for love so deep; look out for me while I'm asleep." And then he slept.

SIX

DAN AND LOUISE shuttled back and forth for a while, staying first at the trailer and then at the farm. But with all their running around, they didn't see much of each other, and their razors were never where they needed them to be. So they talked this over and Dan moved to the farm, selling his house trailer to the farmer Jan Johanson for nineteen hundred dollars.

The trailer marked the point at which Grafton gave way to fields, and Jan decided to clear and plow the lot. He owned all the surrounding land, so this made sense. The trailer he would move to his farm and use as an agribusiness office. Many farms had now developed to the point where they needed such places, with computers and fax machines and file cabinets that would have struck the farmers of yesteryear as a big waste of material. In any case, moving a trailer required a crane and a flatbed truck, and a number of people showed up out of mild curiosity on the Saturday this was to happen.

Snow fell lightly, disappearing as it touched, leaving no accumulation on the hard black dirt of the fields. The air was cold and still. Louise and Dan sat with Henry Hamilton on the tailgate of Henry's pickup. Henry was smoking a pipe that kept going out.

Most of the work was done. The Johanson family worked with utmost efficiency. The trailer was off its foundation with two girders underneath, one at each end. Cables connected the girders to the hook of the crane, which was being operated by Hans Cook. The engine was running and sending up smoke from time to time. Up in the cab Hans was drinking coffee.

Later, Henry would claim to have predicted that something would go wrong, which was true, but what he predicted to go wrong and what in fact went wrong were two separate things.

"What do you think'll happen when they lift that mobile home?" he said.

"The earth will open up and swallow the town," guessed Louise. She wore a red quilted vest and a Cargill cap.

"I'll bet you fifty bucks the thing breaks in the middle," said Henry.

"Tell Jan," said Dan.

Henry went over and raised this issue with Jan, who listened carefully and then said he had talked to the company that had manufactured the trailer about the best way of moving it. Actually, he said, the company was defunct, but he had tracked down its former engineer, who was now retired and living in California and very willing to discuss the problem. Coming from Jan Johanson, this detective work was totally believable.

"He talked to somebody in California," said Henry to Louise and Dan.

Hans Cook took a last sip of coffee, tossed what was left on the ground, screwed the cup onto his thermos, put the thermos by his feet, and took hold of the levers that controlled the crane. Jan raised his hand. Hans revved the crane's engine, and the sound and stream of exhaust sent a current of excitement through the crowd. The crane roared and the cables tightened until the trailer lifted, but then one of the girder clamps broke and the girder dropped, ringing like a church bell against the cinder-block foundation. The trailer rolled crunching and shattering on the ground. All this happened at once and so smoothly that an uninformed bystander might have thought that this was what they wanted. Fortunately no one was hurt. Jan Johanson had his arms folded the whole time, and when the trailer had come to a stop he still had his arms folded, and he said, "Mother… fuck."

A crow coasted onto the field and the snow fell.

"I am not believing that," said Louise.

"I guess that's how they do it in California," said Henry.

Hans, in the window of the crane, shook his head and poured coffee. Louise pulled Dan's hip to hers. "We had some beautiful times in there," she said.

They lived together all winter, and in the spring announced their engagement. People wondered what Louise saw in someone like Dan. Of course, Dan had his merits. He might not have been a great crime fighter, but he conducted himself decently in most situations, which is not true of every cop. He had gray eyes and a melancholy smile. He was tall enough to be a little taller than she was. The question had more to do with Louise, who had developed a certain status apart from the town and its business. She had always said what she was thinking, and seemed to be afraid of no one, except perhaps Mary. The reason she had married Tiny was that most people thought it was a bad idea. So had she tired of that contrary life? Had she changed? Did she want to drive the patrol car? One phrase came to explain Louise's decision. Nurse Barbara Jones said it to the hairdresser Lindsey Coale. "She's come into herself," said Barbara. "Just look at her face. I was looking at her face the other day when she didn't know I was watching. She has come into herself at last."

"Her hair's improved, too," said Lindsey Coale. "It's got all those reddish highlights. I wish she would stop by. A cut, a curl. Anything. People don't understand how dependent hair is on the emotions."

Louise put on a blue dress with white dots and went to see Pastor Boren Matthews of the Trinity Baptist Church. Grafton seemed to get two kinds of religious leaders: simple, good men who understood not one thing about the town, and moody ones who embodied rather than allayed the anxieties of the congregation. Pastor Boren Matthews was of the second category. He and Louise climbed the stairs to the cupola to talk. A .410 shotgun leaned against the wall in a corner.

"We've been having trouble with pigeons," he said. "They live in the bell tower of Sacred Heart and come over here to do their business. I've spoken with Father Wall, but he is no help. I don't know if you're familiar with Catholicism, Louise. But there are people in this town who are doing some very strange things."

"All religions are strange," said Louise.

"But the Catholics take the prize."

"It's like having an imaginary friend."

"You don't have to think of God in human terms," said Boren Matthews. "Some people are comfortable with the general idea of a higher power."

"But that's like giving up. A higher power could be anything. It could be a big paperweight."

"A paperweight is not a higher power."

"I like when they say God is a jealous God. Because you

112

can imagine him storming around Heaven going, 'All right, where were you last night?'"

"Quite an imagination. What brings you here?"

"Dan Norman and I are getting married, and I promised my mother to ask if we can have the wedding in your church."

"It would be difficult for someone who describes God as possibly a paperweight."

"Well, I gave it a shot."

"And there was a time not that long ago when I would just say forget it. But churchgoing is not what it used to be, and frankly, we can't afford to turn anyone away. Do you know how many people we had last Sunday?"

"No."

"Take a wild guess."

"I don't know."

"Come on, guess."

"Fifteen."

"Six."

"Including you?"

"No. With me it would be seven."

"It's not many."

He shook his head, looked out the window. "I'm afraid the Trinity Baptist Church of Grafton will not be around much longer. Look what happened in Pinville. Look what happened in Lunenberg. What they'll do is lump us in with that crowd over in Chesley. And they don't allow gambling or dancing in Chesley. We're very liberal here. We take a laissez-faire attitude all the way. When people get to Chesley they'll be in for a rude awakening."

"Will you still be around in May?"

"Oh, probably."

"Because we were thinking about May."

Pastor Matthews jumped up and crept to the window. "Shh," he said. He picked up the shotgun. A pigeon flew from the roof. "Come back here," he said. "Look, May is fine."

"O.K., great," said Louise.

The minister shook her hand. "Congratulations, Louise," he said. "I must say I've always been attracted to you, mentally and physically."

Then she had to go downstairs and ask the minister's wife, Farina, for a book of ceremonies. Farina was friendly. Her hair was dark, with little waves like those in an unbraided rope. She often sat alone on the steps of the parsonage in the evening. Now she went around the house looking for the book. She could not find it anywhere. She did find an old photograph. In it a young woman smiled, her legs folded on summer grass. She had lipstick and sideswept hair.

"Do you believe that's me?" she said.

"Sure."

"That's on Rainy Lake, Minnesota. My family used to go every summer."

Louise left the parsonage and thumbed through the small notebook she had taken to carrying to keep her errands straight. Then she drove up to Stone City and met Dan at Mercy Hospital to have their blood drawn for the marriage license. They sat in plastic chairs with fold-down palettes for their arms. A nurse they did not know came in and wrapped tubing around their arms. Louise had seen junkies apply this same kind of tourniquet on PBS. The intercom said something and the nurse left.

"Boren Matthews came on to me," said Louise.

"What do you mean, 'came on'?"

"He said he was attracted to me."

114

"Maybe he meant he likes you."

"He said mentally and physically attracted."

"That does sound like coming on."

"I guess he doesn't have any congregation left and it's driving him crazy."

"Do you want me to talk to him?"

"Nah. You know, my arm's beginning to hurt. I don't think you're supposed to leave a tourniquet on if you're not bleeding. Where did she go?"

They removed the bands. The lights throbbed in their eyes. "It's this dress," said Dan. "When you wear this dress the most sacred man would be attracted to you."

"I thought you were the most sacred man."

"It's just a sexy dress."

"This?"

"Yeah."

"I never thought of it that way."

"I guess that's why," said Dan.

The nurse came and drew their blood. It was kind of painful. Louise imagined that the doctors would mix their blood together in the lab and hope for the best. Then they went into the waiting room, where Dan stood at the counter filling out forms while Louise wrote in her notebook.

"What were you just writing?" he said as they walked out, and she handed him a piece of paper on which she had written "Show Me Love" four times.

"I will," he said.

Dan went back to work, and Louise drove to the mall south of Stone City. She bought a pair of pale yellow shoes to get married in. They hurt her feet.

"You want that," said the salesman. "If the shoe didn't feel

115

painful now, it would probably be the wrong size. You could go to a seven. But, Miss, I guarantee you this foot of yours would swim in a seven."

Louise paid for the shoes and left. She followed a mother and daughter out of the store and through the mall. The girl, about two years old and carrying a shoebox, was drawn like a magnet to anything that would break or fall. The mother kept dragging her away from the storefronts. There was a stone fountain in the center of the mall, and here the two rested. The mother read a newspaper while the girl opened the shoebox, took out a new pair of red shoes, and threw them in the water.

Now, at this same time gamblers had set up shop in Grafton. These were two men who drove a dark red Chevrolet Impala and sat all day in the back of the Lime Bucket tavern. They claimed to be from Canada, but their knowledge of Canada was sketchy. Dan knew something about the gamblers but had not yet taken action. It seemed to Louise that many things fell into this category for Dan. A good part of the job of sheriff, the way he did it, was the biding of time.

One day Louise overheard one of the gamblers talking on the phone. There was a pay phone in the Lime Bucket, but these two men generally walked across Main Street to the phone booth by the old bank. This was not what you would call private—the door had been removed years ago to discourage kids from going in there at night and kissing—but it was better than standing by the jukebox with "Third Rate Romance" playing in your ear.

"The angel will bite if it gets aggressive," the gambler was saying. "Sure it will... I did tell you that, honey. You've got to separate them... Yes, I'll hold on, but I want you to go right now and separate those fish… How about in the tank with the mollies… What do you mean? All of them?… Well, what exactly killed them, honey? I am not, I'm not accusing you of anything. I just wish you wouldn't sound so happy when my fish die… Listen, while I'm holding, why don't you put Klaus on… Hi, Klaus. It's Daddy. It's your old man, Klaus… Do you hear me? Are you there? I hear you breathing… Klaus? Hello?"

The gambler left the booth. He dressed with style for someone living out of a Chevrolet Impala. He wore black pants, an ironed blue shirt, and a New York Mets cap turned backward over his ponytail. No one seemed to know his name, but he was called Larry Longhair.

"You're getting married," he said to Louise. "I saw your picture in the paper. I went to get you a present, but the store was closed. Good for you, in any case. Marriage is one of the reasons we play this silly game. Here, have ten dollars."

"Oh, that's all right," said Louise.

"Oh, take it," he said.

"You'll need it for gambling," said Louise. "You and that other guy."

"Richie," said the gambler.

"You can't get away with it forever."

"Maybe you're right," said the gambler. "But in the meantime, I know of a good bet in the ninth race at Ak-Sar-Ben. If I call right now, we can get you in on it. I'll put in this ten, and you put in twenty. Total wager: thirty bucks."

"Some present," said Louise.

• • •

One evening between then and the wedding, Louise came home from work to find sawdust settled like snow on the floor of the bedroom. Dan had dug an ancient string bed out of the attic and lengthened it by cutting and installing new four-by-four side rails. Then he ran six planks from rail to rail, spacing them evenly from the head of the bed to the foot, and bolted plywood to the planks. The mattress rested on the plywood, and the resulting bed was rustic, fragrant, and very high. Louise and Dan got on their backs and slid underneath—it was like being in the basement of a new house, peering up at the joists.

"That ought to hold us," said Louise.

Dan had to go out later and help the fire department burn down a shed on the Lonnie Pratt farm. Sometimes when people had old buildings they wanted to get rid of, they would donate them to the fire department for practice. Dan returned at ten-thirty, took a shower, and came into the bedroom with a white towel draped across his head. "They do all right when they set the fire themselves," he said.

Louise put down the magazine she was reading. She enjoyed the elevated perspective of their new bed. "Climb up here and talk to me," she said.

The women of Trinity Baptist gave Louise a bridal shower in the cafeteria of the old school. Louise, Mary, and Cheryl Jewell sat at the head table. The other women filed solemnly by, leaving packages, and then they sat down and watched Louise open them. She got a popcorn maker, a birdhouse, a carpet sweeper, a shoeshine kit, and a framed poem about the dogwood tree. She got a fishnet heart in which to save ribbons. Inez Greathouse stood and prayed for the marriage. "Louise has a wonderful name," she said. "Because if we take off two of the letters and rearrange the remaining ones, we have the word 'soul.' The Christian soul we know is bound for heaven; and two souls such as Louise and Dan, who commit themselves to God's love, will never falter in life's journey. Oh, there will be fights, because there are always fights. And there will be times when Louise and Dan are convinced their hearts are breaking. We have all been there. But if they have faith, their hearts will not break, and that is God's promise to us all. Amen." After the prayer everyone had small, bitter cups of coffee. When it was over, Louise and Cheryl went to the tavern for a beer.

Cheryl Jewell had come back from Kansas City to be maid of honor. Her presence in Grafton was controversial. She was divorced from her third cousin Laszlo and usually flirted with him when in town. But Laszlo was remarried, to a woman named Jean. Also, Cheryl and Laszlo had a daughter, Jocelyn, who now lived with Jean and Laszlo. And Cheryl was staying with her Aunt Nan, whose house stood right next door to Jean and Laszlo's on Park Street. All these names are not important except to show the delicacy of the situation. Nan Jewell was bossy and opinionated but did not take sides in this matter, as she disapproved of Cheryl and Laszlo equally. Cheryl had sexy gray bangs. She was always in school and always involved with someone unworthy of her time. Currently she was studying botany and dating a chemist named Walt.

"He runs away every time we make love," said Cheryl.

"You know who else was like that?" said Louise, and whispered the name of someone they both knew.

"I mean he literally runs away," said Cheryl. "He puts on tennis shoes and he's out the door. He goes up around the reservoir, down the graveyard, and back, a total of four or five miles. There's something I don't trust about joggers. The blankets are still warm and I hear his soles hitting the pavement. I don't think it's normal. And I also happen to think he has a glass eye."

Louise laughed. "What do you mean?" she said. "You can't tell?"

"Well, sometimes he gives me a look, and I think, My God, those eyes are glass," said Cheryl.

"Dan's eyes seem real," said Louise.

"He's all right," said Cheryl.

"Hi, ladies," said the gambler with the ponytail. He stood at the table, holding a cigarette near his mouth. "Say, Louise, I'm afraid that bet we made didn't pan out."

"I didn't make a bet," said Louise.

"Well, I put that ten dollars in for you. But the horse pulled up lame. Isn't that the way? The race was fixed, too, which is the hell of it. I guess you can't fix Mother Nature, much as we might like to."

"How are your fish?" said Louise.

"Last I heard, the tank had stabilized," said the gambler. "So when's the big event?"

"Saturday," said Louise.

He sent a stream of smoke toward the ceiling, took off his baseball cap, and settled it on Louise's head. "Here's something blue," he said, and moved on.

"Who the hell is that?" said Cheryl.

"Larry Longhair," said Louise. She got up, put money in the jukebox, and played the first and second parts of "Rock Your Baby" by George McRae.

"Remember this?" said Louise.

"I played it when you and Tiny got married," said Cheryl. "Everyone hated it."

"No, they didn't," said Louise.

"It isn't a tune for the French horn," said Cheryl. "I realize that now."

"You were in the music academy. We assumed you knew what you were doing."

"It was an interesting experiment," said Cheryl.

"Much like the marriage itself," said Louise.

"You know, I miss hanging around and talking," said Cheryl. "Sometimes I think I'll get back with Laszlo."

"What about Jean?"

"Yes, well, that's the problem," said Cheryl. She sighed. "I have to tell you. Don't take this wrong. I mean, it isn't negative. But the word around town is that you've changed."

"What do you think?"

"Yes, but not how they mean," said Cheryl.

Louise lowered the visor of the cap and took a drink of beer. "How have I changed?" she said.

"It's not like you're repenting or anything," said Cheryl. "It's more like, O.K. This is the way."

Louise nodded. Rod Stewart sang "Maggie May" on the jukebox. "You know what I never liked about that song?" said Cheryl.

"What?"

"Well," she said, "if it really don't worry him none, you know, when the morning sun shows her age—why even mention it?"

"This is true," said Louise.

Louise stayed at her mother's house the night before the wedding. She lay in her childhood bed, on her side, in the shape of a question mark. At the suggestion of *Hey, Teens!* magazine, she had climbed a stepladder twenty-three years ago and pressed glow-in-the-dark stars to the ceiling. Louise had been greatly influenced by *Hey, Teens!* when she was a

121

teen. She had made and worn easy-to-make clothing that really looked very bad. She had joined the Gary Lewis and the Playboys Fan Club. The stars barely glowed, and she saw them faintly from the corner of her eye.

She fell asleep and dreamed. Louise had simple dreams most of the time. She had little patience for those who would draw her aside and say, "Listen to this dream I had. I was talking on the phone with my cousin, and then it was like I *was* the phone …" Anyway, in this dream Louise and Dan were driving home at night from Morrisville, and Dan took a steep road that Louise had not known about. They glided up through the country. The sky was like a map of the sky, with concentric rings, big blue planets, names and distances printed in white. The road climbed sharply, and the scenery was lonely—a dark house, black pines—but beautiful in the planetary light.

"Do you take this route very often?" said Louise.

"In fact, I never have," said Dan, "but I'm familiar enough with the road system to know this will level out up ahead like a hawk's nest."

It didn't, of course. The car went over the crest of the road and dropped into endless dream darkness. Louise woke, breathing hard. She heard a strange smacking noise and went downstairs. It was one-thirty in the morning, and Mary was mopping the walls of the hallway for the reception. She wore a housecoat with the sleeves rolled up. She had never mastered cleaning, and as she flailed the plaster with the cords of the mop, she seemed to be losing ground.

"I wasn't going to do this," said Mary. "But I started in with a sponge, and don't you honestly think the mop does a better job?"

Louise yawned. "You're paranoid," she said. But she pitched

in, unfolding and setting up three card tables with the distinct and tropical smell of Mary's basement.

They listened to a talk show on the radio and made their way down Louise's list. Their work acquired the intent and wordless pace that can be reached only after midnight. Louise chased cobwebs with a cloth-covered broom. Mary sewed the hem of Louise's dress. Louise taped white ribbons to the lamps. Together they made sandwiches without crusts.

The talk show featured a woman in Rapid City interviewing an agoraphobic. But the guest got nervous and went home halfway through.

"I guess she wasn't lying," said Louise.

"You always had the opposite problem," said Mary. "You never wanted to come home."

Louise sat in the kitchen curling ribbon with the blade of a scissors. "One time I did," she said. "I had a flat tire and it was raining and I didn't have a coat. I remember wishing and wishing I was home. Well, I'm going to bed."

"Don't be scared about tomorrow," said Mary.

"Good night," said Louise.

"Good night."

In the morning they made punch—orange juice, grapefruit juice, pineapple juice, and vodka. Sun poured through the kitchen windows. They stood mixing and sampling until they were happy not only with the punch but with the house, the weather, and the lives they had led so far.

Heinz Miller came over shortly after noon. A retired farmer, he lived next door with his wife, Ranae. He wore a short-sleeve white shirt and wine-red slacks.

"Our cable just went out," he said. "Would you mind if I turn on the ballgame? Got some money on the Twins. It's the top of the third with one man on and nobody down. Our cable went blank. I thought of you."

"How much money?" said Mary.

"Three thousand dollars," said Heinz.

"Good Lord," said Louise.

"How much?" said Mary.

"Three thousand," said Louise.

"I know it's a lot," said Heinz. "I bet it with those guys at the Lime Bucket."

"Well, Heinz Miller," said Mary.

"They used psychology on me," said Heinz. "They made it sound like I wouldn't have any money *to* bet. They said the farm economy is so poor that when a farmer moves into town it's usually to live in low-class housing. So of course I told them all about the house. Like an ass. 'We finished the attic.' 'We put in a breakfast nook.' The next thing I knew we were betting three thousand dollars. But I'm going to ask you not to tell Ranae. I believe it's best she doesn't know. If she found out, I think she would take my gun and kill me."

"You have it coming," said Mary.

"She really has gotten attached to that gun," said Heinz. "And she used to hate it. Couldn't stand to see it. Didn't even want it in the garage. Then the other day I noticed it was missing from the cupboard by the Drano there, where I keep it. Next thing I know, here comes Ranae walking up the street with the gun in her hand. Well, it turns out she's been taking it down to the sand pits every afternoon. So I ask her, you know, why the sudden urge to be a sharpshooter. And she says—get this—she says, 'Heinzie, I'm thinking about doing away with you.' How's a fellow supposed to respond to something like that?"

"She walks to the pits every day?" said Mary. "I should start

124

walking. A lot of people walk these days."

Heinz Miller turned on the ballgame, which was between the Twins and the Tigers. "What do you bet this is fixed," he muttered, and lit a cigarette. "Doctor said I shouldn't smoke, so I got some of these low-tar jobbies."

Louise brought him a cup of punch and took a cigarette. She and Heinz sat on the davenport smoking and watching the ballgame, an ashtray between them. Louise wore a red and white bathrobe, a blue towel around her hair. "Are you coming to my wedding?" she said.

"When is that, honey?" said Heinz.

"Two o'clock," said Louise.

"That you would have to ask Ranae," said Heinz.

"You could at least congratulate me," said Louise.

"Congratulations."

"Thank you."

"How do I pay these men?" said Heinz. "With a check?"

"Hell no, they won't take a check," said Mary, who had been listening from the kitchen.

"You wouldn't think so," said Louise.

"I can't watch," said Heinz. The Tigers had runners on second and third. He turned down the sound and covered his eyes. "What's happening?"

"The count is three-and-one to Tony Phillips," said Louise. "And here's the pitch. Phillips swings. It's a line drive single to right."

She went upstairs and dried her hair. Then she sat on the bed, looking at a framed photograph from her first wedding. In the picture she stood alone in a white dress, day lilies in her arms. Her eyes looked hooded and desirous and empty.

She had been stolen not long after this picture was taken.

Seven of Tiny's friends had grabbed her on the church steps after the ceremony. Bride stealing was traditional but rather pointless in the modern era. They put her in a car and drove fast to Overlook Park in Chesley, where everyone settled on a ledge above the river. She still had the lilies in her lap.

Marijuana and a gourdlike bottle of Spañada were handed around. Dusty light seemed to follow the path of the river, and Louise got loaded on two drags of Hawaiian marijuana. She wondered what had happened to the mild grass of high school—gone forever. Then it dawned on her that these men could throw her off the ledge and into the river. This seemed suddenly very likely, and she had the impression that the notion was blooming in all of them. She wondered if by spreading her arms she could fashion wings from the extra fabric in her wedding dress. Maybe it was supposed to have been a kite in the first place. She could glide all the way to St. Louis, or someplace far like that.

Louise got away without much trouble. She retreated from the ledge, carrying the train of her dress, fingertips touching the twigs and leaves that had hooked in there already. She climbed into a car. The doors and trunk were open and the radio was well into that very long Southern song about the bird who would not change. She started the engine and drove away. A cooler bounced from the trunk at the speed bump in the park. In the rear-view mirror she could see bottles and ice tumbling along the pavement.

Now she took the old wedding picture into the closet, where Mary kept a cardboard barrel of coats. When you were in Mary's house you were never far from a store of old coats. Maybe she knew something no one else did about climate patterns. Louise buried the picture in the coats.

She brushed out her hair and put on her dress. It was yellow with white flowers and a low back. She tied a rose-colored ribbon in her hair, spread her arms, and turned toward the mirror. Her hair was long and brown, and the ribbon made it look coppery.

Henry Hamilton gave Louise away. They walked together down the aisle of the church. He had a bad hip and she had small shoes, so they moved at a slow and stately pace. Henry wore a handsome, deep blue wool suit. It is an unnoted fact of Midwestern life that the old farmer rummaging through pocket T-shirts at Ben Franklin might have a wardrobe like Cary Grant's at home in the attic. The suit smelled like a trunk with faded steamship stickers.

"You look beautiful," said Henry.

"No, you do," said Louise.

The church was plain, but light streamed through the stained glass. Cheryl had done a good job on the flowers, and Louise felt as if she were approaching the edge of a jungle. Pastor Matthews was flanked by the leaves of large plants. Dan and his best man, Deputy Ed Aiken, edged toward the altar as if making their way along a narrow ledge. Dan's tie was crooked and he had a kind of careless happiness on his face. This is the way of men.

"Dearly beloved," said Pastor Matthews. "We are here to unite Louise Montrose Darling and Daniel John Norman in the blessings of matrimony. First I have a few announcements I did not get to last Sunday. Shirley Baker is still in the hospital, as are Andy Reichardt and Bill Wheeler. Bill continues to be troubled by that nasty cough but wanted to thank you for your prayers. Marvin and Candace Ross have a new baby, Bethany; mother and daughter are doing fine. And a note comes from

Delia Kessler thanking everyone for the kindness extended to her following the death of her grandfather Mort ..."

The announcements went on for a while longer, but eventually Louise and Dan got to speak their vows. The pastor raised his hands and Louise felt his palm brush her hair. "With this ring," said Dan, "I thee wed, and pledge my abiding love." They kissed. Louise closed her eyes. She could not define what she was feeling but knew no other way to express it than to say that she loved him. So that's what she said. It occurred to her that you only get glimpses of love, your whole life, just bits and pieces. They kissed again, deeply, unrehearsed. Farina sang a hymn—"O Love That Will Not Let Me Go."

Afterward, everyone went outside. Cheryl and Laszlo walked beneath the poplar trees while poor Jean waited, counting the fingers of her white gloves. Across the lawn, Louise and Dan stood on the sidewalk, receiving the wishes of the people. It was cool in the shade, and wind moved the branches of trees.

Heinz Miller had been forced to go home when Mary and Louise left for the church, and by then his cable service had been restored. He asked Ranae to take a seat in the living room and told her about the bet he had made. They watched the Twins complete a dull and losing effort, and Ranae wept softly. In her mind's eye she saw the departure of all that three thousand dollars could buy for their grandchildren. Toys, games, and bicycles went spinning over the horizon. It's true that the Millers would not have spent the three thousand dollars on their grandchildren, but it gave Ranae a way to measure the loss. The wedding started in the sixth or seventh inning, and Heinz and Ranae did not go. When the game ended, Heinz turned off the television, and they sat in dim light for almost an hour and a half. Three or four times Heinz asked Ranae what she was thinking. Finally she threw a book that hit him on the arm. Then she got up and said, "If you think I'm going to miss the wedding of my friend's daughter, and now the reception, because of you, well, how wrong you are."

They dressed silently and walked over to Mary's house. Heinz was mournful. Ranae was furious at Heinz. They found Louise soaking her feet in a plastic tub at the base of the stairs. She looked wonderful in her yellow dress and bare feet. They hugged her, and Heinz gave her a card with five dollars in it to start them on their way. Mary came over, said how proud she was of her daughter, cried, coughed, blew her nose, and sat down. "By the way, Ranae, I hear from Heinz that you're walking every day to the sand pits," she said. "I would love to go with you."

"I don't think I shall be walking anymore," said Ranae.

"Oh, Ranae," said Heinz. "You'll be walking, for God's sakes. Aren't you being kind of melodramatic."

"Shut up, Heinz," said Ranae.

Sensing the poorness of their own behavior, Heinz and Ranae left the reception after fifteen minutes. They walked across Mary's grass, through the hedge, and into their yard. The red Impala of the gamblers was in the driveway, and the gamblers themselves were looking in the windows of the house.

Heinz put his hands in his jacket pockets. "Say, get away from there," he said, in a formal voice.

"This *is* nice," called the gambler named Richie.

"Are you aware those milk pails by the piano are antiques?" said Larry Longhair.

"That's none of your concern," said Heinz. "Ranae, honey, go inside the house."

Ranae did so. She got the gun from the cupboard by the sink

and loaded it. Her hands were shaking. The gamblers were walking Heinz to the garage. Ranae came down the sidewalk. She raised the gun and fired twice into the sky. She shot out a garage window. The gamblers ran to their car and peeled out of the driveway. Heinz went to Ranae and embraced her. Then something odd happened. One of the bullets that she had shot into the air came down on the sidewalk. Ranae and Heinz looked at each other and hurried into the house.

Louise and Dan went to Solitude Island, in Lake Michigan, for their honeymoon. Although it was May, it snowed almost every day. They stayed in a hotel with gas lighting, narrow rooms, no electricity. Dining was communal in the morning and at supper, and as far as Louise could tell, the only thing people ever talked about was who disliked meat the most. One man who admitted feeding bacon to his dog was asked to leave the table. Louise and Dan had not thought to bring boots and scarves. They kept to themselves and spent a lot of time in bed, with the snow falling on the old hotel. But on the sixth day the weather cleared and the sun came out. They walked through the woods to a cliff by the big lake.

"I didn't know there were places like this," said Louise.

The wind blew in their faces and hair, and that night Dan came down with an earache. The next day his temperature was a hundred and one, and they went to see an island doctor, who told him to put mustard in his ear. Louise and Dan took a ferry to the mainland, picked up some antibiotics in Escanaba, and drove home without stopping. It was eleven-fifteen on a blue and brilliant morning when they got back to Grafton. The gamblers had left town, and soybeans were growing in curving rows where Dan's trailer used to be.

SEVEN

TINY DARLING settled into Colorado life. He found work at a lumberyard in Lesoka, the town where he had arrived by chance. He rescued his broken-down car from the empty highway. The police had put an orange sticker on the side mirror that said, "Give Generously to the Policemen's Benevolent Association." All winter he plowed snow from the blacktop of the lumberyard with a Case tractor. He was thankful for every day that it snowed.

In the spring he began dating a woman named Kathy Streeter from the Farmers Business Bank. She had crayon drawings on her bedroom wall, done by her nephew, who was four or five. The last night Tiny stayed at her apartment, he got up early, untacked the drawings, and left without waking her.

Tiny drove across the state to the town of August. This seemed like a proper Western place, whereas Lesoka had seemed merely depressed. The bar was called a saloon, men wore cowboy hats, women wore long leather skirts with fringe down the seams. Tiny found June and Dave Green's address in the phone book. They lived in a development called Sangria Shores—no water in sight, but maybe that would come later. All the houses in Sangria Shores balanced on gentle hills. The grass was perfect and the sunshine evenly distributed. The Greens had the sort of house that would have been better off had there been fewer construction materials available when it was built. There were red tile roofs, stucco walls, copper downspouts, and intricate wrought-iron railings; and everywhere Tiny looked he saw either a fountain, or an arch, or a combination fountain and arch. A white Mercedes-Benz sat in the driveway. Someone had written "This Is Indian Land" in green along the fenders and driver's door. The driveway curved broadly, with black asphalt and yellow lines. Just as Tiny angled his car between the lines, the mirror that the orange sticker had been on fell off.

He stepped from the car and picked up the mirror. At least it was not broken. June opened the front door. She was tall with dark curls, and wore a long black dress. "I've been expecting you since fall," she said.

"Hi, June."

"Louise warned me," she said.

"What do you hear from her?" said Tiny.

"She got married last month, Tiny. She married Dan Norman in Trinity Church."

Tiny polished the mirror with his sleeve. "I know it's pretty serious."

"It's not 'pretty serious.' They're married."

"Did you go to the wedding?"

"We were in Mexico."

"How was that, June?"

"Very different."

"I'm not saying I own her."

"You got that right," said June.

132

Tiny walked up the steps. "I came all this way—"

She took the mirror and turned it toward him. "I think I've found the problem," she said.

Then Dave Green came to the door. He wore jeans, a turquoise sweatshirt, and glasses with round black frames. He was in shape. "You must be Tiny," he said.

They went into the house. There was probably five or ten thousand dollars' worth of stuff in the front hallway alone. Dave led June and Tiny past a grand piano and bright swirling paintings into something called the Florida room, which was full of waxy plants and cane furniture. Dave poured coffee while June leaned reluctantly in the doorway.

"Honey, sit with us," said Dave. Orange fish swam in a rich green aquarium behind his head.

"I've got to go downtown," said June.

"No, sit," said Dave. "Help yourself to a cruller, Tiny. You must be hungry from your journey. Come on, June. We'll get our bearings and then we'll go from there."

"What happened to your car?" said Tiny.

"The Indians around here are pretty unhappy with me," said Dave.

June sat. She pulled pastry apart and stared at it. "I have to go to the pet store, and the clothes store, and the pharmacy, and the bank."

"See, I work with land," said Dave. "It was my dad's business and now I have it. June and I met in Germany. I was studying overseas."

"The problem is Wild Village," said June.

Tiny looked from June to Dave and back. Probably they were unhappy with each other, and probably this unhappiness could be worked with. "Where?"

"It's an amusement park based on various conceptions of the Old West," said Dave. "It may or may not happen. Wild Village is a long way from becoming reality. A long way."

"Frankly, I wish we had never heard of it," said June.

"So they painted your car," said Tiny.

"Look, I don't blame the Bearpaw Nation," said Dave. "The white man did steal their land. Not me, but my kind. Today we would go to the police. I don't know where to put their resentment. The irony is, Wild Village would pay a lot of Bearpaws a good wage."

June gathered crumbs on the tip of a finger. "I can see where they wouldn't want to wear those uniforms."

"Hey, I didn't like those sketches any more than the next person," said Dave. "But the fact is they were preliminary sketches."

"What's wrong with the uniforms?" said Tiny.

"Look, they were cut too high in the thigh," said Dave. "No one's denying that."

"I'm going," said June.

"Did you know that the gods sometimes appear in disguise to test our characters?" said Dave.

"You always say that," said June.

"I'm just a man," said Tiny.

"What do you want, Tiny?" said Dave.

"I'd like to find work," said Tiny.

Dave Green drove Tiny to a construction site in the mountains. There were pilings, concrete forms, cranes, and trailers. A bridge stood half built across a stream. To the right was a dark green wall of mountain, and to the left a lighter valley. The Mercedes rolled to a stop; Dave and Tiny got out. A thin

134

construction worker pointed with a shovel and laughed at the graffiti on the car. His boots were yellow and big as loaves of bread. Dave beckoned to him, asked his name.

"Milt," he said.

"Milt, I want you to meet Tiny," said Dave. "He'll be taking your job. That's right, you're done. Leave your tools and get on home."

"I don't believe it," said Milt.

"You believe it, Milton," said Dave. "It happened to the Indians. See how you like it."

"I have a family," said Milt.

The foreman came over. "What's the trouble, Dave?" he said.

"Hi, Cliff," said Dave. "I've fired Milt here. Tiny will be taking his place. Any problem with that?"

"What did Milt do?" said the foreman.

"He made fun of Indians," said Dave.

"I thought that was directed at your car," said the foreman.

"Either way, that makes him a smartass," said Dave.

"I have a family to feed," said Milt.

It was not clear who had the upper hand, Dave Green or the construction foreman. A swivel hook and some wire ties happened to be on a stack of rerod nearby, and Tiny picked them up and showed that he could use them. Both Milt and Tiny ended up staying on the job. The foreman, Cliff, seemed all right. Some construction bosses have a sadistic streak, and the whole site then gets that way. Cliff was a fair man, with a big stomach and gray hair. Later that first day, Tiny got to see how he handled a problem. The bridge had wood pilings that had been driven deep into the ground by a pile driver attached to the boom of a crane. Because of rocks and roots it was rare for a piling to go in straight, and by the time you had six of them driven in a row, they looked crooked as teeth. Then they had to be pulled one at a time into a more or less straight line, also by the crane, and secured that way long enough to set up concrete forms and pour a pier on top of them. This securing was done with a come-along run from the straightened piling to another piling across the creek. A come-along is a length of cable with hooks on either end and a ratchet-and-handle in the middle for taking up slack. When you crank up a come-along enough to hold a strained sixty-foot piling, the tension becomes considerable. So a cable broke and the ratchet, weighing perhaps twenty pounds, ripped across the stream with a ghostly sigh and buried itself in sand. This was a case of death finding no one home, and everyone looked at the sky, as if expecting a fusillade of come-alongs. Cliff came out of the trailer. He pulled the ratchet from the creek bank and examined the piling, which had snapped back to its wayward position.

"Let's try that again," he said.

Tiny got a room in a big house in the Mount Astor neighborhood east of August. Tall, bleached grass grew all around. Many members of the crew lived there. It was one example of the overbuilding that had been sponsored by the failed Bank of August. One night Tiny drove over to Dave and June's for supper, and afterward they turned down the lights and prepared for a séance. The founder of August had been murdered in 1894, leaving a fortune in silver that had never been found.

The three Green children were at the movies, and June went around the house putting masking-tape crosses on the doors of their rooms. She wore a denim skirt and a big purple

T-shirt. She explained how you could never expose children to the influence of the underworld and asked Tiny if he had any pictures of children or any children's belongings. He told her about the crayon drawings by Kathy Streeter's nephew.

"Drive by a church tonight before going home," she said. "Go out to the stop sign and make a left. Go through two sets of lights and take the first right past the Cantonese restaurant. That's Highland Episcopal."

"I thought you had to go in the church," said Dave.

"I heard driving by is sufficient," said June. "I remember, because I thought, That's odd."

June brought out the Ouija board. Dave put on some spooky music, and they sat around a glass coffee table. Tiny upended the pointer when he put his fingers on it. He adopted a lighter touch. Asking a piece of heart-shaped plastic to tell you where a dead man had left his treasure seemed as foolish as anything Tiny had ever heard of. But staying close to the Greens seemed important. Eventually something would fall into his hands. The pointer had begun to move. Tiny thought June was pushing it, or Dave, or both of them. He stared at June's legs in a way that might pass for mystical concentration. He thought about the first time they made love, on a blanket beside a corncrib at night.

The Ouija session was kind of a disappointment. What was spelled out was "hajir." June and Dave decided that the *j* could be disregarded. What they based this on, other than pure convenience, Tiny did not know. He was pleasantly surprised at the silliness of rich people, or these rich people anyway, in their spare time.

"Hair," said Dave. "Cut hair. Who cuts hair?"

"A barber," said Tiny.

"A barber cuts hair," said Dave.

"Stop the presses," said June.

"Maybe the guy needed a haircut when he died," said Tiny.

"Maybe the silver was in a barbershop," said Dave.

"This is just speculation," said June.

"I think we're going to have to spend some time with the plat maps," said Dave.

Then Dave led Tiny into the billiard room for some nine ball. The table spread before them like a brilliant green field. Dave seemed unaware of the rack of polished cues, the powder dispenser, the gleaming abacus on the wall for keeping score. Absently he hummed and poured out the Johnnie Walker.

"You're a drinking machine," said Tiny. He had too much talcum on his hands and left ghostly prints on the felt as they played.

Tiny had velocity but not accuracy. Dave patiently won three games of nine ball. June was waiting for Tiny in the front hall, and she walked him to his car. They heard a song begin on the piano. It sounded like things drifting down stairs.

"They say you don't know Dave until you've heard him play," said June. They stood sheltered by the open door of the Parisienne. Tiny kissed her until she pushed him away.

"I think not," she said dreamily.

The church June had directed him to was bunkerlike and modern, with a giant cross that seemed to challenge rather than court the stars. The door was locked but not securely. Tiny stood at the back pew and let his eyes absorb the darkness. The moon shone through tall, narrow windows and reflected from something on the floor at the head of the aisle. It was a vacuum cleaner, which Tiny approached and turned on with his foot. He vacuumed the carpet and thought about Louise.

He had been dispirited and blasé when she engineered the divorce. But now the years they had been married seemed like the central age of his life. He finished vacuuming and stole a silver pitcher from a wooden rail.

The next day, in late afternoon, Tiny went walking on Mount Astor. Many trails branched from the big house. As he walked, a red-winged blackbird flew from tree to tree. This was a breed he knew from home. All else was different. The trees were taller and darker, the land was jagged and in most places could not be farmed. Tiny followed the blackbird along the side of the mountain, and eventually the trees opened, revealing a valley with a cluster of unpainted houses linked by gravel roads. The hillside had been timbered, and Tiny rested on a fallen tree. It was suppertime, with mist in the air over roofs of tin and shingle. An eighteen-wheeler rolled in, crowding the rutted road, and stopped beside one of the plywood houses. The driver climbed down, went around to the other side of the cab, opened the door, and took a small, sleeping child in his arms. He carried the child into the house. Everything was quiet except for the occasional bang of a garbage pail. Dogs roamed the village, searching for something they did not seem able to hold in their memory. Tiny sat for another twenty minutes or so, held by the peacefulness of nightfall, and then headed back to the big house. The trees rose up again, over his head.

Milt the construction worker put a water spider in Tiny's hard hat. This was a hard-shelled spider found on the banks of the creek. The water spider did not bite but would eventually crawl down your forehead or neck, scaring the hell out of you. Everyone laughed when Tiny discovered the joke. He charged the nearest person, who said, "It was Milt!" Tiny put his hands on Milt's shoulders and shoved him down. Milt jumped up and delivered a wild punch. Tiny looked at Milt with deep appreciation. Fighting gave Tiny a feeling like being in his own yard. He knocked Milt's knees out from under him and hit him two times. That pretty much ended the fight. Cliff the foreman took Tiny into the trailer. Cliff had a desk on a raised platform. He rested his elbows on blueprints and looked at Tiny a long time.

"I don't see the enjoyment in your kind of life," he finally said.

"Milt put a spider in my hat," said Tiny.

"Jesus Christ, will you listen to yourself?" said Cliff. "You ain't a man, the way you talk—you're a little goddamned kid. Even your name. Tiny is no name for a human being. What is your given name?"

"Charles," said Tiny.

"Then call yourself Charles. Or Chuck, Charlie, I don't know. Tiny is a mouse's name."

"Why don't you let me worry about that," said Tiny.

"Well, take your time," said Cliff. "Because I'm letting you go. It's not just this. It's a lot else. You've been stealing tools. This we know."

"No, I haven't," said Tiny.

"Charles, accord me the simple dignity of not lying to my face," said Cliff. "If you return them, I won't have you arrested. You can start by handing over that nail apron."

"Don't fire me," said Tiny.

Cliff removed his own hard hat, touched his silver hair, and put the hat back on. "Go home," he said. "Come back tomorrow morning with all the tools. And I mean I had better see every tool."

• • •

On Saturday night, Tiny and Dave Green went digging for the silver. Dave had learned that a barbershop once occupied a vacant lot next to a nursing home in August. Shovels clattered as they dragged them up the basement stairs. It was almost midnight. June was in the kitchen stirring up an Instant Breakfast.

"You're both too soused to find anything," she said.

"The nursing home will want our silver if we don't keep it a secret," said Dave.

"You're soused," said June.

"Who," said Dave.

He and Tiny stepped onto the porch with the shovels and a goatskin flask. "Is there any chance of finding this silver?" said Tiny.

"I just felt like getting out of the house," said Dave.

They drove to the lot, which was surrounded by a shabby wooden fence. Tiny and Dave went through a gate, and Dave took a certain number of paces from the northwest corner. They went to work. Moonlight made everything look like an old negative and seemed to link them to the pioneers.

Dave rested his shovel, pressed the sides of the flask, and drank. The night air had sobered him. He breathed deeply and passed the flask to Tiny, whose drunkenness had continued without pause.

"Why are you really here?" said Dave.

"I want Louise back."

"You're in the wrong state."

"Granted."

"She's not your wife," said Dave. "The court has split you asunder. She is married to an influential man."

"I have goals."

"And if it's a high wage you're after, Aspen pays better than they pay here. Boulder pays better. Denver pays best of all. The situation here could improve if Wild Village goes through, but hell, that's years down the road. June and I have been putting our heads together and thinking maybe you should go over to Denver."

"I like working for Cliff," said Tiny.

"Well, see, that's what I wanted to tell you," said Dave. "I was talking to Cliff, and the sad fact is he really can't keep you on. My initial plan was that Milt would leave, but as you know, that didn't come to fruition."

"June had a say in this?"

"We're the best friends you have," said Dave.

"What did she say?"

"You don't necessarily want to know the exact words."

"Yes, I do."

Dave looked at the crooked fence. "She said she thought you should go to Denver," he said.

Tiny ran a red light that night. He was crossing downtown August when he ran a red light and a truck plowed into the driver's side of the Parisienne. The truck was a delivery vehicle for Bazelon Lighting and Fixtures in Colorado Springs. Tiny had a broken nose; the driver of the truck seemed to have something wrong with his arm. Police converged. An officer brought Tiny into a patrol car and handed him gauze for his nose. Banks of light danced on the dashboard.

"You are Charles Darling?" he said.

"That's right."

"Have you been drinking, Charles?"

"Well, I had some beer with supper."

"You had some beer with supper."

"Yes, a Grain Belt."

"And that's all you had to drink?"

"I had the one Grain Belt."

"How fast would you say you were going upon entering the intersection?" said the policeman.

"I don't know."

"Make an estimate."

"I'm sure I drive around looking at my speedometer every minute," said Tiny.

"I see," said the policeman. "Where do you live?"

"At the foot of Mount Astor."

"Uh-huh. I have a sister lives over that way."

"It's a nice area," said Tiny.

As a result of his drunk-driving conviction, Tiny lost his license and was forced to go eleven times to group counseling in the basement of the courthouse in Sedonia. The approach was psychological. A red banner with letters of yellow felt hung across the front of the room: LIQUOR IS BAD. Tiny did not take any of it very seriously, and one time he raised his hand to ask whether pent-up rage might not come in handy in certain situations. It wasn't until the ninth meeting that something got through to Tiny. The people in the group were taking turns behind the wheel of a video monitor that simulated the warped road perceptions of the drunk driver. You could turn it up—one drink, three drinks, eight drinks, legally dead. Every level ended in a crash, and then a little cartoon man would stagger across the screen with crosses where his eyes should be. When Tiny touched the steering wheel, the machine malfunctioned, delivering an electrical shock that knocked him unconscious.

143

He lay on his back on the floor, dreaming of being on a lake. Ghosts moved swiftly about in small boats. They called his name: *Charles... Charles...* They all got around fine. Only Tiny drifted toward the waterfall. When he reached it, however, he found that he too was a ghost, able to keep going in the air.

PART II

HEAVEN, HELL, ITALY

EIGHT

A CAR HIT Kleeborg one hot and sunny Wednesday as he was walking back from church in Stone City. It was an old blue Galaxie at a four-way stop. A man and a woman got out of the car and stood over the fallen photographer.

"You were in my blind spot," said the man.

His name was Frank. He was a handsome man in a yellow shirt who sold billboard space and breath mints. He had been popular in high school and felt somewhat victimized by everything that came after.

"See my hand?" he said. "How many fingers do I have?"

Kleeborg closed his eyes.

"I hate to think what this will do to our premiums," said Frank. He lit a cigarette and threw the match in the street. "What a fraud that is. What a big racket. You pay and pay every month of your life, and what happens?"

"I never should have let you drive," said the woman. She wiped her brow with the back of her arm. She wore a sleeveless blouse, a short, full skirt, and a pin that said "Grace."

"They raise your rates, that's what," said Frank.

"You know, this is a really old man," said Grace.

"What did they do with the money you've been giving them

147

all along?" said Frank. "But we're not supposed to ask that."

"Here's his glasses," said Grace. "Broken."

"Imagine it's the other way around," said Frank. "Imagine your record is spotless. Imagine you have no violations."

"Will you shut up?" said Grace. "You've hurt him."

Frank smoked his cigarette and paced in a big circle. "Tell you what we could do," he said. "We could say that you were driving. This would be your first infraction, and that way we could stay out of the risk group. What about it? Good idea?"

Grace lifted Kleeborg's feet. He wore penny loafers in which the pennies had drifted from the slots. She put Kleeborg's feet down.

"You drove yesterday," said Frank. "So it wouldn't necessarily be a lie."

"Look at this gorgeous old shirt," said Grace.

"Oh, hell," said Frank. "He doesn't know what day it is. Mister! Hey! He's out like a night light. If there aren't any witnesses, our testimony takes on added weight."

A teenage boy came down from one of the big houses on the bluff east of Eleventh Avenue. "I've called the 911," he said. "I saw everything that happened."

"Good," said Frank. "Great."

The boy knelt and laid a washcloth on Kleeborg's narrow forehead. "Something told me, Go to the window. I was making a sandwich and suddenly—I don't know—it was like, Put down your knife."

"These voices, tell me about them," said Frank.

"Were you driving?" said the boy.

"So many questions."

Three blocks away, the county supervisors were having their weekly meeting. Sheriff Dan Norman had to attend these meetings, although he thought picking up rocks would have been more fun, and surely more useful. For the past five minutes he had been surveying the little white scars on his hands in an effort to stay awake. This was done by a band saw, this by a hammer, this by a fishing knife …

The supervisors were retired people, mostly, and they took their time. Lately they had been toying with a plan, obviously illegal, to unilaterally extend their terms. This allowed them to confer often with county attorney Lee P. Rasmussen, which they seemed to enjoy. "Better run this by Lee," they would say.

Today, however, they were talking about Ronnie Lapoint's plan to build self-storage units next to Lapoint Slough. This was on the low part of Route 29, south of Lunenberg and northeast of Margo. There was some disagreement about the proposal. The chairman of the board of supervisors, Russell Ford, seemed to be in Ronnie's pocket. But other supervisors were concerned about the environmental impact and about the creepy nature of self-storage places.

"I guess my question would be twofold," said Supervisor Phillip Hannah. "Who are these people and what exactly will they be storing? If this is something they can't put away proudly in their own home, my feeling is, should we be providing a place to hide it."

Bev Leventhaler argued that bitterns nested near the slough and that the U-Stow-It building would disrupt their habitat. She was the county extension woman and host of The Coffee Club, which was on the radio every day except Sunday.

"I've got a book with a picture," said Bev. She was slim and pretty, with red lipstick and an attractive overbite. "Can everybody see that? I'll pass it around. Please be careful. It is a library book. What can I say? My husband Tim and I love

149

these birds. I'm not saying they're domestic—they're not—but we've had some success with small feeders fashioned from an ordinary Clorox bottle."

"Thank you, Bev," said Russell Ford, who was picking his teeth with the edge of a matchbook.

Dan put in his opinion. "A lot of people hunt ducks in Lapoint Slough. I hunt ducks in Lapoint Slough. The slough is a game area where the hunting of ducks is encouraged. It was deeded to the county twenty years ago by Ronnie's grandfather, and I don't think he ever anticipated that Ronnie would try something like this. It does not seem wise to me to allow commercial development on the edge of a game area. Who's to say birdshot won't rain down on people using these units?"

Ronnie Lapoint stood and defended his plan. He claimed that family heirlooms make up ninety percent of the contents of self-storage places, that the bitterns would welcome the company, and that if birdshot were to reach the building, which he didn't think it would, it would fall harmlessly on the heavy-gauge corrugated roofing.

Dan did not stay for the whole thing. He slipped out of the courthouse and drove down Ninth, took a left on Pear, and eventually happened on the crowd around Kleeborg.

In addition to Frank, Grace, and the teenage boy with the washcloth, there were now a dozen people who had, like Kleeborg, attended the liturgy at St. Alonzo's, and two young women leading a pack of children on a rope, and some landscapers who had stopped their green truck and were leaning on rakes, watching the commotion.

"It's Dan Norman, Mr. Kleeborg," said Dan. "Louise's husband. Dan. Can you hear me?"

Kleeborg put his hand to his forehead. "I don't know why, but I am reminded of something that once happened to my sister."

"Yeah, what's that?" said Dan.

"She would write letters late at night," said Kleeborg. "Her name was Lydia. She had a strange habit of moving her hands over the page when she was done writing. Well, one night I heard her crying. It was important that our father not wake because he worked for the creamery and had to get up before daylight. So I lit a kerosene lamp and went to see what the matter could be. Kerosene was all we had for lighting, and there were many fires. Well, Lydia had upset the inkwell, and I'm afraid it had fallen. The letter to her boyfriend was ruined and so was her nightdress and the rug beneath her writing table."

"Oh, my," said Dan.

"'Well, Lydia,' I said, 'maybe you'll learn not to move your hands so much when you write.'"

"What did she say?" said Dan.

"I don't remember. I believe she kept crying."

"What happened here?" said Dan.

"I wonder why I thought of that," said Kleeborg.

"You've had a hit on the head, Mr. Kleeborg," said Dan.

"The man in yellow ran me down," said Kleeborg. "I was coming back from the church and he struck me with a car."

The EMTs got Kleeborg onto a stretcher and put a protective clamp around his head. Dan went after Frank. "Sir—were you driving this car?"

"No," said Frank.

"What's your name?"

"Franklin Ray," said Frank.

Dan walked around the Galaxie. It was dark blue and dusty, and there were regular indoor stereo speakers sitting crooked in the back window. This arrangement always struck Dan as pathetic, like a suitcase with a rope handle, or a dress held together by pins. "Is this your car?"

"I would like a lawyer handy," said Frank.

"Then it is your car," said Dan.

"I didn't say that," said Frank.

"Don't go anywhere."

Sheila Geer of the Stone City police pulled up, new Chevy cruiser gleaming white in the light of a summer noon. Although the county stood at the peak of local government, the towns seemed to get better police cars.

"What do we have, Dan?" said Sheila. She was a short and tough sergeant who loved to roar up to a crime scene and ask what they had. Dan had stayed over at her apartment a couple of times years ago, when she had been a patrolwoman and he a deputy. She had more candles than Christmas, and beanbag chairs.

"Apparently there's this Galaxie 500 over here, and it collided with Mr. Kleeborg," said Dan. "There he goes into the ambulance."

"Hey, he took our yearbook pictures," said Sheila.

"Very possibly," said Dan. "My wife works for him."

"Which reminds me, congratulations," said Sheila. "Your wedding and everything."

"Thanks, Sheila," said Dan.

"Louise Darling, right? Her second time?"

Dan nodded.

"You know, I once considered getting into photography," said Sheila.

"Louise does real well with it," said Dan.

"I remember there was a printing paper called Agfa," said Sheila.

"Yes," said Dan.

"Always liked the sound of that," said Sheila. "Agfa. Are you going to take care of this accident?"

"Not if I can help it," said Dan.

"Who's operator number one?" said Sheila.

"Got to be the guy in the yellow shirt," said Dan. "A Mr. Franklin Ray. But he's being all evasive."

"Know the type," said Sheila.

"Some kind of legal scholar," said Dan.

"Oh, yeah."

"Shh," said Dan. "Here he comes."

Frank had his hands in his pockets and was walking like someone out for an evening stroll. "Let me offer you a hypothetical situation," he said. "Assuming I was the driver—now, I'm not saying I was, but just assuming—would I be looking at a moving violation or some other kind of violation? Or are they all moving?"

"Look," said Dan. "I don't have time for this. Either you were driving the car or you weren't."

Frank scuffed his foot on the pavement. "I was," he said.

"Well, you drive like shit," said Dan.

"The old guy leaped in front of the car," said Frank.

"I really believe that," said Dan.

"Come on, sir," said Sheila Geer.

Rollie Wilson approached Dan with a clipboard. He was a farmer, a mechanic, and an ambulance driver. He raised antelopes as a hobby animal. His coat was smudged with oil but his fingernails were scrubbed.

153

"Need your John Henry, Danny," he said.

Dan signed. "How is he?" he said.

"He seems to have a minor concussion," said Rollie. "He'll be all right. They might keep him overnight to make sure. You look terrible, but he looks all right."

"I'll admit to not sleeping well," said Dan.

One of the young women walked by, reeling in the string of children. "I wouldn't push her out of bed for eating a cracker," said Rollie. "You know, I had insomnia there for a while. After our place burned. You remember our fire."

"Vividly," said Dan.

"I'll be honest with you, Dan. I went to see a psychiatrist," said Rollie. "I don't mind telling you that, don't mind it a bit. I've really come around on this question. I used to be ashamed, but shame is so stifling."

"Oh, I know it can be," said Dan.

"I've never been one for talking about myself," said Rollie. "The family I come from, you more or less keep your mouth shut. I bet my father never said a complete sentence to us kids the whole time we were growing up. Not with a subject and predicate—no, sir. But the funny thing is, when I finally got to the psychiatrist, get this, I didn't have to say two words. She wrote me a prescription right off the bat. She said a lot of people can't sleep. This is no lie. She said go home and have pleasant dreams. I was in and out of that place in fifteen minutes."

"Really," said Dan.

"I can write her name down if you want," said Rollie.

"Are you still taking something?" said Dan.

"You bet," said Rollie. "And I sleep great."

Louise was making prints in the red light of the darkroom at Kleeborg's Portraits. She wore blue jeans and a faded blue work shirt.

"Rollie said they might keep him overnight," said Dan. "He was none too lucid when I talked to him. I know that."

"Yeah? Like what?"

"He was talking about his sister spilling ink back in the days of kerosene," said Dan.

"Lydia," said Louise.

"Yeah, Lydia."

"Poor Kleeborg," said Louise.

"You know what we ought to do. Call her."

Louise laughed. "You better have a good phone. She's been dead for years. That's why he goes to church."

"Why?"

"Because of Lydia," said Louise.

"He misses her."

"Yeah, or whatever," said Louise.

When Mary heard about the accident, she rather ruthlessly pushed for Louise to take center stage at the portrait business. But about Mary it was sometimes said that you could no sooner change her than you could teach a badger to fix cars.

She drove out to the farm one scorched evening. The heat had been bad for weeks. The air did not turn over, the sun burned the basin of the Rust River, and events acquired a random quality, separated by rings of heat. And Grouse County was scattered to begin with. Family agriculture seemed to be over and had not been replaced by any other compelling idea.

Louise and Dan were sitting in lawn chairs in cutoffs and loose T-shirts. Louise read the paper and Dan shucked corn. They were expecting relief. They lived on a hill, and whatever wind came from the east funneled through their yard.

"Did you see the six o'clock news?" said Mary. "A gal went to the statehouse dressed in road maps."

"Why?" said Louise.

"I only caught the tail end of it," said Mary. "I thought there might be something about it in the paper."

Louise turned a page noisily. "Doesn't seem to be."

Dan snapped the stem from an ear of corn. "Probably some kind of protest," he said.

"Evidently," said Mary.

"Against the heat," said Louise. She folded the paper, fanned her face, unfolded it, went back to reading.

"Well, I guess," said Mary. "Isn't this something? And tomorrow's supposed to be worse than today. Is Perry Kleeborg out of the hospital yet?"

Louise shook her head.

"Who's he got?" said Mary, meaning for a doctor. "Freiberger?"

"Duncan," said Louise.

"I don't care for Duncan," said Mary.

"A lot of people don't," said Louise.

"Freiberger I like, but Duncan, no," said Mary.

"Kleeborg doesn't mind Duncan," said Louise.

"Louise," said Mary. "I'm afraid this might be it for old Perry. He isn't twenty-one anymore."

"How old is he?" said Dan.

"Eighty-seven," said Louise. "But very spry. He's still the best person I've ever seen with a view camera."

"I don't look for him to be back," said Mary. "I'm sorry, but someone should say it. Let's not forget, the man walked into the stream of traffic. Isn't it time to start thinking about retirement?"

"Kleeborg had the right of way," said Louise.

Dan finished with the corn and picked up a Tupperware bowl full of ice cubes. "She's right," he said.

"Excuse me?" said Mary.

"Frank Ray was in the wrong," said Dan.

"That's the guy who was driving," said Louise.

"There's such a thing as right of way and such a thing as survival," said Mary.

They thought this over. A puff of breeze came along and they turned their faces toward it.

"But that's not the point," said Mary.

"I know very well what your point is," said Louise.

"We both do," said Dan. He broke an ice cube in his teeth.

"But I like the darkroom," said Louise. "I like printing. I like burning and dodging. I like the chemicals and the lights, and I like not being hassled."

"Louise, you like the darkroom. Fine. We know this. This is a given," said Mary. "But the darkroom is not a career."

"You would say that no matter what I did," said Louise. "If I was an opera singer, you would say that wasn't a career."

"Well, I don't think it is a very stable one," said Mary.

A white plastic fan swiveled in Dan and Louise's bedroom. They sat up watching a movie about a bear family. Louise drank a gin and tonic and Dan had a beer. The narration of the movie was from the point of view of the male bear.

"And so, inevitably, our winter sleep comes to an end," he said. "The warmth of the sun calls us from our den."

"Quite the articulate bear," said Louise.

"You know, your mother gives you a hard time," said Dan.

"I do know," said Louise.

The bears were batting salmon through the air. "We just saw this footage," said Dan.

"Is everything all right?" said Louise.

"Yes," said Dan.

"Really?"

"Yeah. Why?"

"No reason," said Louise. "Are you still having trouble sleeping?"

"Are you still talking in your sleep?" said Dan.

"How would I know?" said Louise.

"Well, you are," said Dan.

"It isn't supposed to be a contest," said Louise. "You need to relax. That's why you don't sleep, is you don't relax. Why don't you have a real drink? The problem with beer is that the water content is very high. You know when they say, 'It's the water'? Well, that's right. It is water. Whereas gin is more distilled. Have some of this. Relax."

Dan took a drink and reached over to touch her hair. "Kind of fond of liquor, aren't you?" he said.

"I am," said Louise. "When I was getting ready for bed just now I couldn't wait to tear into this g and t."

"I noticed your clothes flying off," said Dan.

"The trick is just what they tell you—being moderate," said Louise. "Too much will actually wake you up. But a little bit helps. It does me, anyway. One generous drink with lime. Certainly no more than two."

Dan woke up in the middle of the night. It was not just that he was awake. There was always something slightly wrong. Either his ears rang or his bad knee felt tenuous or his teeth hurt, or he had a hard-on that would not go away. It was always one thing but never two things together. Maybe these distractions did not cause the insomnia but instead resulted from it—as if, once he was awake, some bothersome condition was required to keep him company.

Louise was breathing deeply onto his arm. He could see her dark hair beside him. Her breath was strangely cool in the heat, and he seemed to be breathing in time with her. This in fact was going to be the minor problem of the night. With each breath, he was taking in a little less air than his lungs required. You would have thought that breathing was automatic enough, but on this night Dan was going slowly breathless to Louise's rhythm.

He got up, walked around the bed, and sat in a chair. Now he could make out the shape of her back. She was a being of beauty and tenderness from this vantage point, and maybe they should have met a long time ago. He was thirty-seven years old, and even though the county of which he was sheriff was not heavily populated, he had seen the worst things. Every kind of car accident, involving children, involving infants. And motorcycle accidents, in which the drivers seemed to have been fired into the pavement by a giant hand. He had seen people out of their heads and threatening to do their families harm. That happened every drinking night of the year. He had seen the consequences of a murder-suicide, or whatever it was, in an otherwise neat kitchen with a sampler that said, "Bless This Mess." He had a hard time squaring these memories with the plain sight of Louise brushing her hair in the morning, simply taking the hair in one hand and brushing the resulting ponytail with the other; or making a sarcastic statement, with light in her eyes and a glass poised at her lip; or driving the car with her hair tied back and her forearm slung over the door. She was turning now and saying something. He leaned toward the bed. "Wetlands," she said, just that. "Wetlands," in a low voice. And then either the breathing problem went away or he stopped being conscious of it.

Dan put on a shirt and went downstairs to the kitchen. It had been Louise's house, but he was familiar enough with it by now to walk around in darkness. A bar of orange light shone from the dryer, a reassuring reminder that the dryer could be used anytime, day or night. Dan pulled up a chair and turned on a small black-and-white television that sat on a table between the refrigerator and the counter. They got four channels at this time of the night. Ames, Albert Lea, La Crosse, and Sioux City. There was no cable out in the country, and Morrisville signed off at one.

Dan turned the dial with scientific disinterest. Channel 3 had a gold commercial. After a month of little sleep Dan had become convinced that the American people, or at least American insomniacs, loved gold—gold plate, gold filigree, and, most of all, solid gold. On any night you could order bracelets, chains, animals of any species, characters from Les Misérables—all in gold. If you were of a business mind, you could even buy a franchise to peddle this gold to others. And yet in his day-to-day world Dan encountered very little gold, and he wondered, as he sometimes did about all television, whether these advertisements were intended for someplace else and only reached Grouse County by accident. Channel 5 had car racing, followed by an advertisement for a science fiction movie called The Thirty-Foot Bride of Candy Rock,

160

starring an oversized woman in a sexy tunic that was probably fashioned from a tent or a tarp of some kind.

Moving along to Channel 7, Dan found an old movie in which a woman was singing on a strange and shadowy stage. She had dark curls, pale eyes, a transparent veil. She sang with great power. Her voice soared and trembled—it was hard to tell if she was in control. Violinists and harpists played behind her, and candles shook in the hands of the choir. The piece was almost over, climbing toward some destructive note. Then the camera pulled back, revealing that the woman was singing in an amphitheater in a landscape of dark towers and hills. Was this supposed to be Heaven? Hell? Italy? Dan could not say. He made the short journey to Channel 13, where a man with a Southern accent was hacking up a countertop with a kitchen knife to prove the durability of the knife.

• • •

Kleeborg had still not been released that weekend, so Louise and Dan went up to Stone City to see how he was coming along. They had him in Mercy Hospital, an obscure but industrious place where construction was a constant but nothing ever seemed to get built, and where some new machine was always being acquired to do the things that were being done in Rochester or Kansas City.

"I think they forgot me," said Kleeborg.

"You must want out," said Louise.

"Not especially I don't," said Kleeborg. "They bring food. And it really isn't bad food either. I hear it's awfully hot out there. I don't care for the heat."

"How are you?" said Dan.

"Dan, I can't see very well," said Kleeborg.

"What does Duncan have to say about that?" said Louise.

"Well, I don't know," said Kleeborg. "I haven't seen Duncan since the day I came in. This is what I'm telling you. I think they forgot me. But I have reached a decision, Louise."

"What's that?"

"Well, I've been thinking a lot about death."

"Oh, Perry," said Louise. "There's no reason."

"In fact, there is," said Kleeborg. "Because yesterday I had a roommate—his name was Crawford—and last night he died."

"No kidding," said Louise. "What of?"

"No one seems to know," said Kleeborg. "There is a great deal of confusion here. A very great deal. But I have made a decision, and I called my lawyer in today. You know, Ned Kuhlers. And I said, 'Ned, when I die, the studio belongs to Louise. And you see to it, and you do what has to be done.' "

"Perry, this is really, really jumping the gun," said Louise. She picked up a buzzer and pushed it. "And I don't blame you. No one's talking to you, and you're sitting here getting all worked up."

"Well, I talked to Crawford yesterday," said Kleeborg. "Talked to the man a lot. He couldn't go anywhere, and I suppose I took advantage of this. I hope it wasn't what killed him."

Louise went to the door and looked down the hall. "I'm going to go find somebody," she said.

This left Dan and Kleeborg alone.

"She gets so emotional," said Kleeborg.

"Oh, yeah," said Dan. He went to the window. Bulldozers crawled silently through a dusty lot. "So anyway, what did you say to this Crawford?"

"I told him about my sister," said Kleeborg.

162

"Lydia."

"Yes. You see, when we were young, she wrote many letters to her boyfriend," said Kleeborg.

"I remember."

"But our parents did not agree with this," said Kleeborg. "Whether they were correct in their apprehensions I don't know. But they made an arrangement with Dean Ross, who ran the post office and the store in Romyla, in which Dean would hold Lydia's letters for my parents to retrieve when they came into town. Of course, this was unfair to Lydia. But back then you didn't see the strictness about the mail that you see today. Anyway, I don't think a one of her letters got to where she thought they were going."

Dan came away from the window and sat in a chair. "It's a sad story," he said, "but I don't think it would have killed anybody."

Someone knocked on the door. It was not the doctor or nurse as they had expected, but Grace, the woman who had ridden in the car that hit Kleeborg. She crossed the room in sandals and a tight green dress, and gave Kleeborg his broken glasses.

"I'm sorry," she said. "I really wanted to get these fixed. I took them to one place where they said they couldn't help me because the glasses were too old. And I took them to another place where they said that was completely wrong, they weren't too old, and when did I want them. So fine. Then I went back today, and they said, 'Come to find out about it, they *are* too old, and we can't fix them.' I said, 'Thanks. Thanks a lot for wasting my time.' Anyway, here's your glasses, and I'm sorry I couldn't get them fixed, and I'm sorry this whole thing ever happened in the first place."

"Well, thank you, Miss," said Kleeborg. He turned the mangled glasses over in his hands. "I appreciate the fact that you did try."

And then she left, and of course he had to ask who she was, because he couldn't remember. Then Dan and Kleeborg played cribbage.

"Fifteen two, fifteen four, fifteen six, a pair is eight, and nobs is nine," said Kleeborg.

Louise returned and said, "Has anyone been here?"

"Just Grace Ray," said Dan.

He was awake again that night. At ten after three he was sitting at the kitchen table doing the bills when Louise walked into the kitchen in her nightgown. He said hello to her but she only stood by the table gathering the bills in her hands. There was such a calm look in her eyes that Dan understood she was sleepwalking. Once she had all his paperwork, she went out the screen door, letting it bang behind her. Dan followed, being careful not to wake her. The only thing he knew about sleepwalking was that you had to be careful not to wake the person. Louise glided over the grass in the dark. She walked out from under the shadow of the trees, and leaning down she spread the bills on the ground. Then she straightened and looked at the sky. It was a warm, clear summer night. Stars glittered like towns, and the Milky Way seemed to be a real road, going somewhere. After a moment Louise folded her arms and walked back to the house. Dan picked the bills from the damp grass and carried them into the kitchen, where he arranged them according to paid and unpaid and went back to work.

NINE

TINY DARLING came back to Grouse County, as everyone always does. He drove past broken corn stalks, tall blue silos, and the handwritten roadside reminder that Sin Is Death. He tried to imagine these as scenes from a documentary about his life, with a soundtrack by John Cougar Mellencamp. He drove east through Margo and over to Grafton. The Johanson farm looked too perfect in the smoky autumn light. The fields were stripped and the drying bins arranged neatly, like polished steel replicas of the family. "Grafton," said the town sign. "Pop. 321. Stop and Have a Look Around."

Tiny drove directly to Lindsey Coale's beauty shop. Lindsey was sitting in the chair nearest the door, looking out the window at the empty street.

"Hi, stranger," she said. "I heard you went to be a cowboy."

"That's an unfounded rumor," said Tiny, lowering himself into the barber chair. "I worked on bridges in the state of Colorado."

Lindsey fastened a sheet around Tiny's neck with a safety pin. "And how short today?" she said.

Tiny took out his billfold and produced a picture torn from a magazine of a man holding a bottle of after-shave and

165

looking at dolphins in the ocean. The man had wavy black hair.

"Can you make me look like this?"

Lindsey studied the picture and looked at Tiny's red hair. "I can try," she said. "Given your coloring, understand, it won't be identical. But we can give it a whirl."

"I mean the coloring," said Tiny.

Lindsey looked at him uncertainly. "What? You want your hair tinted?"

"I don't know what to call it," said Tiny. "Make it black."

Lindsey Coale turned toward the mirror and lit a cigarette. "May I ask why?" she said.

"For a change."

"Tiny, are you in trouble?"

He leaned forward with his hands on the arms of the barber chair. "Why would you assume that?" he said.

"Because I could go to jail," said Lindsey. "And that's happened."

"I'm not in trouble," said Tiny.

"In Oklahoma," said Lindsey, flipping through a trade magazine. "A hairdresser altered the appearance of a postal employee who had stolen federal checks. The mailman made it out of the country, but the hairdresser went to jail for three months. Here it is. *U.S. v. Hair Skin Nails.*"

"You're reading a lot into it that isn't there," said Tiny. "My life has changed but my hair is the same tired color."

"I understand," said Lindsey. "A lot of people feel that same way. But the fact is I can't help you, Tiny. I don't do tints anymore."

Tiny stood, swept the sheet behind him like a cape, and reached for a bottle on a shelf. "Then what's this?" he said.

"It's conditioning gel," said Lindsey Coale. "Please put it back. Please put it back, Tiny."

"All right," said Tiny. "Here, it's back."

"Do you want a haircut or don't you?"

Tiny unpinned the cloth around his collar. "I do not," he said. He had business in Morrisville, so he might have taken the Pinville blacktop, which headed southwest out of Grafton. Instead, he decided to swing over to Boris to see his mother. This took him by the Klar farm, which he had not visited in almost two years. The house looked about the same. It needed paint more than it had. It was a white farmhouse with a tall gable and a lower ridge. Dan and Louise had hung a tire swing from the elm. Big deal. Dan's gold Caprice was up on blocks. Tiny drove in, sounded the horn several times, waited, and wheeled his car behind the hedge that separated the yard and the barnyard.

He walked into the garage and paused at the window onto the kitchen. Then he raised it and stepped inside. He walked through the house. In the living room he found a shiny blue photo album from the wedding. Tiny carried this back to the kitchen, got some cheese slices from the refrigerator, and ate the cheese while sitting at the kitchen table looking at the wedding pictures. One of Louise embracing Dan generated a pain that seemed to begin in his earlobes and travel down his neck to his shoulder bones and from there into his arms until his elbows hurt. Tiny took the album upstairs to the bedroom. This was completely changed over. What could be as foreign as someone else's bedroom, especially if it used to be your own? The bed was so high it seemed like a children's clubhouse. It was half made, with an airy plaid quilt (new) lofted over tangled sheets, and Tiny could picture Louise running late, pulling on clothes, pausing to finish a cigarette with her shirttail hanging down. The walls had been stripped of paper, the scarred plaster painted white. A cool white nightgown (new) hung on a hook on the back of the door. The room smelled of lemons and soap. Tiny held the photo album to his chest and lay on the bed. He kept whispering Louise's name, and after some time he fell asleep. It was early afternoon when he awoke. The sky was rough and gray, and there had been a loud noise downstairs. Tiny went down the steps quietly and replaced the album. The kitchen window had fallen shut. Tiny lifted it and went out.

The trip from the Klar farm to Boris was all on the gravel, and it had been dry, so Tiny was accompanied by a cloud of rolling dust. His mother's house was in the dead center of Boris. The house had been painted years ago in a flesh tone that must have been cheap to make, judging from the number of poorly maintained places that you see in that shade. There was a long porch to the left of the front door, and this was laden with junk and sinking into the ground. Colette Sandover's house was a mess, and no sense could be made of the disorder. There were engineer boots in the sink, an animal trap shedding flakes of rust on the television set, and stacks of *Photoplay* magazines in the bathtub. Tiny found his mother standing in the backyard weeds, telling a story to some children from the neighborhood.

"And so, the wolf went home hungry," she said. "He was so hungry that he ran around his cave, and the geode that he had worshiped fell upon him. The wolf howled and howled until the townspeople heard his terrible cries. 'Help me, I can't move,' said the wolf. Then the mayor reported to the people, 'The wolf is pinned. He has no food. It is only a matter of time.' 'Good,' said everyone. And they waited three months until they were certain that the wolf had perished. Then they went into the cave, carried his bones out, and made a boat that carried them to the new land across the lake."

"Hello, Mom," said Tiny.

"Go home, children," said Colette. She and Tiny went into the house.

"I don't want to see you," she said.

"Well, this is a hell of a thing," said Tiny.

"I can't give anymore," she said.

"Name something you ever gave," said Tiny.

"When you fell, I picked you up. When you were hungry, I handed you food. There are other examples. I'm not the endless well you seem to think I am. I'll be happy to see you children at Christmas. But that's it. Possibly Easter. Otherwise, I must ask you to keep your distance."

Some parents get their children mixed up, calling one sibling by the name of another. But Colette seemed to have confused Tiny with the offspring of some other mother. "I don't think I've been in this house in five years," said Tiny.

"Christmas or Easter, take your pick," said Colette. "Tell you what. Why don't you choose now and Jerry will have to take the other. What could be more fair?"

"I don't want either one of those."

She sighed. "Well, what do you want? Everyone's needs come before Mother's needs."

Tiny went to the sink, moved the engineer boots, and got a drink of water. "Are you getting enough nutrition and stuff?" he said. "Do you cook for yourself? What do you do?"

"What I cook or don't cook is no concern of yours," she said. "If I were you, I would worry about my own plate. Your

169

father was a fool. Jerry's father was mean, and Bebe's father was weak, but yours was the fool of the bunch."

"A stroll down memory lane," said Tiny.

"And stay away from my meter," said Colette. "I know you've been turning it forward to make it look like I'm using more power than I am."

"Oh, yeah. I do that all the time," said Tiny.

"Christmas or Easter," said Colette.

Tiny went south to Highway 56 and west to Morrisville. His mother was crazy, and maybe insanity was all that he had to look forward to. The drunk-driving people in Colorado had given him the address of something called the Room. This was a counseling group with an office in a brick building above a jazz-dancing studio by the South Pin River. Tiny watched the jazz dancers in their colored tights for a while and went upstairs, where he found two rooms with the sort of sad, anonymous furniture that can be purchased in bankruptcy auctions from coast to coast. There was a metal desk with a wood-veneer top, a green file cabinet scarred by the removal of unknown stickers, and half a dozen flimsy chairs of orange plastic in a seventies contour. Over in the corner Johnny White was hitting golf balls at a putting machine.

"Johnny?" said Tiny.

"Shh," said Johnny. "If this goes in, I'll be a success in life." He hit the ball past the machine and into the baseboard. "That doesn't bode well."

"Johnny?"

"I know you," said Johnny. He had large red eyes that always made him seem either hung over or very sincere. "We used to have belt-sander races in shop class."

"Those were the good days," said Tiny. "Listen, I'm looking for something called the Room."

"You got it," said Johnny. "Tell you what, though. I'm running behind in my schedule. I'm giving a talk up by Margo in about twenty minutes. You want to come along, see what we're all about?"

"All right," said Tiny.

Johnny and Tiny went to Margo in Johnny's Bronco. It was a new truck with a black interior, and although it was only forty-some degrees outside Johnny kept the air conditioner blasting.

"You hear a lot, Tiny—or I hear a lot, anyway—about the twelve steps," said Johnny. "At the Room we don't have twelve steps. We have one step. Step into the Room. Don't leave until you're clean. It's that simple. Once you're in the Room, the idea is always to be moving toward the Door of the Room. This must be gradual. You can't just waltz out, because if you do, you'll fall. By the same token, you do have to step out eventually. Understand?"

"No," said Tiny.

"The Room is not an actual room," said Johnny.

"I'm confused," said Tiny. "If you step in and then step out …"

"Right," said Johnny.

"That right there is two steps," said Tiny.

"Let's not get hung up on the number of steps," said Johnny.

The Little Church of the Redeemer was dark brown with frayed red carpet on the floor. It was four o'clock in the afternoon and Tiny could see the gray hills and board-and-batten cottages out the window. This was an area on the edge of Grouse County where it was too hilly to farm. Joan Gower

171

met Johnny and Tiny at the back of the church. Tiny did not know her. She was a wide-eyed woman with blond hair, and she wore a long white gown with a rose-colored cross on the front. Johnny introduced Tiny and Joan, who sat together in the front of the church as he gave his talk. Tiny turned around a couple times. Some of the people in the audience were blind, and they aimed their ears at Johnny and consequently seemed to be looking right at Tiny. This made him nervous, even though they could not see him.

Johnny White told his own story—the bankruptcy, the divorce, how he missed his kids. He had told the story many times, but now, instead of being merely sad, it established his credentials as leader of the Room. Johnny had grown his hair long enough in front that he could smooth it back to cover his bald spot. But this long front hair tended to fall forward, and as a result he leaned his elbows on the pulpit and kept both hands free for managing his hair. There was a new part in his story, about drinking. Johnny did not really have an ongoing drinking problem. Judging from this anecdote, he had got drunk once and run into some spectacularly bad luck. Maybe this was a nitpicking distinction. He had ended up getting stitches. It's also possible that Joan Gower had not heard Johnny's story before. As Johnny spoke about his children, Megan and Stefan, she took Tiny's hand and held it tightly, and Tiny saw the tears on her face.

At the end of Johnny's talk an old man came up the aisle with a whiskey bottle. "I'm a big drinker," he said. "I fought with George Smith Patton in Sicily but I can't fight this."

"Not alone, my veteran friend," said Johnny. "That's why the Room exists. Most people can't fight it alone. Some can. If anyone here can, I would advise them candidly to hit the road, because they don't need us."

"I just get so thirsty," said the man. "During the day I'm right there. But when night comes on, I don't know, that's when it's bad."

"You're in the grips of a disease," said Johnny. "It's like anything. It's like breaking your ankle."

"Something's broke," said the man.

"We will mend it in the Room," said Johnny. "Out here is the land of make-believe. You might as well uncork that container and have a cocktail."

"Really?" said the man.

"That's how much I believe in what I'm doing," said Johnny.

The man looked at the bottle. "No, I wouldn't feel right."

Afterward, Johnny White stood under a musty tent beside the church and answered questions. There was a great deal of confusion about the Room and why, if it wasn't an actual place, did Johnny talk about going into and out of it. What did he mean by that? And if it isn't a place, what is it? And where? Meanwhile, Joan Gower took Tiny for a walk.

"This is our duck pond," she said. "As you can see, it's almost time to skim for algae. Continuing up the hill, we get a good view of the repairs being done gradually to our church roof. And here are the cottages. Aren't they the greatest? These were manufactured in Sioux City in the nineteenth century for farmers who would come to town on Saturday and wish to stay overnight for church in the morning. In that sense they are the first prefabricated houses, and here they are in Margo. Our campers or residents come from the cities primarily—Chicago, Minneapolis, and St. Louis—and they study with me and Father Alphonse Christiansen. Stepping in, we see the nice detailing and bead-board that tell us these cottages are from a different time. The setup is pretty spartan. We provide a hot plate, a desk, a chair, a dresser, and a plain but sturdy bed. This particular cottage has a nice view of the duck pond that we were just at. Look, some mallards are coming down for a water landing. Oh, hold me. Please hold me."

Margo began as an outpost and has remained one. The houses are far apart and small. Whereas other towns thrived and then dwindled, Margo never thrived and so dwindling was not an issue. Even Boris has more handsome pages in its history than Margo. Margo has the lake, too, just south of town, which you would consider a benefit until you actually stood on its shores. Lake Margo is fed by the same aquifer as Walleye Lake, but as is the case with some siblings, they could hardly be less alike. Walleye is clean and broad and, when viewed from above, is shaped like a big healthy muskrat. Most years it is full of northern and walleyed pike—hence the name—and many a young camper has been sent off to bed with the promise that "we'll get up and fish Walleye in the morning."

Lake Margo, by contrast, has the outline of an elemental protozoan, and though it is deep, it is full of weeds that seem to have evolved specifically to foul the blades of outboard motors. There is a large gasoline distributorship to the east, and after a rain the water sparkles with fragile pastel oil rings. No connection has been proved, and the matter has been tied up in court so long that the county judges are all tired of it and tend to recess defensively whenever it comes up. But the lake often smells of gasoline, which helps explain why Walleye Lake has a thriving tourist business featuring a water slide while Margo has the Little Church of the Redeemer with its falling-in roof and ragbag revivalists.

Tiny and Joan Gower kissed passionately for several minutes, with the gray light coming through the window of the homely cottage. Then Joan straightened her gown and its pale cross and walked down the hill to the church. Johnny and Tiny drove to Morrisville, where Tiny picked up his car and a box of L'Oréal No. 3 Soft Black hair color before returning through the dark countryside. Joan was in the basement of the church playing "This World Is Not My Home" on the piano when Tiny came down the stairs. He stopped and listened to her sing.

This world is not my home
I'm just a-passing through
My treasures are laid up
Somewhere beyond the blue

They made love on the piano bench, on the steps, and in the bell tower, where there has not actually been a bell since the big lightning storm of 1977. Finally they sat in the kitchen, worn out if not exactly satisfied, smoking Father Christiansen's Canaria d'Oros and languidly reading the intimidating instructions that came with the hair dye.

"You don't want to do your eyebrows, do you?" said Joan. "It could cause blindness."

"In that case, no," said Tiny.

"I like when the eyebrows are different," said Joan, and she smiled. Then she read: "Some people are allergic to haircoloring products. Allergies can develop suddenly even though you have been coloring your hair for some time. The simplest and most effective way to find out if you are allergic is to do the following Patch Test."

"Nah, forget that," said Tiny.

He poured the coloring into the developer and shook the mixture while Joan pulled on the transparent gloves provided.

"I know what it is to profoundly change," said Joan. "I wasn't always in the ministry. I was an actress for many years in Chicago. I tried to be, anyway. It's a very hard business to be in. I come from Terre Haute, and when I left there they all warned me. 'Joan,' they said, 'the only way people get ahead in that business is by sleeping around.' So I went to Chicago and I took an acting workshop and I did sleep around to a certain extent but apparently not enough, because it took me two years to get a part in a play. It was called *Au Contraire, Pierre*, a French comedy, and I played a pregnant woman. I had a thing to wear on my stomach and, you know, I really studied for that part, because I wanted to make it special. Wow, this is black. I mean, it's really black." She lathered the coloring into his hair. "Well, for instance, some pregnant women have to lie on their backs for months, and I knew this, so I suggested that it might be comical for me to lie in a bed onstage during the whole play and never move. But they said no, they didn't want that. Don't you think that could have been funny? If it was done right? And I knew that some women have to sit down all the time and put their legs up to keep from getting varicose veins, but they didn't want me to do that either. The last thing that I thought might be interesting was the fact that pregnancy can cause forgetfulness. But instead of asking anyone, because of course they would say no, I just started acting forgetful—you know, as if I couldn't quite remember my lines. I admit it was tricky, what I was trying to achieve. Then one day when I came to the set they told me I had been replaced by another woman, and I should clean out my locker and go."

"You got screwed," said Tiny.

"I agree," said Joan. "Wait a minute. I got some on you. Hold still."

She ran a towel carefully over his forehead.

"Anyway, that night I happened to be in a bar, and I managed to let it slip that I was an actress. Well, this man started talking about a well-known star—or starlet, I guess you'd say—who you always see on TV. He said some terrible things about her and what she supposedly did in order to become famous. I mean, unless he was a bug on the ceiling there is no way he could have known what he was talking about. And the more he talked the louder he got, and the more bitter he got, and it was 'Fuck this' and 'Fuck that,' and the more he reminded me of the people back in Terre Haute and the warning they gave me when I left home. So finally I hauled off and hit him just as hard as I could across the face. But you understand, this is when I knew I had to change. Now we let it sit for twenty-five minutes. Then, let's see… we rinse your hair and apply the Accent de Beauté shampoo and conditioner."

"My scalp feels strange," said Tiny.

Joan Gower pulled the blackened gloves off, one finger at a time. "That means it's working," she said.

Tiny went to see Johnny White. They could hear the music from the dance studio, the bass like a heartbeat. Johnny said there was a possibility that Tiny could get four hundred and twenty-five dollars a month to work for the Room. It all depended on whether he was any good at talking in front of a group. Johnny said it was not that hard, and from what Tiny had seen at Joan's church, this had the ring of truth. Johnny said he would coach Tiny. Tiny would start off talking to kids and gradually work up to the adults. Tiny would be required to wear a tie and to look everyone in the eye at all times. He would be expected to emphasize drugs rather than alcohol, because people were more afraid of drugs. Johnny said there was fair demand right now for speakers in the high schools.

So one Saturday night Tiny found himself sitting at a basketball game between Pringmar and Romyla in his new black hair and a clip-on necktie, waiting for halftime when he would speak. Like many of the smaller gymnasiums in Grouse County, this one was cramped and outmoded, with a rounded ceiling that was so low on the sides that corner shots with too much arc would hit the rafters. Seeing this, Tiny felt less nervous. His efforts might not amount to much, but they could not be sillier than the spectacle of these children in badly fitting jerseys bouncing basketballs off the ceiling. Then the first half ended, a boy and girl swept the yellow floor with push brooms, and Tiny climbed onto the stage and with both hands took hold of a microphone that had been set up in front of the pep band.

"Hello, folks," he said. "My name is Charles Darling and they call me Tiny. You might wonder how I got that nickname. Well, if you think that's strange, you should meet my brother Fats. If you're not home, I'll just slip him under the door. But I jest. What I'm here to talk about today is no laughing matter, which I'm sure you'll agree with, and that's drugs ..." Tiny spoke for fifteen minutes and showed a short film. The reaction was about what he had hoped for, which is to say that most of the students ignored him completely, and then the program was over, and the Romyla pep band played "Cocaine," and Tiny walked off the stage and sat down. The Room distributed questionnaires the following Monday in health classes at the Romyla and Pringmar high schools. After getting the responses back and reading them, Johnny White said they were basically what you would expect, although a handful of students had seemed to get a favorable rather than an unfavorable impression of amphetamines, which is something Tiny would have to work on.

And he did work. He had never worked so hard on anything, with the possible exception of his big plan (never carried out, for lack of a decent accomplice) to steal fifty-five miles of copper wiring from the Rock Island Railroad. And, although he had hopes of getting paid, this had not happened yet. He had money left from Colorado and was also trying to launch a new business in which he would go from town to town washing windows. Squeegee and bucket in hand, Tiny thought he had found an unfilled niche, but others did not see it that way. Most people gave Tiny quizzical or suspicious looks and told him to keep moving. Some people with filthy windows got angry, asking, "What are you trying to say?" Once in a while he got a taker, but not often. The whole thing seemed misunderstood and forlorn as Tiny drove the empty plain between the towns.

In this sense the window washing blended well with the high school talks, which Tiny did more of as the weather got colder. He gained confidence, as Johnny had said he would. Minor problems no longer fazed him. In Stone City, for example, before the biggest audience Tiny had yet faced, his tie slipped from his collar and fell to the gym floor, and he was able to laugh along with everyone instead of, say, heaving the podium into the crowd. Another time, there was some kind of scheduling mistake and he had to sit through a play rehearsal on the stage of the Grafton gym. Tiny did not mind, because he was feeling somewhat distracted and this gave him the opportunity to settle down. The drama featured Claude Robeshaw's son Albert and an Asian girl whose name Tiny did not know. (This was Lu Chiang.)

"You say it," said Albert.

"You say it," said the girl.

"In this scene—"

"Don't say it like that," said the girl.

"Why don't you say it," said Albert.

"Go, 'In this scene, Melville's hero relays part of his daring plan to the mysterious and dark-haired Isabel,'" said the girl. "Put a taste of suspense in there."

Albert repeated the introduction, and he and the girl took their places on a wooden bench.

"This strange, mysterious, unexampled love between us makes me all plastic in thy hand," said the girl. "The world seems all one unknown India to me."

"Thou, and I, and Delly Ulver," said Albert Robeshaw, "tomorrow morning depart this whole neighborhood, and go to the distant city."

"What is it thou wouldst have thee and me to do together?" said the girl.

Albert stood. He put his hand on his narrow chest. "Let me go now," he said.

The girl rose and wrapped her arms around Albert. "Pierre, if indeed my soul hath cast on thee the same black shadow that my hair now flings on thee... Isabel will not outlive this night."

The girl collapsed and Albert held her by the waist. They began making out. A handful of students clapped and whistled and stamped their feet, and a teacher said, "What did I say about the kissing. Pierre and Isabel! What did I say!"

Tiny began his talk by acknowledging the damage he had done not only in this gym but elsewhere. He blamed it all on drugs and alcohol, and examined in some detail the breakdown of his marriage and the pain involved in a bad hangover. He did not dwell long—he never did—on the concept of the Room, because no one understood it, and he did not understand it himself. His tie stayed in his collar, and when he asked for questions Jocelyn Jewell stood up with a high school yearbook and said, "Is it true that you graduated in 1969?"

"Yes," said Tiny.

"Do you remember by any chance the caption on your senior picture?"

"No, ma'am," said Tiny.

"Well, I have it right here. 'If trouble were sand, I would be a beach.' Can you tell us about this?"

"I'd say it was self-explanatory," said Tiny.

"I also have something else, and this is a comment, not a question," said Jocelyn Jewell. "Do you know the part in the film you showed where the boy is writing the letter to his parents?"

"Yes," said Tiny.

"And he goes, I forget what it was exactly, something like, 'Dear Mom and Dad, I'm having a great time in college but I need more money for drugs.'"

"Right."

"I just think that's kind of unrealistic. Because I don't think anyone would come out and say that."

"Yeah, maybe not," said Tiny.

The next question was from Albert Robeshaw. "With so much emphasis on drugs, don't you think it makes our country look pathetic or something?"

"It takes a big nation to admit it has large problems," said Tiny.

Then Dane Marquardt stood, but Albert Robeshaw did not sit down. "I want to second what Albert said. Our country is pathetic," said Dane.

"Where would you go, assuming you could go anywhere?" said Tiny.

"Copenhagen," said Albert.

"I would, too," said Dane.

"What's the drug situation there?" said Tiny.

"It's much better than this dump," said Dane Marquardt.

"It was founded in the eleventh century," said Albert Robeshaw. "It has a temperate climate."

Principal Lou Steenhard walked up to Tiny and took the microphone. "Mr. Darling is a drug counselor, people, not a travel agent," he said.

"Well, I'm not really a drug counselor either," said Tiny. "They call me a drug lecturer."

"I have a question about drugs," said Albert. "You know when they fry the egg on television and say this is your brain on drugs? Well, I wonder how effective that is. Because I just get hungry for eggs."

It was cold and windy when Tiny left the gym. Winter was coming and he was glad. To him it was the most honest of the seasons. He drove to Morrisville and stepped into the jazz-dancing salon underneath the Room. There were mirrors everywhere, and with his hair and his tie he really didn't look like himself. He danced along with the perspiring women for a minute and then went upstairs. Johnny sat on the edge of his desk, spinning the cylinder of a six-shooter.

"How'd it go, buddy?" he said. "Don't worry. This is a limited-edition replica."

"I feel like if I got through to one person it was worth it," said Tiny.

"I know damned well you did," said Johnny. "But don't worry about that. We're putting you on the payroll next week."

"That's good," said Tiny.

"You're going to do some grown-ups," said Johnny.

"Jesus, John, wonder if I'm ready," said Tiny.

"You've got what people are hungry for," said Johnny. "Straight talk." He pretended to draw and fire the gun, and then laid it on the desk. He brought out a camera.

"We need your picture for an identification card," said Johnny. "It's really kind of nice. I put mine in a leather holder so it looks like a badge."

"I was just thinking of something," said Tiny. "How about if I go over to Kleeborg's Portraits in Stone City?"

"We don't have the money," said Johnny. "We're saving up for an overhead projector."

"I'll pay," said Tiny.

"This wouldn't be because Louise works there," said Johnny.

"Partly," said Tiny.

"I'm not going to tell you how to live," said Johnny. "But let's say you go over there and, who knows, an argument of some kind should occur. I would hate to see you throw away your good work. Because the Room would fire your ass, and I know it, because that's how I got this job. So my advice would be to let me take your picture."

"All right," said Tiny.

Johnny turned the focusing ring of the camera. "Hold that face," he said.

Joan Gower climbed the attic stairs with a flashlight at the Little Church of the Redeemer. It was cold and she rubbed her arms, making the light dance in the rafters. She bumped the worn plywood figures of the Nativity scene and continued to the back wall, where, under a dim and diamond-shaped window, there were three trunks, each bearing her name. She had labeled the trunks years ago, when she was spelling her name Joän. These were her things from Chicago. She had to open all the trunks before she found the canvas pillow that she had worn in order to perform the role of the pregnant woman in the French farce. It had two straps, one for her hips and one for her back, and utilized a crude and early form of Velcro. She belted the rig over her jeans and sweater. Then she put on a long, gray houndstooth coat that she had worn all the time back then.

Joan went down the steps carefully. The hard part in the play had been to accept the weight as part of herself, and in turn to project that acceptance beyond the edge of the stage. The cast had been much nicer to her when she appeared to be pregnant, even though they knew it was an illusion. She walked through the drab church and out the side door. She got a rake from the shed and began combing the algae from the duck pond. The clouds were like the pieces of a broken blackboard. Sometimes Joan wished she had stuck with her acting a little longer. Of course, there was nothing that said she couldn't get back into it. Even now, anyone driving by would have thought for all the world that she was a pregnant woman walking in the hills. No one did drive by, however. The ducks followed her around the edge of the water. "I am big as a house," she said.

Meanwhile, Tiny was standing in the reception area of Kleeborg's Portraits. He felt as though he had completed a long journey to reunite with Louise, although he might not have a lot to show for it. Tiny rang a bell and waited quite a while. Eventually Kleeborg came out. He had thin white hair and large wraparound sunglasses. Gesturing with the squeegee, Tiny offered to wash the windows.

"I got a guy named Pete who comes around in the spring," said Kleeborg.

"With windows like these, I wouldn't wait until spring," said Tiny. "I mean, it's up to you. But come over here. This is not good."

"I don't see very well since my car accident," said Kleeborg.

"Maybe there's someone else who can take a look," said Tiny. "I'm not saying this because of the money. I'm saying this as a friend."

"We've come this far with Pete," said Kleeborg. "Goodbye."

Tiny left the office and stood on the sidewalk. Kleeborg's was on the ground floor of a three-story building with an awning. The door opened and Louise stepped onto the sidewalk. Her hair was pulled into a ponytail. She held a little paintbrush in her hand.

"Hi, Lou," said Tiny.

"What happened to your hair?" she said.

"I had it dyed," said Tiny. "What do you think?"

"It's dark all right."

"Thank you."

"What do you want?"

"To see you."

"Here I am," said Louise. "Happy now?"

TEN

KLEEBORG WAS STANDING at the window when Louise came in. "That window washer didn't want to take no for an answer," he said.

They watched him get into the rusted Parisienne. "He had no intention of washing the windows," said Louise. "Well, I mean, he may have. Who knows? But that's Tiny Darling."

"You're kidding," said Kleeborg.

"Would that I were."

"I thought he joined the Seabees."

"No, he sure didn't."

The car pulled from the curb.

"He's right about the windows," said Louise.

"I don't see where clean windows is going to get us any business that we wouldn't get otherwise," said Kleeborg.

"I tend to agree," said Louise.

"Well, I'm going up," said Kleeborg. He lived in an apartment above the studio. "Take care of yourself."

"Good night, Perry."

She turned out the lights, locked the doors, and headed for home. But she had only gone a few blocks when Tiny's headlights swung into her rear-view mirror. She cut across the train yard, but he was not falling for anything. He didn't try to run her off the road but just maintained a certain distance. Finally, out in the country, she pulled over and rolled down her window. Tiny got out of his car, walked up beside her.

"What a messy car," he said.

She picked up a bottle cap, as if considering the evidence. "Twist off," she said.

"Do you remember when we were in high school?" said Tiny.

"We weren't in high school at the same time."

"You weren't a freshman when I was a senior?"

"I'm afraid not."

"Well, anyway. In my senior interview, they asked, 'What is your pet peeve?' And do you know what I said? Do you remember?"

"No," said Louise. "And please get your arm off the door."

"People who think they're better than others."

"Oh, everybody said that. And better isn't the issue. You want me to say I was wrong. Fine. I was wrong. I wrote the book of wrong. Now stop following me. You know, we never should have got married. Our marriage was... misguided."

"You liked my owl tattoo."

"Yeah, there's a solid foundation."

"You forget the good times," said Tiny. "You have dismissed them from your mind."

"It's hard to conduct a life and not have a few good times, if only by chance," said Louise.

"I cooked for you when you were sick," said Tiny.

"Never once did you cook for me in six years."

"I most certainly did make Kraft Dinner that time you were sick."

188

"Why? Because you were hungry," said Louise.

She went home to an empty farmhouse. Dan was seeing a therapist at that hour for his insomnia. Louise ran a steaming bath and undressed. She balanced a *Redbook* magazine and a package of Twizzlers on the rim of the tub.

For a half hour she soaked. Then the candy was gone and *Redbook* fell into the water. She retrieved the magazine and hung it over the towel rack to dry. She washed and conditioned her hair, rinsing with a red Hills Brothers coffee can.

Dan came home. She lay on the bed in a white robe, watching square dancing on television. The men had their hands on the women's waists as they danced among hay bales. This aroused her vaguely. Dan took his badge off and put it on the dresser.

"Check out the petticoats," said Louise.

"Ooh la la," said Dan.

"So how was the therapist? Did she fork over the sleeping tablets?"

"She said I should try sleeping outside the house."

"It's cold out there," said Louise.

"Well, she didn't mean outdoors," said Dan. "She meant a motel, I guess."

"Who's going to pay for that?" said Louise.

"I told her it was impossible," said Dan.

"We're not even fighting, not really."

"I told her that."

Louise turned on her side in her robe. "I seriously hope you did."

Dan's eyes changed as she said this. They got deeper somehow, seemed to focus on something inside her. His hand brushed her throat; he kissed her.

"I mean, Jesus, go for a simple sedative," she whispered.

She woke in the dark of night and reached for Dan, finding no one. She got out of bed and went downstairs. Dan was reading *Arizona Highways* on the davenport. Mary always gave them her copy when she had finished with it.

"Look at this house," he said. He folded the magazine and showed her. "It's supposed to be haunted."

"By what?" said Louise. "The lonely ghost of a restless sheriff?"

"You don't see a figure in the window?" he asked.

"No, darling," said Louise. "It's a reflection."

Late fall was a busy time at Kleeborg's. One Saturday morning Louise drove down to Morrisville to take some publicity pictures for Russell Ford's RV dealership.

In the photographs Russell's nephew was to embrace a young woman in front of a mobile home. When Louise arrived, the girl was sitting on a spackle bucket in a strapless dress of black and gold.

"Hey, Maren," said Louise, for it was Maren Staley, the young woman who had come into Kleeborg's a year and a half before to have her high school picture taken but had been too hung over to pose. Next to Maren's name in the yearbook was a drawing of a person in a barrel with shoulder straps. The caption said, "Nothing to Wear." Now she was sober and pretty, grown up, leaning forward, shielding her sternum from the icy breeze.

Louise got a flannel shirt from her car and gave it to Maren. Russell's nephew Steven drove up. He was a handsome kid wearing a tuxedo. He had very little resemblance to his Uncle Russell.

The session was dogged by problems. Maren's shoulders

got goosebumps. The lights flickered because of a bad connection that could not be isolated. Maren was supposed to hug Steven's neck, but with her arms raised that way, the edge of her bra could be seen above the side of her dress.

"Fix her undershirt," said Russell Ford. He stood beside Louise, speaking into a megaphone.

"I'm right here," said Louise. She went over and pinned the bra to the dress.

"And another thing. The trim is bent," said Russell.

"What trim?" said Louise.

"On the motor home," said Russell. So then there was another delay while Russell went to find an unmarred example of this particular model he wanted in the advertisement.

Maren put Louise's flannel shirt on and bummed a cigarette. Louise looked in her pack. "There are six," she said. "Take them." The two women climbed into a silver trailer like the ones in which the astronauts used to recuperate after coming back from the moon.

"What are you up to?" Louise asked.

"I'm in community college now," said Maren. "I've changed a lot, Louise. College has changed me, and this is causing problems for me and Loren. Do you remember Loren?"

"He was your boyfriend, right?"

"That's what the problem is about," said Maren. "I say that I've changed. An example would be that now I love the music of Van Morrison. I listen to *Veedon Fleece* and sometimes I could just cry. So the other day Loren and I were driving around and he goes, 'Put on some of that Don Morrison.' I mean, it breaks your heart."

"People drift apart," said Louise.

"I'm in a two-year program, and then I can take my credits

191

and go anywhere," said Maren. "I may go out to the West Coast. In *Cannery Row* by John Steinbeck the author talks about a marine biologist named Doc. And reading this, it suddenly dawned on me that I have never put my feet in salt water. And I think that's something I would enjoy doing, given the type of personality I have. Evidently you can float motionless in the water and there is no way you can sink. Being a poor swimmer, I like the sound of that. So I'm considering California schools, which are all free. What college did you go to?"

"I didn't," said Louise. "I graduated from Grafton High School in the class of seventy-four. We had this guidance counselor who was really more like a fortune teller. Instead of giving advice, he would make these mysterious predictions. He said, 'Louise, you will work in a small shop.' So I guess he got that right."

"Photography is so intense," said Maren.

Russell opened the door and looked in. "Let's go," he said. "Mercury's falling."

Steven and Maren resumed their embrace. Russell threw his megaphone to the ground. "Now the dress looks bunchy," he said.

"Oh, you look bunchy," said Louise. "Steven! Put your hand on the side of the dress! Where the pins are! Perfect. Let's take some pictures."

A crowd had gathered on the sidewalk during the photo session. There had been a rumor for years that Sally Field was going to direct and act in a farm movie that would be filmed in Grouse County, and whenever anything resembling acting occurred in public, people would come together and look around hopefully for Sally Field.

This movie had been rumored for so long that the plot had changed from a young farm woman with cancer to a middle-aged farm woman with cancer. But through it all Sally Field never came to Grouse County, and she never would, and the whole thing was one of those grass-roots misunderstandings that refuse to go away.

Rumors can last a long time in Grouse County, or they can come back seasonally, like perennials. Take the one about Mary's trees, which, being on the edge of Grafton, tend to collect a lot of ice during winter storms. About once a winter, word spreads that a photographer is coming down from the Stone City newspaper to take pictures of Mary's ice formations. And soon all the parents have dragged their kids over to Mary's place with instructions to get their ass out there and build a snowman. But the afternoon unfolds, and the word proves false, and the sun sets on a poignant landscape of half-finished snow creatures.

Anyway, the crowd at Russell Ford's photo shoot had now been joined by Louise's friend Pansy Gansevoort, who airbrushed for Big Chief Printing and had an impressive mane of ginger-colored hair that would have made her a colorful extra in the Sally Field movie that was not to be.

Pansy waited for Louise to finish her work. "Hi, hon," she said. "I just came from Eight Dollars." This was a sprawling store on the edge of town where every item had that price.

"What did you get?" said Louise.

"Two blouses, a case of Cheetos, and a bowling ball," said Pansy.

"What kind of bowling ball costs eight dollars?" said Louise.

"This is what we're going to find out," said Pansy. "Want to go to the Rose Bowl?"

"I'm not a good bowler," said Louise, "and you bowl league. I mean, come on."

"I'll give you pointers," said Pansy.

So they went bowling, but Pansy's tips did not help. Louise was one of those uncanny bowlers who seem to throw directly into the gutter. That afternoon she even managed to make the classic error of rolling a ball after the pin-sweeping gate had descended. The ball cracked into the gate, and everyone stared, and a guy from the alley had to catwalk down the lane divider.

Still, the beers were tasty. Pansy and Louise sat at the scoring table and discussed their partners but did not seem to be speaking the same language. The sadism of Pansy's boyfriend had given way to something more common— just a lot of threats. And Pansy threatened him back, so this amounted to progress in Pansy's view.

Her stories involved either herself or the boyfriend cowering in a corner while the other one broke things by throwing them on the floor. Once Pansy's boyfriend had even entered the kitchen with a pistol, which turned out to be a starter's pistol but could have been real for all Pansy knew.

In comparison, Dan's not being able to sleep or Louise's feeling that something was not right sounded minor.

"I would leave the man," said Louise.

"We have a history," said Pansy.

"What's the point if you end up with a broken nose?" said Louise.

"It's not like that," said Pansy.

"It sounds just like that."

"I love him so much."

"Maybe it isn't love," said Louise. "Maybe it's more of a sadness that you get used to."

Louise was speaking very freely with Pansy. This is sometimes known as "the beer talking," although beer usually speaks in rougher tones. Amid the clatter of falling pins Louise was getting plastered in that loving and rose-colored way you can on afternoons in October.

At one point she swung her legs from beneath the table and, admiring the cuffs of her clean blue jeans and her rented shoes with their red suede and olive suede, she said huskily, "I love these fucking shoes."

Eventually Pansy and Louise emerged from the Rose Bowl into the slanting light. Pansy produced from her bowling bag the shoes that Louise had rented.

"What a nice thing," said Louise. She sat down on the curb and put the shoes on.

"You're right about not being able to bowl," Pansy said, "but I still like you."

Louise drove home slowly on narrow and little-used roads, reminded of the mechanical way she used to walk when as a teenager she would try to get across the living room and upstairs without her mother knowing she was drunk.

She and Dan had a fight when she got home. He was grilling peanut butter sandwiches for supper.

"I wish you wouldn't reach into the bread and tear out pieces of slices," he said.

"I lost my head," she said. She sat in one chair, her feet in the bowling shoes on another.

"That therapist I went to called," said Dan. "She thought maybe you should come in for an appointment."

"She's so perfect," said Louise.

"It's up to you," said Dan.

"Marriage counseling after six months," said Louise. "Not too very promising."

"It isn't marriage counseling," said Dan.

"Especially with divorce so easy to get," said Louise. "I did it not that long ago. They probably still remember me."

"Oh, cut it out," said Dan. "Where were you this afternoon?"

Louise was crying. "Look at my shoes and guess," she said.

"What's wrong?"

"You married me because I chased you," said Louise. "My mother said, 'Don't chase him, Louise.' But I did, I chased you."

"You didn't chase anyone," said Dan.

"Do you think I'm blind?" said Louise.

"What?"

She wiped her eyes on her sleeve. "I should have been a lot cooler about the whole thing."

"I don't see why."

"Look," said Louise, "do you love me?"

"Yes," said Dan. With the spatula he put grilled sandwiches on a plate. "Don't cry," he said. He had a way of becoming wooden and emotionless just when she needed him to be the opposite.

"I will if I want," said Louise.

The next day Louise felt terrible. All day at work she had to talk to some historic preservation people about a photographic survey of houses. Talk, talk, talk, and then they wanted coffee. They were very concerned with authenticity, and seemed to be scrutinizing Louise to see if she was authentic.

Then Louise went over to Russell Ford's and rented a trailer. She thought this could be the separate roof under which Dan might get some sleep, and by doing this good deed she could make up for the fight.

Russell gave her a discount, but still all she could afford was a tiny trailer made in 1976. Inside, there was just enough room to turn around. Russell said he would tow the trailer to the farm and set it up for seventy-five dollars.

"And that's treating you like a sister," he said.

Russell's nephew Steven delivered the trailer two days later. He put a carpenter's level on the fender and turned a crank on the hitch until the trailer was square. He filled the water tank, hooked up the electricity, showed her how the tiny appliances worked.

"Do you think I have a chance with Maren?" he said.

The question sounded to Louise like one you would ask the Magic Eight Ball. "There is always a chance," she said.

She enjoyed preparing the trailer for Dan. She cleaned it all up and made the bed with new sheets, pillows, and a quilt. She put beer in the refrigerator and cattails in a vase on the table. She plugged in a lamp with a warm yellow shade.

By the time Dan came home she had changed her mind. She opened the door and looked down at him.

"What's this, baby?" said Dan.

"I want to stay," she said. "I fixed this up for you, but I want to stay."

It would be wrong to say that the little trailer solved all their problems. But Dan began to sleep once he had the bed in the house to himself. It is true that his therapist had finally come through with a prescription. He and Louise ate together, and every night had the pure emotions of parting.

One night Dan knocked on her door and read for her a speech he was to give at a seminar on domestic violence.

"Sometimes we get a mistaken notion of what is strong," said Dan. "Why? Television, for one reason. We see a man lift five hundred pounds over his head, we see another man tear up the phone book of a large city. It becomes easy to conclude that this is what we mean by 'strong.' But turn off the set. Aren't the real strong men and women right at home, looking out for that family? What do we mean when we say 'strong'?"

• • •

Kleeborg's Portraits won the bid to take pictures of old houses. For Louise this amounted to long walks with a camera around the nicer parts of Stone City.

Not everyone understood the purpose of the project. Some people dressed up, gathering the kids and the dogs in the front yard. One thin old gentleman with a steep-roofed house built in 1897 showed Louise the spools in his garage. He had attached dozens of small sewing spools to the walls and ceiling and connected them by taut loops of string, so that when he turned on an electric motor the spools all spun at once and the knots on the strings danced back and forth.

"Wow," said Louise.

"Each one stands for someone I know," said the man.

Louise went to see Dan's therapist. The office had a soft chair and a huge inverted cone of an ashtray. A handle on the side of the chair operated a footrest, enabling Louise to raise and lower her feet as needed.

She had expected the therapist to be a bombshell, but the woman seemed tired and normal instead. Her name was Robin Otis.

"Where are your parents?" she said.

"My mother lives in Grafton. My father is dead," said Louise.

"How old were you when he died?"

"Well, how old was I. Sixteen," said Louise. "He had a heart attack while getting ready for a party."

"Such loss at a young age," said Robin.

"Yes, well," said Louise.

"Do you remember the last words he said to you?"

"He said for us to have a happy New Year."

"Do you get along with your mother?"

"You could say that," said Louise.

"Tell me about the trailer. I am curious about this. Why did you claim it for yourself?"

"I don't know," said Louise. "It seems familiar. It's clean. It's warm. I don't really know."

"Hmm," said Robin Otis.

"Why, does Dan want it?" said Louise.

"I can never read him," said Robin.

"Tell me about it."

"He's like some incredible ice cube or something."

"I think he wants to stay married," said Louise.

"I have no doubt of it."

Louise walked out of her office through a hallway that served as a waiting room not only for the therapist but for a dentist and an accountant.

A couple sat between a stack of hunting magazines and another stack of *Highlights for Children*. Louise pushed a button and stood waiting for an elevator.

"All I'm saying is that we don't necessarily need to get into specifics about sex," said the man.

"Ho ho, you wait," said the woman.

As part of the architectural survey, Louise took a picture of a palm reader's house on Pomegranate Avenue. The house was built from rocks of all sizes. The roofline curved like a roller coaster. A sign out front said, "Mrs. England Palms and Cards." It was an eclectic house, and the woman who came to the door had huge arms and fogged glasses.

"I'm here to take pictures of the house," said Louise.

"Let me shut off my story," said Mrs. England. She went through an arched doorway, leaving Louise in the front room. The house seemed perfectly silent.

"Nice place," Louise called.

There were framed oval mirrors and a painting of a man with a hammer. Turtles and newts dragged themselves across a sandy tank. A map of the solar system hung on the wall, with a marker saying, "You Are Here."

"Mr. England built this house," said Mrs. England. "He built houses all over Stone City, but he considered them very tame. He was happy enough to build the houses that people wanted, but he also wanted the chance to build a house that would satisfy his need for self-expression. This is his portrait. He was a wild man who perished in the war."

"I'm sorry," said Louise. Mrs. England took her by the hand and led her to a purple davenport.

"He used the materials of his region and got it all at cost, and I loved him," said Mrs. England. "How late are you?"

Louise sat down. "Eleven days," she said.

"You have a lot to think about."

Louise sank into the davenport. "How did you know?"

"By touching your hand," said Mrs. England. "Didn't you read my shingle? I guess you assume it's all fake. Well, it isn't all fake. I should say not."

"I don't get it," said Louise. "Can you tell from the temperature?"

200

"Oh, it's complicated," said Mrs. England with a wave of her hand.

"Am I pregnant?" said Louise.

"I couldn't say for sure that you are," said Mrs. England. "But I do know how you can find out. You go down Pomegranate another five blocks, and you will come to a Rexall's."

"Yes," said Louise.

"They've got little kits that you can do at home," said Mrs. England.

The pregnancy tests were on a shelf between the condoms and the sinus pills. Louise compared the brands without the first idea of what she was looking for. She passed over two tests that could be accomplished in one step, because that did not seem like enough steps. Another featured a plastic wand that was to be held in the "urine stream," and she rejected this as well.

Most of the kits were fifteen dollars, but some were eleven, and she ruled out the less expensive ones on the theory that something must account for the price difference, and after all, she wasn't going to be buying a pregnancy test every day of the week. Beyond these judgments, she went strictly by the design of the packaging. Almost all of the boxes had red lines or red words, as if invoking nostalgia for the menstrual cycle. The model she chose suggested urgency and yet, she thought, not outright panic.

On her way to the counter Louise checked to make sure the package had a price tag, so the clerk would not take a silver microphone and ask all over the store for a price check on the pregnancy test. The salesboy rang up the purchase with the blank and undiscerning face that they must teach in salesboy school. She might have been buying a key chain, or toothpaste, or flashbulbs, instead of embarking on the mystery of life.

ELEVEN

DAN TOOK Russell Ford duck hunting that winter because he wanted something from him. He had no reason to expect trouble; Russell claimed to be a pheasant hunter, and whether the game is pheasant or ducks there are certain rules.

It was just before five o'clock on a Sunday morning in November when Dan drove up to Russell's house. Russell lived in the area known as Mixerton, which took its name from the Mixers, a utopian society that existed around the turn of the century but broke up under the strain of constant squabbling. There is nothing in Mixerton now, really, except the Mixerton Clinic and some houses.

Rain fell steadily. It was the kind of rain that might fall all day—fine weather for ducks. Dan sat in his car looking at Russell's house. The wipers went back and forth as he unscrewed the metal lid of his thermos. Steam rose from the coffee. Hunting was considered recreational, but when you got up in the dark to go hunting, the act seemed to acquire unusual gravity. The radio played softly "Hello, It's Me" on the second day of a Todd Rundgren weekend.

Russell came out of his house with a shotgun and a box of doughnuts. He was a fat man, and in fact his nickname used to be Fat before he got to be chairman of the board of supervisors and received once again his given name. He was dressed in the mixed greens of camouflage.

He opened the door and slid into Dan's police car. Dan could tell that Russell's costume was stiff and new. "Brought you some breakfast," said Russell.

"And I thank you," said Dan.

"I wonder about this using the cruiser for off-duty."

"My car is broke down," said Dan.

"You always say that."

"It always is."

"Why don't you take the thing to Ronnie Lapoint and have it fixed? Good God, you make twenty-two thousand dollars a year."

"I've been thinking I could cut some corners by working on the car myself. I got a Chilton's manual and a good ratchet set, but it seems like there's always something to sidetrack a person."

"I know that feeling," said Russell. He looked around the car as Dan pulled onto the road going south. "I guess you don't have a dog."

"No. That's true."

"I would have thought for some reason that you had to."

Dan took a bite of a doughnut. "Not if you have waders and the water isn't deep."

Russell shook his head and folded his arms with a great scratching of material. "See, there, I'm learning," he said.

"I used to have a dog," said Dan.

"That right?"

"His name was Brownie."

"I remember that dog," said Russell.

"He was good."

"What ever happened to him?"

Dan slowed for a corner. "Well, that was a funny story. He ran away, and I never did find out where he went."

"Isn't that something."

"He must have got in a car with somebody. Because you know dogs will always come home. I heard a thing on Paul Harvey the other day where a dog walked all the way from Florida to Quebec looking for his owner."

"Quebec, Canada?"

"They just said Quebec. I assume it's Canada."

"If they didn't say, it probably is Canada."

"That's what I thought."

"Son of a bitch. Now, that's interesting. What did he do, take the interstate?"

Dan shrugged. "I don't know. We also have the white dog on the farm. But he isn't a retriever. I don't really know what kind of dog he is."

They parked on the southern end of Lapoint Slough and walked to Dan's blind, a distance of about half a mile. They moved along with their guns resting on their shoulders. Russell was slightly ahead of Dan—he could not stand walking behind anyone. Rain drummed their hats. The sky was dark except for a line of red light on the eastern horizon. Grass batted their legs, the ground rose and fell beneath their boots.

"Be looking for a fence," said Dan.

"What fence is that?" said Russell.

"Lee Haugen's," said Dan.

"That's east of here. Way east."

"No. We're not talking about the same fence."

"Hulf," said Russell, or something like that, as he ran into the fence.

"That's the one I mean," said Dan.

Dan's blind was a plywood shed separated from the water of the slough by a screen of marsh grass. He had decoys inside and with Russell's help carried them down to the water.

Russell and Dan sat in the blind smoking cigars and watching the clouds turn gray and white. The rain seemed to fall a little harder as the light came up. Soon they could see across the water to the other side. Dan reached into the blind and brought out a bottle of blackberry brandy. They each had a drink and shuddered.

Dan laughed. "It is pretty bad," he said.

"It's bitter," said Russell.

"That brandy belonged to Earl Kellogg. And I don't think I've hunted with him in two years. Every now and then I'll have a drink, but there always seems to be the same amount left."

Russell took out a box of shells and loaded his gun, which was a twelve-gauge with a bolt action and modest carving on the stock. A good part of hunting's appeal is loading the shotgun. The shell is very satisfying, its coppery base and forest-green plastic. The weight and balance seem natural, as if shells grew on vines.

"Where are the ducks?" said Russell.

"You have to be patient," said Dan. "This is the time when you can sit and think. That's what I like about duck hunting— the thinking."

"That's pretty deep," said Russell. "What do you think about?"

"I just let my mind wander," said Dan. "But I'll tell you what you should think about, and that's making Paul Francis a constable."

Russell ignored this. "Tell me what we do when the ducks come in."

"Don't get flustered. Don't turn your safety off until you're shouldering the gun. If you think something is too far away, you're right—it is."

A flock came in after a while with beaks and webs reaching for the water. Dan and Russell stood and fired. They got three, and Dan waded into the slough to retrieve the birds. There were two males, with green velvety heads and copper breasts, and a speckled brown female. All the wings had traces of blue. These were mallards, and Dan felt the exhilaration and sadness of having killed them, as if he were a wheel in the machine of the seasons.

Then a long time passed with no action, although they could hear gunfire from other places around the slough. Russell clipped his fingernails, Dan laid his gun down and leaned back on his elbows. He thought about Louise. She was two months pregnant, and according to a book they had, the baby was an inch and a quarter long and the heart was beating. Dan considered for a moment the outlandish fact of reproduction, and it struck him that even Russell had been a fetus at one time, hard to visualize as this might be. Then Dan thought how one day his and Louise's child would be as old as Russell, who had to be at least sixty, and that by then he, Dan, would probably be dead, and Louise probably would be as well, and he hoped that the child would not be too upset at their deaths—wouldn't turn to booze, or get gouged by the funeral men. A plain pine box would be fine with Dan. He considered the large number of people who would be satisfied with a plain pine box versus the fact that he had never seen such a box, let alone seen anyone buried in one, except in historical dramas on television. In this county even paupers went to their graves in a coffin that looked like it could withstand rifle fire.

Dan decided to get away from this line of thinking by lobbying for the hiring of the pilot Paul Francis as a constable.

"In the first year this would cost us twelve thousand seven hundred dollars," said Dan. "That includes thirteen hundred for state police training school in Five Points, eight thousand for estimated part-time salary, twenty-one hundred dollars for flight insurance, and approximately thirteen hundred for medical insurance."

"This is just the kind of thing that I'm always railing against. What in hell are we doing paying medical insurance for a constable?"

"This is a very conservative policy," said Dan. "He has to be dying, practically, before it kicks in."

"So why have it?"

"The state requires it."

"That fucking state," said Russell, and then he ranted about the state for a while.

"The way it is now, we can't fly anywhere," said Dan. "We used to be able to fly, but the insurance company has now decided that they will not insure our flights because Paul is freelance. So we would be able to fly again, and sometimes we need to fly. Secondly, Earl, Ed, and I all work at least sixty hours a week, without overtime. Now, for me, that's not really a problem, because I'm management. But if AFSCME were to find out about Ed and Earl, they would definitely have a grievance, and defending that, as you know, would cost a lot more than hiring Paul Francis and giving these guys some relief. Now, I'm not going to call AFSCME, but can I guarantee they'll never find out? No, I can't. And the third point is, once Paul is licensed to fly as a constable—and I checked into this, so I know—he will be able to fly for other county functions too. Say you want to go to, I don't know, a conference in the Ozarks. Well, you jump in the Piper Cub and Paul Francis takes you down there. Sounds kind of nice, doesn't it?"

"I just cannot see adding a constable when all the county towns are getting police of their own."

"You're wrong about that, Russ," said Dan. "Five of the towns don't have any police coverage at all. Ever."

"The trend is toward town police."

"Like where? Grafton?"

"I'm not talking about Grafton, or Boris, or Pinville, or any of those ghost towns—Lunenberg is another—where they can't sell houses."

"We are in those towns all the time," said Dan. "They are the county."

"Let me tell you something, Dan," said Russell. "Twenty years down the road, there won't be a sheriff's department as we think of it now." And as he said this he made a slashing gesture with his right hand. "There might be a sheriff, and I say *might,* but he'll be mostly a figurehead. And this was ordained many years ago, when Otto Nicolette had the opportunity to solve the Vince Hartwell murder but could not before the Morrisville police stumbled on the weapon by pure chance. Ever since that time, the sheriff's department has been like, like, well, you know what it's like. And I don't mind telling you that, because I said the same exact thing when you first ran for sheriff back in… whenever it was."

"You and that Hartwell business," said Dan. "Living in the past."

"Don't slight the past. People were better back then. I remember those times with great fondness. Today I look around me and I don't see much. By the way, did you know that Johnny White is thinking about running against you next year?"

"Good," said Dan. "He's not much of a threat." This was a fairly common opinion to have about Johnny White. When you looked at his experience it was hard to see what it was that might justify his being sheriff. He had run that restaurant in Cleveland that went bust. He had been an assistant in the county clerk's office. And he now ran the Room, but he didn't get much respect for this position of authority because his father, Jack White, was on the board of directors and provided a lot of the money to run the thing.

"Well, Jack is a friend of mine," said Russell. "We often play pool together at the cigar store in Chesley. Eight-ball, last-pocket, scratch-you-lose. He may seem scattered, but I wouldn't sell him short."

"You mean Jack."

"Yeah," said Russell. "You're right, by and large, about Johnny. He was a file clerk for the county there for a while, and I happen to know that some pretty important papers have yet to turn up. But he's not doing that anymore. He's leading that group of addicts called the Wall or the Hall or something. They have taken the abuse issue and are running with it."

"The operation seems pretty specious," said Dan, "but who knows? Maybe they do some people good."

"They do Johnny good," said Russell. "You know who his partner is over there, don't you? Tiny Darling."

"I've heard that," said Dan.

Probably they should have left earlier than they did. That's easy enough to say in retrospect. Either way, everything would have been all right had Russell followed Dan's advice about not shooting at distant targets. After the first few passes by the mallards and teals, the banks of the slough were more or less exploding with gunfire, and no duck with any instinct at all was going to come near the water until sundown. But unable to leave well enough alone, Russell raised his gun to the sky and fired at something overhead, then swore that he had brought a duck down at the curve of the slough to the north of them.

Dan was skeptical. "It would just fall," he said.

"No, it coasted."

"Then you didn't hit it."

"I'm pretty sure I did."

"If you hit it, it would fall."

They retrieved the decoys, put them away, gathered their things, and went looking for the duck that Russell claimed to have hit. They never did find it, but they did scatter a dozen or so red-winged blackbirds and a large and unfortunate waterfowl, which got up with a slow and graceful ripple of wings only to have Russell Ford shoot it.

"Russell, quit shooting."

"Got you, son of a bitch."

"Don't shoot anymore."

Russell walked over to the bird and picked it up by the neck. It was gray and brown with a long body, reedy legs, a black patch on the head. "It's a goose," guessed Russell.

"I don't think so."

"It might be in the goose family."

"It's a crane, I'll bet you anything."

211

Russell folded the bird carefully in his arm. "You've been hard to get along with this whole trip," he said.

There was nowhere to go now but the Leventhaler farm. Bev and Tim lived in a cedar house on Route 29 north of the slough. They were very proud of their house, and when they invited you there they would mention it specifically, as if it were something marvelous that had just appeared one day.

The rain had stopped and the sun was coming through the clouds in discernible rays. The Leventhalers had just got back from church. They attended the Methodist church in Margo. Their children were running across the wet grass in green and red coats.

Being the county extension woman, Bev was practical and utilitarian, but she loved birds with a passion. It was brave of Russell to go to Bev with an illegal kill, but she was the only one Dan or Russell could think of who would know the species.

Bev and Tim asked Russell and Dan into the kitchen for waffles and coffee. The waffles were from a real iron—Bev showed how easy it was to keep the batter from sticking and burning. Tim, a serious-looking young man with wire-rim glasses, was known as the Tile Doctor, because he ran crews who installed drainage tiles in fields around the state. He spoke about the uncertainties of the tiling business and about a kid who had mashed his fingers between two tiles not that long ago but was back in school and playing the clarinet in the University of Wisconsin marching band.

Then Russell said, "Bev, we got a problem. There's something in the trunk of the car. Well, it's a bird. There's a bird in the trunk of the car that perished by accident."

Bev wiped her mouth with a red and white napkin. "What happened?"

212

"I shot it," said Russell. "I think it's a goose. I hope it's a goose.

I don't know what it is. Dan doesn't agree with me. We need to get some kind of ID on this bird. So naturally we thought of you."

Bev's radiant smile had faded, making everyone sad. She left the room. Tim said, "Where did this happen?"

"At the slough," said Dan.

"Maybe I'll call the kids in," said Tim.

"Why not," said Russell.

Bev came into the kitchen with a bird book and an old sheet, and they all went outside. Dan opened the trunk. The lid came up with a soft *whoosh*. The bird did not look bad. A shotgun from medium range often does little apparent damage.

"It's a great blue heron," said Bev.

"It doesn't seem that blue," said Russell.

Bev sighed. "They're not."

"Well, what's the sense of that?" said Russell. "Why call something blue if it isn't? I mean, I should have known. I should have made sure. I'll admit that. But it's not like I went out of my way to shoot a great blue heron."

"They're really beautiful when they fly," said Bev. "The neck folds into an S, and the wings move so slowly you can't understand what keeps them in the air. Do you know what I mean?"

"It was over in a heartbeat," said Russell.

"They are just intensely beautiful birds."

"All right. I fucked up."

"Shh," said Bev. She wrapped the bird in the sheet. "We'll bury him underneath the willow tree. There's a shovel by the side door of the garage."

"I'll grab it," said Russell. He hurried off.

"Well, I guess I'd better report this," said Dan. "I mean, you can't not report it because it's Russell Ford, can you? There are game laws and that's that. Maybe I should take the bird for evidence."

"Oh, Dan, no," said Bev. "I mean, no. And what? Put it in a room, on a table, with a bright light? No."

So they buried the heron under the willow tree at the Leventhaler farm. Dan and Russell drove away without talking. The day had been a fiasco. On the radio Todd Rundgren sang "Can We Still Be Friends?"

Russell pleaded not guilty to killing the heron. He said it was an accident, and that the county had no case without intent. The law did not require intent, but Russell didn't care; he had public relations in mind. He said he and Dan had been searching for wounded game when the heron burst from the grass. He said he had merely raised his gun as any sensible hunter might have, positioning the animal in his sights in case it was something legal to shoot, and that his gun somehow went off, fired itself, an accident. People were doubtful. "A gun just doesn't up and fire itself," said Mary Montrose. "No gun I've ever seen." A hearing was scheduled for February.

This would be, as it happened, Russell's second prosecution in the many years that he had been a supervisor. The first was in 1970, for assaulting a young teacher whose political opinions Russell did not agree with. Russell had a restaurant in Stone City at the time, and the teacher, Mr. Robins, and a seventh-grade class were picketing the restaurant for using paper napkins with blue dye, which would pollute the water when the napkins were thrown away, instead of white napkins with no dye. Russell ended up paying a seventy-five-dollar fine on that one.

Both of these cases were embarrassing to Russell, and one might wonder why they were allowed to proceed, since he was such a big shot. But people in Grouse County have an enduring mistrust of those who would put themselves above others, and they are vigilant. There used to be a saying painted on the railroad bridge south of Stone City: "Better to be Nobody who does Nothing than Somebody who does Everybody." And it was only in the last ten or twelve years that this had faded so you couldn't read it.

• • •

If Russell Ford was angry at Dan for pushing the issue of the dead heron, he did not let on. In fact, he saw to it that the board of supervisors sent Paul Francis to the state police training school at a time when Russell was still being ridden pretty hard by the Stone City newspaper, which printed, for example, a large illustration showing the many differences between the mallard duck and the great blue heron, including size, coloration, shape, and manner of flight.

The police school at Five Points was situated in a former Baptist Bible camp in the southern part of the state. Dan went along as Paul's sponsor on the first day of the two-week course. He did not have to appear in person, but his father lived in Five Points and Dan figured he would take the opportunity to see him.

To get to the main lodge of the police campus you had to cross a ravine on a rope bridge. The bridge swayed as Dan and Paul crossed it, and Paul accidentally dropped his shaving kit into the ravine. The office was not open when the two men arrived, and they stood under a large oak tree in the dead grass. With a pilot's sense of curiosity Paul spied something red in a knothole on the tree and reached in and brought out a moldy pocket version of the New Testament that must have been there since the days when the camp was occupied by Baptist children. Being a religious man, although a Methodist and not a Baptist, Paul felt that this discovery meant he was on the right track. But Dan could not shake the uneasy feeling that the police and trainees milling around in sunglasses and the uniforms of their respective towns were about to be asked to sing "Michael, Row the Boat Ashore," and so once the lodge had opened he delivered the check that was signed by Russell Ford, shook Paul's hand, wished him luck, and left.

Dan's father was a retired pharmaceutical salesman named Joseph Norman. A stern, sorrowful man, he lived in a yellow bungalow on two acres of thick and untended trees. His first wife had drowned while on a picnic at Lake Margo in 1949, at the age of nineteen. His second wife, Dan's mother, was also dead. She died five years ago. Joe Norman's job had taken him all over the upper Midwest but had seemed a relatively small position in a region where many men, through no special effort of their own, had wound up running farms of hundreds of acres. He was once reprimanded for failure to account for some pharmaceuticals but there were no hard feelings, and he retired on a full pension.

Joe Norman had tried various hobbies, but few had worked out. He had golfed but his eyesight was not good, and when he ran a motorized cart into the corner of the clubhouse, his membership was restricted. Then he tried woodburning, but lost interest once he had put decorative brands on every wooden item in the house. Now he carried a video camera everywhere, and so far nothing terrible had happened. When Dan visited, which was not often, his father would play tapes for him on the television. "This is a Buick LeSabre bought by a friend of mine, and here he is washing it... This is Denny Jorgensen, who delivers the mail... Some people don't like Denny. Denny and I get along fine."

This time Joe played a tape of wild animals eating white bread and cinnamon rolls at night under a floodlight in the back yard. This was fascinating at first, and then weirdly monotonous.

"Look at the raccoon, how he uses his hands," said Joe.

"Boy, I guess," said Dan.

"They call him the little thief," said Joe. "Well, I say 'they.' I don't really know who calls him that. I guess I do."

"We missed you at the wedding," said Dan.

"I wasn't feeling that good."

"I've got a picture," said Dan, reaching into the pocket of his shirt.

"There's a pain that comes and goes in my eye. I don't know what that's about."

"This is Louise."

"She's a very pretty girl, son."

"You can keep that," said Dan.

His father got up and stuck the picture to the refrigerator with a magnet. On the television, skunks were shimmying around with slices of bread in their jaws. "Well, have you been to the doctor?" said Dan.

"What is a doctor going to say?" said Joe.

"Maybe he'll be able to figure out what's wrong."

Joe pulled out a drawer in the kitchen counter and rummaged through it. "I'm old," he said.

"That's no attitude," said Dan. He took from a coffee table an orange rubber ball covered with spiky nubs. "Didn't they use these for something in the Middle Ages?"

Joe looked up. "That's for my circulation. I don't know what you're talking about."

"As weapons," said Dan.

Joe finally found what he was looking for and brought it into the living room. It was a Polaroid of the headstone of Dan's mother's grave.

"See a difference?" said Joe.

"What am I looking for?"

"I had them redo the letters."

"Oh… O.K. How did that come about?"

"I happened to be at the cemetery when some fellows came by offering the service. And do you know what the problem is? Acid rain. It turns out that acid rain is eating away at the stones. It's the same thing that's happening to the statues in Rome and Vienna."

"So what did they do exactly?" said Dan.

"Well, they had what I would call a router."

"And it helped?"

"I'm not saying it leaps at you across the cemetery, but yes, there's a difference."

"What does a thing like that run you?"

"It's paid for."

"Well, it sounds a little bit like a con."

"You could see the erosion."

"I believe you," said Dan. On the television the animals scattered and Joe himself came onscreen, casting more bread into the yard. His back and arms seemed stiff. He wore a red plaid shirt, gray pants with suspenders.

"When did you film this?" said Dan.

"Last night," said Joe.

Dan left his father watching the tape of the greedy animals, and on his way back to the highway he visited the cemetery where his mother was buried. He knelt and examined her stone but could not tell any difference in the letters, which said, "Jessica Lowry Norman, 1922-1987. What a Friend we have in Jesus." His mother had died of a heart attack on Flag Day in an ambulance on the way to the hospital. One of Dan's strongest memories of her was the time she broke a knife. The three of them were eating supper one evening when there was a loud clatter and his mother inhaled sharply. A stainless steel table knife had broken in the middle, separated blade from handle, cutting her hand. She cupped the base of her thumb in a napkin and hurried to the sink. There was a perfect silence in the house except for the running of the water. Dan had never heard of a table knife breaking under normal use, or any use, and the whole thing seemed to suggest or represent some deep psychic turbulence in his mother.

The cold weather took a long time coming that winter. It snowed maybe three times before Christmas, and the snow did not stick. The fire department wore shirtsleeves while stringing lights across Main Street in Grafton. It was sixty-three degrees for the football game between the Stone City Fighting Cats and the Morrisville-Wylie Plowmen, and the game drew nine hundred fans, although Stone City had a bad team that could do nothing with a conventional approach and was reduced to trying desperate sleight-of-hand plays that resulted in losses of six to thirty-six yards. Dan waited until two weeks before Christmas to cut a tree. He paid twenty dollars and walked across the hills of a tree farm outside Romyla. The sky blazed with a blue so strong that he could hardly take his eyes away long enough to look where he was going. Louise was three months pregnant, beginning to show. Accordingly Dan selected a full and abundantly branched tree. "Tree" is maybe even the wrong word; it was more like a hedge. Dan lay with his back on needles, sawing through the trunk. He dragged the thing over the grassy fields and struggled to confine it to the bed of a borrowed pickup.

The tree took up the whole north side of the living room. Dan had to run guy wires from the window frames on either side of the tree to keep it from falling. At first the large tree seemed wrong somehow in the house. Why this was so Dan could not explain. Either it seemed like the tree of a showoff or, by its sheer expanse, it revealed something sinister and previously unknown about the whole concept of having a Christmas tree. The only thing to do was decorate it. Being the kind of people they were, Louise and Dan had not really considered what they would use for decorations. Louise found some ornaments that dated back to her days with Tiny, but they decided not to use these, and in fact burned or at least melted them in the trash burner. They went over to see Mary, who gave them six boxes of bird ornaments that she had got years ago and never opened. Louise hung these one afternoon while Dan straightened a snarled ball of lights that had been seized in a drug raid and stored for several years in a closet at the sheriff's office. Louise glided around the tree, breasts and belly pressing sweetly against a long colorful dress. The flimsy silver birds responded to air currents, turning and glittering when doors were opened or closed.

So all in all it was a good Christmas, though Louise was still spending her nights in the trailer by the garage. Robin Otis had advised against changing anything that was working and especially not during the holidays, a stressful and for many people a hideous time to begin with. So it was that Dan woke alone on a windy Christmas morning and made bacon, eggs, and coffee with "God Rest You Merry, Gentlemen" playing quietly on the radio. The broadcast had that strange, nobody-at-the-station quality that you don't find at any other time of the year. Louise came over at about seven forty-five in a nightgown, robe, and sneakers. There was no snow on the ground. She kissed Dan on the neck, and the smell of sleep in her hair made him shiver. Out the window above the sink, the sky was the yellow color of dust.

They exchanged presents at the breakfast table. He gave her a coral necklace and earrings, and she put them on, and she gave him a long gray and purple scarf that she had knitted, and he put that on. They went upstairs to bed and stayed there until one o'clock, when it was time to watch college football. Louise had turned into a dedicated fan of college football since becoming pregnant. She felt that the college boys played a better game than the pros, because in college the plays seemed more earnest and at the same time less likely to work, and therefore more poignant when they failed.

She had watched the games every Saturday and knew the names of eight or ten colleges in Arkansas alone. She had developed a science of upsets. California teams always upset Great Lakes teams. Any college with "A & M" in the name could upset any college whose name ended in "State." Teams called something "Poly," on the other hand, might come close to an upset but would always lose in the end. The higher the male cheerleaders could throw the female cheerleaders, the more likely a team was to be upset, all else being equal. Michigan State was in a class by itself, a school that existed for no other purpose than to have its football team upset. As

221

her pregnancy progressed, Louise was both emotional and forgetful. She could not keep track of the score and grew pensive whenever a kicker, with his forlorn minimal face guard, squared his shoulders to try a field goal.

In the middle of the afternoon Dan and Louise walked up to Henry Hamilton's place with a bottle of Grand Marnier. They all sat on the sun porch drinking it—even Louise had half a glass—and listened to the strange unseasonal wind.

Elsewhere in the county the public forms of Christmas were being observed. Paul Francis had drawn his first flying assignment since becoming a certified constable, playing Santa's pilot to Russell Ford's Santa for the benefit of a group of poor children from the Children's Farm gathered on the tarmac at the Stone City airport. The plane rolled from wing to wing as it came down to land, leading the children to speculate with genuine excitement about the prospect of Santa crashing in flames before their eyes. But Paul got the plane down all right, and Russell climbed out in a red suit and white beard and that shiny black vinyl belt that seemed to have been added to Santa's wardrobe sometime in the seventies. He gave out dolls and footballs and colored pencils, and one little boy said, "We already got colored pencils," so Russell took back the gift, boarded Paul Francis's plane, and, grabbing a microphone that did not work, said, "Clear the runway for departure."

And over at the Little Church of the Redeemer in Margo, Johnny White and Tiny Darling were trying to cook Christmas goose for forty-five declared alcohol and drug abusers who participated in the programs offered by the Room. Two things that people fail to understand until it's too late about the cooking of goose are how long it takes and how much grease is produced. So at four-thirty, with a church full of hungry addicts, Tiny and Johnny huddled in front of an oven, stabbing at a tough goose in a gently swirling lake of grease. "Probably we should spoon some of this off," said Tiny, and using an oven mitt that looked like the head of a goat, he attempted to pull the pan toward him. This little bit of motion spilled grease onto the grate of the oven, where it ignited with a fiery gust that singed Tiny's forearms. Johnny shoved Tiny away from the oven door and blasted the goose with a fire extinguisher. When the fire was out, they tried to scrape the foam and ash from the main course, but this proved futile and the celebrants had deviled ham instead of goose with their string beans and sweet potatoes. But they had waited so long that even deviled ham seemed good, and they ate hungrily in the basement of the church.

In February, as scheduled, Russell Ford went to Wildlife Court to face the charge of shooting a protected species. Wildlife Court met on the second Tuesday of every month, presided over by Ken Hemphill, a retired judge and permanently tanned outdoorsman who ran his court in the affable style of Curt Gowdy on *The American Sportsman*. In the summer months the court mainly concerned itself with fishing violations, but during the winter most of the defendants were young or middle-aged men who had been keeping illegal trap lines. One innovative step taken by Ken Hemphill had been to order the surrender of any trap line deployed without a trap stamp, and defendants were accordingly required to bring their traps to court in case the verdict should go against them. Thus it was that in the cold months Wildlife Court became a sort of purgatory of downcast men wearing Red Wing boots and orange coats and clinking their chains up and down the aisles of the courthouse. Dan ordinarily enjoyed this spectacle, but today he was testifying.

Russell's lawyer was Ned Kuhlers, a mousy man who represented so many people in Grouse County that he more or less ran the court docket, and when he went on vacation the system slowed to a crawl. Ned's strategy was simple. He tried to show that the witnesses for the prosecution could not know what they claimed to know. First he emphasized that Bev had not been at the slough and so could not say firsthand who shot what. Her response was typical of the flustered citizen trying to defend her common-sense conclusions only to be told that common sense has no place in the judicial system. "But he told me," she said. "We had just finished our waffles and he said that he had shot this bird that he could not identify. I mean, I suppose that's hearsay, but for heaven's sakes, it's hearsay from the guy who did the shooting."

"I'm afraid I object to that," said Ned.

Judge Ken Hemphill chuckled softly. "Overruled," he said.

Dan took the stand next. Ned spoke to the bailiff, who went out and returned after several minutes with a large stuffed bird. There was a moment of surprise as Ned held the bird up before the members of the jury.

The jury foreman, who had seemed uncertain of his role throughout the trial, said, "Excellent taxidermy."

"Sheriff," said Ned. "You have testified that Russell shot a waterfowl. I would ask you now to look very carefully at this example, who comes to us courtesy of the folks at the Stone City Museum of Natural History. Please take your time, because this is important. Is this the same species as the bird that you have testified was shot by Russell?"

Dan looked at the bird. It was gray and spindly with a red mark over the eye. The courtroom was hushed. "I don't know," said Dan.

"In other words," said Ned, "it might be, or it might not be? What kind of answer is that? Don't look at Bev. We want your opinion, Sheriff. Isn't it true that you don't know what kind of bird Russell shot?"

"I'm not an ornithologist," said Dan. "I think the two birds are similar. But whether it was this exact one, no, I don't know."

"Sheriff," said Ned Kuhlers, "what if I were to tell you that this is a sandhill crane, who spends his winters in Texas and Mexico. And what if I were to tell you there is virtually no way a sandhill crane could have been in Lapoint Slough on that day in November."

"What does that prove?" said Dan.

"What indeed," said Ned. "The defense rests."

The jury deliberated all morning and all afternoon. At twelve-thirty they were given a lunch of deli sandwiches, cole slaw, and chips. At three they requested a snack and received two bags of pretzels and some Rolos. At four-thirty a message came from the foreman informing Judge Hemphill that one of the jurors was on a salt-free diet and that this should be kept in mind when ordering the evening meal. At this point Russell entered a plea of *nolo,* or no contest, and Ken Hemphill called the jury in and told them they were free to go home and make their own suppers.

TWELVE

THE GROCERY STORE in Grafton closed in the spring.
No one had really expected Alvin Getty to make a go of it.
There will always be people who are drawn to a business on
the skids and, given the chance, will take the thing over and
finish it off.

That winter everyone had known what was happening. The
shelves emptied while novelty displays appeared in an effort
to jolt the store from its decline. You could get jam made by
Trappist monks but not the bread to spread it on.

Later, Alvin had the idea that some new form of pudding
would turn things around. "This will create a light and happy
atmosphere," he told Mary Montrose. "Come on, admit it—
it's a popular dessert."

Mary did not want the store to fail, so she couldn't decide
whether to nod encouragement or laugh. She and Alvin had
never got along. That fight they'd had over his dog, King, was
no coincidence.

"There is hardly a grocery store in the world that doesn't
sell pudding," said Mary.

"Not in ready-to-eat canisters."

"I'm afraid you haven't done your homework."

"Not with a little spoon attached."

"I don't know about the spoon," said Mary.

"The spoon is what makes it," said Alvin.

Then he tried lending videos. By this time the store commanded so little respect that few customers bothered to return the tapes they had borrowed. Alvin lost three copies of *Fatal Attraction* in the first week, and they were not his to lose. One morning in April while walking up to get her mail, Mary saw a fat guy in a Cubs jacket lugging Alvin's cash register out of the store.

"What happened?" Mary asked.

"We're closed," the man said.

"Where's Alvin?" she said.

"I don't know."

"Is the store out of business?"

"What do you think?"

"I think it is."

"I'll give you a loaf of bread for a nickel," said the man. "You won't find a better deal than that. Could you open the door on that car? I also have some nice rib eyes."

"Rib eyes to eat?"

"No, for a doorstop—of course to eat."

Mary opened the passenger door of a black Eldorado and the man eased the cash register onto the seat. "I knew Alvin wouldn't last," said Mary.

"I don't know this Alvin," said the man. "I try not to know them. I'm what you call in the industry a take-down man. In other words, I come in and take everything down. It's no easy life. People get emotional when everything they have is on the auction block. Once a guy pulled a gun on me. It's better for all concerned if I don't know them."

"I had hoped somebody else would take over," said Mary. "Every town needs a grocery store."

"Today, who wants the hassle," said the take-down man. "The best you can hope for in these little one-horse places is some sort of mini-mart."

"Fine," said Mary.

"I don't mean to be callous," said the man. "I'm the bad guy in this situation. I know it."

Mary picked up her mail—a bulb catalogue and a letter saying she had won a vacation home in Florida, a Jeep Wrangler, or a radio. She walked home discouraged. Services were leaving Grafton like seeds from a dandelion. Twenty-five years ago the town had two taverns, three churches, a lumberyard, a barbershop, and a bank. Of these, one tavern and two churches remained. On the plus side, Lindsey Coale had opened the beauty shop and a man named Carl Mallory had put up a quonset in which custom gun barrels were said to be manufactured. Ronnie Lapoint had expanded the body-work part of the gas station, but since he owned and operated stock cars it was not always clear whether the welding you saw him doing produced income or simply amounted to doodling.

Mary had an aerial photograph somewhere of Grafton in the happy days of the early sixties. How dramatic and instructive it would be to enlarge it and wave the enlargement around at the next council meeting. It was as if they had all been sleepwalking through the decline of their town. She looked in the boxes at the bottom of the basement stairs. She found June's Barbie suitcase, Louise's lunch pail, the black ice skates of her late husband, Dwight. These things were musty and faintly sad compared with how she remembered them.

She rested for a moment on the green and white cardboard box in which the *World Book Encyclopedia* had once arrived, full of facts and pictures for the girls.

After a while Mary realized that she had heard something. She climbed the stairs with hurting ankles. The living room was full of ivy and afternoon light. She stood at the picture window and saw a wren on the ground outside. This was not unusual. Birds had been smacking into the picture window lately. Mary considered it part of the season. They get to mating and not watching where they're going and smack. She had thought about hanging a fake owl in the window but heard they can cause crows to congregate in your trees.

She went out to the garage and found a snow shovel with which to scoop up the wren, but when she got around to the front of the house it had evidently dusted itself off and flown. Or it had been carried away by a dog. Then a delivery van pulled up. "Package for Mary Montrose," said the driver. He unloaded four boxes that June had sent from Colorado— hand-me-downs for the baby Louise was seven months pregnant with.

Louise waited for an ultrasound examination at the Mixerton Clinic. This was located in the former Mixers Hall, five miles southwest of Stone City. The building was low and rambling, made of sandstone, and strangely modern for something built at the turn of the century. The Mixers had not lasted long but undoubtedly had their share of good ideas. For example, they developed an elaborate system of body language, enabling them to be quiet most of the time. They opposed the planting of wheat, because beer and whiskey could be made from it, although this was somewhat contradictory, since they did drink beer and whiskey. The community fell apart soon after World War I, but some of the Mixer offspring are still alive, and every once in a while you will see an obituary along these lines:

PRINGMAR WOMAN DIES
WAS CHILD OF MIXERS

Louise wore a white T-shirt, a pink and white dress, and a rust-colored canvas jacket. Her bladder was full, and she sat in an indirectly lighted room with three other pregnant women who also had full bladders. To prepare for a sonogram, you were required to drink three big glasses of water and refrain from peeing. Otherwise, Jimmy, the kid who ran the ultrasound machine, might not get a clear picture of the baby. Holding so much water was not an easy task for anyone, let alone a pregnant woman, and now one of the women began sobbing softly, and a nurse named Maridee entered the room and reluctantly placed the key to the bathroom in her hand, with the instruction not to give the key to anyone else. Another woman tried to take their minds off the pressure inside by telling how she always found playing cards on the ground. She wore a blue maternity shirt with a ruffled collar. Her eyes were big and glazed. "I don't know what it is," she said. "I can't explain it. I wish someone could explain it to me. Other people find quarters. If they're lucky they find a dollar. My brother found ten dollars at the movies. Ten dollars! But me, I find the seven of diamonds. I find the jack of clubs under my shoe. The other day, for some reason I was thinking about New Mexico, and when I got in the car what do you think I found? A matchbook that said 'New Mexico.'"

"I thought you were going to say a playing card," said Louise.

"That's what I mean," said the woman. "That was the only weird thing I ever found that wasn't a playing card."

Jimmy had long curly hair and a gold tooth. He used to tune up the ambulances, but his life had changed when he read a sign posted in the cafeteria about the growing field of sonography. "I'm glad I did it, don't get me wrong," he said. "But I do miss the camaraderie. In the motor pool we used to play softball behind the middle school. I was a scrappy player and always found a way to get a hit. Singles, doubles, take the extra base. That I miss."

"Maybe they would still let you play," said Louise, who was on her back with her dress pulled up over her taut round abdomen.

Jimmy shook his head and applied blue gel thoughtfully to her stomach. "Tried it," he said. "You'd be surprised at the turnover down there. I didn't hardly see nobody that I recognized. And then I fell down running after a screaming liner and tore up my knee."

"That's too bad," said Louise.

"It was like a telegram saying youth is over," said Jimmy.

He put plates of film into the top of the machine. The screen was just off Louise's right shoulder. She turned her head to see. Jimmy skated the transducer over her skin, pointing out the fluttering chambers of the baby's heart and the curve of its spine. Louise wished that Dan would walk in. He was supposed to be debating Johnny White before the Lions Club in Stone City.

"What are we looking for?" said Jimmy.

"Due date," said Louise. "Dr. Pickett thinks I'm big."

"O.K."

Jimmy made some measurements by moving an electronic

star across the screen. "I get May the twenty-first," said Jimmy. "Hey, do you know the sex?"

"No."

"Do you want to?"

"Well, do you know?"

"Maybe."

"I don't want to," said Louise.

"O.K."

"No, I don't think so." She believed the baby was a girl.

"It's up to you."

"I mean, in a way I'd like to." She had a feeling and wanted to leave it at that.

"There's her hand."

Louise held her breath. The baby's fingers moved, making white sparks on the blue screen.

After the sonogram Louise went to see Cheryl Jewell, who had flown in from Kansas City the night before. Jocelyn, Cheryl's daughter, was about to begin rehearsals for the starring role in the senior play at Morrisville-Wylie High School.

"I didn't have a sonogram when I was pregnant with Jocelyn," said Cheryl. She stood at the counter of her Aunt Nan's kitchen, making chocolate malts in an old green mixer.

"They're not bad," said Louise.

"Don't they feel strange?"

"Not really," said Louise. "You get used to them."

"And did you have that other thing?"

"Amnio?"

"Yeah."

"Amnio was tough."

"That's what I heard," said Cheryl.

"It's true."

"Here's your malt," said Cheryl. "My doctor was pretty laid back. I had a blood test."

"I don't mind medical things," said Louise. "I'll tell you what I don't like."

"What don't you like?"

"When people you hardly know want to touch your stomach. I find this happens more and more."

"Oh, yeah. I remember that."

"People who would never ask to touch your stomach if you weren't pregnant."

"Let's hope not."

"Here's what I do," said Louise. "As they go for my stomach, I step back and shake their hand."

"You should write to Ann Landers with that clever tip," said Cheryl.

"My way would be too polite for Ann Landers. She'd advise you to say, 'Keep your hands to yourself, bub.' "

"'Cut out the funny business, mac.'"

They laughed and drank malt from cold aluminum glasses. Cheryl said, "Here's what used to bother me. When I was pregnant, it seemed like an awful lot of people would look at me and say, 'Whoa, somebody's been busy.' Like they were imagining me in bed or something."

"People don't know what to say," said Louise.

"Well, they shouldn't say that."

"It's like they're embarrassed. It's like you're doing something embarrassing in public just by being pregnant."

"Just by being," said Cheryl.

Mary called her friend Hans Cook to drive the hand-me-downs out to the farm. He came over in coveralls and a St. Louis Cardinals baseball hat.

"I wear this on the days I don't wash my hair," he said.

"Well, that's pleasant to know," said Mary. "You are getting on the shaggy side."

"Lindsey Coale does not do a good job with men," said Hans. "This is nothing against Lindsey. With women there's no one better. She just doesn't have the knack for cutting male hair."

"Why don't you go to Morrisville?" said Mary. "That's where everything is now."

"You know, in olden times everybody had their hair like this," said Hans.

"You go live in olden times," said Mary.

Hans loaded the boxes into the back of his pickup. "I don't mind the lifting, and it's none of my business, but this seems like a lot of stuff. How big is a baby? About like so?"

They discussed the question for a while, moving their hands to show the possible sizes. Eventually Mary conceded that June had perhaps been overly generous.

"How is June?" said Hans.

"She seems well," said Mary.

"What's her husband's name again?"

"Dave Green."

"That's right."

"He just put an addition on their house."

"Mr. Moneybags," said Hans.

"Let me tell you something about Dave Green," said Mary. "It's true that he has more money than you and I will ever see in a lifetime. But as for common sense, you and I have riches untold compared to Dave Green. Did you ever hear about the time he flew to Hawaii by accident?"

235

"No."

"By accident. I mean, my God, think of all the people with legitimate reason to go to Hawaii and no ticket."

"They say rich people are unhappy."

"That's all hype."

"I'd give it a whirl," said Hans. "I would be the exception that proves the rule."

"You would be happy whatever you're doing. You're a happy man. Some would say too happy."

"I never will be rich, though."

"Well, I don't suppose you will."

"The little man's got a hard row to hoe in this world."

"As does the big man," said Mary.

Hans yawned. "What were we talking about?"

"Louise."

"I admire her a lot," said Hans. "Nothing bothers Louise. Things roll off her back."

"To an extent. Somewhat. She has Dan. She has a baby on the way. I believe without question that Louise and Dan love each other. Now, am I saying there haven't been ups and downs? No. Every relationship has ups and downs."

"I heard they weren't living together," said Hans.

"Well, see, that's wrong," said Mary. "They live together. She might sleep in her little trailer. That's eccentric but it's not the end of the world. You of all people ought to agree with that. She'll move to the house when the baby comes. Who said this, anyway? It sounds like a classic piece of Lime Bucket exaggeration."

"I forget who said it," said Hans. "Should we go?"

"Let me get my coat."

Wind swept the countryside, and the pickup bounced along

236

on gravel roads that were, as Mary would say, "washboardy" from the winter snow and the spring rain. Halfway to the farm, the tailgate banged open and the boxes fell from the truck.

"Trouble in paradise," said Hans as he pulled over. He and Mary stepped down from the truck. Two of the boxes had broken open, their contents spilling into the ditch. Red, yellow, and gray clothes were all over the lush grass.

"Guess I didn't get it shut," said Hans.

"Say, maybe not," said Mary.

They walked down into the ditch and gathered the clothes. This was on the south side of the road, where the abandoned utility poles were leaning so badly that you had to duck to get under them.

"They ought to do something about these," said Hans.

"I have said that for years," said Mary.

Hans scooped up a pair of corduroy overalls. "She may want to give some of these a spin in the dryer," he said.

"There is a bootie by your foot," said Mary.

Hans secured the boxes with rope and slammed the tailgate. As an afterthought he walked back to the ditch and unscrewed six insulators from the electric poles. The insulators were heavy and made of rounded blue glass.

"If Louise washes these out, she'll have a perfectly usable set of drinking glasses," he said.

Louise found the cardboard boxes in the kitchen when she got back home. It looked as if June had sent every piece of clothing ever worn by her two children, from infancy to the present. There were also many toys—roller skates, Lincoln Logs, alphabet blocks.

Louise sat down and shook her head. Sometimes June seemed in rather light touch with reality. And some of the clothes were damp, as if they had been rained on in transit. Louise decided to wash everything. The insulators she did not know how to interpret. She lined them up on the kitchen table.

When Dan came home, the first thing he did after putting his gun away was to walk over to the table and examine the insulators. "What are these?"

"Mom left them," said Louise. "My guess is they are paper-weights."

"We don't have this much paper."

"What do you think they are?"

"Insulators," said Dan.

"Well, obviously."

"They're from the utility poles up the road." He picked one up and turned it in his hands. "Maybe they're supposed to be drinking glasses."

"Wouldn't they fall over?"

"You sand them or file them."

"That's something we'll get to right away."

"Hey, how did the ultrasound go?"

"Oh, I wish you could have been there. The baby looked at her hands."

"Is everything all right?"

"Yes."

"How's the heartbeat? Did the guy talk about that?"

"Jimmy said she has a really good heartbeat."

"She?" said Dan. "He said 'she'?"

"He said 'her.'"

"No kidding. Maybe they just do that, you know, as a non-sexist thing."

Louise shrugged. "Could be. I told him I don't want to know."

"That takes a lot of restraint."

"Thank you. Did you have your debate?"

"Yes," said Dan. "And I have to say, I cannot see anyone going into the privacy of the booth and pulling the lever for Johnny White."

"You'll win the primary," said Louise.

"He'll go Independent after that," said Dan.

"Really?"

"Sure," said Dan. "Jack would never put up the money if he was just going to drop out. And everybody is aware of that. The Lions were treating him with kid gloves like you wouldn't believe."

"Give an example."

"Foot patrols," said Dan. "As you know, we have three people working a county that is two hundred and ninety six square miles. And Johnny says they should be on foot. Say, what a good idea. We'll walk from Morrisville to Romyla when somebody wraps their car around a tree. But these Lions, they lap it up. Johnny says we're understaffed. The Lions nod seriously. Well, no kidding. But I don't have a printing press. I can't make money."

Louise washed out an insulator, poured a beer into it, and handed the insulator to Dan. "Don't worry. Johnny won't win."

"He's calling himself John," said Dan. "John White."

"He can call himself John Shaft, he still ain't gonna be elected," said Louise.

"Miles Hagen is one thing. I don't mind Miles Hagen. At least he was a police officer at one time."

"Who is Miles Hagen?"

"The guy the Republicans always put up."

"Isn't he deaf?"

"No."

"Who am I thinking of?"

Dan said he didn't know.

"Johnny won't get past the primary," said Louise.

"Like I say, he'll become an Independent."

"So that's what's up his sleeve."

"Yeah, I just said that."

Louise smiled. "I guess I'm not paying attention," she said. "I keep thinking about the baby moving her hands. It was about the coolest thing I've ever seen."

"I wish I would have been there."

"Let me tell you something else," said Louise. "They gave me a handout on anesthetics, and I've decided I don't want to be knocked out. I want to be awake. Whatever you do, don't let them knock me out."

"I won't let them knock you out," said Dan.

"You have to be my advocate," said Louise.

Dan cooked hamburgers and broccoli while Louise dropped baby clothes into the dryer. After supper, while they were doing dishes, Claude Robeshaw dropped by to advise Dan about the campaign. Claude was still very influential among Democrats around the county.

Dan and Claude sat down at the kitchen table, and Claude lit a cigar and rolled it slowly on the edge of an ashtray. He tipped his head back and looked downward through his glasses to read Dan's campaign brochure. He said nothing, leading Dan to think that he must hate it.

"First thing I'd do is schedule a pancake supper in Grafton," said Claude. "Grafton is the heart of your support and the geographical heart of the county."

"I've done that," said Dan. "Actually it's a spaghetti supper. Jean Jewell has agreed to play the folk guitar."

Claude shook his head.

"You don't like the guitar," said Dan.

"I have no problem with the guitar," said Claude. "I haven't heard Jean play but, in general, music is good."

"Jean is amazing," said Dan.

"No, it's spaghetti I don't like, and I'll tell you why," said Claude. "Pancakes are cheaper to make. Thus you raise more funds, and after all, it is a fundraiser. Pancakes are easy on the system. If you keep a person up all night because your spaghetti sauce hasn't agreed with them, they tend to remember. Lastly, spaghetti has a foreign connotation that you avoid altogether with pancakes. Steer clear of tacos for the same reason."

"Oh, come on," said Dan.

"Do you remember Everett Carr?" said Claude.

"The name is familiar."

"He was a state senator, and once upon a time at a campaign supper he served a goulash that made a number of people ill. When Election Day rolled around, we had a new state senator."

Louise took an armload of clothes from the dryer. "That's the dumbest thing I ever heard," she said.

"It is dumb," said Claude. "It's very dumb. Politics is a dumb game."

Louise went upstairs. She felt slightly strange about the election, having gone out with Johnny White, married Tiny, and then married Dan. She felt as if she were exerting some

241

improper influence on public affairs. She felt like the sun to their revolving planets.

Dan had painted the baby's room a deep and soft color called Shell Ivory. It was a small room with a dresser, a wicker rocker, and a boxed and unassembled crib that leaned against the wall.

Louise folded the clothes and put them in the drawers of the dresser. They felt great in her hands. She loved the softly coarse fabrics, the pebbled rubber feet of a pair of pajamas. She looked into the mirror above the dresser. Could she be a good mother after all the false starts and wrong turns? She had her doubts. But she also had a feeling she rarely got—of life as a path leading directly to this moment. She was rocking in the chair and thinking about this when Dan and Claude came clinking and clanking up the stairs with beers and a socket set.

"We're going to put up the crib," said Dan.

This took longer than might have been expected. Twenty minutes after starting, they were still sifting through the pieces and frowning at the instructions. Dan would say, "Fit cotter pin A to post flange D," and then he would repeat the words "cotter pin A" very slowly, and he would ask Claude if cotter pin A didn't look shorter than the other cotter pins in the instructions, and if so, where was the damned thing. But they worked on, joining the pieces and components in a painstaking and bewildered fashion, until all of a sudden they were done, with pieces left over.

"Maybe those are extras in case you lose some of them," said Claude, but they didn't look like extras, and the gate on one side would not lower the way it was supposed to. "Push that side up against the wall," said Claude. "Then it won't matter if it opens or not." This is what they did, and then they sat on a braided blue and white rug in the middle of the floor, drinking their beers and talking about the weather, as Louise rocked gently with one hand resting on her stomach. The baby kicked, turned, settled.

Claude finished his beer and stood. "You two seem good," he said. "Now I have to go see Howard LaMott, the fire chief. He wants to talk about my son Albert."

"What did Albert do?" said Dan.

"He put cake in the boots of the firemen," said Claude.

"That sounds like Albert," said Dan.

"Howard claims this delayed them responding to a fire."

"Howard LaMott is a big windbag," said Louise.

"I'll hear him out," said Claude.

He left. Louise and Dan went down the hall and to bed. Dan read aloud from a book called *Planets, Stars and Space*, which he had found in the attic with the inscription "For Jeannie with love on her ninth birthday, July 20, 1962." Dan remembered hearing somewhere that infants in the womb liked being read to.

"Considering its influence upon the lives of people, animals, and plants on the earth," Dan read, "the moon is the second most important object in the sky. It is the illuminator of the night. It is responsible for the month as a calendar unit, and, working with the sun, it produces the important rise and fall in the earth's waters—the tides. In ancient times, calendars depended solely upon the moon, and lunar calendars are still used by many people for religious purposes. The dates of Easter and Passover are determined by the motions of the moon.

"Because the moon goes around the earth instead of around the sun, it is not a planet, even though it resembles the planets in many respects. It is a satellite, one of 31 in our solar system."

• • •

While this was going on out at the farm, in town Mary went to see Alvin Getty. Alvin lived in a tall and nearly paintless house, one block north of the park and not far from the Three Sisters of the Jewells. Mary almost tripped on an uncoiled Slinky on the sidewalk. She saw Alvin standing on the porch in the hazy glow of a bug light.

"What's happened to the store?" said Mary.

He took a long drink from a bottle of Falstaff beer. "I've persuaded new investors to lend me their backing," he said.

"Alvin, you are bankrupt."

"Says who?"

"Well, aren't you?" said Mary.

"Pammy," called Alvin. "We have company."

Pam Getty was in the kitchen. She had black hair and moved heavily in a quilted housecoat. Mary could see her through the open door.

"It's Mary Montrose," said Alvin.

"Leave me alone, Alvin," she said, searching violently through the pantry. "I'm making a Fizzy and I don't want any of your shit."

"Hi, Pam," said Mary.

"Pam, Mary is speaking," said Alvin.

Pam's hands shook as she got the Fizzy into water. "I don't care. That was my money."

"It was both of our money," said Alvin. "Why not cool it for one second and say hello to a guest in our house."

"Not after what she did to King," said Pam. She left the kitchen, and Mary did not see her again.

"Pam is angry at the world tonight," said Alvin.

"It was not me that let a biting dog run loose," said Mary.

"You were hard on that animal," said Alvin.

"I don't think so," said Mary. "But I'm not here about King."

"There is no reason to panic," said Alvin. "Pam and I are working closely with our creditors. We will be open again on Monday, and if not Monday, then the following Monday. Everyone will get their groceries in due time."

"But people are hungry now," said Mary. "Alvin, they took your cash register. The store isn't going to open again."

Alvin sat on the steps. "No, it probably won't," he said.

"What happened?" said Mary.

"People didn't shop."

"Goodbye, Alvin," said Mary.

Alvin shook her hand. "Go quietly," he said.

"And yourself."

Mary walked through Grafton in the dark. Two cars sat in front of the Lime Bucket, looking lonelier somehow than no cars. The rest of Main Street was deserted except for a dented maroon van by the old Opera House. Vans disturbed Mary, although she could not have said exactly why. She passed through the business district and into her neighborhood. In the windows of the houses she could see people washing dishes, huddling before the flickering fire of television, reading magazines in chairs. Arriving home, Mary found her back door standing open. She turned on the light in the kitchen as she always did, put her keys on the counter, and went into the living room. A deer stood not ten feet away, eating from the tangled vines of her ivy plant.

In the broken light Mary could see the steely black eyes and the stiff bristled hair along the shoulders. She could see the mouth tearing the dark leaves that she had been growing for years. The deer was not afraid of Mary. It wanted the ivy and

245

would have it, that simple. It looked at her out of the corner of its eye. It smelled like a river. The head butted the coffee table as the teeth made that soft ripping sound. Mary turned and left the way she had come. She raised the garage door, got into her car, locked the doors. She did not know what to do. She had been a schoolteacher early on in her career and had always taught the children that the answers were near at hand for those who would look. But at this moment she didn't know where to look or what she would find.

THIRTEEN

THE SENIOR PLAY was set in the fifteenth century. Jocelyn Jewell had won the role of "the ill-fated Maria," who would be bitten by a spider during the play and who would dance herself down to exhaustion and finally death. The spider was played by Dustin Tinbane of Morrisville.

Louise and Dan would have stayed home but for the involvement of Jocelyn. Louise was expected to deliver the baby in seventeen days. She wore a long black dress and a necklace of red beads to the play. Her cheeks were rosy and her hair hung thick and dark down her back. Under her arm she carried a green pillow, with which she hoped to cushion the hard dark bleachers of the Grafton gym.

Dan held Louise's hand as they walked up the sidewalk. His thoughts were drifting, and the weather could not make up its mind. The sun balanced on the edge of the fields. The light was thin and clear, falling against the bricks of the school. Cheryl Jewell came up behind them and put her arm around Louise's shoulders. Cheryl wore a pink hat with light green stitching. "This reminds me of being late for typing," she said.

The Grafton School had been one of the last old prairie schools, and although the classrooms were empty the building remained in decent shape. Three stories, each with a band of windows, rose between piers on the east and west. The top of the east pier had been the principal's office, and the top of the west pier the Red Cross room, containing one chair, one desk, and one bed for children who were not feeling well or for young women with their periods. The gym, round-roofed and democratic, stood on the east end, connected to the school by a low lobby with oak doors. GRAFTON was spelled out—for pilots—in large yellow letters on the black roof. Only fragments of letters could be seen from the ground.

Dan, Louise, and Cheryl entered the lobby. Display cases held loving cups, oxidized to a smoky color, that had been won by people who were now either dead or very old. The shop and hygiene teacher Richard Boster sold tickets beneath a banner saying, "Tarantella—A Musical—Cast And Directed By Edith Jacoby." Mr. Boster was an absent-minded teacher who habitually scratched the backs of his hands and who once totally confused a class of ninth-graders by saying that during sex the penis gets "hard and crusty." Now he pushed three tickets across a counter. "They've got quite a production this year," he said.

But this was said every year, and indeed it was hard to imagine a senior play so lame that it would not be considered outstanding. There were a couple of reasons for this. Coming on the eve of the students' entry into perilous adulthood, the senior play took on the power of an omen. To find fault with a particular drama would be like jinxing the new generation, and no one wanted to do that. Also, people came to see the senior play who might not see another live drama all year, and for them even theatrical basics, such as lighting, costumes, and shots fired offstage, could be dazzling. It was backward in a way—children acting sophisticated for the benefit of adults—but in Grouse County, as elsewhere, theater was not universally accepted as a worthwhile activity beyond the high school level. Making up stories, acting them out—people just got uneasy. Out in the country if a man were to go into a tavern and say he could not play cards that night because he was going to see *Finian's Rainbow,* it would be an odd moment. But anyone can go to a school play.

The basic plot of *Tarantella* was the proven one of lovers who are separated and die. Jocelyn Jewell played a maiden who falls in love with a young shopkeeper. The shopkeeper agrees to cater a banquet for a haughty and powerful judge but instead escorts the maiden on a picnic after her date falls through. On the picnic they find an intriguing spider and put it in a jar. Meanwhile, the banquet is a disaster, the judge's political hopes are dashed, and the judge, frustrated, kills the shopkeeper in a duel. The spider then grows to human size and bites Jocelyn, sending her into a dancing mania.

Thanks to Jocelyn Jewell, who seemed to be good at everything she tried, it really was quite a production. The singing was strong if sometimes uncertain, no one fell down during the dance sequences, and Edith Jacoby, whom a third of the audience could see standing in the wings, kept the action going and seemed particularly skilled in the staging of loud arguments. But Dan was not paying much attention and lost track of the story. Something had happened the night before that he could not stop thinking about.

The phone had rung late—say, ten or ten-thirty. It was Sergeant Sheila Geer of the Stone City police. "Can you meet me at Westey's Farm Home?" she whispered. Dan drove over. It took twenty minutes or so. The yard was sparsely lit, and

Sheila's cruiser had the parking lights on. Dan could see the outline of her head in the car.

Sheila suggested they go for a walk. The yard was enclosed by a chain-link fence, but Sheila had a key, as one who patrols the area well might. She led the way past cinder blocks, clothesline posts, and the dull black blades of tractor tires.

Finally they sat together on a bench swing. "Let's talk about the election," said Sheila.

"O.K."

"Look, there's someone on your side who should not be trusted," said Sheila.

"There aren't that many on my side," said Dan.

Then Sheila said that Deputy Earl Kellogg was providing department files to Johnny White. "I can't prove this in a court of law," she said. "But they consider you vulnerable. They think the cases go against you. You remember the heavy machines that disappeared."

"Of course."

"And the gamblers."

"Right."

"And Quinn. That baby Quinn."

"What about him," said Dan.

"I don't know," said Sheila. "They think the mother should have been prosecuted."

"We never found the mother."

"Yeah, except everyone knows you did."

"All right," said Dan. "This was a woman with mental disorders going back years ago. She was not capable of deciding for herself. And you're going to prosecute her? Why? Put her name all over the paper? There's no reason... And besides, read the charter. Prosecution isn't up to the sheriff."

"They know her name. They know everything about her."

"If they make an issue out of her, they will be sorry," said Dan. "And you can tell Johnny I said that."

"We don't have contact."

"You know a lot for not having contact."

"Well, I can't say. I really can't say."

"Earl's worked seven years for me," said Dan.

"I always wondered why that is."

"He knows the county better than anyone, and he's very good at stopping fights."

"I think he sells pornography."

"He doesn't sell," said Dan. "He has a collection of his own, but selling, no."

"He goes to a club called the Basement, in Morrisville, to watch the strippers."

"How do you know?"

Sheila shrugged. "Word gets around."

"The Basement is legal entertainment," said Dan. "You may not think much of it, but it isn't grounds for dismissal."

"And that poor wife of his, home knitting blankets."

"Quilts," said Dan.

"I think you kept him around too long," said Sheila.

"If what you say is true."

"You might check his cruiser."

"Why are you telling me?"

"I never wished you bad luck."

They got up and walked along, with Sheila's flashlight glancing over sawhorses and garden carts. A cellar window of Westey's was broken. They went in the back door with guns drawn, but found no one.

"Children must play," said Sheila.

251

Now Louise was clutching his arm. Jocelyn had started her final dance, in a long dark skirt and white blouse. The skirt traced poignant circles in the air.

This was the last of five performances, and there were many curtain calls. Jocelyn's face shone as she lifted the hands of her fellow actors. The lights came up on a gym full of roses and weeping teenagers. Jocelyn was in the middle of a group that would take some time to disperse. Cheryl said she would wait but Louise and Dan should go. Louise smiled uncertainly and started walking up the stairs to the stage.

"That's not the way," said Dan. He took her hand.

At home they had dried venison and salad, but Louise ate only a few bites. She put her fork down beside her plate and reached for the back of her neck to unhook the red beads.

"I think I did too much today," she said.

Dan looked up from the records he had taken from the trunk of Earl's cruiser. "What all did you do?" he said.

"Mom and I went to the Lighthouse to eat," said Louise. "We got some bumpers for the crib. And then the play."

Dan took a drink from a bottle of beer. "Why don't you go lay down," he said.

"Don't be mad at me."

"I'm not mad."

"You have been all night."

"I want you to lay down and take care of yourself."

Louise pushed her chair back and stood by the stove. She put her hands on her stomach. "You know what I think it is. I think I've lightened. The baby feels much lower. This is what happens as birth approaches. The baby moves down into the canal. I was reading about this."

"Lightened," said Dan.

"Put your hand on my stomach."

"It won't be long, will it?"

"No, darling. I am going to lay down."

"Why don't you."

Dan read for a while and then sat staring at the knobs of the stove. Waves of light seemed to wash over him. How many times he would remember this moment, these waves of light in the kitchen. He went upstairs and massaged Louise's back.

"I feel a little sick to my stomach," she said. "That's what I get for eating at the Lighthouse."

"Maybe a bath would make you feel better."

"Yeah," she said.

The faucet turned with a loud squeak and water thundered into the bathtub. When Louise got in she closed her eyes and rested her head on the back of the old claw-foot tub. She smiled faintly, her dark hair veiling the porcelain.

"Dan, I might be in labor," she said quietly. "I think I'm contracting, and I'm kind of scared."

"Really," said Dan.

"It hurts," said Louise. He helped her gently to her feet and wrapped her in a big green towel, her favorite. But before she was dry she asked him to leave the room, and as he stood outside the door he could hear her throwing up.

"Louise," he said.

"Why did I have to eat that goddamned food."

Dan went into the bedroom and called the hospital. A nurse came on the line. She had the low and steady voice of those who make their living reassuring people at night. "Is the pressure rhythmic or would you say it is steady?"

"I don't know," said Dan. "She's throwing up. She had some food that didn't agree with her."

"Who is her physician?"

"Beth Pickett," said Dan.

"Is Louise close by?" said the nurse. "May I speak to her?"

Louise stood in the hallway with the green towel around her shoulders. Dan brought the phone to her. She listened. She touched her stomach with spread fingers.

"Yes," she said. "Very much so."

They had to drive three miles on gravel roads to get to the hospital; there was no getting around this. They could pick up the blacktop in Chesley. Louise felt sick and took the ride badly. She wore the dress she had worn to the play. A cooking pot rested on her knees in case she had to vomit. The pot had black marks in the bottom from times they had burned popcorn. Dan flashed the blue lights but went very slowly to keep Louise out of pain. Even so, she leaned heavily on the armrest of the cruiser and sometimes asked him to slow down.

Due to a construction project, the logic of which was not readily apparent, the Mercy Hospital emergency room entrance had been moved since the last time Dan had been there. They followed a makeshift sign, winding up at a pair of dark doors; Louise sat in the car while Dan tried them. One would not open and the other would, but the area beyond was empty and Dan turned away. Then the door opened again and a security man appeared. He was in silhouette and Dan could not make out his features. "This is right," the man said. Dan helped Louise into the hospital and down a corridor until they found the emergency room. Louise slumped in a small chair at the admissions counter, and a man with drowsy eyes looked at her and then into a computer screen. "Are you in labor?" he said.

"I don't know," said Louise.

"Who's your insurance carrier?"

"Danny, I'm going to be sick," said Louise.

"What's going on?" said Dan. "Blue Cross—for Christ's sake, don't make her wait because of paperwork."

"We're not," said the man. "When they are ready to take her, she will go."

Soon a tall pale nurse with platinum hair and red lipstick helped Louise into a wheelchair, and guided the chair to a large treatment room curtained into sections. The lights were low. Someone moaned softly in a corner. The nurse helped Louise onto a gurney, took her blood pressure, listened to her account of what had been happening.

"Is the pressure cyclical, like a rhythm?" the nurse asked.

"I don't know anymore," said Louise. She lay on her back, looking at the ceiling. "I don't think so."

"All right," said the nurse. "Let's listen to the baby." She touched a stethoscope to Louise's stomach. The heartbeat often took a moment to locate. "How far along?" she asked.

"Thirty-six weeks," said Louise.

"Hmm." The nurse moved the head of the stethoscope. Her dark brows knit and a dazed little smile appeared on her face. "This baby's hiding from us." Her voice was musical, forlorn. "This baby is hiding from us."

The pale nurse left and came back with a stout, swift nurse who said nothing to Louise or Dan. She took a stethoscope from the pocket of her coat and listened for the heartbeat.

Dan stood on the other side of the gurney. "What's the matter?" he said.

"I can't tell you," she said. Turning to the pale nurse, she said, "Get a monitor." She folded her stethoscope and put it away. The nurse rolled a fetal monitor in. Then Dr. Pickett arrived.

"Beth, we're glad to see you," said Dan. "They're saying something about the baby hiding."

"Shh," said Dr. Pickett. She fastened the belt of the monitor around Louise's stomach and stared into the green and black pattern of the monitor screen. Then she said, "There is no heartbeat."

"Sometimes it takes a while to find," said Dan.

"The baby… is not alive."

"No," cried Louise.

"I am sorry."

"Bring her back," said Louise, her voice full and breaking, like the peal of a bell.

"Louise …"

"Ah, Jesus," said Dan. "What happened?"

"I don't know yet," said Dr. Pickett. "There are things that go wrong. We will find out before this is over."

Louise sat up, pulled the black dress over her head, and threw it fiercely across the room. "You're not even trying!"

"I'm going to try very hard," said Dr. Pickett. "Please settle yourself now."

"How can this be," said Dan. "What will happen?"

"Louise will go into labor and deliver the baby," said Dr. Pickett.

"I can't go through labor," said Louise. "I can't go through labor with a dead baby."

"And I'm not going to operate for a dead baby," said Dr. Pickett. "I'm not going to endanger you more than you already are."

Louise pressed her hands against her eyes. "It hurts," she said. "Oh, how it hurts me."

"We're going upstairs, Louise," said Dr. Pickett. "We'll make it hurt less."

The sturdy, reticent nurse put an IV needle in Louise's arm. Then both nurses, Dr. Pickett, and Dan hurried Louise to the elevator. Dan rolled the IV stand along as they ran down the hall.

A big stainless-steel elevator took them to the fourth floor. Louise's room was the last one in a long, wide corridor with rooms on the left and tall windows on the right. Louise was placed in the bed.

"I want to go home," she said.

"We can't for a while," said Dan.

They gave her a drug to induce labor, and when labor came it was more than she could take. The pains tore at her lower back and she called out for relief. Dan had read of something called back labor, and he supposed this was back labor. How strange, how misguided, that the body would go ahead trying to give birth when the baby was dead. An anesthesiologist gave her morphine, which did nothing. Later he came back to give her a shot in the spine called an epidural.

"Don't knock her out," said Dan. "She doesn't want to be knocked out."

"She may sleep because the pain has stopped," said the anesthesiologist. "But she won't be knocked out. Now please go while I give the shot. Please go."

"She wants me here," said Dan.

"Dan, get out, it's all right," said Dr. Pickett.

Dan left the room, and the door clicked behind him. He stood in the corridor looking down at the parking lot. Trees moved darkly and rain spattered the glass. A car turned slowly on the asphalt. There was a row of lights on the grass beside the street, and as the car went by, the lights went out one by one by one.

• • •

The epidural did its job, and Louise drifted into sleep. Now they had to wait just as anyone who is in labor must wait. A yellow chair stood in the corner, and Dan pulled it over by the bed. It was heavy and cumbersome as if a reclining chair were a wonder of heavy-gauge mechanics. Dan put his feet on the rail of the bed and tried to sink into a dream but the medical people kept coming and going in their soft shoes and whispering clothes. They used a door on the opposite side of the room from the corridor in which he had watched the lights going out. Dan dreamed that he was carrying the yellow chair along an empty highway. He went into a gas station, where a man with white hair said, "I make sculptures of pipe, which everyone likes." But Dan knew this was a dream and knew that the hospital was not a dream, so he awoke more tired than if he had really been carrying the chair, and the lights of the room seemed to drain his heart.

Louise was asleep, but he knew if he spoke her name she would answer. At four-thirty they gave her something to bring her blood pressure down. Dr. Pickett came in and taped one plastic bag to the wall and another to the frame of the bed. She said the bags contained antiseizure medicine. She told Dan that Louise was suffering from preeclampsia; the placenta had evidently separated from the wall of the uterus, and the baby must have died immediately.

"She is very sick," said Dr. Pickett. Her face glowed and her eyes were light blue. "The only cure is to deliver the baby."

It took two more hours for Louise's cervix to dilate sufficiently. Dan went into the corridor from time to time.

The light was coming up over Stone City. The delivery room filled with doctors, nurses, carts of gleaming instruments.

"All right, Louise," said Dr. Pickett. She said it loud. "I know this is not easy, not what we had planned. Is it, Louise? Is it?"

"No it isn't."

"That's for sure," said the doctor. "But we have a job to do, and for that to happen you must help. We have talked about breathing and pushing and resting. I want you to do what you can. We need you to push, not now but soon. Do you think you can?"

"Yes."

"You do."

"Yes I do."

"All right. Then here we go."

Dan held her hand so tightly he could not feel where his hand stopped and hers began. She bore down when told to, her lips and eyes pressed shut, and then gulped air as if rising from a dive. Her green eyes were alive, her brown hair matted on her temples. "Stay with me," said Dan. He washed her face with a cloth. After a while she could not push anymore. Dr. Pickett used suction to help bring the baby out. Dan was afraid she would come out in pieces but she didn't. She fell into the doctor's wiry arms, and only after she had been carried away and some minutes had passed did Dan stop hoping that somehow the heart had been beating and they had missed it all along.

"Is it a girl?" said Louise.

"Yes," said Dr. Pickett. "A beautiful girl."

Thinking back, Dan was never sure how soon it was after this that Beth Pickett presented him with a form to sign allowing the transfusion of blood. "She has lost too much," said the doctor. "You see, she was hemorrhaging and it was dammed up behind the placenta. That's why her tummy was so hard, because of this bleeding."

"You said delivery would end it," said Dan.

"She lost a lot in the course of delivery, and what she has left is not clotting," said Dr. Pickett.

"What are you saying? Is she bleeding to death?"

"It is a serious situation. I think she will be all right if we do what we must. But, as I say, it's quite serious."

"Well, Christ," said Dan.

"Don't despair," said Dr. Pickett. "I've dealt with preeclampsia before, and I know we can bring Louise around. But right now she needs good blood and plasma, so please, Dan, let's go."

He signed the transfusion form and turned to the bed. There was dark blood all over the floor. People had tracked it around the room. He could see their footprints, the zigzag serrations of hospital shoes. Louise was pale and still. He went over and whispered about the transfusions.

"All right, Dan," she said. Her eyes were badly swollen. He kissed her, and she smiled sadly, and he sat down in the yellow chair.

She kept bleeding. The first transfusion was followed by more. Envelopes of blood hung from the IV hook and drained into Louise's arm. They had rigged a catheter to collect her urine, but the collection bag remained empty, and different doctors came in to observe the strange emptiness of the catheter bag. Dan saw Dr. Pickett leaning against the wall, saying something no one could hear.

Louise knew they were pumping blood through her. There didn't seem to be any secret about that. Her heart raced to keep up but it could not. And her vision was failing. There was a big gray spot in front of her eyes. The spot was dense and uneven, like the nest of a paper wasp, and she could not see around it. She pulled Dan to her.

"I love you," she said. "But my eyes hurt and I am closing them."

"All right," he said. "I'm right here."

She touched his face, which was very hot. Closing her eyes, she imagined or saw a red light glowing under her pale gown. She knew this light so well that she could have laughed. It was the safe light from Kleeborg's, which enabled her to see what she was doing without damaging the prints. Now the light rose from her chest and it was as if she were inside it. Being in this light was as natural as going to a window to learn the weather. She could see the doctors, the nurses, and Dan from a place slightly above them. Dan gripped the rail of the bed and stared blankly at a bloodpressure monitor. He looked like hell, bathed in the warm red light but not knowing it. Louise drifted up. The ceiling would not hold her. She felt powerful and free from pain. She could go or she could stay, and the decision was hers. It did not scare her to go. It made her curious. She had lost the baby, and nothing would hurt. She saw a house on a road. It was dark, guarded by trees. She knew the house, had dreamed of it the night before she and Dan were married. The lane went up from the road, cushioned with pine needles. There was a plank porch and a brass knocker shaped like a deer. Whatever was in the house hummed. She could go in or not, her choice, but once through the door she could not return. She looked away from

261

the house. The lights of the doctors cast a ragged glow in the darkness. Dan was holding her hand. The house hummed louder and the boards trembled beneath her feet. But she didn't want to go without him, without knowing him.

So she would always believe that it had been her choice to come back. And her body did regain its balance slowly over the next three or four hours. Her kidneys began to work, her blood to clot. The shift changed, and a woman in fresh green clothes mopped the floor. Louise had received twelve units of blood and plasma in all. Dr. Pickett smoked a cigarette in the cafeteria. Dan stared at the dust that floated in the corridor. Louise's voice was low and hoarse, her eyelids swollen. In the late morning nurses brought the baby into the room. They had washed her, wrapped her in a blanket, placed a white cap on her head. Dan held her. Her features were delicate, her eyes closed. She did not seem to have been in pain. Her hands would have been strong. Dan cradled the baby on the bed beside Louise, but with the tubes in her arms and with the blood-pressure cuff Louise could not hold her. Dan sat with the baby in the yellow chair for a long time. "Tell her what's happening," said Louise. Dan held her some more. He did not know what to do. He gave her back to the nurses.

Mary Montrose and Cheryl Jewell came to see Louise. They pushed her hair gently from her face and held her hands, but were not allowed to stay long. They wandered from the room, lost in disbelief and wonder.

Louise would not leave the delivery room for days, because Dr. Pickett felt the equipment and staff there were better able to deal with her. Her blood pressure remained high. Around the hospital she was a curiosity. Eye doctors and kidney doctors and blood doctors came to examine and question her. One day Dr. Pickett asked the extra doctors to leave because she needed to speak to Dan and Louise alone. Dan thought he knew what this was about, and his heart pounded. Undoubtedly it was among Pickett's duties to find out why they had not got to the hospital sooner on the night the baby died—to find out who was at fault. But all she said was that they should get counseling.

On the third day Dan was sitting in the sun of the corridor when Joan Gower came around the corner with flowers.

"I'm awfully sorry," she said.

"Hello, Joan," said Dan.

"Did you name the baby?" she said.

Dan looked out at a blue sky with small clouds. "Why do you ask?"

Joan was pulling her hair into a ponytail these days, with a few strands left to curl forward. "They have to be named to go to heaven. Otherwise they become a spirit, called a taran, in the woods."

"Just be quiet," said Dan.

"It can be a private name, known only to you."

"Please go."

"I was so sorry when I heard."

"Thank you."

"You couldn't stop it."

"Thank you."

"You couldn't."

"We'll never know."

"I know you think you could, but it's not true," said Joan. "I brought you these flowers. They're from me and Charles."

"Get them out of here."

"Don't take it all on yourself."

"Please, will you take them out of here."

"I will leave them at the desk in case you should change your mind."

He watched her go. They had named the baby. They had named her Iris Lane Norman.

When Dan went home, he found the beer bottle still in the bathroom where he had left it. He took it out to the kitchen and threw it against the wall as hard as he could. The bottle did not break but put a hole in the plaster that is still there today. Dan went outside and sat on the steps. The white dog ran from him.

Ed Aiken picked him up and they went to see Emil Darnier in Morrisville. Darnier Funeral Home was the biggest house in town, with white columns and red bricks, and when Darnier handled a funeral it was a little like the Holiday Inn handling a funeral. Emil's daughter met them at the front door and led them down to the basement, where Emil's son took over, escorting the two men through a long cinder-block hall with metallic purple caskets. Eventually they were face to face with Emil, who had a clipboard in his hand and a hearing aid. The three men sat around a low table. Emil smoked a little cigar.

"I want a simple wooden box," said Dan.

"For infants there is only one," said Emil. He puffed, and spoke around the cigar. "It is white and like so." He showed with his hands.

"What's it made of?" said Dan.

"Oh, I don't know. It isn't plywood. I want to say particle board, but that isn't right, either. Let me see if I can find one. Tony! Tony! Where is that kid? Usually I have to order them, but sometimes we have them around. Let me go see."

While Emil was gone, Ed explained how he, Earl, and Paul Francis were keeping the sheriff's office going.

"That sounds good," said Dan.

Emil came back with a case that seemed hardly bigger than a shoebox. Dan lifted the lid and closed it.

"Well, I don't know about this," he said.

"What?" said Emil.

"It seems flimsy," said Dan. "I don't know about this at all. I could make something sturdier than this at home."

"If you want to use another box, it is all right," said Emil. "If you want to use this box, that is all right as well. You can use whatever box you are comfortable with. What we need to know is where and when. This is the standard infant casket. There is only one. Our wish is to help. We take no payment when an infant has died."

Dan and Ed stood and shook Emil's hand. They left the funeral home. It was cold and windy.

"It isn't such a bad box," said Ed.

"Oh, I know," said Dan.

"I'm not sure you should focus so much on the box."

That evening when Dan got to the hospital, Louise was lying in the dark in her new room on the sixth floor.

"My milk has come in," she said. Her breasts were large and hot. But Dr. Pickett had said the milk would go away in a short while when it became clear that no one was going to drink it.

"Isn't that a relief?" said Louise. "It will go away." Her voice had taken on a ripe, red quality because of all the crying she had been doing. Dan hugged her, and when he stepped back the front of her green gown was wet.

Dan went home that night and tried to build a coffin. He cut the parts out of pine, but his measurements were off just enough that nothing fit together. He could have assembled the box, but it would not have been right. So he didn't. He stacked the pieces in a corner of the basement and went upstairs. He drove over to Earl Kellogg's place in Wylie. Earl sat in a lounge chair. The news had just ended and he was looking at television. His wife, Paula, was on the couch. The walls were covered with her quilts, including the one of Kirby Puckett which had been featured in the *Stone City Tribune*.

"I'm sorry to bother you so late," said Dan.

Earl turned down the sound. "It's a repeat, anyway. How are you, man?"

"We could not believe it when we heard," said Paula. "We just sat here and looked at each other. How is Louise?"

"She's going to be all right," said Dan.

"What caused this?" said Earl.

"They don't know," said Dan. "It's called preeclampsia, and they don't know why it happens."

"We burn our lights in a wilderness," said Paula.

"I still can't believe it," said Dan. "I mean, I know it happened, but I don't believe it."

"You look pretty bad. Would you like a beer?"

Dan nodded. "Yeah," he said.

"We'll get you a beer," said Earl.

"Thanks," said Dan.

The child was buried at the cemetery north of Grafton known as North Cemetery. It has another name no one uses, which is Sweet Meadow.

Louise and Dan went down to Darnier's in the morning. The baby wore a white gown and lace cap. Under her crossed hands they put a locket with Lake Michigan sand from their honeymoon and a photograph of the two of them, taken while Louise was pregnant. Then they each kissed her and closed the lid of the white box.

Emil Darnier brought the infant to the cemetery in the long black hearse. The back glided up to reveal the tiny casket. The walls of the inside of the hearse were burgundy. The grave was under a willow not far from the stone of Louise's father and grandparents. It was the fourteenth of May, warm and mild.

Emil thought the way to get the box in the ground was for him and Dan to stand on either side and let it down with two ropes run beneath it. But Dan said, "I don't want the box to tilt."

"They never do," said Emil.

"Why?"

"I been doing this a lot of years."

"I will lower her with my hands. The hole isn't that deep."

"It's deeper than it looks."

"I don't want the casket to tilt."

"That's how people hurt their back."

"I'm in pretty good shape."

"It's not the weight so much as it's an awkward reach."

"Let's not argue," said Dan.

"No," said Emil.

Dan knelt on a towel beside the grave. The hole was not really very deep. It didn't have to be for such a small casket. He could not help but think of the winter frosts which would go three or four feet down. But now it was warm and the light poured from the sky.

There was a large turnout from Grafton, Pinville, and Wylie, people they knew from town and people they knew from their jobs. Louise had asked Henry Hamilton to read the

Scripture, and he had brought his family Bible, an enormous gold book that threatened to fall from his hands. "Behold, he that keepeth Israel shall neither slumber nor sleep," read Henry. "The Lord himself is thy keeper; the Lord is thy defence upon thy right hand; so that the sun shall not burn thee by day, neither the moon by night."

Louise sat in a lawn chair in the shade. Dan held the coffin throughout the ceremony and then put it in the grave. Louise stood and dropped a white rose on the box. Bumblebees cruised heavy-headed through the leaves of nearby bushes. Everyone lined up to turn a shovelful of earth. This baby is hiding.

Dan and Louise were the last to leave after the service. Louise put dark glasses on. They did not feel like going home, so they drove over to the nature walk by Martins Woods. They made their way through the trees and along the river, coming out in the prairie grass, which was golden in the sun. Then they drove to Walleye Lake and parked on the shore, looking at wind moving across the water. They didn't say anything, holding hands between the seats of the Vega. The colors were vivid and real, but they felt that somehow they could see these scenes and no longer be part of them.

PART III

LOVE REBEL

FOURTEEN

LOUISE GOT BETTER but did not go back to work. Perry Kleeborg hired Maren Staley for the summer and was teaching her to take pictures. Maren came out to the farm from time to time because there was so much that Kleeborg did not know about running the studio, although it was his name on the door.

Maren would report to Kleeborg that Louise's coloring was poor and her eyes still seemed puffy or that she was suffering from headaches or that she was still taking blood-pressure medicine. Kleeborg would then order some Texas grapefruits or California oranges and have them delivered to the farm in cardboard boxes that would sit in the garage unopened, bearing bright pictures of their contents.

Louise walked in her sleep. She would go down into the cellar, and wake in the morning with dirty feet. She would take out and rearrange the food in the cupboards. Several times she woke in the middle of the night certain that she had heard a baby's cry. She was out of bed and on her bare feet before she could think twice. She felt a stirring in her breasts even though her milk had long since gone away.

She did not take the crib down or change the baby's room back to a spare room. People offered to put the baby's things away, even people she did not know well—the implication being that whoever was going to do the job, it should be done. She figured it must have been a custom at one time because mothers could not bear to do it. But the quilts and rocker and crib and dresser were the only day-to-day proof that there had in fact been a baby. Louise felt, or maybe imagined, the impatience of the outside world. She and Dan would wake early, as light crept into the room and mourning doves issued their three-part calls in the yard. At that hour time seemed to have stopped, and therefore seemed not to be carrying them any farther away.

Dan always had something to do. He emptied the trailer of her things and towed it behind the barn. Dan said the trailer now seemed like a terrible joke, although the loss of the baby did not seem to have anything to do with the trailer. He put in longer hours as sheriff. He would speak to anyone on any topic. He rewrote the shift system, which had become twisted and ridiculous over the years. Dan campaigned hard for the sheriff's primary. Some people thought he was a little out of control or had some weird look in his eyes. But on June first he won the primary, and Johnny White, as predicted, filed enough signatures to run as an Independent.

One Sunday not long after the primary, Louise walked around the barn to see the trailer. The air inside was hot and still. She sat there, heat-stunned, sweating, drinking a beer, which she was not supposed to do. A wasp buzzed against the window. As she looked through the dusty glass, a bale of straw tumbled out the door of the haymow. She walked to the barn. It was cooler inside, and dark, smelling of ammonia and old wood. She climbed the ladder past the floor of the haymow, past several layers of straw, and into heat again. Dan was wrestling a bale in the sunlight streaming through the door.

"What are you doing?" she said.

He stopped and rested. "Fixing the straw."

Louise looked at him. He was shiny with sweat and covered in bits of straw. "What's wrong with it?" she said.

"It wasn't stacked evenly, so the corner was about to give way," said Dan.

"I wouldn't worry about it," said Louise. "It's Les Larsen's straw."

"I know it," said Dan. "I know it is. It just bothers me to see something done so badly."

"Why did you come up in the first place?"

"Who else is going to?"

Louise left the farm in August to go with Mary up to Seldom Lake in Minnesota. Mary went for two weeks every year because her sister and brother-in-law, Carol and Kenneth Kennedy, ran a camp on the lake.

It was late on a Friday when Louise and Mary arrived. The air was cool and they drove a winding dirt lane past tall black trees. Louise had not been here for years. As a child she had regarded Kenneth and Carol as exotic.

The house came into view, big as Louise remembered, lights burning in the windows. Kenneth and Carol rose from rocking chairs on the dark porch. They showed Mary and Louise to their cabins, and the four walked back to the house. Carol, Mary, and Louise sat at the kitchen table as Kenneth handed out cans of beer from the refrigerator.

"Well, it sure is good to see you two," said Carol. She was tall like Mary, but heavier, and had an oval mark on her cheek from playing with a soldering iron when young.

"You know, I had forgotten a lot of it," said Louise.

"We're really not the same place you would remember," said Carol.

"We built the rec center in eighty-two and the bathhouse in eighty-six," said Kenneth. "In five years we've more than tripled our dock space."

"Wow," said Louise.

"I am looking forward to fishing," said Mary.

Kenneth had been standing with his hands on the back of a chair, and now he pulled the chair out and sat down. He was one of those skinny, aging caretakers you see carrying boxes and rakes and things from place to place at motels and camps all over the country. "We wanted to talk to you about that," he said.

"What?" said Mary.

"We... How should I say this? We made a mistake," said Kenneth. "It was in the spring. We've always been blessed with good fishing here. Well, you know that, Mary. And I guess we just—"

"I'm sure you noticed there aren't that many cars for the middle of summer," said Carol. "This is why we can give you separate cabins."

"Are you going to let me tell the story?" said Kenneth.

"Tell it," said Carol.

"We pushed our luck," said Kenneth. "That's what we did. We pushed it. As you may know, we went to Finland last year."

"You sent me a postcard," said Mary.

"Mary, it was so beautiful," said Carol.

"Anyway, we went," said Kenneth. "Naturally we tried the fishing. In fact, we were able to write the trip off. But that's neither here nor there. So. We were especially impressed by a fish called the bandfish. It's a real fisherman's fish, if you know

274

what I mean, and we arranged to have some shipped back live as a transplant."

"Long story short, they chased the other fish out of the lake," said Carol.

"That's right," said Kenneth. "All that's left is scrup."

"Is what?" said Louise.

"Scrup," said Kenneth.

"That's the local scavenger fish," said Carol.

"Back home, Louise, a scrup would be called a chub or a sucker," said Mary.

"I got you," said Louise. "What happened to the bandfish?"

"Well, this is what really makes us mad," said Carol. "Once the other fish were gone, they left."

"After we shelled out all that money to bring them here," said Kenneth.

"Where did they go?" said Louise.

"We don't know," said Carol.

"They could be anywhere," said Kenneth. He laughed and the others joined in. "It would be funny, if we didn't need the income."

"Did you know I'm delivering newspapers now?" said Carol.

"You were doing that before," said Mary.

"I feel bad you came all this way," said Carol. "Of course, we had thought that by now some kind of fish would have returned. Because they feed on scrup. That's why we didn't call you and tell you not to bother."

"It's not a bother," said Mary. "We're glad to be here."

"What would you like to do?" Carol asked.

"What would I like to do?" said Mary. "I don't care what we do. We don't have to do anything. I want Louise to get some rest, and beyond that I want to do whatever you want to do."

"There must be something," said Carol.

"There isn't," said Mary.

"Louise, what about you?" said Kenneth.

"Oh, I don't really care," Louise said. "I thought it might be nice to do some hiking while we were here."

"Hiking?" said Mary. "I think you'd better take it easy. I'm not sure how much hiking you should do."

"We have lots of trails," said Carol.

Mary and Louise walked a curving cinder path to the point where it forked, and said good night. Louise's cabin was stone, and had a soft blue light above the door, which was painted red with six panes of glass near the top. Louise ran her hand along the rough cool walls and went inside. Fireplaces built of sandstone blocks stood at either end of a big open room. There were bookcases and window seats with linen pillows. Above one fireplace was a deer head mounted on a wooden shield. The ceiling was made of wide boards resting on rough rounded logs. Louise hung her shoulder bag on a hat rack made of deer feet. She washed her face and brushed her teeth. Carol wrote poetry for the local newspaper, and taped to the inside of the medicine cabinet was one of her pieces, called "May Day," which went,

> *Workers rejoice 'round the world;*
> *In U.S., baskets for the girls!*
> *Which way better?*
> *Sure don't know—*
> *It is interesting,*
> *Though!*

The bed did not utilize any deer parts, and the sheets were stiff and cool on her feet. She thought about Mary and Carol, and how they did not always get along. Louise thought they had got more antagonistic in recent years, but it may have been that she was noticing it more. The turning point, Louise thought, had been the tablecloth Carol sent Mary for her sixtieth birthday. It was a white embroidered tablecloth. Mary said it was beautiful and that the pattern reminded her of some blue napkins she used to have. Louise thought nothing of this, but in several days Mary called and asked her to come over. She had dyed the tablecloth blue, or tried to, and cut it into jagged pieces.

"What should I do?" said Mary.

"What did you do?" said Louise.

"I don't know what to tell Carol."

Louise examined the remnants of the tablecloth. "Just say you purposely destroyed the tablecloth she gave you."

"It was not on purpose," said Mary.

"Well, you didn't leave much doubt," said Louise.

"To color something is not to destroy it," said Mary. "People color things every day. The dye must be defective. I should go to the store and demand my money back."

"You are amazing."

"It could be something wrong with the fabric," said Mary.

"Don't say anything to Carol," said Louise.

But for some reason she did. When Carol and Kenneth came down that Thanksgiving, Mary brought out the blue squares and laid them on the table. "What do you make of this?" she asked Carol.

"Your whole life, no one has been able to trust you with good things," said Carol. "That's what everyone used to say.

'Don't give Mary anything you value.' Why do you think I got an ample trousseau when Kenneth and I were married, and you and Dwight got a shoe tree? A shoe tree! Did you ever stop and consider why that might be?"

"A shoe tree is not all we got," said Mary.

"You got a shoe tree," said Carol.

"You know damned well we got some beautiful porcelain," said Mary.

Of course, the two sisters were capable of friendship. They enjoyed playing cards and trying to remember what had happened to people they knew from the old Grafton School in the forties, before the war took away the boys.

"Guess who I saw the other day," Mary would say.

"Who?"

"Bobby Bledsoe."

"Didn't he play baseball with Dwight?"

"Yes, he did. Every town had a team back then."

"Not Boris."

"Well, not every town."

"Didn't Dwight and Bobby get arrested?"

"They got arrested in Davenport."

"What was that about?"

"They would never say."

"Bobby Bledsoe …"

"Now, do you remember Nick Bledsoe? You remember Bobby. What about Nick?"

"Yes! Poor Nick had braces on his legs."

"That's right. Bobby was a good ballplayer and Nick had the braces."

"I liked Nick better than I did Bobby."

"Bobby was all show."

"But not Nick. Nick was kind."

"Nick would do good deeds without seeking recognition."

"I wonder what happened to Nick."

The next morning Louise woke early and went outside in her robe. The grass was cold and wet on her feet as she walked down behind the cabin to a stream that must have run to the lake. Moss covered the banks, and a bridge made of rope and boards crossed the stream not far above the water and the round stones in the streambed. Louise walked onto the bridge and lay face down with her forehead resting on her fists. Between the boards of the bridge she could see the water coursing over the worn-down stones.

The sun came through the trees and belled on the water. Louise lay there shivering in her robe. She could hear the rushing sound of the water and the sound of her own breath, which rose as steam past her ears. Her breasts felt large and unfamiliar against the wooden slats. She wondered if they would ever go back to their former size. She felt or imagined a pull between the water in the stream and the water in herself. She considered how it is taken for granted that water gets to go wherever it wants. Sometimes water got in the basement of the farmhouse, and she and Dan once had to have the fire department pump it. "How can we keep it out?" she had asked Howard LaMott. "Oh, it's *going* to get in," he said. Now a dragonfly hovered under the bridge. She saw momentarily the blue wires of its wings. Then it was gone.

She got up and went inside. From her suitcase she took the blood–pressure cuff and stethoscope that she had brought along on the advice of Beth Pickett. She hooked the stethoscope in her ears, fastened the cuff around her upper left arm, placed the black bulb in her left hand, pumped the cuff up to one hundred and sixty, and slowly let the pressure escape. Where the thumping began in her ears was the high number, where it stopped the low. Later, she lay on the unmade bed and chose a thin green book from the nightstand. The book, called *The Assurance of Immortality*, was published in 1924 and written by a man named Harry Emerson Fosdick. She opened the book and read this: "A traveller in Switzerland tells us that, uncertain of his way, he asked a small lad by the roadside where Kandersteg was, and received, so he remarks, the most significant answer that was ever given him. 'I do not know, sir,' said the boy, 'where Kandersteg is, but there is the road to it.'"

On the second day of her vacation Louise found a pair of hip boots in the closet of her cabin, and on the third day she put them on and walked up the stream. The cold water pressed against the rubber of the hip boots, and the rocky area near the bridge gave way to smooth sand where the stream widened. Clouds moved fast across the sun; the light and the shade swept across her path in alternating bands. A muskrat dived into the water, and a stranded orange traffic cone had washed down from somewhere. She waded awkwardly to the bank and stood there crying for a half hour. Her tears fell into the stream. She wiped her nose with the back of her hand, and washed her hands in the water.

When she got back, Carol and Mary were waiting to take her fishing. Carol suspected that the bandfish were still in the lake, but grouped together as if preparing for a counterattack from the other fish they had driven out. So the three women went across the lake in a Boston Whaler and dropped anchor not far from a shady spot under a weeping willow on the far bank. Looking back at the camp, they could see the tiny figure of Kenneth carrying something across the grass.

"Cast at the tree," said Carol.

"I'm afraid I'll get tangled in the branches," said Louise.

"There's no way," said Carol. "I've put too much lead on the line. You couldn't reach it if you tried."

They cast for a long time with no response. There was a light breeze, and swallows dipped over the water.

"How are you, Louise?" said Carol.

"I'm good," said Louise.

"Mary said you've been waking up early."

Louise squinted and dropped her lure into the dark water beneath the tree. "Yeah."

"Well, why don't you come along on my paper route?" said Carol. "I'd be glad for the company."

"I don't think that's very advisable," said Mary.

"What time do you go?" said Louise.

"Four o'clock," said Carol. "It's a pretty time of day."

"That might be fun," said Louise.

"Louise, you just cast right over my line," said Mary. "All right. Don't move. Hand me your rod and reel."

"Where?"

"Hand it to me."

"You're not tangled," said Carol.

"And I'm not going to be," said Mary.

It was not long before Louise was running Carol's route on her own. There were seventeen papers every day except Sunday, when there were forty-eight. Carrying a pair of snips in her hip pocket, she picked up the newspapers in the parking lot of a natural-gas substation next to a bean field in the middle of nowhere. She liked the sound when the yellow nylon band that had held the bundle together broke. She would often be there waiting when the guy who brought the papers to the substation arrived. His name was Monroe, and he was a bald man who stood in the back of his truck in a white canvas apron. Sometimes he would ask after Carol. He never seemed to quite understand why Louise was doing the route. That was all right with Louise. "Carol is taking a little vacation," she would say, smiling up at Monroe, waiting for her papers like someone about to take Communion. Then Monroe would toss the papers out of the truck and they would land with a slap on the pavement.

All the customers lived in the country and had mailboxes, so after picking up the papers and breaking the band, Louise never had to get out of the car. She drove Carol's old beige Nova, which had a bench seat and an automatic transmission on the column. Carol had demonstrated how to drive and deliver newspapers at the same time. You sat in the center of the seat, left hand on the steering wheel, left foot working the pedals, right hand flipping open the mailboxes and putting the papers in. Louise liked driving this way. She had a much clearer sense of where the car was in relation to the ditch.

For most of the route the sun lit the sky from below the horizon. This light was either white or pale blue, and the trees were black against it. Louise listened to the radio. She had to dial away from the bland and voiceless junk preferred by Carol. She and Carol were destined to fight a war of the frequencies for some time. Louise found a station out of somewhere in Wisconsin that played stark Irish songs about the difficulties of that poor land and its wretched inhabitants.

There was a town to the north of Seldom Lake, and after the papers were delivered Louise drove there for coffee and hash browns. She sometimes went into a consignment shop near the diner to look at the children's clothing. She found some incredible buys, and she bought a tiny yellow dress, which she hung on a deer hoof back at the cabin. The woman behind the counter was indifferent to what happened in the store and did not seem to notice or care whether Louise bought anything. One day the telephone rang in the shop, and the woman picked it up and listened, then said, "Don't call me here, Susan. I mean it... I understand that, but not here. Goodbye." Within seconds the phone rang again. "All right, Susan," she said. "I'm not joking with you. I am very serious." Louise edged toward the door, knowing, as anyone would, that the phone would ring again. "This is too much. My God, Susan, it has to stop!"

When Louise got back to the camp, Carol was waiting outside her cabin with a bundle of overalls tied with string. "These are my old ones," she said. "They haven't fit me for years, but they should be about right for you. They'll keep the ink off your clothes now that you're doing it every day."

After the two weeks that Mary always stayed, they decided to stay another two weeks. This was what Louise wanted, and Mary said that whatever Louise wanted was fine. Louise knew on some level that her staying away would bother Dan, but she avoided that level by making her letters to him kind of impersonal. They were reports of her days. He called sometimes to find out when she was coming home, but she never gave a definite answer.

Being an older newspaper carrier, Carol also was responsible for supervising the paperboys and papergirls in the towns around Seldom Lake. So one night she asked Louise to come up to the house and help put together the packets for a subscription drive. Each carrier was to receive a manila envelope full of information. They had just started when the telephone rang and Carol went to answer it. Then Mary came in to make a drink, and Louise was working alone in the living room.

"Now what does she have you doing?" said Mary.

Louise explained.

"Well, Jesus Christ," said Mary.

"What's wrong with that?" said Louise. She licked an envelope.

"You are here to rest," said Mary.

"I am putting sheets of paper in envelopes," said Louise. "What is your problem?"

"I don't have a problem," said Mary.

"You sure act like it," said Louise.

"Well, I guess I am mistaken once again."

"What is wrong with you?"

"What do you think?" said Mary.

"I don't know."

"Do you think you're the only one who's sad?"

"No, I don't think that."

"That baby should be here."

"I cannot believe you."

"She should be, Louise."

"She is mine. Don't you bring her into this."

"I think she's already in this," said Mary. "I wanted you here because you were sick—not to run a paper route and pretend everything is fine."

"Oh, I don't want to talk to you anymore," said Louise.

Right about this time Carol came back into the room. "Come on," she said. "That was Kenneth. He's down at the boathouse. The fish have come back."

"What fish?" said Mary.

"Hurry," said Carol. And Louise and Mary were so embarrassed to have been surprised in the middle of their fight that they went along.

The dock system was complicated, and although they could see Kenneth standing out there against the dark water, getting to him was like going through a maze.

Hundreds of fish were swimming just beneath the surface of the water, forming a river of silver in the moonlight.

"What kind of fish are they?" said Louise.

"Northern pike," said Kenneth.

"I am going home in the morning," said Mary. "Good night, everyone."

Louise and her mother had fought before, of course, but they had never really had the ready option of putting hundreds of miles between them. Louise stayed on at Seldom Lake. Her cabin had a gas heater that she began using in September, with the red and yellow leaves batting against the windows. She kept doing the paper route, and ran the subscription drive herself. She handed out all the packets and sat with the carriers in Carol's car as they looked over the prizes they might try for.

"Let me ask you something," said one boy with owlish glasses. "Me and this girl were pen pals all summer. So she always signed her letters by saying 'Love you always,' and I did the same. But now that we're back in school she won't even look my way. Not only do I not think she will love me always, I don't even think she loves me right now. So I was going to get her a present, and I see that if I get three new subscriptions I win a stuffed dog with an AM/FM radio inside."

Louise looked at the picture of the dog. "Yes, but can you get three subscriptions by the contest deadline?" she said. "This is a pretty small town, and right in the instructions they say don't shoot for the moon."

"I think I can," said the boy. "But what about that idea? Would you like a dog radio if you were a girl? I mean, you *are* a girl. Would that sort of thing appeal to you if you were my age?"

"Let's see," said Louise. Her opinion was that the item shown would probably not be a very good dog or a very good radio. She looked at the paperboy and said, "If I was your age, I would really want this."

With Louise handling the paper route, Carol had hoped to write more poetry. She had a lot of ideas about autumn. But once the northerns had returned to the lake, so did the customers, and Carol and Kenneth found themselves working from dawn until nine or ten at night to keep the place running. And Louise, being Louise, did what she could to help out.

FIFTEEN

ELECTION SEASON came to Grouse County, bringing unusual weather. The leaves hardly changed color and fell abruptly, almost overnight. Miles Hagen, the Republican candidate for sheriff, ran his usual campaign, with no chance of winning, no desire to win, and no particular platform beyond advocating the construction of a new jail on the northern bank of the Rust River in Chesley.

This land was owned by one of his relatives, but Miles was a handsome and venerable figure who had propped up the two-party system for years, and the proposal would never get anywhere, so no one cared.

Dan Norman campaigned sufficiently but with a distance between him and the voter. One Monday morning he went to the Valiant Glass Company in Wylie and shook hands at the factory gate with the men and women of the seven-thirty shift. It was a clear October day, and the workers were reluctant to leave the light so late in the year.

"With winter coming up," said a fat man in worn overalls, "I guess my biggest concern is my mailbox. I live west of Boris, and every snowfall without fail the county plow comes barreling along and knocks my mailbox down. Yet when I call the county recorder's office to straighten this out, I invariably reach a curt young woman who gives me the runaround."

The proper response was obvious. Dan should have taken the man's name. He didn't have to do anything with it. He could even throw it away once the man was out of sight. But standing at the plant gate, he should have written down that name. Instead, he said, "Well, see, you're calling the wrong people. The recorder doesn't have anything to do with the snowplow. Try Public Works."

Meanwhile, Johnny White, the Independent candidate, seemed to have a chance. His theme, that Dan had been a do-nothing sheriff, did not sway many voters, who for the most part were not looking for a keyed-up or hyperactive sheriff. But Johnny had a large advertising budget, and the repetition of his name and face made him seem more plausible. He also had an indignant, cheated style that appealed to some.

As the election neared, Johnny wondered how to use what he considered his secret weapon: Margaret Lynn Kane, the mother of the abandoned baby Quinn. According to the file Earl Kellogg had given Johnny, a judge in Family Court had assigned her to a halfway house in the eastern part of the state. She was thirtynine years old and a graduate of Romyla High School. Her parents were dead, she had cousins in San Diego who did not remember her, and her thought processes were faulty and unrealistic.

Now, Johnny had boxed informally in high school: a group of friends would gather and spar behind the school, pretending to enjoy it. One time, Johnny knocked down a better boxer but couldn't remember how—which hand, what sort of punch. The fall was like a gift from the blue, and so were the facts on Margaret Lynn Kane. He felt that these smudged and typewritten secrets must be useful. But he was not sure how. He did not want to confront the woman at the halfway house. He did not want to talk to her. All he wanted was to announce her existence in some dramatic way.

Tiny and Johnny talked strategy over beers at the Lime Bucket in Grafton. Little could be done without Shannon Key, the reporter who covered health, agriculture, and politics for Channel 4. And she liked Dan Norman, judging from when she interviewed him on TV. Even if there had been a bad accident, she would smile ruefully, as if wishing she could have ended up with him. She had already refused to run some of Johnny's charges against Dan, saying they were "unsubstantiated."

"Hey, if I say something, I don't care what it is, it's news," said Johnny.

"That's right," said Tiny.

"If I say the moon is made of, you know, fiberglass."

"Right."

"Now, if she wants another opinion, I can live with that. But at least report the charge. She's the media. This is her job. She's not hired to make fine distinctions."

Tiny finished his beer and swirled the foam around the bottom of the glass. "Why don't we go to the halfway house?"

"They wouldn't let us in," said Johnny.

"We could have a press conference. We could set up in the street or on the sidewalk with the building in the background."

"I like that… "

"In a way," said Tiny, "it would be preferable if they didn't let us in."

"I don't want to go in," said Johnny. "I had a cousin in one of those places. I remember she bit her wrists. She'd have these bite marks. Spooky girl."

"Who's that?"

"Connie Painter."

"I know Connie."

"She was fucked up, man," said Johnny, and he seemed lost in thought. "Anyway, I don't know if Shannon Key will go for this. She'll say Quinn is old news. She'll say anything to keep from helping me."

"You don't have to tell her what it's about," said Tiny.

The next day they were driving around Morrisville in Johnny's Bronco when they saw Shannon Key sitting on a bench in Roosevelt Park and eating an apple while a crew set up around her. Johnny pulled over and said he wanted to schedule a press conference out of town.

"First of all, we don't travel out of our viewing area," said Shannon. "Second of all, the rule for political coverage is you gotta make a press release and hand it in. Third, you're parked on our cable."

Johnny put the truck in drive and eased it forward. "You don't want to miss this."

Shannon bit the apple. "Maybe I do and maybe I don't."

"It will explode what's left of Dan Norman's campaign," said Johnny.

"Oh, likely," said Shannon.

"Even you can't save him," said Tiny.

"Hey, Charles—I'm impartial," said Shannon.

"The hell if you are," said Tiny.

Shannon sighed. "When is it?"

"What does your schedule look like?"

"I'm free on Friday. I'm not free on Saturday. Monday is doubtful. Tuesday is out of the question."

"Friday."

"Look, I'll bring it up. I'll see if we want to do something. You realize that, under the Fairness Doctrine, Dan would get equal chance to respond."

"Good," said Johnny.

Johnny campaigned with his kids that night at the Town Hall in Pringmar. He flew them in from Cleveland whenever possible. Sometimes Lisa, their mother, would come along, sometimes not. Her attitude toward Johnny had improved through therapy.

Megan and Stefan bolstered Johnny's image. Without them he was considered by some to be a lightweight. He knew this and had reconciled himself to it, although he still suspected that a polling firm working for him had inadvertently helped popularize the label. His kids granted him the minimal substance necessary to be a father.

He interviewed them in public, drawing out their concerns about the world. It turned out they had many concerns about the world; Johnny was surprised. These two children, aged twelve and nine, viewed the world as a place verging on disaster. Sometimes he cast them in skits with a law-enforcement theme. In Pringmar that night, on the stage of Town Hall, Megan played deputy sheriff to Stefan's dope fiend.

"What are you holding, son?" said Megan. "Grass, snow, dust, smack …"

"I'm not holding anything."

"… speed, reefer, Quaaludes, crack …"

"Are you deaf? I don't have drugs."

"Then I guess you have nothing to fear from a drug-sniffing German shepherd."

"Ha—Grouse County doesn't have a canine program."

"It does since Sheriff John White was elected."

At this point, Jack White's beagle spilled onto the stage, barking and running circles around Stefan, who had a plastic bag of hamburger in his jacket.

Megan found the bag and held it up to the light. She handcuffed her brother. "Just as I thought—drugs."

"Everything's changed since Sheriff John White came in," complained Stefan.

"Now you'll go to jail, with access to the counseling you need."

Megan dragged Stefan offstage, leaving the dog to eat the hamburger. The audience got a kick out of the whole thing, and the serious lesson probably sunk in as well. Then Johnny came out and gave his speech. "Some will tell you my campaign is negative," he said. "What does negative mean except I'm against it. In this county we have a sheriff who lets three out of four crimes go unsolved. We have a sheriff who lets gamblers and dope dealers run free. Am I negative about these things? Yes …"

Afterward, Johnny took Megan and Stefan out for supper at a club in Stone City, with oak tables and primitive country murals on the wall. Johnny ordered wine and made a show of trying it in the presence of the waiter, although he would not have rejected the bottle unless there was something terribly wrong with it.

He leaned back in his chair and asked the kids to tell him about their lives in Ohio. And they did, for a while, but soon their stories trailed off and they began fighting. Megan accused Stefan of lying to make his life sound better. Stefan said Megan always put their mother in tears. Megan stabbed Stefan in the arm with a fork.

Johnny tried to divert their attention. "Look, here comes our food," he said, as Stefan punched Megan in the back. Megan gasped for air. Finally Johnny yelled, "All right, that's enough! I said enough!" For he had found that the kids hated to be embarrassed in public even more than they hated each other.

Friday came. Johnny and Tiny drove across the state, stopping for coffee, stretching their legs like old men. The halfway house was located in a former jail in a pretty town ten miles from the Mississippi. The term "halfway house" had made Johnny expect a small bungalow, an overgrown yard, torn shades. But this was a big brick building with chestnut trees and a leaf-covered yard. Johnny parked on the street in front of the jail, which had been part of the state correctional system until budget cuts. Half a dozen people tended the yard. They moved heavily and with troubled expressions.

"I guess these are the inmates," said Johnny.

"Slaving away," said Tiny.

"Maybe it's work therapy."

"Yeah, right."

"You should try to be more positive."

They were early. Johnny turned on the radio and listened blankly to the hog reports. "I saw a funny show on television last night," he said.

Tiny bit his thumbnail. "Yeah?"

"This guy was telling some great jokes."

"Like what?"

"Well, they weren't really jokes. They were just, like, remarks. I can't really remember them."

"I see," said Tiny.

293

They sat in silence for ten minutes. Tiny read a newspaper. Johnny took a folder from above the visor and looked through it.

"Wait a minute," said Johnny. "Look at this." He handed Tiny a photocopy of a picture of Margaret Lynn Kane. The contrast was very high. "Now look at the woman over by the yard cart," said Johnny. "My God, I can't believe it."

The woman wore a red sweater, baggy tan pants rolled at the cuffs, and dirty white sneakers. She glanced up with dark and unguarded eyes, raking.

"It could be," said Tiny.

"She's the right age," said Johnny. "I mean, look at her face. You can just tell. You don't get a face like that for nothing."

"You could be right."

"I know I am," said Johnny, pressing a blue bandanna to his forehead. "But we don't want to talk to the media with her standing there. I mean, Jesus, she'd hear what we were saying. She might freak out."

"I'd hate to think what she would do."

Johnny put the folder back above the visor. "I can't believe we found her."

"She's looking right at us," said Tiny. "She's coming over."

"What could she want?"

"I don't know."

"Hey," said the woman. Tiny rolled down his window. "Hey, listen to me. You have to move your vehicle. There's a truck coming for the leaves. This is where the truck comes. You can't park here."

"Who do you work for?" said Tiny.

"Rudy Meyers," said the woman. "That's what I'm trying to tell you. In about two minutes he's going to be pulling in here to load his truck. That's why you have to move."

"You don't live in there?" said Johnny.

"God no, I don't live in there," said the woman. "That's the nut house. What do I look like, a nut?"

"Not at all," said Johnny.

"Do they have a Margaret Kane?" said Tiny.

"We don't know," said the woman. "We keep the yard nice. That's all we do. These are dangerous people, mister. If you want their names you have to go inside."

Johnny turned the truck around and parked across the street from the halfway house. The rakers began combining their leaf piles. Johnny stared at them. "You know, the more I think about this, the more I don't want to do it."

"I was just going to say the same thing," said Tiny.

"The woman has trouble enough."

"Let's get out of here."

"It's Dan Norman's fault. It's time to pull the plug."

"Channel 4 will be here any time."

"We did come all this way," said Johnny. "But we learned something. We learned that this was a bad idea. Dad is not going to be happy. That's inevitable. So be it."

Johnny jammed the gearshift down, backed up, and sped away. Leaving town, he and Tiny saw the television van in time to turn down a side street where they would not be found. They laughed, imagining Shannon Key's bewilderment, and got back on the highway. But the Bronco didn't have much gas, and Johnny had to stop after several miles and fill up. The tank was large, and there was a reserve tank, and by the time both were full the bill was forty-four dollars. This figure seemed to underscore the folly of their efforts and, discouraged, they rode twenty miles in silence and then stopped at a tavern. They drank Tuborgs and played bumper pool until they felt all right again. There were other ways of defeating Dan Norman. They forgot all about Quinn's mother.

She had, in fact, been at the halfway house. She watched the yard workers at about the same time Tiny and Johnny did. Standing at the window of her room, on the second floor, she looked down through the glass and bars, then went to her desk, opened a journal bound in blue paper, and began to write. The journal had been given to her by her doctors, along with a mirror and a doll. They wanted her to look at the doll and remember the baby. They felt that memory and tranquilizers were the way to health. But she did not want to remember, and she had no interest in dolls. She had put the one they gave her under her bed, in the center of the space beneath.

"I am always hungry these days," she wrote. "Promised food, we do not get enough. The yard people have been here since morning. They miss so many leaves it seems to make things worse instead of better. They sit on the sidewalk eating their lunch and I want their chips. I would like to go out and rake with them. They probably never took care of a place alone. They probably never had a house to themselves. Raking would be a way for me to make some money and buy a clock radio. I know I have mentioned this before but I really want one. There is something about me that waking up I want to see a clock and hear a radio. Without them it is hard to come out of a dream."

SIXTEEN

SHERIFF DAN NORMAN, in street clothes, painted campaign signs in his office on the Saturday night before the election. Some of his signs around the county had been knocked down or painted over, and therefore he needed new ones. The signs were nothing fancy. They said things like DAN NORMAN IS ALL RIGHT and VOTE EXPERIENCE VOTE DAN. The idea was simply to get his name out there.

As he was painting, a call came in from the Morrisville police. They had people out with the flu and required assistance at the strip club called the Basement. A man there was ranting and making trouble. Ed Aiken was on duty but was investigating a burglary in Lunenberg, so Dan decided to handle the call.

The Basement was on the west side of town, downstairs at the old Union Hotel. It is the law in Morrisville that strip joints must be underground, which makes it harder to see in. The Union Hotel was boarded up, but the Basement was not as rough a bar as it once was. Workers used to come down from the pin factory around the corner carrying straight pins and ready for trouble. There is still a bar magnet near the

297

front door, under the legend "Leave Pins Here," although the last true pin came off the assembly line in 1969.

Dan drove over to the hotel and went downstairs, showing his badge to avoid the cover charge. Irv London and Chris Doren of the Morrisville police already had the guy handcuffed. He wore blue jeans and a gray sweatshirt. His name was Sterling, and he was the sort sometimes found around strip shows—the drunk, sentimental tough guy who wants to rescue the dancer or reclaim her innocence for her, regardless of her feelings on the subject.

London and Doren were escorting Sterling from the bar when he twisted loose and began knocking over tables. Dan and the two officers surrounded Sterling and let him get it out of his system. "Barbara, don't let them take me," he yelled.

Outside, they frisked him for weapons. "Who is this Barbara?" said Irv London. "The sign says Pamela Ardent."

"That's a stage name," said Sterling. "Don't you know anything?"

"You're under arrest and have the right to remain silent," said Chris Doren.

"In fact, we wish you would remain silent," said Dan.

"I've cut my lip," said Sterling. "Wonderful. I'm bleeding."

Irv and Chris took Sterling off to jail and asked Dan if he would talk to the dancer. So Dan returned to the hot and smoky club, where the customers and bouncer were putting tables and chairs back. Pamela Ardent stood with one hand on her hip, punching songs into the jukebox.

Dan went to the bar and ordered a martini. Since Louise had gone north, he had developed an appreciation for the gin that she so admired. He stood with his back to the bar and surveyed the action. The house was not full, and as it was a long and narrow space, Dan was reminded of the cheap prints of the Last Supper that seemed to hang so often on the walls of houses in which there had been trouble. Fires, breakns, and beatings made up the dinner theater of the Disciples.

The Basement smelled like a museum of cigars, and on the ceiling there was a spotlight with a painted-glass disc that turned slowly, changing the light on the stage from red to blue to yellow.

The dancer was supple and bored, with brown hair cut short and curled behind her ears. She danced as if she'd had lessons a long time ago. She straddled a wooden chair turned backward, thrust a hip forward while tilting an imaginary hat over her eyes, and strode the stage with her thumbs hooked under her arms. She wore a tiny black outfit with glittery swirls.

Dan went back to see her after the show. Her dressing room doubled as a storeroom, and she sat surrounded by aluminum kegs, looking into a cracked mirror wired to the wall. She had dressed in corduroy jeans and a sweater, and was cleaning her face with round pads of gauze.

"Do you know that man?" said Dan.

"No, look, I'm from Florida," she said.

"Is your name by any chance Barbara?"

"My name is Marnie Rainville. I'm from Fort Myers, Florida. And I don't know what this guy's problem is, but he ain't nobody I know."

"Is there any reason somebody might call you Barbara?"

"Yeah, if they're crazy. Which I wouldn't rule out."

"I believe it," said Dan. "Do you have a license?"

She laughed. "You don't need a license to dance."

"A driver's license."

She sighed and began looking through her purse. "I've been doing this three years," she said. "All over the United States and Canada. I like the South a lot. I like the Midwest too, but I could do without the cold. Did you ever go home to a cold room? That I could live without, easy. Not that I'm looking for company. That's the last thing I need. I'm talking about the weather."

"What's Fort Myers like?" said Dan.

"What's it like?"

"Yeah."

"Oh, man. It's beautiful? It's warm? The sun shines every day? What else? The grocery stores are very clean, with aisles of beautiful fruit? Someday I'll go back in style and they'll all come out to greet me. That's the Fort Myers I know. Someday I'll return to the land of decent weather and get out of this godforsaken deep freeze at last."

"I hope your wish comes true," said Dan.

"Oh, it will, believe me."

They shook hands, and Dan left the bar and went back to the sheriff's office. He picked up the radio. "Morrisville, come in, Morrisville."

"Go ahead."

"Yeah, Dan Norman here. Will you tell Chris or Irv that I talked to the stripper at the Basement but she doesn't know the guy. Her name isn't Barbara or Pamela. It's Marnie."

"Marnie?"

"That's right," said Dan. "She's from Florida and she's going back home just as soon as she can."

"Maybe we should take up a collection."

"Why don't you do that."

"Ten-four."

300

He went back to painting his signs. It seemed as if in the short time he had been gone, someone had moved them. His mind wandered from the election frequently these days, and possibly he had just forgot where he left the signs. Then Mary Montrose and Hans Cook showed up.

"We're on our way home from the movies," said Mary.

"What did you see?" said Dan.

"The one where the fellow makes his children very small," said Mary.

"Well?" said Dan.

"Hans liked it. I was somewhat disappointed."

"It wasn't anything extraordinary—just a good yarn," said Hans.

"To me, once you knew they were small, there was no place for the movie to go," said Mary.

"What do you think of my signs?" said Dan.

"Pretty good," said Hans.

"They say Johnny White has a following," said Mary.

"Have you seen his commercials?" said Dan.

"How could you miss them?" said Hans. "They're saturating the airwaves."

"The people get the sheriff they want," said Dan. "That's why it's a democracy."

Mary sat on the bench, and Hans went in back and stood in a cell with his hands on the bars.

"I'm innocent, I tell you," he said.

"I wouldn't give a nickel for Johnny's crew," said Mary. "He was on the news the other night, talking about alcoholic this and alcoholic that. Why, he's no more alcoholic than the man in the moon. My uncle was an alcoholic, and believe me, I know what they are."

Dan dipped his brush in paint and paused with it halfway to the sign he was working on. "I tried to make that very point to the League of Women Voters. I'm not sure they understood me. And then he produced that DWI arrest from Cleveland in 1982. Well, that doesn't prove he's an alcoholic."

"Of course it doesn't," said Mary. "You've got to cut him down to size, just like this fellow did to his kids in the movie. If it were me, I would look him smack in the eye and say, 'Johnny, you're a goddamned phony.'"

"I did use some fairly strong language at the League of Women Voters," said Dan.

"I bet you didn't call him a goddamned phony."

"No, that's true," said Dan. "I am wary of dwelling on the alcoholism claim."

"I can see that," said Mary. "It's kind of a no-win situation."

"I'm going to talk to Claude Robeshaw," said Dan.

"He might know something," said Mary.

Then they were silent a moment and could hear Hans humming the song "Una Paloma Blanca."

"What do you hear from Louise?" said Dan.

"Not a lot," said Mary. "Carol says she's all right, but I don't know. My family—they should do a long-term study. This is really why I stopped, Dan. I think you should try going to get her."

"I have tried," said Dan.

"Well, try again," said Mary.

"I went up a couple weeks ago," said Dan. "I asked her to come back. I really pushed the issue. But she wasn't ready. Well, I guess you know she's delivering newspapers."

"Yes," said Mary.

"Evidently she supervises a number of younger carriers,"

said Dan. "One of them has come down with mono. So she wants to run this girl's route for her until she's better."

"Hell, Dan, mono can go on for months," said Mary.

"I know it."

"This is Carol's doing," said Mary. "I'm not saying the girl doesn't have mono. She may have mono. I'm no doctor. But you have to understand Carol. Carol is an enigma. Carol is a very lonely lady. She wanted children, but instead of having children she has sunk all her energy into this fishing camp."

"It's a pretty nice camp," said Dan.

"No one's denying that," said Mary.

The next morning was Sunday, and Dan went for a drive in Louise's Vega. It was clear and cold; there was frost on the windshield. Louise had always kept a cluttered car, and the floor and the bead-covered seats had tissue dispensers, paperback books, and beer bottles on them. It seemed to Dan that he had married her without knowing her, did not know her now, and might never know her, but that these things she had thrown off had some magical power over him.

There was a guy who always sold flowers on Sunday from a cart at the intersection of Highway 8 and Jack White Road. Dan almost never saw anyone buying flowers. There was hardly room to stop.

Dan bought a mix of flowers, violet and orange and white.

"I'll bet these are for that girl," said the man.

"Excuse me?" said Dan.

"She was with you last week. About this high."

"You're mistaken," said Dan.

"Sure she was."

He drove up to North Cemetery. Larkin Brothers of Romyla had set the gravestone late in the summer. Brian Larkin carved the inscription, which read:

IRIS LANE NORMAN
BY THIS MAY I
REMEMBERED BE
MAY 7, 1992

It was a small, flat stone of blue-gray slate, its surface about flush with the ground. Brian Larkin said this was how an infant's grave should be. It was a good stone, but because it was horizontal, the leaves and dirt that landed on it in the normal course of cemetery life tended to stay. Ants traveled the grooves of the letters. You would think rain would wash it clean, but sand floated onto the slate and remained in delicate whorls after the rain had evaporated.

Dan took the flowers from the car, along with a bucket and chamois cloth. There was an iron pump in the middle of the cemetery, and he pumped water into the bucket. Over at the grave he removed the flowers that he had left the week before and dipped the chamois in the water. He washed the stone and dried it with a red handkerchief and put the new flowers down. He took the old flowers to the iron fence bordering the cemetery and tossed all but one over the fence into the grassy ditch. The flower that he kept he threw into Louise's car with everything else. Then he went back and took a last look. Already a leaf had landed on the stone. The task was never-ending. He sat with his back to a tree and wondered if Iris had felt pain or perhaps only a fleeting sensation of something changing. He remembered her face as untroubled. Actually he was forgetting her face.

The nurses had given them Polaroid snapshots, but these did not do her justice.

Dan had Sunday dinner with Claude and Marietta Robeshaw. You can't miss the Robeshaw farm if you go from Grafton to Pinville. The barns are light blue and a porch wraps around the big white house. For years the place was known as the one with the "Impeach Reagan" banner on the machine shed, but with Reagan gone back to California, that had been put away. The house was plain and spare inside, except for mementos of JFK, whom Claude had met once in Waterloo. Among their collection, the Robeshaws had two dozen Kennedy dinner plates, an autographed copy of *Why England Slept,* and a rare tapestry of PT 109. Young Albert liked to tell his friends that Kennedy himself was in the attic.

Of the six Robeshaw children, Albert was the only one still at home. The rest were grown and moved away. On Sundays, combinations of them came home to eat. Today Rolfe, Julia, Nestor, and Susan had returned with spouses and children.

So the meal had to be big, and the cooking was done mostly by the women. The exception would be Nestor cooking the Swiss chard, but this is deceptive. Nestor liked cooking Swiss chard, and it was assumed that if he were to walk away from it for any reason, one of the women would have to take over before it burned. Nor would anyone ask Nestor to cook anything but the Swiss chard. In other words, his sisters, wife, and mother might be there cooking beside him but did not have his freedom to pick and choose. Let's take Susan, for example. She had been assigned the cooking of the yams. If she did not feel like cooking yams, too bad—she had to anyway. The bad part of this arrangement for the men was that they had nothing to do. They sat around listening to Vaughan Meader records and drinking Claude's Olympia. In the old days they would have been out threshing.

At the Robeshaw table the food and the eaters were opposing armies, and if you did not overeat, you were considered a traitor. Marietta reacted to the words "No, thank you" with a hurt and puzzled smile, as if you had cursed her in a foreign language. She also had rules for how and when things were to be passed, and nobody understood these rules, so they were constantly being broken.

Talk was fragmentary amid the pings and scrapes of cutlery. Nestor and Rolfe argued about hybrid grain.

"They have oats now that will grow on rocks."

"That's crazy talk."

Claude buttered some bread and said, "I've seen things I never would have expected. Take that deal they got out West."

"What deal is that, Papa?" said Julia.

"You know, that Biosphere," said Claude. "That big pillow in Arizona."

"A *pillow?*" said Susan, the vehement disbeliever.

"It's a sealed environment in which they are trying to evolve a new society," said Albert.

"What's wrong with the one we have?" said Marietta.

"It just never would have been done years ago," said Claude. "Nobody would have thought *to* do it."

"Did I hear that thing was leaking?" said Dan.

"Leaking?" said Susan. "Leaking what?"

"I don't know," said Dan. "Some gas."

Rolfe rolled a potato onto his plate. "Carbon monoxide," he said, so decisively that he was clearly guessing.

"Isn't that interesting?" said Helen, schoolteacher and wife of Rolfe. "Like car exhaust."

"That's right."

"Do they have cars?" asked Nina, who was married to Nestor.

"Yes," said Nestor.

"They're trying to make do without cars," said Claude. "That's the whole idea."

"They drive the same model Buick that we do," said Nestor. "The Skylark."

"This sure is good food, Mama," said Julia.

"Food tastes better off these forks than any other forks," said Nestor.

"Why is that?" said Julia.

"It's a toxin in the silver," said Albert.

After dinner Marietta and Helen did a mountain of dishes while Claude took a nap and the children played football on the grass. The game was two-hand touch, which everyone seemed clear enough about, but Rolfe tackled Dan hard, for no reason.

The wind was knocked out of Dan, and though Rolfe said he was sorry, the issue was not resolved. Later, when Dan passed the football so that it hit Rolfe in the forehead, the two had to be held back to keep them from fighting. Albert came to Dan's defense. "Knock Rolfe down," he said.

The game ended. Claude was up from his nap and standing on the front porch with his hands inside the bib of his overalls. He and Dan took a walk down the lane to hear the drying fans on some grain bins built over the summer.

"You're in trouble," said Claude.

"I know it," said Dan.

"The Whites have done more with TV than has ever been done in this county," said Claude. "I wouldn't be surprised if half the people think Johnny is already sheriff."

"I've run a good campaign," said Dan.

"You have, in a sense," said Claude.

"I can't control what people think," said Dan.

"You know, they talk about the old days and the smoky rooms where things got decided," said Claude. "And I'm not saying we weren't highhanded at times. But at some level we wanted to do good for the community. Why? Because our hearts were in the right place? Hell, no. Our hearts were in the same place as anybody's heart. But we needed people to be for us, and this was the only way we knew how. Nowadays the parties are worthless and everything is television. Claude Robeshaw doesn't mean a goddamned thing to Jack White."

"I think the western half of the county is mine," said Dan.

Claude took a cigar from the pocket of his jacket. "Can I ask you something? Where is Louise?"

"At her Aunt Carol's, in Minnesota."

"People wonder," said Claude. "They get ideas. They make assumptions."

"It's none of their business," said Dan.

Claude lit a cigar and smiled indulgently. "No, that's right. That's right. But still…"

"Even if she wanted to come back, I wouldn't put her in the campaign," said Dan. "People know who I am."

Claude blew a smoke ring and patted Dan on the back. He closed his eyes, sniffed the air. "Somebody's burning cobs," he said. They walked out into the evergreen grove, where parts of old machines lay rusting in the white grass.

Marnie Rainville called the sheriff's office late on the afternoon of election eve. Marnie said the guy who had interrupted her act was at that moment coming up the back stairs dragging a big suitcase.

"Where are you?" said Dan.

"Home," she said. "I don't go in until six-thirty. Typically I have an early supper and then do some yoga until showtime. I was putting the milk away when I saw him coming up to my building."

"Don't let him in," said Dan.

"Shall I pretend not to be home?" said Marnie.

"Yes, good idea," said Dan.

"I better shut off the radio."

"Do."

She did so, and came back to the phone. "I'm at Two Forty-six East River Street, apartment nine. Come down the alley between River and Railroad. I'm at the top of the stairs."

"Don't open the door," said Dan.

He barreled across town with siren and lights. He turned on the police radio, but instead of the emergency band got the local FM station. He had been meaning to get this radio looked at.

"Are you the type of person who never forgets a face?" said the announcer. "Do someone's features stay in your mind for months at a time? Or do they begin to fade after a matter of days? If the latter is true, scientists say, you are like the great majority of the rest of us. So why not order an attractive reminder of your loved one, in the form of a portrait photograph from Kleeborg's Portraits of Stone City."

Marnie Rainville lived by the railroad tracks in a building that Dan had not even known was residential. He ran up the

309

fire escape she had called the back stairs. He did not wish for the woman to be in danger, but a rescue might help his frame of mind. The door to apartment number nine was open and he ran in, only to find a man kneeling on a threadbare piece of carpet.

"It's all right, Sheriff," said Marnie. She sat on a chair in the corner of the room, surrounded by cardboard boxes. "I was wrong. I tried to call you. It's only a guy selling vacuum cleaners. I'm sorry to drag you out here, but I saw that big suitcase and I guess I got scared."

"You did the right thing," said Dan.

The man on the carpet looked at Dan over his shoulder. "You're welcome to join us," he said. "This is not, repeat not, a sales pitch. I love this cleaning system so much I have to show it off. I would imagine that a floor covering can really take a beating in law enforcement."

"Just say your piece," said Dan.

"Imagine never being troubled by dingy carpets again," said the salesman. "I have just emptied on Marnie's carpet a mixture of ashes and soot such as you might find on a chimney sweep's boots at the end of the day. Although come to think of it, you don't see many chimney sweeps anymore. I wonder why that is."

"I don't know," said Marnie.

"Because they still have chimneys."

"How much longer will this take," said Dan.

"But I think we can all agree that no ordinary vacuum cleaner can touch grime like this," said the salesman. He turned on the vacuum cleaner and made several passes over the rug. The machine roared and hissed and shot water everywhere. The soot and ash had left a shadow that would not come up.

"There," said the salesman.

"It's still there," said Marnie.

"For all intents and purposes it's gone," said the salesman. "I think any reasonable person would agree that no ordinary vacuum cleaner could come as close as this one has."

Dan ordered the guy to pack his case and go. "Are you all right?" he asked Marnie.

"Yes," she said. "If you have a minute, you could help me carry a few things down to the car. As you can probably tell, I'm moving on."

"Where you going?" said Dan.

"Home," she said.

"Florida?"

"I've never been to Florida," she said. "I didn't mean to lie to you. But when you get into your act, sometimes it's hard to keep straight who you are."

Dan carried some things down for her. After several trips he dropped a box of dishes at the base of the fire escape. He and Marnie stood on either side of the box, looking to see what was broken.

"I'm sorry," he said.

"It's all right."

They leaned toward one another but stopped just short of kissing.

Dan went back to the office. The shift ended. He turned the office over to Ed Aiken, gathered his signs, and put them in the back of the cruiser.

He drove around the county, pulling over every so often to pound in a sign. He liked to put them near points of interest— corncribs, bridges, trees, things you might glance at anyway.

The temperature had fallen steadily all day. The ground was freezing and the wind had come up. The cruiser shuddered on the high ground north of Mixerton.

Dan left a trail of signs in Lunenberg, Romyla, Chesley. He came to the crossroads from which he could either go west toward his house or south into Boris. The sun was nearly down. He had signs left, but wondered if they would last in Boris and Pringmar, which were not Dan Norman towns.

As he sat by the side of the road considering this question, he looked off across a field and saw a windmill, known as Melvin Heileman's windmill, although Melvin Heileman himself was dead. The windmill no longer pumped water, but the dark blades still turned in the wind.

Dan got out of the cruiser. He crossed the steep ditch and climbed over the barb-wire fence with a sledgehammer and sign saying DAN NORMAN DEMOCRAT. As he walked up toward the windmill, a gust of wind took the sign from his hands. He dropped the sledge and ran, but the sign sailed like a bird over the prairie. It went a long way and finally settled into a marsh, where Dan had to stop chasing it. He stood, out of breath, hands on his knees. Blue stars glittered in the sky, and he thought of his daughter in the cold ground. He spoke her name—Iris, Iris—but heard only the sound of wind.

SEVENTEEN

SIXTEEN THOUSAND people voted in the sheriff's race—a good turnout. The Republican candidate, Miles Hagen, who had run for sheriff in every election for twenty-eight years, took nine percent of the vote. In his concession speech he argued, as always, that the county tax levy was illegal under Articles I and VI of the United States Constitution.

The remaining votes were closely divided between Dan and the Independent, Johnny White. Dan beat Johnny by three hundred and thirty-seven votes in the machine totals. Johnny called for a recount, which took two days and reduced Dan's margin by a handful of votes. Still to be considered were the absentee ballots, which as a rule help the incumbent. Then there was a flurry of panic—the absentee ballots could not be found. They turned up eventually, in a shoebox in the recorder's office. They were counted, Johnny conceded, and Dan was declared the winner of a third term as county sheriff.

Tiny went to a hayride put on by the White family at Walleye Lake. It was a Friday night and cold as hell with the wind coming off the lake. This had been planned as a victory hayride and then changed to a farewell hayride. Walleye Lake always had its share of hayrides. One fall they were tried without hay, but there were many complaints.

The rides were to begin and end at the park across from Town Beach. When Tiny arrived there was already a small crowd, mostly people who relied on Johnny's father, Jack, in one way or another for financial help. Johnny stood by the bandshell stairs.

"I don't feel like going up," he said.

"Skip it, then," said Tiny.

"You don't think it's necessary?"

"If you don't want to go, why go?"

"Won't people expect it?"

"Who cares what they expect?" said Tiny. "You don't owe them anything. I'll say this, though—the longer you stand here, the more they will expect it."

"I really thought I was going to win. That's what bothers me. I thought I would be making another speech entirely. I even have it prepared. Here it is—three pages, single-spaced. I might as well make paper airplanes."

"That would be funny."

"Do you think I would have been a good sheriff?"

"Sure."

"I think I would have been a *real* good sheriff. And obviously, a lot of people agreed."

"Speak from the heart," said Tiny. "That's what you always told me."

Jack White walked across the park from the place by the road where his draft horses were hitched up and ready. "Let's go," he said.

"I don't know what to say," said Johnny.

"Get the hell up there."

314

"And say what?"

"Tell them about your back."

"Oh, Dad. I don't want to overstate the back business."

"There's got to be a reason," said Jack.

"What about your back?" said Tiny.

"See?" Johnny said. "Tiny didn't even notice."

"He hurt it the last week of the election," said Jack.

At that moment Lenore Wells approached the three men and said, "Can we get started? My feet are very cold. I have a circulation problem I've had all my life. My mother used to call me Little Whitefingers, and I don't know how much longer I can stand here. If Johnny is going to speak, then it seems to me he ought to get up there."

"He's having trouble with the stairs on account of his back," said Jack.

"What about his back?" said Lenore.

"Nothing about it," said Johnny.

"I don't know about Johnny's back, but I can tell you that my feet are turning into blocks of ice."

"I will introduce him," said Tiny. He went up the stairs and into the bandshell, through a forest of music stands and fallen leaves. "I remember when Johnny White first told me of his desire to run for sheriff," Tiny said to the crowd. "To be honest, my response was one of skepticism. I said, 'Are you kidding me?' And he lost. He did lose. But not by that much. And don't forget, we were trying to replace an incumbent sheriff with someone who had good ideas but, let's be honest, not a lot of law enforcement experience. This is no reason to hang our heads. Sure, we'd all rather be at a victory celebration, but for every winner there is a loser. So let's cheer up and give a warm hand on a cold night to John White."

Tiny stepped back, yielding the stage to Johnny. People clapped but in a hesitant or halfhearted way that underscored the common perception that Johnny had his chance and would never run a serious campaign again. Watching Johnny's narrow back in a green windbreaker, Tiny was seized by the perverse notion to push him off the edge of the stage.

Johnny told a story about hurting his back while playing with his children. He said the injury was a bit more serious than run-of-the-mill back injuries, and the chiropractor had warned him to go to bed for two weeks, but he had finished the campaign even though his back hurt every morning when he got up and every night when he went to bed. He said that nonetheless the campaign had been the best and most alive time of his life. Johnny thanked them all and said he loved them all.

Then he waved and everyone clapped again and jogged across the grass to where Jack had the draft horses Molly and Polly hitched to the haywagon. People had to wait in line, and wondered aloud why Jack had not brought two or three wagons so they could have their rides faster and get home to their warm houses. But there was only one wagon, and the horses would only go so fast. Tiny curled his fingers in his gloves and shifted from foot to foot. Steam rose from the broad backs of the horses, and through the steam Tiny could see the blue lights of the Lake House tavern up the street. He wished he were in there playing cards and drinking a big glass of brandy. Then he climbed aboard the wagon and sat down among a group of strangely festive people who sang Christmas carols, although Christmas was almost two months away and it was hard to see the connection between the little town of Bethlehem and Johnny's all but fraudulent campaign for the office of sheriff. Tiny glared at the happy carolers and lit a cigarette.

"Put that out," said a stocking-hatted man who had been leading the singing. "This is hay, for God's sake."

After the hayride was done, a few people went back to the Jack White farm northeast of Grafton. Tiny tagged along—it was a case of no one saying he couldn't. He had always wanted to be part of a small group that went somewhere following a larger event. There seemed to be a vague suggestion of sex in that. Tiny had never been in Jack's house. The layout was odd and not very handy. Appliances didn't seem situated for human use, and the kitchen, dining room, and living room met in an open space where everyone kept bumping into each other.

Tiny stood in a corner drinking and minding his own business but getting a general feeling of not being wanted. Johnny's exwife, Lisa, who was at the house with Megan and Stefan, kept scowling at him. Tiny was dressed nicely, but something was definitely bothering the woman. While talking to Johnny, she had pointed across the room at Tiny and then at the door and then made shoving motions with her hands, so it was pretty clear to Tiny what was going on.

Later, he made a margarita and brought it to her as a peace offering. "Have a drink," he said. "And by the way, that's a very nice dress you're wearing."

"I don't want a drink."

"It goes very well with your shoes."

"What?"

"The dress and the shoes."

"Who asked you?"

"It's a spontaneous comment."

317

"Johnny and I used to have a restaurant," Lisa said. "We had a restaurant in Cleveland, Ohio. And there would be people like you hanging around all the time."

"And they were your friends?"

"Oh, no. Far from it. They wanted us to close our restaurant. They were supposed to do whatever they could to get us out of the food business. They broke our windows. They bent our utensils. They set fire to our dumpster."

"I wouldn't break your windows," said Tiny.

"You might not break my windows. You might leave my windows alone because you get money from my ex-husband's father. But I heard one of your jobs in the campaign was to destroy Dan Norman's signs. Don't deny it. And I let Johnny know in no uncertain terms what I thought of that kind of thing. I asked him how he could ever, ever, ever put my kids in campaign events when at the same time he had hired people to go around destroying personal property like they did to us in Cleveland."

"And what did he say?"

"Oh, some excuse."

"A campaign sign is not the same thing as a window," Tiny said.

"I never should have come back here. I sure never should have let the kids come back. It was all a mistake. Give me that drink after all, you Cleveland son of a bitch."

Tiny gave her the drink and walked away. Jack White then asked him to come out to the stable. This was a warm and softly lit barn with shining bits and halters. Molly and Polly were blocking the corridor between the two rows of stalls. Their eyes were big as plates, their winter coats a shaggy white. Jack now went around tapping on their shins and cleaning their hooves with a metal pick. The horses breathed placidly.

"Would you please go up and throw down some straw?" said Jack quietly.

Tiny did so. When he came down he said, "I don't think Lisa cares for me."

"Ah, she's nuts," said Jack. "I wouldn't worry about her. Being married to Johnny was more than she could handle."

Tiny opened a jackknife and cut the twine on one of the bales. "Did you want to talk to me?"

"If you have a rock that is part of the pavement, and it keeps the road from wearing away, that rock is providing a use. But once it works loose from the pavement and wedges in a horse's hoof, it has to be pried out and discarded."

"The campaign is over," said Tiny.

"Right."

"Johnny said that no matter what happened in the campaign, I would still have a job in the Room."

"'Johnny said,'" said Jack. "If Johnny jumped off the Sears Tower, I suppose you would be the next in line."

"I have things I want to do."

"We all have things. What we're looking for now is people with training."

"I could get training."

"I mean people with training now, who can hit the ground running with training."

"What kind of training?"

"The kind they have in college."

"Johnny doesn't have training."

"Yes he does."

"Not from college."

"Johnny has some college."

Tiny distributed straw in the horses' stalls. "You owe me a check," he said.

"You didn't get that yet? Well, don't worry. Thanks for helping me with the bales. I think it's time for you to go home."

"I'm thinking."

"There's nothing to think about. It's not a situation that requires thought. I'm going in the house. You have to leave."

"Tell me something," Tiny said. "You like horses. Given the size of a draft horse, why don't they just stomp everything?"

"Man controls the oats."

"If I got training, could I get back in the Room?"

"If you got training, you would have the same chance as anyone else who had also got training."

"So fuck off is really what you're saying."

Jack put Molly in her stall and closed the door. "Yeah."

Tiny shook Jack's hand. Then he went out to the Parisienne and drove home. He was living these days with Joan Gower in a basement apartment at the Little Church of the Redeemer. At first Tiny and Joan had kept this arrangement a secret from Father Christiansen, but then Tiny climbed up on the roof of the church and patched the leak, and after that Father Christiansen agreed to look the other way. It's true that the patch would not last. In Tiny's uncertain life, one of the things he knew for sure was that the only true way to fix a roof is to reshingle the whole thing. There were already drips forming over the choir sometimes when it rained. But Tiny did not have much expectation of being around when the thing gave way for good.

It was late when Tiny got home, and not only was Joan awake but she was hard at work stripping the green paint from a chair. After reading an article on adoption, she had decided to adopt a child. Tiny was not sure of the details; if he understood right, a person from the state would be coming at some point to interview Joan about her intentions. But this visit had been postponed several times, and Joan seemed to be in a perpetual state of fixing up the apartment for this mythical state person who never arrived. She was scouring the chair with steel wool in the kitchen. A garbage can was in the center of the floor, filled with paint-sodden pads of steel wool. The smell of paint stripper was strong in the apartment. Tiny opened the refrigerator and took out a can of Old Milwaukee and sat down. "They have kicked me out of the Room," he said.

"What will you do?" said Joan.

"I don't know."

"In the past you would turn to stealing."

"Something to fall back on."

"Au contraire. I mean, just the opposite. You used to, but I don't think you will anymore."

"You go right on believing that."

"You seemed to be doing so well."

"They want somebody with training."

"You've been to the college of hard knocks."

"I tell you what, I think I'm still enrolled in that fucker," said Tiny. "I wonder if we should crack a window while you're doing this."

"Please watch your language."

"You may not be able to smell the paint stripper, but when you come in from outside it's very strong."

"I did have the door open awhile but it was too cold. I was going to make some supper but I got started doing this, and you know what? I'm not the least bit hungry."

"You're high as a bird. That's why."

Joan laughed and lifted a blond curl from her forehead. "I might be a little tuney."

"'Tuney'? What does that mean?"

"You know. Feeling it."

"You made that up."

"You never heard 'tuney' before? Where did you come from, the Outer Limits?"

Tiny drank some beer. "I hate to be the one to say this, Joan, but those adoption people are going to take one look around the church and they're going to say, 'This woman is in a cult.' "

She scrubbed the arm of the chair with steel wool. "You can't see the future."

"I mean, you *are* in a cult."

"Why are we tax exempt? If we're a cult, as you say we are. Hmm? Answer me that."

"I'm not an accountant. I don't know why you're tax exempt. I don't know that you are tax exempt. I don't have the training to know such things."

"This chair is going to look excellent."

"Oh, yeah, Joan," said Tiny. "They're going to love that chair so much they'll put a little kid right in it."

Joan looked under the sink until she found her white Bible. "Behold ye among the heathen," she read, "and regard, and wonder marvelously: for I will work a work in your days, which ye will not believe, though it be told you."

Tiny took the Bible from Joan.

"Hey," she said. "That's Habakkuk."

"You use this thing as a crutch," he said. "Any point of view can be found in here somewhere. Listen: 'The range of the

322

mountains is his pasture, and he searcheth after every green thing.'"

"That's beautiful," said Joan.

"But what does it prove?" said Tiny.

"It doesn't have anything to prove. It's the word of God."

"And you are drunk on paint stripper."

"Oh no, it's beautiful, Tiny. Please read it again."

Tiny took Jack White's remarks about training to heart. He went to the community college outside Stone City to sign up for a night course on drugs and how they work. The campus had been built in the sixties, under the egalitarian architectural theory that no building should be any better than any other building. Tiny had to wait in line behind two young women—a tall one in embroidered denim and another one with straight black hair—who were looking at the course catalogue.

"I'm thinking about Rock Poets," said the taller one.

"Who are they doing this semester?"

"Tom Petty and Wallace Stevens."

"What else?" said the girl with black hair.

"Well, there's psychology."

"You're good with people. You'd smoke that puppy."

"And there's Luddites."

"What's Luddites?"

"The Luddites were people in England who went around destroying textile looms."

"Why?"

"I don't know. But it sounds interesting, doesn't it?"

"Very interesting."

Eventually it was Tiny's turn. "You're sure this is the course you want?" said the registrar.

"Yep."

"This isn't the course to get you off drugs. That's a different course, held in another building. This course has science in it."

"What are you trying to say?" said Tiny.

"I'll also tell you that if you're taking this course to meet women, you can forget it," said the registrar. "People have ideas about night courses, but we don't run that kind of college."

The class met on Tuesday nights. The teacher was a doctor named Duncan. He came into the class pushing a slide projector. Two dozen people sat at small desks.

He introduced himself and began, writing on the chalkboard as he spoke. "Amphetamines belong to the chemical class of alkylamines. They have the formula $C_9H_{13}N$ and a molecular weight of 135.20 in the basic form. Most amphetamines are isomers of the fundamental structure. Another group created by rearranging this basic amphetamine is called amphetamine derivatives, and comprises a long list of chemical names beneficial to really no one but the pharmacologist. These drugs are primarily different from their predecessor in that the NH2 is turned back and bonded with the alpha carbon group, like so. It's kind of a neat trick …"

The doctor talked like this for a long time and Tiny found himself staring at the back of the young woman ahead of him. She had a very short haircut and there was something alluring and even moving about her bare neck. He wanted to touch the brushy dark hair behind her ears, and so he did.

She looked at him. "Stop it," she whispered.

Dr. Duncan turned off the lights and began a slide show. Tiny wondered what had made him touch the woman's hair.

He seemed to be getting more emotional. The other day, hearing "The Wreck of the Edmund Fitzgerald" on the radio, he had found himself anxious, as if he had relatives aboard the doomed ship.

Dr. Duncan clicked the slide carousel. A photograph of a hamster running inside a wheel came on the screen. "We also find increased arousal, increased motor activity, decreased appetite, and mood amelioration or happiness," said the doctor. "This happiness, however, is fragile. Heavy users can experience paranoia or even amphetamine psychosis." The picture changed to one of the Statue of Liberty. "How did that get in there?"

When the class had reached the halfway point Tiny began to seriously wonder what he was doing there. He knew the Whites would never hire him again. It was rumored, in fact, that Jack was breaking all ties with the Room. With no reasonable hope of employment Tiny had enrolled in the class more as a way of changing his luck. He was over forty now. Something had to give if he was going to make the mark he felt capable of making.

The lights came up. There was a break and everyone had coffee. Tiny tried to speak to the short-haired woman but she only smiled and slipped away. Then the class resumed.

"How do amphetamines work?" said Dr. Duncan. "Imagine a mighty kingdom that communicates by means of a special group of messengers. What if all those messengers lost their way at the same time? The kingdom would fall into disarray, wouldn't it. The messengers would wander from house to house, delivering the same news over and over like a zombie."

An elderly woman raised her hand. "I'm sorry—I don't follow that at all."

"O.K.," said the doctor. He held up a chart of the brain and tried again. A thick black line outlined the brain; the chart looked like the map of a prison. People took notes, rubbed their chins thoughtfully, and Tiny felt utterly alone. The woman with short hair had moved to another desk. He imagined her going home. She would drive a Trans Am to an apartment in a nice old building in Stone City. There would be a cat, a robe and slippers, record albums on a shelf. She might as well have lived on Mars.

There was a big fire that night. Tiny could see red light in the sky from Highway 8 between Chesley and Margo. He turned at Jack White's corner and followed the light south. It turned out that Delia and Ron Kessler's place was burning. Coming down the hill he could see the yellow flames with the North Pin River in the background. A number of spectators had already parked by the corncrib across the road from the Kesslers'. There were trucks and firefighters from Grafton, Wylie, and Pringmar, but fire showed in all the windows of the house, upstairs and down. Two sheds were also burning, and the family stood hypnotized between the swing set and the fire trucks. A cage full of chickens rested on the ground. The chickens were quiet, and reflections of fire danced in their eyes. Three windows shattered as Tiny walked behind the Kesslers, and then Tiny heard a faint and strange melody. Ron Kessler was singing: "If that mockingbird don't sing, Papa's going to buy you a diamond ring. And if that diamond ring gets broke, Papa's going to buy you a billy goat ..."

Dan Norman and Fire Chief Howard LaMott of Grafton stood together in black rubber coats with yellow bands on the sleeves, looking into the fire, faces dirty with smoke.

"What happened?" said Tiny.

"We don't know," said Howard LaMott.

"Did they all get out?"

"We think so."

"Good evening, Sheriff," said Tiny.

"Howard, what about spraying water on the machine shed?" said Dan. "The house is a loss. Let's save what we can. Don't you think?"

"I agree," said Howard LaMott.

"I'm sorry, Tiny," said Dan. "What did you say?"

"Just good evening."

"Oh. Good evening."

"How is Louise?"

"She's all right."

"I was sorry to hear about her troubles. Joan and I sent some flowers."

"I know."

"Can I help in some way?" said Tiny.

"No," said Dan.

Tiny walked away from the burning house. It seemed that something in his mind was also burning. When he got home, Joan was lying on her side in the bed with her face turned from the light. She was crying.

"What's wrong?" said Tiny.

"The adoption guy came."

"What'd he say?"

"He didn't even come in. He gave me some papers to fill out but he wouldn't come into the apartment, and he said that even if it worked out, it would be nine years before I could get a baby."

"That's what he said? Nine years?"

"If it worked out."

"In nine years you might change your mind."

"I worked so hard and he wouldn't come inside."

"Maybe he said five years."

"I said please come in. I said have a cup of coffee. He said it didn't matter at this point."

"Did he say anything at all about the church?"

"He said it was an odd place to live."

"Fuck him, what does he know."

Joan turned onto her back and reached for Tiny's hand. "They don't make it easy on people who live in odd places, do they, Charles?"

"No, Joanie, not really, they don't," said Tiny.

Then Tiny left the bedroom. He went out to the kitchen to sit in the chair that Joan had stripped to plain wood. He sat there and drank until he fell asleep, and while he slept he dreamed of the fire in the windows of the Kesslers' house. When he woke up it was nearly morning, and the light was on the windows of the church.

EIGHTEEN

IN MINNESOTA that winter Louise slept with a pair of knee socks under her pillow, and when she woke she pulled the socks on and got out of bed. She sat at an oak trestle table drinking coffee and listening to the wind that roared around the cabin.

She set her clock radio to begin playing at four in the morning. "Brandy (You're a Fine Girl)" would come on, or "Knock on Wood," or "The Long and Winding Road."

Getting dressed took a while. There were many layers, and with each one her motions became more cumbersome. She had always loved winter clothes. She loved boot socks, quilted underwear, cracked-leather mittens with fleece cuffs. They were dear to her, lifesavers.

She downed the last of her coffee with mittens on and went outside. The season lay like an ocean over everything. Branches snapped and cabins groaned. The Nova, kept in a quonset hut, always started—sometimes she had to open the hood first, take off the air filter, and spray ether into the carburetor.

She did Carol's motor route and then went into town to deliver the papers of the girl who had mononucleosis. The windows were dark, the streets icy and hard. The north wind gusted over pools of street light. She might have been delivering newspapers to houses that had stood empty for a hundred years.

The rural people mailed their subscription fees to the newspaper, but in town you had to collect. Louise went door to door with a green zippered bag for the money. Some people would ask, "When is Alice coming back?" as if Louise had done something to her. Or they would get out the ticket she had given them the previous week, to make sure they weren't being cheated. It occurred to Louise that people in your own area generally seem friendly, and people in other regions of the country do too; but that people in neighboring states seem cold and cruel.

The girl with mononucleosis was named Alice Mattie. After collecting, Louise took the money to her house. The Matties lived in a small house near a river, and their yard was like an ice-skating rink. Alice's father worked for the highway department and her mother had a bad back, a very bad back. She usually lay in a lawn chair in the middle of the kitchen. She had a small face and would crane her neck to see what was going on. Alice was a thirteenyear-old with shimmering red hair. She was always playing Nintendo, and tried to get Louise to play, but Louise could not get to the higher levels.

One day, not long before Christmas, Alice gave her a present. Louise unwrapped the package and found an Advent calendar.

"You open a different door every day," explained Mrs. Mattie from her lawn chair.

"I can't wait to try it," said Louise.

That night after supper Louise and Kenneth played backgammon in the kitchen of the main house. Kenneth talked to the dice. "Come on, six and three," he would say. Louise did not know whether to hang back or hightail it out of Kenneth's inner table. As she played, she ate Cheetos and absently wiped her fingers on the shoulders of her sweatshirt. Before she knew it, all the Cheetos were gone and Kenneth had only had a handful. She said good night to Kenneth and Carol and trudged up the hill to her own cabin. After taking her coat off and building a fire she went into the bathroom, and in the mirror saw the streaks of orange dust on her sweatshirt.

"What has become of me?" she said.

She turned the water on in the bathtub and sat on the toilet lid while steam climbed to the ceiling. She smoked a cigarette delicately, flicking ash into the sink. When the tub had filled, she undressed and got in. "Ahhh," she said. She had slipped on the ice at the Matties' and bruised her hip. After her bath she sat staring into the fire and drying her hair. Then she lay on the bed and looked at the Advent calendar. It was a manger scene. Mary had a ball of light behind her head, and the Wise Men looked impatient, as if they had somewhere else to go. She held the calendar in her right hand and slowly flexed her wrist several times. Then she threw the calendar across the room and into the fire, where it gave off a green light as it burned. She screened the fire and went to bed.

Ice fishing and hunting kept the camp going in the winter months. Louise would go up to the top of the hill and see the huts that dotted the lake. She could not understand why anyone who was not seriously hungry would ice fish. The men went into their freezing little booths at dawn and came out in midafternoon. Some of them drank a lot; Louise cleaned their cabins and had to carry the bottles out. The ice fishermen were not as sociable as the hunters, who had parties and laughed loudly deep into the night. When Louise lay awake listening to the faint sound of laughter through the frozen trees, she knew a hunter was out there.

She had developed a strange habit that often disturbed her sleep. She would wind up with her wrists crossed beneath her chest, sleeping like Dracula, only on her stomach. This position cut off her circulation so effectively that she would wake with a start, certain that some kind of stroke had rendered her hands forever useless. It took a good five minutes for feeling to return to the point where she could turn on a light or push herself up in bed, so she would lie on her back, panting and staring at her hands.

Johnny White showed up just before Christmas for a week of ice fishing. He seemed totally surprised to see her. Carol and Kenneth said that Johnny had been coming up here for years, first as a child with Jack and then on his own. He had an elaborate ice-fishing shack with a generator, a refrigerator, and a kerosene heater. Louise and Carol and Kenneth helped him drag the shack across the ice on a blustery crystalline morning when the temperature was about eleven degrees. One day Johnny showed Louise the ropes of ice fishing. It still seemed boring. They had some brandy, and Louise laughed at his campaign stories, and then Johnny asked her, "What are you doing up here?"

"People think Grafton is all there is," said Louise. "It's not. You can leave Grafton for a few months without the world ending."

"You ought to go home," said Johnny.

Louise had made small mistakes in her pregnancy, but she did not believe that these mistakes had killed the baby, or that because of them she deserved to lose the baby. It was surprising the number of people who seemed to think it would be a comfort to Louise to hear that if she had taken some simple step they had read in a magazine, she would have a living child today. People did not want to think that anything was precarious. Birth was supposed to be a given. Advertisements for baby toys and food and clothes kept coming in the mail after Iris died. The companies must have known that some of the promotions would reach people who had lost children. Tough, must have been their attitude.

There was a house on Alice's route Louise could rest in. It was a big house with an enclosed porch where Louise would sit reading the front page of the newspaper. The paper seemed to specialize in explosions around the globe and odd stories about animals. So one day Louise was reading about a hawk in Florida who had flown off with a man's portable telephone and figured out how to push the automatic redial button. The man's mother was getting a lot of hangups in the middle of the night. "It's a unique situation and we're not happy," said a spokesman. While Louise read this, the front door came slightly open. She stood and, feeling the heat from inside, entered the kitchen. She removed her wool hat and mittens and pushed back her hair. There was a stairway leading from the kitchen, and she went up. She opened one door and then another until she found a man and a woman asleep in their bed. The air was humid. Someone was snoring. A humidifier bubbled and steamed. Louise rested her hand on a dresser beside the door and found it slick with water. The woman rolled over and flopped her arm around the man. Louise decided the humidifier must be broken to put out this much water.

The following Saturday, while collecting, Louise found the couple home and sitting in their kitchen. She laughed out loud when she thought of asking if they'd got their humidifier fixed.

"What's funny?" said the man.

"Nothing."

"When is Alice coming back?"

"Soon, I hope."

Later that day Louise dropped the collection at the Matties', and Alice asked her to watch television. They sat cross-legged on the carpeted floor of Alice's room with cream sodas. The show that Alice wanted to see was not on. Instead an announcer said, "We interrupt our regularly scheduled program in order to bring you a holiday concert of the Applefield High School Chorus, under the direction of Warren Monson."

The students came on right away, clearing their throats and straightening full-length robes of red and white. Louise and Alice could hear the baton of Warren Monson tapping a music stand.

"Do you know these kids?" said Louise.

"They're older than me," said Alice.

The girls' voices were clear and strong, and the boys carried the bass and baritone parts earnestly, like lumber that had to be stacked. Together the voices seemed unbearably beautiful to Louise, and during "O Come, O Come, Emmanuel," she began to cry. She leaned forward until her forehead and arms touched the carpet. God knows what Alice thought. But she said, "It's all right, Louise. Don't be upset. Oh, dear."

Alice resumed her paper route on New Year's Eve. Mrs. Mattie drove her around, wearing a back brace. Louise went along to see how they did.

Carol and Kenneth were going to a party that night, and Louise would be heading south in the Nova. She was going to catch a bus in Hollister and leave the car at the depot for the Kennedys to pick up on New Year's Day.

She sat in a wicker chair in Carol's bedroom while Carol tried on dresses for the party. Louise told her which ones she liked and didn't like.

"I want to thank you for all your help around here these past months," said Carol. "We are going to miss you so much."

"I'll be lost without my newspapers," said Louise.

"I can't believe it's New Year's."

"Me neither."

"Where does the time go?"

"Away."

"Did you call Dan?"

"No."

"You should."

"I got him a shirt with horses on it."

"Those are nice."

"He won't like it."

"Don't be surprised if things seem strange at first."

"Probably."

"Come July it will have been twenty-seven years we've run the camp," said Carol. "And right after it opened I had a guy come up to me. 'Carol,' he said, 'you know the trail from the cabins down to the water?' And I said, 'Yeah, I know it,' and he said, 'Why didn't you cut it straighter? It meanders, Carol.' See, he was an engineer, and everywhere he looked, he saw the straight lines that people could have made but failed to. And I said, 'I thought that was straight,' and he said, 'Well, it isn't.' And I said, 'You get your own camp and you can make the trails any way you want.' "

Louise laughed. "You didn't really think that trail was straight."

"It used to be straighter than it is now," said Carol.

Louise went back to the cabin for a last look around. The Nova was packed and running. She got in and drove to

Hollister. It took about forty-five minutes. She parked the car and carried her things into the bus depot, where an old man was sweeping up. She sat expectantly on a wooden bench, but the place was empty except for the custodian.

"Where you going, Miss?" he said.

"Stone City," she said. "There is a bus at six-twenty."

"Not on New Year's Eve, Miss," said the man with the broom. "There are no buses on New Year's Eve except the Prairieliner to Manitoba, which left at four-thirty."

"Oh, fuck, you've got to be kidding," said Louise. "They said there was a bus."

"There was—the Prairieliner."

Louise kicked her bag in despair. "When does one leave for Stone City?"

"Tomorrow morning at nine thirty-three," said the man. "And I'm sorry, but you can't stay here overnight. I'm sweeping up, and when I'm done I'm going to lock the doors."

Louise picked up her shoulder bag and the box with Dan's shirt in it and went out the door. The town square in Hollister was empty in the dying light except for some kids who were climbing a statue of a Greek goddess with wings and large breasts. As Louise watched, they put a party hat on her head and a cigarette in her mouth. Then the boys dropped expertly to the ground and scattered as a police car roared into the square with blue lights glinting off the darkened windows of the town. It took a moment before it registered with Louise that the side of the police car said "Grouse County." And then she had the crazy misfiring thought that this was a coincidence—that Dan or one of the deputies had come all this way chasing a criminal or tracking a clue. And by that time Dan was out of the car. He hugged her, lifted her off her feet. "Let me take you home," he said.

NINETEEN

AND so they went back home where, one day in January, Albert Robeshaw and Armageddon held a practice on the stage of the high school lunchroom in Morrisville. They were playing a song about snowmobiling called "(Look Out for the) Clothesline." Albert banged out a series of minor chords on the guitar and stopped abruptly when the foreign-exchange man Marty Driver walked up and rapped on the stage.

Everything about Marty Driver was unacceptable in a young person's eyes. He walked unacceptably, made unacceptable facial expressions, wore unacceptable clothes. He was that kind of adult, from Kansas City. On this empty midwinter afternoon he wore a tentlike down coat and an absurd furry hat.

"I am looking for Miss Lu Chiang," said Marty.

"There's a rabbit on your head," said Albert.

"Am I supposed to laugh?" said Marty.

"I wouldn't," said Albert.

"Nobody likes ridicule," said Dane Marquardt.

"Especially when it's aimed at them," said Errol Thomas.

"You could try pretending to be surprised," said Albert.

"You know, take the hat off and go, 'Jesus Christ! It *is* a rabbit!' and try to win our confidence by being a good sport."

"Not that it would work," said Dane.

"It would be too, oh, what word do I want?" said Errol.

"Pathetic," said Dane.

"That is the word I want."

"What about Miss Lu Chiang?" said Albert.

"He's her boyfriend," said Errol. "Whatever you have to tell her, you can tell him."

"Oh, I can?" said Marty.

"Are you going to send her home?" said Albert. "Because she doesn't want to go."

"Are you Albert Robeshaw?" said Marty.

"As a matter of fact, I am," said Albert.

Marty opened his briefcase and took out a copy of the school newspaper. "You're quoted in this article, 'Love Rebel Chiang Questions Authority.'"

"That's full of inaccuracies," said Albert. "And we didn't know it was on the record."

"Just tell me where to find her," said Marty.

"We're not foreign students," said Dane. "You don't have any power over us."

Marty Driver took his down coat off and left the lunchroom, but soon came back with the principal, Lou Steenhard, who moved quickly in his V-neck sweater and string tie. Albert, Errol, and Dane sensed that Marty Driver posed some kind of threat to Mr. Steenhard.

"You boys will have to leave," said the principal. "There's going to be a meeting in here."

"Where are we supposed to go?" said Dane.

"I don't give a damn," said the principal.

"The last time we tried to go in the gym, they said we couldn't," said Errol.

"That's right, because of the trampoline," said the principal.

"Chiang doesn't want to leave," said Albert.

"Shut up," said the principal.

Actually Chiang had no choice. She had been an exchange student for two years now and had applied for more time. This had been denied. Marty had her plane tickets in his pocket.

Armageddon cleared out of the lunchroom, and soon Chiang and her host family, the Kesslers, joined Marty and Lou Steenhard at a table underneath a sign saying, TAKE ALL YOU WANT BUT EAT ALL YOU TAKE.

The Kesslers—Ron, Delia, Candy, Randy, and Alfie—sat smiling at Chiang. Since their house had burned down they were living with Delia's mother in Wylie. It was crowded, and the summoning home of Chiang was fortunate in that sense. The relationship between the exchange student and her hosts had been a prickly one. At first Chiang had felt the family was cynically using her as a workhorse. Later, she grew used to caring for the chickens and saw the henhouse as her own province.

Now the Taiwanese girl stood at the head of the table in a tan skirt and red sweater, pretty and composed. If she felt as resistant to leaving as Albert had said, she did not show it.

"To the Kesslers I offer my gratitude and my sincere hope that the rebuilding goes quickly," she said.

"We'll be all right, babe," said Delia. There were tears in her eyes. The onset of goodbyes can paper over so many differences. She gave Chiang a T-shirt that said, "Corn & Beans & Rock & Roll."

In return, Chiang gave the Kesslers a portrait that she had painted of the chickens. Ron accepted the painting. He wore

339

the standard uniform of the farmer: baseball cap with seed logo, tight long-sleeved button shirt, blue jeans low on the hips.

"This can go by the piano," he said.

Lou Steenhard stood and shook Ron Kessler's hand for no particular reason. He cited Chiang's accomplishments in scholarship, music, and basketball. The Morrisville-Wylie Lady Plowmen had won the Class AA sectionals with Chiang in the forward court. It is possible that this played a part in her unusually long tenure.

"We will miss Chiang," said the principal. "She was active in Year Book, Glee Club, and Future Farmers of America. She was part of Mrs. Thorsen's science class, which studied the eclipse of the sun. I want to read a brief passage from her report on this phenomenon, in which she quotes a Chinese philosopher named Hsün-tzu. This is kind of out of the blue, but I want to give you a sense of the young lady. 'When stars fall or trees make a noise, all people in the state are afraid and ask, "Why?" I reply: There is no need to ask why. These are changes of heaven and earth, the transformation of yin and yang, and rare occurrences. It is all right to marvel at them, but wrong to fear them. For there has been no age that has not had the experience of eclipses of the sun and moon, unreasonable rain or wind, or occasional appearance of strange stars.'"

The principal then went to the doors of the lunchroom and signaled in the cheerleaders, who wore the blue and gold colors of the school.

That night Albert and Dane heard through the grapevine that Marty Driver was staying at the Holiday Inn in Morrisville. They went over, found a car with Missouri plates, and bent the antenna into the shape of the numeral four. That was for the number of people in Armageddon when Chiang had sat in, as she sometimes had. But the gesture seemed empty and even a bit mean, and they left unsatisfied.

Albert Robeshaw seemed to lose motivation daily now that Chiang was leaving for certain. He gazed at the *Fur-Fish-Game* magazines that in his youth had promised a bracing and enjoyable world, but he could not retrieve that confident feeling. He lay crossways on his bed, feet on the wall, dipping snuff and listening to Joe Cocker records. When one record ended he would get up, spit tobacco into a 7-Up can, and put on another. His aging parents learned the words to "The Moon's a Harsh Mistress" by heart. Marietta said that hearing Joe Cocker sing made her depressed.

One night she called up the stairs. "Come down, Albert. Turn that noise off and come down. Your father wants to talk to you."

Claude was in the kitchen fiddling with their old ice cream maker—a wooden-slatted bucket with a crank on top.

"Goddarned thing doesn't want to work," he said.

"Did you ask to see me?" said Albert.

"I did." They sat at the table. Albert had the album cover for *Mad Dogs and Englishmen.* "What the hell's your problem," said Claude.

"Nothing."

"Don't give me that."

"Why? Because I listen to music? I happen to like music."

"I like boxing, but I wouldn't want to see two people boxing in my bedroom for four and five hours at a time."

"Good analogy."

"Why don't you join Mother and me in the family room?" said Claude. "The *Mod Squad* reruns are about on. I was going to make ice cream if I can get this thing to work."

Marietta took Albert's hand. "Don't you want to see Line, honey? Don't you want to see Julie? And that other guy."

"I've seen all the episodes," said Albert.

"Chiang is a peach," said Claude. "Your mother and I know that. But she's not the only one in the orchard."

"I don't buy that whole philosophy," said Albert. "It seems so morally empty."

"You feel that way today," said Marietta. "Tomorrow is another day."

"I will tomorrow, too."

"The next day, then," said Claude.

"No day."

"What are you supposed to say to a kid like this," said Claude.

"Tell him about the time we made paper mâché," said Marietta.

"You can tell it as well as I can."

"I don't remember it."

"I'm going upstairs," said Albert.

"You don't want any ice cream?" said Claude.

Albert sighed and studied the picture of backup singer Rita Coolidge on the album cover. Her hair sat on her head like a halo. He felt that the hippie era must have been intriguing. "I want to go to Taiwan," he said.

"You can forget that," said Claude.

"No, I can't."

"Honey, you don't know anything about Taiwan," said Marietta.

"I know the language."

"The hell if you do," said Claude.

So he spoke Chinese, and Marietta and Claude looked at him as if birds had landed on their ears.

"That means, 'I like you, let's have more cold beer.'"

"We're losing our boy," said Marietta.

"We are not," said Claude. "Listen, how far do you think he'll get on remarks like that?"

"Chiang's uncle can get me a job in a bicycle factory."

"You haven't been talking to her family," said Claude.

"Why not?"

"Oh, my God," said Claude.

"What?"

"If we decide to send you to Taiwan, we don't need help from anyone."

"Does that mean I can go?"

"No."

"You take help from the government. You participate in crop set-aside."

Claude glared at Albert, got up, slammed the top on the ice cream bucket. "Do you have any idea what your grandfather would have done to me for talking the way you do?"

"Smacked you around," said Albert glumly.

"That's right. And when he smacked you around, you knew you had been smacked."

"Didn't you kind of dislike him? Deep down."

"I respected him."

"Well, I guess. In a sense. Like you would a scorpion."

"You are going to the University of Iowa," said Claude. "Just like Rolfe did, just like Julia did, just like Albert did."

"I am Albert."

"What did I say?"

"Albert."

"You know who I mean."

"You mean Nestor," said Albert. "Susan didn't go to college."

"Susan was pregnant."

"Really?"

"Well, she had the baby. They generally go hand in hand, for Christ's sake. Do they teach you anything in that school?"

"We learned what an oligarchy is and how it differs from a plutocracy."

"And how is that?" said Marietta.

"Oh, I don't know," said Albert.

They sat quietly for a while. Claude ground the crank on the bleached green bucket.

"Can I have the car Friday night?" said Albert.

"What's Friday?" said Claude.

"The last time I can take Chiang out on a date."

"I don't see why not," said Claude. He checked the progress of the ice cream. "Well, hell," he said. "Marietta, look at this."

"What?" She walked over and looked.

"There's rust all in here. There's rust in my ice cream."

"That isn't right," she said.

Albert walked upstairs and closed the door. He put the needle of his record player on the song "Space Captain."

> *Once while traveling across the sky*
> *This lovely planet caught my eye*
> *Being curious I flew close by*
> *And now I'm caught here 'til I die*

344

Claude banged on the ceiling. Albert sighed, shut off the music, circled the room, opened a tall green paperback called *Cold Mountain,* by the poet Han Shan.

> *Above the blossoms sing the orioles:*
> *Kuan kuan, their clear notes.*
> *The girl with a face like jade*
> *Strums to them on her lute.*
> *Never does she tire of playing—*
> *Youth is the time for tender thoughts.*
> *When the flowers scatter and the birds fly off*
> *Her tears will fall in the spring wind.*

Albert went to see Ned Kuhlers, the well-known Stone City lawyer, and got a speeding ticket on the way, up north of Walleye Lake. Kuhlers's office was on the seventh floor of a building next to the park. Albert went up and entered the office. On the wall were diplomas and a flier for a martial arts class that the lawyer taught.

Albert had to wait a long time, and moreover, he did not get a sense of anyone else occupying Ned Kuhlers's time as he waited. The office was overheated. Beads of sweat appeared on Albert's face. A woman in a yellow suit went in and came out some time later, crying into a red handkerchief. Albert was then called in to explain his problem.

"Here is this girl everyone likes, and suddenly they want to ship her back to Taiwan when she herself doesn't want to go," he said.

"Uh-huh," said Kuhlers. He was looking out the window and perhaps not listening at all. "My God. There's a guy down here with the biggest dog I've ever seen."

"It could be a case with a lot of publicity," said Albert.

"God, what is that? A malamute? Malamutes are supposed to be big. I don't know what this is, but it sure is big. It's as big as a horse."

"If you looked into it, I'll bet you would find that Marty Driver has done things very sloppily."

"Just out of curiosity, is the girl mainland Chinese?"

"She's from Taiwan."

"Mmm," said Ned. He cracked his knuckles and shook his head. "You know what I think, Albert? I think you should go with the prevailing opinion. I don't pretend to be an expert in international law. Never have. But I'll bet you a hundred bucks that if this Monte from Kansas City—"

"Marty."

"—that if this Marty guy, whoever, wants to send her home, he can do it. It sounds like what we call an open-and-shut case. And you know what I mean by that, don't you? I open my mouth and the judge tells me to shut up."

"You don't think there's a case."

"I think you got a case of the blues," said Ned Kuhlers. "Let me tell you a little story. My first girl was so good to me. I just loved her. You know, I hadn't ever been laid, and she walked me through it. Patient, sweet, you name it. She said baby, don't worry about nothing. I still love her. But one night she called me up and said, you know, she really wants to come over. And I told her I don't want no company tonight. I don't know what got into me. Imp of the perverse, I guess. Maureen was her name. I tried calling her again but she wouldn't have it. You can't blame her. That was how many years ago. Thirty, forty years, whatever it is. I still think about her."

Albert was looking at his speeding ticket. The cop had mistakenly written in Albert's date of birth as the date of the infraction. Albert showed Ned.

"I couldn't have broken the law on this day. I was in the hospital being born," said Albert. "They can't make me pay this."

But Ned disappointed Albert once again, saying that in the case of a clerical error, the police could in fact rewrite the ticket at any time. "In other words, pay the two dollars."

"It's sixty dollars," said Albert.

"Pay."

It rained on Friday. There had been a forecast of snow for several days, but by this time no one was taking it very seriously. People's guards were down. It seemed as if winter was going to rain its way into spring.

Albert did his chores around sundown. He had to feed the hogs and check the watering systems at three locations. He came home, showered, and shaved. He dressed in thin blue pants, a white shirt, and gray jacket. In the kitchen he almost fell over the new electric ice cream maker that Claude had bought. The freezer was full of ice cream and still the thing was humming away.

He picked up Chiang and they drove out on the dirt road that connected Wylie and Boris. Here they had hidden a cooler in the ditch. Albert ran to it with an umbrella over his head and got a bottle of Boone's Farm. They sipped wine as they drove up to Chesley, listening to the radio.

They had the Friday night shrimp at a supper club called the Lifetime. Ruby Jones tended bar there. She was a cousin of the nurse Barbara Jones and known for carding infrequently. She was very popular with underage drinkers.

Yet the Lifetime had a quiet and almost elegant atmosphere. There were not many fights, and even when there were, the tactics were gentlemanly and afterward the participants would say, "What were we fighting about? We weren't even fighting." It's hard to say how places acquire the feeling found within them. Ten years before, Lifetime and Rack-O's, which is outside Romyla, had been on more or less of an even footing. They were both close enough to Stone City to draw upon its sizable population, but far enough away to be regarded as country places. So explain how Lifetime became genteel while Rack-O's deteriorated into a haven for dopers.

There is no answer. It's just interesting.

Lifetime had indirect yellow lighting, red Naugahyde booths, and blue-green felt tables for billiards and cards. When young people came here, they imagined hopefully that this was the environment in which adulthood was conducted. There was a jukebox with a thick and buzzing sound, full of Al Green records. Albert and Chiang played these songs, knowing they could not stay together.

"We could get a loft in Morrisville and I could work at the pin factory," said Albert.

"Are there such places in Morrisville?" said Chiang.

"There are abandoned factories, that's for sure. It would just be a thing of finding one with an apartment."

"You have to continue your schooling."

"Why?"

"Because you are smart."

"Sometimes I don't feel very smart."

"Would we still be allowed in school if we lived together?"

"You can if you're pregnant. Ravae Ross proved that beyond a shadow of doubt."

"I'm not pregnant."

"If you were, they wouldn't split us up."

"Albert, the foreign-exchange people answer to no one."

"On the other hand, working in the pin factory could be very boring."

"Come to Taiwan," said Chiang. "I want to show you my room. I want to show you my bed. I want to show you the path I walked to my old school."

"And I want to see them," said Albert. "I know I could build bicycles. I made a lamp in shop once. There were little strips of metal on it. It's not the same as a bicycle, but still, I would probably do pretty well."

"If my uncle can do it, you can, easily," said Chiang.

There was a dance floor with sawdust, and they walked out onto it and moved to the music. She seemed light and strong in his hands. Even during the fast songs they did not let go of each other.

Later, they got involved in a card game. The game was a local variation of poker called Russ Tried Screaming. No one knows how the game got this name, although there are some speculative guesses. The deal moved to the left, and the dealer called the game. In a low game you didn't want anything you normally wanted.

Chiang was the only female playing but so skillful with cards that she quickly won the respect and courtesy of the gamblers. You could tell they were going out of their way to avoid certain words that came naturally to them. One of the gamblers was a man called Mr. Steak because, it was said, you could always win enough money from him to buy a steak dinner.

Meanwhile, the rain was turning to snow. When Albert and Chiang left, Albert having won nine dollars and Chiang twentythree dollars, the snow was falling in heavy feathers that caught in their eyelashes.

"Look," said Albert. It was the sort of snow that appears to fall from an especially great height.

"This is the snow of goodbye," said Chiang.

In retrospect, they should have stayed in Chesley. Someone would have taken them in. Thousands of people wound up stranded that night. But the center of Chesley at this moment was sheltered from the wind. And for this reason Albert and Chiang did not know what they were getting into.

They left Chesley in Claude's station wagon. By the time they reached Melvin Heileman's corner, visibility was so poor they could not see the windmill. The wind had combined with the ragged snow to produce a blinding curtain on all sides.

Albert turned west onto the gravel road leading to Grafton. Some would ask later why they had not gone back to Chesley. They had been drinking and maybe their judgment was not the best; also, it was only eight or nine miles from where they were to the Robeshaw farm. Anyone who has ever ridden horses knows how strong the pull is toward the barn.

There were no other cars. Chiang said she could see the road fairly well from her side of the car. She suggested that Albert let her steer. Albert could not understand why the visibility should be better from her side. He suspected that she was just saying this because she did not trust his ability to drive. He said that if anything happened and it was later learned that she had been steering while he worked the pedals, they would look like fools. She was thinking about survival and did not realize what a serious thing it is to look like a fool in Grouse County.

They went in the ditch.

"I think we have to walk," said Albert.

"If we do, we will die," said Chiang. "We must bundle up and wait here for help."

"Like who do you have in mind, Chiang?" said Albert.

"I don't know," said Chiang. "Someone will happen by. All those card players. Someone must be going our way. I can't leave this car."

They sat for a while with this disagreement like a block of ice on the seat between them. The wind gripped and shook the car. Albert climbed in back. He found a blanket, a hat, a pair of gloves, and some flares.

"I'm going to walk now," he said. "I will find a place and come back for you."

"How far is it?"

"I don't know," said Albert. "I'm not sure where we are. We could be in a couple places." He slipped the blanket onto Chiang's shoulders. "I'll find a place where we can stay, and then I'll be right back. Don't think I won't. And don't shut off the car, because it won't start again. Remember that. Don't shut off the car. I'm going to crack this window a little bit."

"Goodbye," said Chiang.

"I'm really glad you ended up at our school," said Albert.

The hat blew off his head and disappeared in the storm. He crossed a bridge but had no idea what bridge it was. The wind screamed, a thousand-voiced choir. He covered his ears with his hands and found the back of his head thick with ice.

He prayed not to die, promising in return to treat everyone decently in the future. His hands and feet became numb, and he felt that the line between the storm and himself was getting blurry. He imagined Chiang in the car, bathed in

351

warm orange light. He imagined the orange light on her hair. Her eyes were closed. His love.

Then he remembered a time when he was very young and very sick. He did not remember what he was sick with. He woke dry-mouthed with a dizzy fever. The shades were drawn and the light coming through them had taken on their orange color. His siblings were outside throwing rocks at the window. He went downstairs and told Marietta. She went outside and came back in shortly after. A chill moved through the house. "See, Albert?" she said. She had one of Claude's hats in her hands, upside down and full of hailstones. "It's only bad weather," she said.

Albert stumbled and fell to one knee. He was tired and, having fallen, was not sure which way he had been going. This is how it happens, he thought. Then something pushed against his shoulder. He turned to see a large dog whose white fur blended almost perfectly into snow.

Louise and Dan were making out as the storm began. Wind worked its way through the caulking on the bedroom windows, and a candle flickered on the nightstand. They felt warmth and longing in the house with waves of snow moving past the yard light. They had missed each other, but even that did not account for the desire they felt right now.

Since Louise had come back from Minnesota, they had treated each other tenderly and helpfully. If they were in the kitchen, one would say to the other, "Do you want scrambled eggs? What do you feel like?" Or if Dan had to be out late, he would pull into the driveway, see the bedroom light on, and know she had waited up for him.

Now they slid their clothes off and made love slowly and lovingly. Dan liked the colors of her hair and skin, the long smooth arc of her back, the sound of her breath. He thought that he would never know anyone like her. They came in a moment of stillness, wrapped in each other's arms and seeming to summon everything that had happened to them, good and bad. Their lives rushed in at them, and this is what they were holding on against. They slipped away into sleep. The candle burned lower and lower before going out.

It was about two o'clock when Louise woke, hearing what she thought was a cat trapped in the storm. It was a moaning sound, followed by glass breaking out of the front door. They put on robes and went down and let Albert Robeshaw in. He was practically insensible, frozen half to death.

Louise dried his hair with a towel, made him tea, peeled the frozen jacket off his back. She turned the oven on and sat him in a chair before it. Dan took broken glass from the window frame, as he had done in his trailer when Louise broke in, and with duct tape fastened a piece of cardboard where the window had been.

When Albert's teeth stopped chattering and he was able to make sense, he told Dan and Louise that Chiang was still in the car. His hands were wrapped around the cup of tea. He did not know how far he had come.

Dan got a coat, gloves, and a large red hunting hat for Albert, and they all dressed and went out to the cruiser. They had not gone very far when the car shuddered and failed.

"Now what do we do?" said Louise.

"Only one thing to do," said Dan.

"How far is it, Albert?" said Louise.

"I don't know," said Albert.

"What were you near?"

"I couldn't see."

"Walking is crazy—Chiang is right," said Louise. "Henry has a tractor with a cab."

"It will probably kill too," said Dan.

"It's diesel," said Louise. "It can't. There aren't any spark plugs."

Henry Hamilton was awake and listening to the storm. He let them in and rummaged in a kitchen drawer until he found the key to the tractor.

"Albert, why don't you stay here," he said.

"No, I can't, Mr. Hamilton."

Louise drove with Dan and Albert on either side. The cab had a good heater, and the visibility was better this high above the road and looking down through the headlights. After a half mile the lights picked up the side of Claude's yellow station wagon.

The car had gone into the ditch at a right angle to the direction of the road, which gives you some idea of how disoriented Albert and Chiang had been. The lights were off. The car might have been abandoned for days.

Albert and Dan climbed down from the tractor and waded through the drifts. The station wagon was not running, and in fact had killed within five minutes of Albert's leaving. Dan opened the door. Chiang was lying across the seat, wrapped in the blanket that Albert had given her.

"I thought you had forgotten me," she cried.

Dan carried her to the tractor. He could feel her shivering. He boosted her up the ladder and into the cab, where Louise hugged her and laughed and said how do you turn this thing around.

The storm lasted three days. A lot of livestock died because of the cold and the fact that in many cases no one could get to

354

them. The pheasant and deer populations also suffered large losses and would take several seasons to come back.

On Saturday, the second day, Dan and Albert walked through the driving snow out to the road where the cruiser had died. They lifted the hood and found the engine packed solid with snow. They scooped and chipped this away, pulled the battery, and took it back to the farm for recharging. In this way they at least got the car off the road. That afternoon the snow let up a little. Dan went into Morrisville, where he would spend the next two nights dealing with car accidents and heart attacks and other emergencies of the storm.

Henry came over to the house with bread he had baked. He, Louise, Chiang, and Albert ate thick slices of bread and played Monopoly all afternoon and well into the evening. Louise won, with hotels she deftly distributed on the green and yellow properties. Henry specialized in the inexpensive places and seemed content with the low-key game they afforded. Albert was one of those players who land on Chance and Community Chest all the time, play an interesting game, and go out fast. Chiang owned the railroads and utilities.

At nine o'clock they walked Henry home and then came back, and in Louise and Dan's room watched a movie called *Two-Lane Blacktop* on television. It was funny and pointless, with a lot of driving. James Taylor said nothing, but kept looking at people with absolutely no expression on his face. Louise, Albert, and Chiang drank beers, made jokes at the screen, dozed on the bed. Louise got up to shut off the television after the movie had ended, and Albert and Chiang lifted their heads sleepily, wondering where they were. "It's all right, stay," said Louise. She got a blanket from the closet, covered them up, and crawled under the blanket herself. They slept deeply and without dreams in the bed that Dan had built.

TWENTY

THE SPRING was rainy and farmers could not get their crops planted on time. They complained bitterly, projecting a loss of yield. It was always too wet or too dry for farmers, said Mary Montrose. You would never hear a farmer say, "Yes, everything is perfect." She was working on a Grafton comprehensive leash law, which she hoped would become a model for other towns. Instead of "choke chain" she used the term "training collar."

Perry Kleeborg drove out to the farm one day in a straightforward attempt to get Louise to come back to the job. The little man wore his big sunglasses behind the wheel of a lavender Chrysler New Yorker. It was hard to see how he kept getting his driver's license year after year, and in fact he did not. He walked up to the house with a box of prints for Louise to examine. Business was not great at the old studio. Most of what he showed Louise looked out of focus, and she said so.

"Maren is in over her head," said Kleeborg. "She has not yet mastered the rudiments of photography, and now she wants to reorganize the back shop. She wants to move the enlargers where the dryer is. She wants to put the light table where the enlargers are. I don't know why she wants these things. I ask but she cannot tell me. She just thinks it will be handier somehow, as if by magic. I tell her there isn't any magic, only hard work every day of the week. She is a young person with a lot of new ideas. Some good and some bad. I suspected the pictures might be soft, but with my eyes acting the way they do, it is an easy thing to overlook."

"Don't let her move things around," said Louise. "She may not realize it, but that is a pretty efficient layout."

"That's what I told her," said Kleeborg. "The problem is that her job has not been well defined. We were operating under the assumption that you would be coming back any moment. When you didn't, I found myself giving her more and more responsibility, until now she wants to put her personal stamp on the operation."

"Let me ask you about these prints from the horse show," said Louise.

"I thought you might."

"The horses are stepping out of the frame," said Louise.

"Well, yes," said Kleeborg. "Yes, I spoke to her about these. And we gave the horse people a special discount. But this is what I say. Maren is not ready. She's a year or two away. And that's if she stays. She talks constantly of California. California is the place to be. California is the ideal. Louise, you must come back. I meant what I said about you inheriting the business, but if you don't come back soon, there won't be any business left. I can't tell you how many times we wanted to call you up in Minnesota but decided against it because it would be a toll call."

They had been sitting on the steps of the house, and now they got up and walked along the bluestones that Dan had arranged into a path. Red, yellow, and violet flowers grew under the kitchen window. A red-winged blackbird flew into the bushes on the edge of the yard.

"I'll come back," said Louise.

So she went back to work. And one sunny day she and Maren were loading the van for a photo session at the elementary school when Louise said, "Hey, just from curiosity, why did you want to move the enlargers?"

"What enlargers?" said Maren. "I don't want to move any enlargers."

"You know," said Louise, and she repeated what Kleeborg had said Maren wanted to do.

Maren closed a tripod and slid it into the back of the van. "I never said any such thing. As if I would want to move the enlargers. They're fine with me right where they are. As if I would want to move the light table. I don't care where the light table is. Perry's a nut."

They drove over to the elementary school in Walleye Lake and spent the morning taking pictures of kids. Maren got them laughing and Louise snapped the shutter. In the van on the way back to Stone City they rolled down the windows and dangled their arms in the sunlight. Maren closed her eyes, smiled, and said, "This is what California is like every day of the year."

As Mary Montrose had once predicted, Jean Klar came back to the farm. She did not want to reclaim the Klar homestead but to sell it. The farmhouse and two acres went to Louise and Dan, and the rest to Les Larsen.

There had been for some years a problem with water getting in the basement, and once they owned the house, Louise and Dan got Hans Cook to come with a backhoe to lay a line of tile around the foundation. They had called the Tile Doctor, Tim Leventhaler, but he put them off until Dan realized that Tim was not going to mess around with a job this small.

So Hans and Dan were working on it. "Hey," said Hans, "remember when we moved your trailer?"

"Oh no," said Dan. "I had no part in that."

Hans laughed. "You know, I saw that old trailer the other day," he said.

"It's at the landfill, right?" said Dan.

"The guys use it for a shed," said Hans. "And they love it. Because, you know, those harmless bastards were sitting out in the rain."

"Did they replace the windows?" said Dan.

"They took the broken glass out."

"How long has it been since that thing rolled?" said Dan.

"Well, what," said Hans. "Two years anyway."

"More than that," said Dan.

"That's right, because it was snowing," said Hans.

Louise came out with sandwiches and coffee, and they took a break and sat around the backhoe. "The coffee is really weak because we're out of coffee," said Louise.

"I've been meaning to invite you guys over for supper," said Hans. "I don't know if Mary has told you, but I'm making my own cheese these days. You wouldn't believe what all goes into the making of cheese."

"Milk," said Louise. "What else?"

"I got a compact-disc player, too," said Hans.

"Let me ask you something," said Dan. "How much of a difference is there really?"

"I tell you, it's like night and day."

360

The tiling took them late into the afternoon. It was dirty work, but the dull terracotta tiles made a satisfying noise when they clinked together in the trench, ready to carry the water wherever Dan and Louise wanted it to go. Hans drove the backhoe home, fed his cat, and took a bath. He eased himself into the tub. It was difficult, sometimes, being such a big person. He got dressed, took a small tab of LSD, and drove over to Mary's house, where they grilled hamburgers behind the house with the spring light fading over the fields.

"Put some tile down with Dan and Louise today," he said.

"Well, that's what Louise said," said Mary.

Hans turned the hamburgers and extinguished some flames with the squirt bottle he kept handy for that purpose.

"How did it go?" said Mary.

Hans looked across the yard. "Wonderful," he said. Darkness was settling. The trunk of a white birch glowed softly against the grass. "One of these days I'm going to make a birch-bark canoe."

"Why?" said Mary.

"Oh, dream of mine," said Hans. "When I was young—now this is going way back—I thought it would be a good trick to retrace the journeys of the French fur traders. Come down the Mississippi to Cloquet, La Crosse, Prairie du Chien—all those places."

"That sounds like something you would do," said Mary.

"It might be overly ambitious," said Hans. "What I'd like to do now is make the canoe and go from there."

After supper they drove up and around Walleye Lake. Hans leaned back in the driver's seat and drove slowly, with his big hands cradling the bottom of the steering wheel. From the parking lot of the restaurant at the western end of the lake,

361

they could see the lights of houses on the north shore. The lights shone twice, once in the air and once in the water.

"Pretty night," said Mary.

The restaurant was called the Sea Breeze, although it was a thousand miles from any ocean.

That was also the week that Tiny Darling fell and skinned his knuckles in the grocery store. He was walking along pushing a shopping cart and wearing the blue and gold corduroy jacket of the Future Farmers of America. For reasons unknown even to him he got the sudden notion to throw all his weight on the cart and give it a shove. Instead of carrying him along scooter-fashion, the cart flipped, dragging him down the aisle. People hurried to help him to his feet, as if he had been the victim of something other than his own crazy idea.

After getting the groceries, Tiny had to pick Joan Gower up and bring her home. They were still living in the basement of the church in Margo, and Joan served three nights a week as a volunteer at the Saint Francis House animal shelter in Wylie. It was a bit of a jaunt from Margo to Wylie, and Tiny wished that she had found an animal shelter or some other volunteer outlet closer to home. On the other hand, if his car had not broken down, he would not be driving her car, and therefore would not have to pick her up no matter where she went. So it was his fault, and yet he was angry with her. It was with an oppressive sense of his own unfairness that he drove down to Wylie. The dogs barked and pressed against the bars when he came in. "Down, Spotty," said Tiny. "Down, Spike."

Joan got to wear a white coat as a volunteer for Saint Francis House, and with the large glasses she had taken to wearing, she looked professional. Tiny thought but had not proved that the glasses had regular glass in them. Her hair was pinned on top of her head, and she carried an empty clipboard under her arm.

"This is Tuffy," she told Tiny. "This is Rebel. This is Eleanor Rigby."

Joan opened Tuffy's cage and knelt at the door. "Tuffy is six weeks old. She's half Lab and half Belgian Tuveren, and the last of her littermates just found a home. So if she is acting kind of downhearted today—and I think she is—that is why. Here, Tuffy. Are you feeling lost this evening? Say 'I'm kind of lost.' Say 'I'm kind of lost and wondering where everybody went.'"

"Let me pet it," said Tiny.

A few minutes later, Joan locked the building and they walked across the dark driveway. The stars were out in the cold black sky. Tiny backed Joan's Torino out while Joan folded her white coat neatly in her lap.

"Remind me to wash this when we get home," she said.

"You put a lot of effort into Saint Francis for something that's volunteer," said Tiny.

"Yeah," said Joan. "But think about this. When payday rolls around, those dogs have no idea who's getting a check and who isn't. I mean, they don't even know what a check is. And that's the way you have to look at it."

"I suppose," said Tiny.

They went back to Margo via Grafton, and as they passed through town they saw Louise's car parked at Hans Cook's place on the main drag. Hans lived in an old cement house opposite the grain elevator. Many years ago the house had been a gas station, and there were still cylindrical red and green pumps with cracked faces and weeds growing around them.

Tiny slowed down. "Guess whose car that is," he said.

Joan touched the frame of her glasses. "I don't know."

"Louise," said Tiny.

"I thought she was gone."

"I thought so too, but I saw her the other day at the bank, so evidently she's back."

"Did you go up to her and say hi?" said Joan.

"I'm sure."

"You should," said Joan. "Show her you're over that time. The divorced couples I admire are the ones who still talk on the phone. Who exchange birthday cards."

Tiny snorted mildly and eased the car onto the highway. The farmland rolled away from them, vast and dark and empty. "Whoever told you that is lying," he said.

"You can't speak for all couples everywhere," said Joan.

"Ninety-nine percent," said Tiny.

The right back tire blew out on the highway to Margo, and the car whumped to a stop. Tiny opened the trunk, in which there were three plastic lambs. "Those are mine," said Joan. They were the standard lambs, in a resting position, suitable for religious purposes or yard decoration. Tiny took the lambs from the trunk and put them on the shoulder. He dug out the jack and the spare tire. Joan brought him the manual—and her having the manual twenty years after the car was built and a good ten years after it had begun falling apart seemed as much a demonstration of faith as anything she had ever done during a church service. Tiny went about changing the tire, and Joan rummaged in the trunk.

"I don't want you doing that while I'm jacking the car up," warned Tiny. In his voice was the righteousness of having caught her doing something procedurally wrong and possibly dangerous.

"I'm not," said Joan.

"Yes you are."

"You're not even touching the jack."

"I'm about to."

"When you start, I'll stop."

"Just cut it out, Joan," said Tiny.

"I'm getting the flares out."

"Don't."

"Yes." She gathered the flares like sticks of dynamite in her hands and went around pushing their metal anchors one by one into the sandy shoulder. Then she removed the caps and scraped the elements to life. The flares hissed and burned with a hollow red light. Joan rested on her knees. Tiny knelt by the car, the lambs around him, and the hollow light touched them all. Joan knew that no matter how long she lived or how soon she and Tiny went separate ways, she would remember this.

Meanwhile, Hans brought the food to the table. He had roasted a chicken with dressing and potatoes and onions and carrots. Mary and Dan and Louise sat around a card table in the living room. Candles burned as the four friends ate the delicious food.

Dan told about a program adopted by the county to promote calmness and civility among public employees.

Mary had read in *Reader's Digest* about an Indian man who could slow his heart to a standstill by thinking about it.

Louise said she sometimes wondered if she or Dan didn't have powers of mind over matter, because so much of their silverware was bent.

Hans said he had dreamed recently that he was standing in

the parking lot at the Burger King in Morrisville and all of a sudden he just took off flying.

After supper Hans insisted that they all take turns lying on the davenport with eyes closed and listening to his compact-disc player through earphones. He said this was the only way you could fully appreciate the quality of the sound. When it was Dan's turn, he lay down and Hans fitted the earphones into his ears. The music was that of a single flute whose notes broke and reverberated in open space.

"That's R. Carlos Nakai," said Hans afterward.

Dan and Louise said good night to Mary and Hans and drove home. They watched part of a movie on television about a band of mountain climbers who because of an avalanche were forced to choose between taking a daring route to the top of the mountain or just forgetting it and returning to base camp.

"Are you snow-blind? It is madness," said the scientist.

"If it is madness, then I am mad," said the handsome leader.

"It is a madness that I share," said the bold woman, who wore a furry white collar.

"Were it shared by the world, it would still be madness," said the scientist.

Louise lay on the bed, working her shoes off with her toes. "Gee, I wonder what they'll do," she said.

"The scientist dies."

CHARACTERS

(In order of appearance)

Dan Norman	county sheriff
Louise Darling	photographer's assistant
Charles (Tiny) Darling	thief
Earl Kellogg, Jr.	senior deputy sheriff
Ed Aiken	junior deputy sheriff
Rollie Wilson	ambulance driver
Henry Hamilton	notary public
Jerry Tate	postal worker
Paul Francis	crop duster
Mrs. Thorsen	science teacher
Mary Montrose	Louise's mother
Hans Cook	Mary's beau
Heinz and Ranae Miller	Mary's neighbors
Tim Thompson	barrel racer
Pete	martial artist
Perry Kleeborg	photographer
Maren Staley	apprentice
Johnny White	Independent candidate
Lisa White	divorcée
Megan and Stefan White	children
Howard LaMott	fire chief
Alvin Getty	grocer
Nan Jewell	matriarch
Mrs. Spees	pet dealer

Joan Gower	proselyte
Lenore Wells	sad woman
Quinn	abandoned infant
Albert Robeshaw	lead guitar, vocals
Claude and Marietta Robeshaw	Democrat farmers
Nancy McLaughlin	night administrator
Beth Pickett	ob-gyn doctor
Lu Chiang	student from Taiwan
Ron and Delia Kesslers	host family
Jocelyn Jewell	equestrian
Cheryl Jewell	heiress
June Montrose Green	Louise's sister
Roman Baker	veterinarian
Jack White	horseman
Russell Ford	county supervisor
Pansy Gansevoort	airbrusher
Dianne Scheviss	airbrusher
Shannon Key	television reporter
Ronnie Lapoint	stock car driver
Beverly Leventhaler	county extension woman
Colette Sandover	tax evader
Bettina Sullivan	public defender
Father Zene Hebert	radio preacher
Marie Person	woman in pickup
Lindsey Coale	hairdresser
Larry Longhair	gambler
Dave Green	Colorado realtor
Frank Ray	billboard salesman

Grace Ray	passenger
Lee P. Rasmussen	county attorney
Tim Leventhaler	the Tile Doctor
Lydia Kleeborg	Perry's late sister
Sheila Geer	police sergeant
Robin Otis	marriage couselor
Mrs. England	palm reader
Vince Hartwell	murder victim
Joseph Norman	Dan's father
Ken Hemphill	Wildlife Court judge
Miles Hagen	token GOP candidate
Paula Kellogg	quilter
Carol and Kenneth Kennedy	camp owners
Alice Mattie	papergirl
Margaret Lynn Kane	mother of Quinn
Marnie Rainville	stripper

ABOUT THE AUTHOR

Tom Drury has published five novels and written short stories for McSweeney's *Quarterly Concern*, *A Public Space*, *The New Yorker*, and more. He is the recipient of Berlin Prize and Guggenheim Fellowships. Drury's work has been translated into German, French, and Spanish.

Drury has lived in Iowa, Massachusetts, Connecticut, Florida, California, Brooklyn, Iowa again, and, currently, at the American Academy in Berlin.

WORKS BY TOM DRURY

The End of Vandalism
The Black Brook
Hunts in Dreams
The Driftless Area
Pacific

Issues in Religion and Theology 1

The Messianic Secret

Edited with an Introduction by

CHRISTOPHER TUCKETT

FORTRESS PRESS | SPCK
Philadelphia | London

First published in Great Britain 1983
SPCK
Holy Trinity Church
Marylebone Road
London NW1 4DU

First published in the USA 1983
Fortress Press
2900 Queen Lane
Philadelphia
Pennsylvania 19129

Library of Congress Cataloging in Publication Data
Main entry under title:

The Messianic secret.

  (Issues in religion and theology; 1)
  Reprint of articles originally published 1958–1976.
  Bibliography: p.
  Includes index.
  Contents: Introduction/Christopher Tuckett—The purpose of Mark's Gospel/ Nils Alstrup Dahl—The blindness of the disciples in Mark/Joseph B. Tyson— [etc.]
  1. Messianic secret (Bible)—Addresses, essays, lectures. 2. Bible. N. T. Mark— Criticism, interpretation, etc.—Addresses, essays, lectures. I. Tuckett, C. M. (Christopher Mark) II. Series.
BT245.M47   1983   226'.306   83–5499
ISBN 0–8006–1767–3

British Library Cataloguing in Publication Data
The Messianic secret.—(Issues in religion and theology; no. 1)
  1. Bible N.T. Mark   2. Messianic secret (Bible)
  I. Tuckett, Christopher   II. Series
  226'.306   BS2585.2

  ISBN 0–281–04052–4

Filmset by Northumberland Press Ltd, Gateshead
Printed in Great Britain by Richard Clay (The Chaucer Press) Ltd, Bungay, Suffolk

Contents

Acknowledgements

Nils Alstrup Dahl, "The Purpose of Mark's Gospel" is reprinted by permission from *Jesus in the Memory of the Early Church* (Minneapolis: Augsburg, 1976) 55–60. Copyright © Augsburg Publishing House 1976.

Joseph B. Tyson, "The Blindness of the Disciples in Mark" is reprinted from the *Journal of Biblical Literature* 80 (1961) 261–8 by permission of the author and *JBL*. Copyright © *Journal of Biblical Literature* 1961.

T. Alec Burkill, "Mysterious Revelation" is reprinted by permission from *Mysterious Revelation: An Examination of the Philosophy of St Mark's Gospel* (New York: Cornell University Press, 1963) 319–24. Copyright © Cornell University Press 1963.

Georg Strecker, "The Theory of the Messianic Secret in Mark's Gospel" is reprinted by permission of *Studia Evangelica* and the author. Original publication as "Zur Messiasgeheimnistheorie im Markusevangelium" in *Studia Evangelica* 3, TU 88 (1964) 87–104. Copyright © Georg Strecker 1964.

Eduard Schweizer, "The Question of the Messianic Secret in Mark" is reprinted by permission of the author. Original publication as "Zur Messiasgeheimnis bei Markus" in *Zeitschrift für die neutestamentliche Wissenschaft* 56 (1965) 1–8. Copyright © Eduard Schweizer 1965.

Ulrich Luz, "The Secrecy Motif and the Marcan Christology" is reprinted by permission of the author. Original publication as "Das Geheimnismotiv und die Markinische Christologie" in *Zeitschrift für die neutestamentliche Wissenschaft* 56 (1965) 9–30. Copyright © Ulrich Luz 1965.

William C. Robinson Jr, "The Quest for Wrede's Secret Messiah" is reprinted by permission of the Union Theological Seminary. Original publication in *Interpretation* 27 (1973) 10–30. Copyright © Union Theological Seminary 1973.

James D. G. Dunn, "The Messianic Secret in Mark" is reprinted by permission of Inter-Varsity Press. Original publication in the *Tyndale Bulletin* 21 (1970) 92–117 (reprinted, slightly abbreviated, in the *TSF Bulletin* (Summer 1974) 7–14). Copyright © Inter-Varsity Press 1970.

Heikki Räisänen, "The 'Messianic Secret' in Mark's Gospel" is reprinted by permission from *Das "Messiasgeheimnis" im Markusevangelium* (Helsinki: Lansi-Suomi, 1976) 159–68. Copyright © E. J. Brill 1976.

The Contributors

CHRISTOPHER TUCKETT is Lecturer in New Testament Studies at the University of Manchester. He is the author of *The Revival of the Griesbach Hypothesis* (1983) and a frequent contributor to journals of biblical scholarship.

NILS ALSTRUP DAHL is Emeritus Professor of New Testament at the Yale University Divinity School. His *Das Volk Gottes* was published in 1941. Three volumes of his essays have now been translated into English: *The Crucified Messiah* (1974), *Jesus in the Memory of the Early Church* (1976) and *Studies in Paul* (1977).

JOSEPH B. TYSON is Professor of Religious Studies at the Southern Methodist University, Dallas, Texas. He is the author of *A Study of Early Christianity* (1973), and is a regular contributor to theological journals.

T. ALEC BURKILL was until his retirement Professor of Religious Studies at the University of Zimbabwe. In addition to *Mysterious Revelation* (1963), he has published another collection of essays on Mark's Gospel, *New Light on the Earliest Gospel* (1972).

GEORG STRECKER is Professor of New Testament Studies at the University of Göttingen. He is the author of *Das Judenchristentum in den Pseudoklementinen* (1958), *Der Weg der Gerechtigkeit* (1962) and a volume of essays, *Eschaton und Historie* (1979).

EDUARD SCHWEIZER was Professor of New Testament Theology and Exegesis at the University of Zürich from 1949 to 1978. A number of his books have been translated, including his commentaries, *The Good News according to Mark* (1971), *The Good News according to Matthew* (1976) and *The Letter to the Colossians* (1982).

ULRICH LUZ is Professor of New Testament Studies at the University of Berne. After a period as *Assistent* to Eduard Schweizer in Zürich, he held a Chair at the University of Göttingen for several years. His *Das Geschichtsverständnis des Paulus* was published in 1968, and a major commentary on Matthew is forthcoming.

WILLIAM C. ROBINSON Jr is Taylor Professor of Biblical Theology and History at Andover Newton Theological School. He is the author of a study of Luke's theology, *Der Weg des Herrn* (1964) and a contributor to journals of biblical scholarship.

JAMES D. G. DUNN is Professor of Divinity in the University of Durham. He is the author of *Baptism in the Holy Spirit* (1970), *Jesus and the Spirit* (1975), *Unity and Diversity in the New Testament* (1977) and *Christology in the Making* (1981).

HEIKKI RÄISÄNEN is Professor of New Testament Exegesis in the University of Helsinki. In addition to *Das Messiasgeheimnis im Markusevangelium* (1976), he has published another study of Mark's Gospel, *Die Parabeltheorie im Markusevangelium* (1973) and several articles on Paul.

Series Foreword

The "Issues in Religion and Theology" series intends to encompass a variety of topics within the general disciplines of religious and theological studies. Subjects are drawn from any of the component fields, such as biblical studies, systematic theology, ethics, history of Christian thought, and history of religion. The issues have all proved to be highly significant for their respective areas, and they are of similar interest to students, teachers, clergy, and general readers.

The series aims to address these issues by collecting and reproducing key studies, all previously published, which have contributed significantly to our present understandings. In each case, the volume editor introduces the discussion with an original essay which describes the subject and its treatment in religious and theological studies. To this editor has also fallen the responsibility of selecting items for inclusion – no easy task when one considers the vast number of possibilities. Together the essays are intended to present a balanced overview of the problem and various approaches to it. Each piece is important in the current debate, and any older publication included normally stands as a "classical" or seminal work which is still worth careful study. Readers unfamiliar with the issue should find that these discussions provide a good entrée, while more advanced students will appreciate having studies by some of the best specialists on the subject gathered together in one volume. The editor has, of course, faced certain constraints: analyses too lengthy or too technical could not be included, except perhaps in excerpt form; the bibliography is not exhaustive; and the volumes in this series are being kept to a reasonable, uniform length. On the other hand, the editor is able to overcome the real problem of inaccessibility. Much of the best literature on a subject is often not readily available to readers, whether because it was first published in journals or books not widely circulated or because it was originally written in a language not read by all who would benefit from it. By bringing these and other studies together in this series, we hope to contribute to the general understanding of these key topics.

The series editors and the publishers wish to express their gratitude to the authors and their original publishers whose works are reprinted or translated here, often with corrections from living authors. We are also conscious of our debt to members of the editorial advisory board. They have shared our belief that the series will be useful on a wide scale, and they have therefore been prepared to spare much time and thought for the project.

DOUGLAS A. KNIGHT
ROBERT MORGAN

Abbreviations

BJRL	*Bulletin of the John Rylands Library*
CBQ	*Catholic Biblical Quarterly*
ET	English translation/English translator
EvQ	*Evangelical Quarterly*
EvT	*Evangelische Theologie*
ExpTim	*Expository Times*
HTR	*Harvard Theological Review*
Int	*Interpretation*
JBL	*Journal of Biblical Literature*
JSOT	*Journal for the Study of the Old Testament*
JTS	*Journal of Theological Studies*
NovT	*Novum Testamentum*
NTS	*New Testament Studies*
RB	*Revue Biblique*
RGG	*Religion in Geschichte und Gegenwart*
SE	*Studia Evangelica*
TDNT	G. Kittel and G. Friedrich (ed.), *Theological Dictionary of the New Testament*
TLZ	*Theologische Literaturzeitung*
TU	Texte und Untersuchungen
TynBul	*Tyndale Bulletin*
ZNW	*Zeitschrift für die neutestamentliche Wissenschaft*
ZTK	*Zeitschrift für Theologie und Kirche*

Introduction
The Problem of the Messianic Secret

CHRISTOPHER TUCKETT

It is a well-known feature of the gospel tradition, especially of the Gospel of Mark, that Jesus is frequently portrayed as seeking to maintain an element of secrecy about his own person and work. This feature is usually known today as the "messianic secret", a term which derives from W. Wrede's classic study of this aspect of the Gospels.[1] As a result of this work, Wrede has been described as the forerunner of form criticism and redaction criticism,[2] and in terms of method, the influence of his book has continued right up to the present day.[3] However, the details of some of his individual arguments are now questioned, and with regard to the messianic secret itself, there is still no unanimity about its correct interpretation.[4] It seems therefore desirable to set the various views represented in this collection of essays in context by giving a brief history of research into the messianic secret.[5]

Prior to Wrede's work, few nineteenth-century critics had seen any difficulties in using the Gospels to rediscover an earthly Jesus, unencumbered by later ecclesiastical dogma. The earlier studies of Holtzmann and others[6] had convinced the majority of scholars of the literary priority of Mark's Gospel. However, this was then often taken as an indication of Mark's historical reliability.[7] In particular, discussion of the secrecy texts in Mark was assumed to concern only the historical question of why Jesus might have enjoined secrecy on others. The most frequent answer was that Jesus was seeking to avoid popular ideas of messiahship with their political overtones. A number of "lives of Jesus" were written, all based for their chronology on the Marcan outline, and many of these centred on the idea of Jesus' gradual revelation to others of his own basic conviction that he was the Messiah. Jesus became conscious that he was the Messiah at his baptism, but in the first stage of his

1

ministry he kept this secret. When the demoniacs recognized him, Jesus ordered them not to spread their knowledge to others so that the correct evaluation of his person might develop gradually in peoples' minds. Slowly the disciples did become aware of Jesus' true identity, this growth in understanding reaching its climax in Peter's confession at Caesarea Philippi. This marked a great turning point in Jesus' ministry, and inaugurated a new period when Jesus had to try to free the disciples from Jewish nationalistic ideas of messiahship and to teach them about the necessity of his suffering. Jesus still kept his identity hidden from the crowds until his miracles led to public recognition (cf. Mark 10:47), and finally Jesus accepted the crowds' acclamation of him as the messianic king at the entry into Jerusalem. Jesus acknowledged his messiahship publicly before the high priest and was crucified as "King of the Jews".[8]

Basic to this type of reconstruction is the idea of development, with a chronology very heavily dependent on Mark's account. Some of the weaknesses and inadequacies of these "lives" were devastatingly exposed by A. Schweitzer in his magisterial survey, *The Quest of the Historical Jesus*. Schweitzer showed how much each author had read into his reconstruction details which were not there in the Gospels, and in doing so had made a Jesus in his own image. Schweitzer's fundamental criticism of these reconstructions was that they failed to take seriously the vital element in Jesus' life, viz. eschatology. Eschatology was not a dispensable "husk" which could be discarded to get back to a true "kernel" of Jesus' teaching about the universal fatherhood of God. Rather, Jesus was a strange figure of first-century Judaism whose life was dominated by the belief that the final, eschatological events were about to break in and bring an end to the present world order. Thus, according to Schweitzer, Jesus sent out the twelve on a lightning preaching tour to warn others, not expecting that they would return before the End (cf. Matt. 10:23). However, events did not bear out Jesus' expectations: the disciples did return with no sign of the End coming. So Jesus decided to go to Jerusalem in order to take upon himself the "messianic woes", which were the necessary prelude to the coming of the new age, and thus force the arrival of the Kingdom.

Schweitzer's theories, which make Jesus into something of a disappointed apocalyptic fanatic, will not be repeated here in detail. What should be observed, however, is that Schweitzer's own reconstruction of the life of Jesus was based on precisely the same methodological presuppositions as those of the older nineteenth-century critics. For Schweitzer too had a basic trust in the chronology of the Gospels: Mark's historical sequence, if suitably expanded by the Matthean discourses, was basically accurate and could be used to reconstruct the course of Jesus' ministry. His objection to the older critics was merely that their reconstructions were bad ones, failing to give due weight to the importance of eschatology in Jesus' life and work. His criticisms did nothing to suggest that the whole enterprise of producing a developmental life of Jesus was inherently impossible. Such a claim is implied by Wrede's book, and it is this which makes his work so important.[9]

One of Wrede's concerns was the question of whether Jesus saw himself as Messiah (1971, 1), but it was not this that formed the starting point, or even the major part, of his discussion. Rather, Wrede started with the Gospel of Mark, and with the way in which it had been used by nineteenth-century critics to produce a "life of Jesus". Wrede said that one's primary aim must be to find the meaning and intention of Mark himself, before jumping too hastily to conclusions about the underlying history (1971, 5f).[10] Wrede, like Schweitzer, pointed out how much had to be read into Mark's account before it could yield any neat developmental story. The theory that Jesus wanted to purify Jewish ideas of messiahship is nowhere hinted at in Mark (1971, 15). The secrecy commands fail to fit any scheme of either a gradual growth in understanding by the disciples, or a gradual revelation by Jesus: the theory that Jesus kept his identity secret initially founders on Jesus' explicit claim to be the Son of Man at the start of his ministry (1971, 18; cf. Mark 2:10,28);[11] the confession at Caesarea Philippi can scarcely be the result of a steady growth in understanding by the disciples, since immediately prior to this they are still as blind as ever (8:15ff) and afterwards they remain equally blind (1971, 16). Any idea that Caesarea Philippi formed a great turning-point in Jesus' ministry, with Jesus then starting to teach the disciples about the necessity of the passion, founders on what Wrede saw as a clear prediction of the passion already in the bridegroom saying (2:19f), so that the passion predictions (8:31; 9:31; 10:33) cannot be seen as introducing any new teaching (1971, 21). Wrede thus rejected the old developmental view of the life of Jesus as having no real support in Mark's Gospel. Rather, Mark's whole presentation was dominated by the idea of secrecy, and this could not be satisfactorily explained away by any theory of a growth in understanding, or a steady process of revelation.

Wrede proceeded to analyse the various elements in Mark which, he claimed, were associated with the secrecy motif, and in this he included a very large number of features from Mark. There were Jesus' explicit commands to silence addressed to the demons (1:25,34; 3:12), to those who had witnessed the miracles (1:43f; 5:43; 7:36; 8:26) and to the disciples (8:30; 9:9); Wrede also included instances where Jesus tried to keep his whereabouts a secret (7:24; 9:30f) as well as the attempt by others to silence Bartimaeus (10:47f) (1971, 34ff). These injunctions to silence had been analysed individually by earlier critics, and different explanations for each had been suggested: Jesus might have banned the demons from speaking because they were not on the side of God; Jesus did not wish to have a reputation as a miracle worker; Jesus wanted to avoid false ideas of messiahship, etc.[12] For Wrede these were all unsatisfactory, primarily because such individual explanations could at best only deal with part of the evidence, and the stereotyped form of this feature in Mark suggested that the evidence should all be explained in the same way (1971, 37). Wrede then examined the secrecy charges in great detail, and argued that they were all unhistorical. For example, the injunction to silence after the raising of a girl assumed to be dead (5:43) could not possibly be taken seriously (1971, 50f). Thus he claimed that all these commands were later additions to the tradition.

Wrede also included with the secrecy charges the feature which he called "cryptic speech": e.g., there are instances in Mark where Jesus gives private instruction to only a few people, and some miracles are performed with only a chosen few watching (1971, 53ff, cf. Mark 1:29ff,35; 5:40; 7:17; 10:10). In these cases Wrede was undecided about the question of historicity. However, a clearer case seems to be provided by the so-called "theory of parables", by which Mark's account appears to make Jesus teach in parables in order deliberately to hide his meaning from the crowds (1971, 56ff, cf. Mark 4:10–13; 4:33f). Here Wrede claimed that this could not possibly be historical, since Jesus had never used parables to obscure his message but only to illuminate it (1971, 62, appealing to the work of Jülicher on the parables). Further, since this feature of Mark was to be taken with the other secrecy charges where the issue was Jesus' identity as Messiah, Wrede felt justified in interpreting the "mystery" of 4:11 in the same way: the "mystery" which is withheld from the outside world is the recognition of Jesus' messiahship (1971, 60).

Wrede found the key to all these secrecy passages in the command after the transfiguration, ordering the three disciples to remain silent about what they had seen until after the resurrection (9:9). Wrede claimed that this time limit was intended to apply to *all* the secrecy charges:

> During his earthly life Jesus' messiahship is absolutely a secret and is supposed to be such; no one apart from the confidants of Jesus is supposed to learn about it; with the resurrection, however, its disclosure ensues. This is in fact the crucial idea, the underlying point of Mark's entire approach (1971, 68).

Wrede applied the same explanation to the theory of the use of parables too: the veiling of their meaning was only temporary, and this in turn suggested the true interpretation of 4:21f, which Wrede took as a reference to the revelation of the true meaning of the parables "*after the resurrection*" (1971, 71, Wrede's italics).

Wrede claimed that another theme closely related to the explicit injunctions to silence and the statement about the purpose of parables was the motif of the failure of the disciples to understand Jesus. Here again Wrede rejected the old view that Jesus had tried to teach his disciples gradually. The passion predictions, he claimed, were all unhistorical, since their detailed prophecies, corresponding so precisely to subsequent events, looked like later Christian creations; in any case the fact that the disciples seemed to have been totally unprepared for Jesus' death implied that they had not received any prior instruction (1971, 82ff). There was no evidence of any progression in understanding by the disciples, since they remained totally uncomprehending throughout Jesus' ministry.[13] Further, the motif as it appeared in Mark depended on Mark's literary composition (cf. 8:17, referring to the literary details of the feeding miracles) and hence could not be historical (1971, 104f).

Thus Wrede's conclusion was that all the various aspects of the secrecy theory in Mark were unhistorical. All the secrecy elements in Mark were later additions to the tradition, and reflected the view that "real knowledge of what Jesus is only begins with his resurrection" (1971, 114).

Wrede also considered various elements in Mark which appeared to contradict the secrecy theme: e.g. the parable of the wicked husbandmen *is* understood (12:12), and sometimes Jesus' commands for silence are disobeyed (1:45; 7:36f). However, Wrede claimed that these were no real problem for his theory. Jesus' life story must have been considered worth telling, and hence the veil of secrecy could not have been drawn totally over it. Thus, to a certain extent, it was inevitable that concealment and revelation should coexist (1971, 124ff).

As far as the origin of the secrecy motifs was concerned, Wrede stated quite categorically that these were not due to Mark himself (1971, 145).[14] The various motifs in Mark were too variegated in nature to be the work of a single individual (1971, 145).[15] Although Mark may have agreed with the ideas, they must have originated in the larger circles which influenced him.

After considering the secrecy motifs as they appear in the other three Gospels, Wrede offered an explanation for the origin of the secret in Mark. He suggested that the clue to the whole phenomenon was to be found in what he thought was a very primitive Christian belief that Jesus only became Messiah at the resurrection (1971, 215ff, referring to Acts 2:36; Rom. 1:4; Phil. 2:6ff). However, subsequent Christian reflection led to the rise of the belief that Jesus' earthly life had also been messianic. Wrede therefore suggested that the secrecy motifs were the result of the coming together of these two views, so that Jesus' life was now described as messianic, but with the proviso that this could only be made public after the resurrection.

> It (the secret) can be characterised as the after-effect of the view that the resurrection is the beginning of the messiahship at a time when the life of Jesus was already being filled materially with messianic content. (1971, 229)

Similarly, Mark's picture of the disciples' failure to understand Jesus was a reflection of the revolution in their thinking which the appearances of the risen Jesus caused in them.

One corollary which Wrede drew from his historical explanation of the secret was that, if his theory was correct, then the secret could only have arisen at a time when no explicit messianic claims by Jesus were known. Thus Wrede claimed that his analysis gave "a positive historical testimony for the idea that Jesus actually did not give himself out as messiah" (1971, 230).

Wrede's book has been significant out of all proportion to its size. Whether one agrees with his detailed theories or not, he opened the way to seeing the Gospels as reflecting the beliefs of the early Church, quite as much as reflecting the historical career of Jesus. Nevertheless, his work was by no means universally accepted. Perhaps the most controversial aspect of his total theory was his assertion that Jesus had made no messianic claims, and many thought that Wrede's thesis could be refuted, at least in part, by pointing to messianic elements embedded in the tradition.[16] Such a criticism does not really deal with Wrede's case. His theory was primarily an analysis of *Mark's* Gospel, seeking to show that the secrecy elements were secondary intrusions into the story. His conclusions about the lack of any messianic claim by Jesus was only a corollary tentatively drawn from his attempt to explain the origin of the secrecy motifs. Showing this corollary to be false might show that Wrede's historical explanation was mistaken; but that does not, and cannot, of itself discredit his analysis of Mark's Gospel.[17]

One of Wrede's earliest critics was Schweitzer, who included a discussion of Wrede's book at the end of his *Quest of the Historical Jesus* (328ff). Schweitzer had already published his own theories about the life of Jesus (Schweitzer, 1925), and in his later work he saw no reason to revise his opinions, and indeed he took the opportunity to compare and contrast his own views with those of Wrede. Schweitzer agreed with Wrede in rejecting the psychologizing approach of the nineteenth-century critics. He agreed that the text should be taken as it stood. He agreed too that Mark's text appeared to be full of conflicting elements, which he described as reflecting two basic ideas, one natural and one dogmatic (1954, 335). Further, the secrecy motif was an integral part of the dogmatic element in the tradition. However, at this point, Schweitzer and Wrede parted company. For Wrede, the "dogmatic" element was all unhistorical, and Schweitzer described this view as "thorough-going scepticism". For Schweitzer himself, the dogmatic element was historical and to be explained from the eschatological outlook which dominated Jesus' life and work. Schweitzer labelled his solution "thorough-going eschatology", and claimed that his and Wrede's views were the only possible ones: "tertium non datur" (1954, 335).

Schweitzer criticized Wrede by referring to various features in the life of Jesus which were messianic, e.g. the triumphal entry and the confession before the high priest (1954, 339). Further, he pointed to the difficulty of explaining how the resurrection itself could have given rise to the belief that Jesus was the Messiah: claims that John the Baptist had been raised did not necessarily carry with them any claim that he was the Messiah (1954, 343). Thus Schweitzer looked for the origin of the secrecy charges in Jesus' own life. He claimed that Jesus knew himself to be the Messiah, but that his messiahship was understood in wholly futurist terms. Jesus thus had to keep his identity hidden since his messiahship would only be fully realized in the future when the Kingdom of God came (1925, 185ff). Jesus spoke of his future role as that of the "Son of Man", referring to the time when the Messiah would come as Judge (1925, 191). For others, Jesus and the Son of Man were two different people;

the fact that they were the same was what constituted Jesus' secret (1925, 191f). It was this secret which Peter unwittingly stumbled on at Caesarea Philippi as a result of what he had seen at the transfiguration (Schweitzer was forced to rearrange the Marcan chronology at this point [1925, 174ff; 1954, 380ff]). Thus before the secret could be divulged too widely, Jesus had to go to Jerusalem to force the arrival of the Kingdom by himself undergoing the messianic woes. Jesus was betrayed to the authorities by Judas, the content of what Judas betrayed being the secret itself: Judas told the Jewish leaders that Jesus had identified himself as the coming Messiah (1925, 216f). Thus Jesus was condemned to death for the blasphemy of claiming to be Messiah.

The weaknesses of Schweitzer's position are clear today. His reliance on the synoptic chronology has been vitiated by the work of the form critics. Further, Schweitzer can scarcely be said to have been true to his own avowed principles of taking the text as it stands and not reading between the lines (cf. his rearrangement of the transfiguration story, or his claim to know what it was that Judas betrayed). So too form criticism has shown that the early Church did adapt the tradition as it was handed on in a way which Schweitzer rejected almost *a priori* (1954, 338).

Nevertheless, if Schweitzer's total theory has found little support, several details of his arguments against Wrede have been used by others. Among these is the argument that the resurrection is insufficient in itself to explain the rise of the belief that Jesus was the Messiah.[18] In Germany several of the early critics of Wrede agreed with Schweitzer in seeing the origin of the secrecy motifs in the life of Jesus, even if some were prepared to admit that the secrecy theory might have been secondarily expanded in the tradition. For example, J. Weiss and Wernle both conceded that some of the secrecy elements were secondary,[19] but claimed that the basic idea could be traced back to Jesus' own ministry. Wernle claimed that some of the secrecy charges were due to Jesus' desire to preach about God and the things of God, rather than about himself (1917, 334). For Weiss, some of the secrecy charges were intelligible in the life of Jesus and reflected the belief, common to Jesus and the earliest Church, that Jesus' messiahship was futurist, i.e. Jesus would become Messiah at a future date (for the earliest Church this was the resurrection) (1903, 45ff). Thus not all the secrecy charges in the tradition were unhistorical. In particular, Weiss claimed that the command to silence in 1:25 was probably historical, even though he conceded that the general statements in 1:34 and 3:11f might be secondary (1903, 53,146f).[20]

Weiss also claimed that the command to silence after Peter's confession (8:30) was historical, and he adopted the traditional theory that Jesus was here seeking to avoid political ideas popularly associated with messiahship.[21]

In England, opposition to Wrede was far more unequivocal in asserting that the secrecy elements in the tradition stemmed from Jesus. Schweitzer's results, which affirmed the historicity of the gospel narratives, were generally found to be more acceptable than the radical scepticism about the question of historicity which Wrede's results seemed to offer.[22] The most influential attack was that of Sanday (1907, 70–6). Sanday's language was intemperate,[23] but effective: indeed one modern writer could even say that "Sanday said all that really needs to be said about Wrede".[24] However, Sanday's only real argument of substance was the argument of the inadequacy of the resurrection to explain the rise of the belief that Jesus was the Messiah. Sanday's own explanation of the secrecy elements in the Gospels changed over the years. In an article in 1904, he adopted the traditional view that Jesus was modifying the popular idea of messiahship, from one involving military warfare to one of suffering service.[25] In his later lectures of 1907, Sanday inclined more to Schweitzer's idea of Jesus' messiahship being partly futurist: the secrecy charges reflected Jesus' reserve about making messianic claims, since "although He was the Messiah, the time for entering upon His full Messianic functions was not yet" (1907, 119). And this idea that messiahship involves a future role, or at least an as yet uncompleted task, has been supported by others since Sanday as explaining Jesus' reserve about himself.[26]

By far the most common explanation of at least part of the secrecy complex in Mark amongst those who would trace its origin back to Jesus himself has been the traditional view that Jesus wished to reinterpret the popular idea of messiahship, and to avoid any political overtones inherent in the title.[27] Such a theory runs into difficulties as a comprehensive treatment of Wrede's case. It involves a certain amount of reading between the lines: Mark himself gives no suggestion explicitly that the title "Messiah" needed modification before being acceptable to Jesus. Wrede himself had already pointed out that a more natural way for Jesus to have proceeded would have been to have given some explicit teaching on the subject rather than simply enjoining silence.[28] Further, such an explanation can only apply to some of the texts considered by Wrede. It *might* be appropriate in explaining the secrecy charge at 8:30,[29] but not in explaining other passages, e.g. the commands to silence after miracles. Thus

9

many who adopt this type of explanation for 8:30 have to give different explanations for other secrecy texts.[30]

Others have seen the secret in more comprehensive terms within the life of Jesus. For Schniewind, the secret was not something confined to single verses: rather, it underlay every synoptic pericope (1963, 56; cf. Taylor, 1954). Schniewind explicitly took up the ideas of Bultmann who had presented the picture of Jesus as the prophet of the End-time whose message signified the presence of the eschatological time of salvation (Bultmann, 1951, 3–32). For Bultmann this implicitly involved a Christology.[31] Schniewind turned this round and identified this implicit Christology with the messianic secret. Thus the secret consisted of the fact that eschatology had now become joyfully present in Jesus' own proclamation, in his call to repentance and in his offer of forgiveness (1952, 6). Yet the one who brings the offer of the presence of the Kingdom is the non-royal Messiah coming with the powerless word. "The secret of the reign of God is the secret of the word" (1952, 10). Nevertheless, despite the force of much of what is said about Jesus here, this does not really tackle the question of why the secrecy motifs appear in the way they do in *Mark*, apparently often in editorial, rather than traditional, passages.[32]

Not unrelated to Schniewind's approach was that of Lohmeyer, who also saw the secret as underlying the whole tradition. He too traced the idea back to Jesus himself, but admitted that Mark had developed the idea considerably.[33] For Lohmeyer, Jesus was both an ordinary man among men, and also the Son of Man, the eschatological bringer of salvation. The messianic secret is the result of the juxtaposition of these two radically different roles in the person of Jesus. In Jesus, the Son of Man has become man and hence there is an inherent duality in Jesus of hidden and revealed, exalted and lowly, divine and human. Any such duality in the tradition led Lohmeyer to interpret the text in terms of a Son of Man Christology.[34] But as Son of Man, Jesus is still essentially part of the divine realm rather than the human, and as such he is opposed by this world and finally rejected.[35] Thus Lohmeyer reinterpreted the "messianic" secret as a "Son of Man" secret. However, he never really developed his theories about how the secret was seen by Mark. Further, there was a basic assumption in his work that when what is eschatological, or other-worldly, enters human history, it must take the form of a *hidden* reality (cf. Sjöberg, 1955, 122f) and this is by no means easy to maintain in the light of Jewish apocalyptic ideas in general.

At this point the work of Sjöberg becomes important. Sjöberg, like Lohmeyer, sought to find the roots of the secrecy motifs in the Son of Man title, but he went further in trying to show why Jesus as Son of Man must be a hidden figure. Like Lohmeyer, Sjöberg conceded that Mark might have developed some of the secrecy elements in the tradition, but the fundamental idea went back to Jesus himself and to the ideas associated with the title Son of Man which he adopted (246). Sjöberg claimed that the idea of hiddenness was inherent in Jewish apocalyptic beliefs about the Son of Man–Messiah. He referred to the idea, found in some later rabbis, of the Messiah living on earth, hidden and unrecognized (72–80). Although the evidence for this was late (post-Christian), Sjöberg claimed that these examples showed how the concept of a hidden Messiah could arise within Judaism (82). A closer parallel to the gospel accounts was to be found in the apocalyptic figure of the Son of Man. The Jewish evidence, especially 1 Enoch and 4 Ezra, showed a basic idea of the Son of Man as a heavenly being who would remain hidden until revealed to all at the eschaton (48f). There was too the general belief that, although apocalyptic secrets would be fully revealed at the end of time, God had already revealed these secrets to a chosen few (1ff). This then was the background for the secrecy elements in the Gospels: Jesus on earth was the Son of Man, but he was only revealed as such to a chosen few, whilst from the rest of the world he must remain hidden.

Sjöberg's theories have not gone uncriticized.[36] The idea of a hidden Messiah on earth is not attested prior to the 2nd century A.D.[37] The dates of 1 Enoch and 4 Ezra may also provide a problem if these writings are to be used as evidence of pre-Christian ideas.[38] But in any case, the Son of Man in 1 Enoch and 4 Ezra differs significantly from the Gospels' presentation in that in the former the Son of Man remains inactive in heaven, whereas in the latter Jesus is active on earth.[39] There is thus no real parallel to the idea of a Son of Man, or Messiah, hidden but active on earth prior to the eschaton. Moreover, the secrecy charges in Mark are, almost without exception, quite separate from references to Jesus as Son of Man; rather the two strands in Mark, i.e. secrecy and Son of Man, seem unrelated.

This then is a brief survey of some of the attempts to deal with Wrede's case by locating the origin of the secrecy elements in Mark's Gospel in the ministry of Jesus himself. The most forceful modern presentation of the view that the secret is basically historical is the article of Dunn reprinted here, where Dunn seeks to give a broader justification for the theory that Jesus was seeking to modify tradi- tional ideas of messiahship, by referring to a wider selection of texts than just the secrecy charges themselves. However, in all these attempts to deal with the messianic secret, it still remains question- able whether Wrede's case has been met on its own terms, viz. as an analysis of *Mark*. How do the secrecy elements function for Mark, and why do the secrecy charges appear in the redactional strand of the Gospel?[40] E.g., Dunn allows the possibility of a re- dactional secrecy motif in 1:34 and 3:11f, but he does not develop this further.[41] The significance which Mark saw in the secret still therefore requires an explanation.[42]

Wrede's book has always been more favourable received in Germany than in England. In England, discussion has often centred on the question of historicity, and many have been content to trace the secrecy elements back to Jesus himself. In Germany, since the rise of form criticism, there has always been a greater willingness to accept some, if not all, of Wrede's evidence as indicating the existence of secondary elements in the tradition. In particular, the form critics Bultmann and Dibelius accepted much of Wrede's theory, even though some of the details were changed significantly.

Bultmann adopted Wrede's theory enthusiastically. Indeed he believed that the theory proved quite conclusively that Jesus had never claimed to be Messiah. (See especially his 1919 article.) Although always claiming to be adopting Wrede's results *in toto*, Bultmann made one significant alteration in that he assumed that the secrecy theory was due to Mark himself, whereas Wrede had claimed that it was pre-Marcan.[43] Many have agreed with this altera- tion to Wrede's original theory. However, this then creates difficulties for Wrede's explanation about the origin of the secret, as stemming from the juxtaposition of a non-messianic and a messianic view of Jesus' earthly life. For Mark himself seems unaware of a non- messianic view, and hence Wrede's historical explanation requires modification.[44] However the need for such a modification was not recognized by Bultmann himself. Bultmann endorsed Dibelius' de- scription of Mark's Gospel as a "book of secret epiphanies", and he characterized Mark as "the union of the Hellenistic kerygma about Christ ... with the tradition of the story of Jesus" (1963, 347f). This assertion by Bultmann, if taken very broadly, has been extremely influential, as we shall see.

Dibelius too endorsed Wrede's theory in some respects, although he also made some modifications. He claimed that the number of features which Wrede had included from Mark should be reduced.

E.g., the withdrawal of Jesus from the crowds to perform miracles (cf. 5:40; 7:33; 8:23) is nothing to do with the messianic secret but is simply a standard feature in such miracle stories (Dibelius, 93f); on the other hand, the injunctions to silence after the miracles *are* part of Mark's messianic secret (73f).[45] Like Bultmann, Dibelius ascribed the secrecy theory to Mark's own redaction, but he interpreted it differently. For Dibelius, its origin lay in Mark's concern to explain the fact that Jesus' messiahship had not been universally recognized. Mark used the secret to show

> why He was not recognized as Messiah by the people and why He was opposed, despised, and finally sent to the cross. In this way the gospel of Mark was written as *a book of secret epiphanies* (230).

This is one of the classic presentations of the so-called "apologetic" explanation of the secret, i.e. seeing it as a device to explain to later readers Jesus' conspicuous lack of success. It is a type of explanation which has always had considerable support, and is represented in this volume by the contribution of T. A. Burkill.[46]

However, as an explanation of all the secrecy elements in Mark as assembled by Wrede, the apologetic theory is not entirely satisfactory. Wrede himself said that he considered the theory at first, but rejected it on the grounds that Mark's presentation of the secret "at no point awakens the impression that in this we are dealing with an apologetic evasion" (1971, 226).[47] Above all the apologetic theory fails to account for the element of revelation which exists alongside the element of secrecy in Mark. The commands to silence are sometimes broken (1:45, 7:36f); and Jesus' condemnation to death in Mark is not the result of any secrecy being imposed: on the contrary, it is precisely due to the veil of secrecy being lifted (14:61f). Thus Jesus' lack of success cannot be due simply to lack of knowledge on the part of the crowds and the Jewish authorities arising from the secrecy charges: for Mark's own presentation shows that such knowledge *was* at times available to others. The apologetic theory can provide a good explanation for the saying about the purpose of parables in 4:11f, but the conjunction of messianic revelation with messianic secrecy is more difficult.[48]

If then the breaking of the secret causes difficulty for the apologetic theory, it was precisely this which formed the basis for the interpretation of H. J. Ebeling, in what is sometimes called the "epiphanic" interpretation of the secret. Ebeling claimed that Mark's Gospel is to be understood as primarily kerygmatic, i.e. as an expression of the kerygma in Mark's day. Attempts to use the Gospel to discover anything about the underlying history of Jesus' own ministry are simply inappropriate to the nature of the gospel material. The messianic secret must therefore also be interpreted in terms of the kerygma. As far as Mark was concerned, there was no question but that Jesus' life was seen as messianic, as the epiphany of the Son of God. Hence there was no possibility that any of the secrecy elements could be trying to hide this fact. Thus these elements were all interpreted by Ebeling as literary devices which simply highlight the glory of Jesus and stress the epiphanic nature of the events concerned. So, for example, the main point in the commands to silence is not the commands themselves; rather the stress is on the way in which such commands are repeatedly broken, and the commands simply highlight the irresistible way in which Jesus' fame spread (115ff). Similarly, the failure of the disciples to understand Jesus' teaching is merely a stylistic device which conveys to the reader the idea of the transcendent nature of the revelation being given (146ff). The Marcan theory about parables serves a similar aim: the characters in the text differ, in that the disciples are distinguished from the outside world which does not understand; nevertheless, the basic idea remains the same: the readers are shown that they too belong within the circle of those to whom the mystery has been revealed, and this implies both their privileged position as well as the responsibilities entailed (179ff).

Ebeling's interpretation brought into prominence Mark's own kerygmatic purpose; so too it took seriously the element of revelation which exists alongside the element of secrecy. Nevertheless, his theory has won little support as the means of explaining all the secrecy elements in Mark,[49] though some have adopted this type of explanation for part of the evidence.[50] Ebeling's approach was undoubtedly very one-sided in driving a deep wedge between kerygma and history, as if the latter had no place in discussing the former. If Mark was so interested in the present kerygma, *and* so uninterested in past history, it is strange that he should have chosen to dress up his version of the kerygma in a form which appears to be a description of past history.[51] Further, the theory runs into some difficulties within the Gospel itself. The key to Ebeling's interpretation was the fact that some commands to silence are disobeyed. But this does not cover all the secrecy charges, since at times there is no mention of their being broken. Ebeling was thus sometimes forced to read an implied breaking of the command into the Marcan text. E.g. the order in 5:43 was seen by Ebeling as so clearly historically impossible that the reader *must* have assumed that it could not be obeyed.[52]

But the text itself gives no justification for this. The time limit in 9:9 also causes difficulties for Ebeling, as Strecker points out.[53] The apocalyptic idea which Ebeling referred to, of a secret to be universally revealed at a future date, does not provide a true parallel to the text of Mark here: in other apocalyptic literature the time of revelation is future, whereas in Mark the time in question is now past.

The tension in Mark between secrecy and revelation thus causes difficulty for both the apologetic and epiphanic interpretations of the secret. In Wrede's theory, this tension was closely connected with the temporal distinction: the period before the resurrection is the time of secrecy, but after Easter a new situation arises. The significance of the resurrection as marking the boundary line between secrecy and revelation has also been stressed by Percy (286ff). Like Wrede, Percy claimed that the secret was due to the coming together of two streams of the tradition. However, he disagreed with Wrede's claim that one of these streams had viewed Jesus' life as unmessianic, for the secret in Mark was not just an auxiliary concept and appeared to be more far-reaching than Wrede's theory implied (280). So Percy suggested that the secret was the result of one stream of tradition, which had always viewed Jesus' life as messianic, being met by another which had reflected more deeply on the importance of the cross and resurrection. Thus Percy claimed that Mark's Gospel is to be interpreted as very similar to the Pauline kerygma (cf. 1 Cor. 2:8; 2 Cor. 13:4; Phil. 2:7f), where Jesus' earthly life is to be seen as one of humility and lowliness, and his true glory only dates from the resurrection. In Mark, "lowliness" is replaced by "secrecy", but the basic idea remains the same.[54] Thus the disciples *could* not see Jesus' true glory prior to Easter, and given this understanding of the importance of the cross, the secrecy charges and the general failure to understand Jesus during his earthly life appear as a necessary part of the story.[55] The time limit set to the period of secrecy in 9:9 is thus taken very seriously. The period of secrecy is Jesus' earthly life and is now past. A very similar view is represented in this collection of essays by the article of G. Strecker.

Nevertheless, it is not clear that this view can solve all the problems of the secret. There are difficulties raised by those points in Mark where the secret is broken *prior* to Easter (cf. 1:45; 7:36).[56] Further, if it is true that the secret belongs primarily to the past, then it is not clear why Mark should have taken the trouble to stress it so much in his Gospel, and it becomes doubtful whether it has kerygmatic significance.[57]

This interpretation has clear links with Bultmann's claim that

15

Mark is setting the stories about Jesus in terms of the (hellenistic) kerygma. Others have tried to develop Bultmann's insight along different lines. One extreme example of this has been the comprehensive interpretation of Mark's Gospel by J. Schreiber in terms of a gnostic redeemer myth. Applied to the secrecy elements in Mark, Jesus' hiddenness and his failure to be understood are compared to the ideas in the gnostic myth where the redeemer is unrecognized by the supernatural powers (cf. 1 Cor. 2:8) (Schreiber, 156f). However, this theory has been heavily criticized. Without going into the vexed question of whether there was a pre-Christian redeemer myth, Mark's Gospel lacks vital elements in the proposed scheme: there is no idea of pre-existence in Mark, nor is there any typically gnostic cosmology reflected in Mark; further, the distinctive feature of Mark is that Jesus *is* recognized by the supernatural powers but not by men.[58]

If the attempt to interpret Mark in gnostic terms has found little support, Bultmann's thesis has been fruitful in a slightly different direction. Probably the most decisive contribution has been that of H. Conzelmann. Conzelmann accepts Wrede's analysis of the secrecy texts as indicating that they are secondary additions to the tradition. However, he rejects Wrede's explanation of their origin, referring to what has become the standard critique of Wrede's original theory, viz., that Mark's material was never understood non-messianically (1968, 42). Conzelmann ascribes the secret to Mark, and says:

> His contribution does not consist in his forcing non-messianic elements into a framework of christological belief, but rather in his putting together a mass of materials already understood christologically in such a way as to conform to the kerygma (understood in the sense of the secrecy christology) (1968, 42).

He says that, "It is not the non-messianic character of the units in the tradition which causes the evangelist trouble, but rather their messianic character", so that the secret represents "an expression of a positive understanding of revelation" (1968, 42f). The secret is thus the means whereby Mark *controls* the Christology of his tradition by pointing to the cross (cf. 1970, 181f). Only by such a means can Mark prevent his account from becoming a series of unambiguous epiphanies of a divine being,[59] or, in Conzelmann's famous words, "the secrecy theory is the hermeneutical presupposition of the genre 'gospel'" (1968, 43).

Clearly Conzelmann's interpretation has much in common with the theory of Percy and Strecker: both stress the centrality of the cross for

Mark as the determining factor in any interpretation of the life of Jesus; so too, both claim that a true understanding of Jesus is only possible after the resurrection. Nevertheless, there is an important difference: for Strecker and others, the secret is a matter of past history alone; for Conzelmann the secret still applies in the present:

> The faithful – i.e. the readers of the book – are shown the mystery in such a way that it remains veiled from the world even after Easter. It can only be grasped through faith, i.e. in the church. To those without it remains hidden (1969, 139).[60]

This theory, that the secret reflects the central importance of the cross as the only valid key for interpreting the person of Jesus, has found widespread support.[61] It is represented in this volume by the article of E. Schweizer, who also stresses the importance of discipleship, of "following" Jesus in the way of the cross. This pastoral aspect of the secret is also brought out by others: the disciple too must follow in the same way of humility and service as his master.[62] Thus, according to this interpretation, the secret is Mark's way of developing his *theologia crucis*. The cross and resurrection are thus the "ending" of the secret in that they provide the key to the interpretation of the whole, and indeed the story itself is told in such a way as to lead up to this ending.[63]

One very popular further development of this theory has been the attempt to specify in more detail the Christology which Mark is seeking to control by the secret. Many have seen Mark as deliberately opposing a specific Christology in his community, usually described as a *theios anēr* Christology, i.e. a view which sees Jesus primarily in terms of a great miracle worker and the possessor of supernatural power.[64] In this respect reference is often made to D. Georgi's study on Paul's opponents in 2 Corinthians. Many would claim that there is a close link between the Christology of Paul's opponents and the Christology which Mark is seeking to control: both profess a *theios anēr* type of Christology and couple this with a belief that the same miraculous powers have been handed on to the community. The most thorough-going interpretation of Mark's Gospel along these lines is that of Weeden, who sees Mark's attitude as one of outright opposition to such a Christology. Others, such as Luz, would see Mark as trying to correct the views of his community rather more gently, by incorporation rather than by outright opposition.[65] In either case Mark is seen as taking the stress away from the miracles and pointing to the cross as the decisive event for reaching a true evaluation of Jesus.[66]

17

Overall, the theory that the secret is Mark's way of stressing the centrality of the cross is very attractive. It takes seriously the results of form criticism which sees that a non-messianic Jesus tradition is hard to envisage; it also takes seriously the time limit set in 9:9 (even if it has to interpret this as referring to only the possibility of under-standing after Easter); above all it seeks to explain the relationship between history and kerygma which is involved in the writing of any "Gospel".[67] Nevertheless, there are still problems. Why do some of the miracle stories lack a secrecy charge (e.g. 5:1–20)?[68] Why too are some of the secrecy charges disobeyed whilst others are not?

These are the main lines of interpretation of the messianic secret in Mark. Many have followed Wrede in assuming that the texts which he collected are all to be explained in the same way. This has frequently been contested by those who would see the secrecy elements as originating in Jesus' own ministry.[69] However, even amongst those who would see Marcan redaction at work in some parts of the secrecy material, there is one part of Wrede's evidence which is often discussed separately from the rest. This is the motif of the disciples' lack of understanding. Many would claim that this should be considered separately from the other secrecy passages. For example, Tyson points out that, in the rest of the secrecy material, people recognize Jesus' true identity but are forbidden to publicize it, whereas the disciples have a wrong conception of Jesus' nature.[70]

Very diverse positions have been adopted with regard to this apparently unfavourable portrait of the disciples in Mark. One view which has attracted a lot of interest is that the disciples represent a group within Mark's own community, and Mark's unfavourable picture represents a polemical attitude towards this group. This view is represented in this volume by the article of Tyson, who claims that the disciples represent the Jerusalem church of Mark's day: these Christians have too narrow a view of messiahship (conceiving of it solely in royal terms), and fail to give central importance to the cross. The view that the Jerusalem church is under attack in Mark is also shared by others.[71] By far the most thorough-going explanation of Mark along these lines is that of T. J. Weeden. Weeden does not specify the geographical location of Mark's opponents, but he sees them as represented by the disciples in the Gospel, and, like Tyson, he sees them as having an erroneous Christology. Peter's confession at 8:29 shows that he only under-stands Jesus as the Christ on the basis of the miracles: it is thus the confession of Jesus as a *theios anēr*. Weeden believes that the opponents based their claims on resurrection appearances which gave them positions of privilege and power. By contrast, he claims, Mark writes his story in such a way as to deny any resurrection appearances to the opponents at all: the transfiguration, claimed by the opponents to be a resurrection appearance, is put back into the ministry of Jesus, and the secrecy charge of 9:9 shows how such a claim by the opponents might arise (news of the story only originated after Easter) but also that it is false. The silence of the women at the tomb (16:8) shows that the disciples never received the angels' message and so can never have seen the risen Jesus.[72]

Such a reading of Mark is not without its difficulties. This wholly negative view of the disciples had already been rejected by Wrede,[73] and it involves a certain amount of forcing of the evidence. The ending of Mark (cf. 16:7) suggests a theophany and hence a restoration of the disciples, rather than their final rejection.[74] Further, negative features about the disciples are balanced by equally positive ones.[75] It is thus by no means clear that the disciples' role is one of implacable doctrinal opposition to Jesus.[76] Thus other critics would see the disciples' role in Mark more positively.[77] Also it may be that not all the passages originally listed by Wrede in this category have the same function: some may be using the motif of lack of understanding simply to highlight the importance of the miracle or teaching in question, and not all the passages suggest that the incomprehension is culpable.[78] Thus although the theory that Mark may be trying to correct another christological view by the secret is widely accepted, the refinement which would identify the disciples with the proponents of such a Christology is more difficult to sustain.

The problem of the unity of the secrecy motifs has also been raised by others, independently of the question of the disciples' incomprehension. We have seen that all the main explanations of the meaning of the secret in Mark explain different parts of the evidence very well, but each has its own difficulties. Thus a feature of some recent discussions of the problem has been the questioning of Wrede's initial premiss that all the secrecy texts must be explained in the same way, and the adoption of different explanations for various parts of the evidence. The most influential attempt to do this is that of U. Luz, who distinguishes two distinct motifs in Mark. The commands to silence after miracles are to be interpreted in the light of their being broken, and hence they simply highlight Jesus' glory as a miracle-worker (i.e. an "epiphanic" interpretation for this part of the evidence); however, the commands to silence which concern Jesus' identity (1:34; 3:11f; 8:30) are *not* disobeyed, and these show that Jesus' true identity can only be understood in the light of the cross.[79]

There has been a tendency among others to discount Mark's theological contribution almost entirely. For Trocmé, Wrede's collection of texts is really only a hotch-potch of unrelated material. He claims that the secrecy charges after miracles are the exception rather than the rule and are probably pre-Marcan; the commands to the demons are simply a suppression of praise from those who cannot be disciples; the failure of the disciples to understand has nothing to do with a *messianic* secret; the private instruction given to the disciples is never christological, but simply serves as a literary device to highlight the particular teaching involved. "In other words, under close scrutiny, the theory of the Messianic Secret simply vanishes for lack of evidence" (1973, 10). The most recent full-length discussion of the problem is that of H. Räisänen, whose concluding chapter is reproduced in this volume. Räisänen too questions the unity of the secrecy motifs. Different explanations probably apply in different cases. The "real" messianic secret only includes the commands to silence about Jesus' identity (1:34; 3:11f; 8:30). Räisänen argues that these texts are probably redactional, and he tentatively adopts a solution similar to that of Percy, that Jesus' true identity is only recognizable after Easter. However, he says that one should not exaggerate Mark's own theological contribution: there were many, at times contradictory, elements in the pre-Marcan tradition, and Mark may have been content to hand these on, rather than impose a consistent, theological viewpoint on the material. A similar view is taken by R. Pesch in his recent commentary on Mark. Pesch quotes Räisänen's conclusions extensively to show agreement with his own views. However, he goes even further than Räisänen in ascribing 3:11f and 8:30 to the pre-Marcan tradition. Thus only 1:34 is taken to be due to Mark's redaction. Mark is, for Pesch, the "conservative redactor", not the creative theologian which modern redaction critics have suggested.[80]

If the idea of the existence of the messianic secret in Mark is not rejected as a modern invention, there is still the problem of whether the secret should be regarded as an isolated phenomenon within early Christianity. Precise parallels in Judaism are not easy to discover, as we have seen. Wrede himself pointed to a few similar features in the Fourth Gospel, but concluded that "the actual idea of the messianic secret seems to have had only a short history" (1971, 244). This has been questioned in J. M. Robinson's recent article (1978). Parallels for some parts of the secrecy complex in

Mark, viz. the parable theory and the belief that Easter marked the dividing line between secrecy and revelation, are now amply documented from the Nag Hammadi texts. Jesus' mysterious teaching is there interpreted to the chosen few, usually after Easter. Robinson thus questions whether Wrede was right to concentrate primarily on the silencing commands and the question of Jesus' identity. Further, he points to the fact that in 8:32 Jesus speaks "openly", prior to Easter. Thus Robinson argues:

> There seems to be in Mark an effort to push back the hermeneutical turning point from Easter to the point in the so-called public ministry when Jesus began to teach kerygmatically ... It may be that we have to do here with what was in substance the rationale for the *genre* Gospel, as an emergent orthodoxy sought to validate Jesus prior to his death as a source of ultimate interpretation and not just as what emergent Gnosticism could all-too-readily dispense with, a coded text (1978, 142).

This attempt to use the Nag Hammadi texts to illuminate the messianic secret no doubt merits further discussion. Clearly there are problems of dating: how far is it legitimate to use these later gnostic texts as background for the earlier canonical Gospels? With regard to Robinson's specific points, it is possible that Wrede placed too much stress on the silencing commands. But these commands are still part of the secrecy complex in Mark, and it is not clear how they are illuminated by the gnostic texts. Moreover, 9:9, which comes after the "open" teaching in 8:32, still suggests that Easter will mark a significant turning-point in the revelation of what is secret. Nevertheless, Robinson's essay may show where further insights into the significance of the messianic secret may be gained.

This survey shows that there is a wide divergence of opinion about the correct interpretation of the secrecy elements in Mark. Most critics today would probably agree that Wrede's original explanation of the secret is not tenable, and that he tried to explain too many features of Mark's Gospel by his theory. (E.g. the secrecy charge in 1:25, and the privacy motif in the miracles, are probably standard features of such stories.) However, unanimity ends there. The problems of how much in Mark should be considered as part of the "messianic secret", how much goes back to Jesus, whether it is right to explain all the secrecy texts by a single theory, etc., are all questions which continue to receive different answers. There has been a recent trend, especially amongst American scholars, to use the methods and insights of literary criticism in analysing the gospel texts, and it may well be that such an approach may shed further light on the messianic secret in Mark.[81] Insights from the field of sociology may also be fruitful,[82] and the Nag Hammadi texts, now fully available in translated form, may enable us to extend the background against which we can interpret the Gospels.

The problems of the messianic secret in Mark is not of academic interest alone. Some earlier critics of Wrede's book believed that the conclusions which he drew about the lack of any messianic claims by Jesus undermined the basis of Christian faith. Others who have been more prepared to accept this feature of Wrede's theory would see the secret in Mark as the result of later Christians struggling with the problems of their faith in new situations. The latter approach makes the messianic secret no less relevant for contemporary Christianity than the former. For only in dialogue with the past, and with Christians who struggled to respond to their own situation, can Christians today begin to work out what their attitudes should be.

NOTES

1 Wrede, 1971. The term "messianic secret" has become the conventional English equivalent of the German *Messiasgeheimnis* (the term which Wrede used in the original title of his book in German in 1901) and so has been used here. However the German word *Geheimnis* carries the sense of "mystery" as well as "secret", so that a rigid translation of *Geheimnis* by "secret" is sometimes misleading.

2 The importance of Wrede's work is particularly stressed by Bultmann, 1964, 41f. Cf. also W. C. Robinson, pp. 97f here.

3 Cf. D. R. Catchpole's review of Wrede's book, *EvQ* 46 (1974) 55f.

4 Cf. the comments of W. G. Kümmel, *Introduction to the New Testament* (London: SCM/Nashville and New York: Abingdon, 1975) 91: "The aim of the evangelist in introducing the dogmatic theory is in no way clearly perceptible", and Luz: "The messianic secret is still a mystery" (p. 75 here).

5 Histories of research are to be found in Ebeling, 1939; Percy, 1953, 271ff; Clark, 1962; Blevins, 1965; Glasswell, 1965a; Minette de Tillesse, 1968, 9–34; Aune, 1969, 1–13; Räisänen, 1976, 18–49; Powley, 1979. However, nearly all of these are either not in English, or not easily available to the general reader, being in the form of unpublished theses.

6 H. J. Holtzmann, *Die synoptischen Evangelien* (Leipzig: Engelmann, 1863); B. Weiss, *A Manual of Introduction to the New Testament* (ET London: Hodder & Stoughton, 1888), both building on the earlier studies of C. G. Wilke, *Der Urevangelist* (Leipzig, 1838) and C. H. Weisse, *Die evangelische Geschichte* (Leipzig, 1838).

7 This is of course a non sequitur: the fact that Mark is earlier than the other Gospels can show nothing about its historical reliability in absolute terms.

8 See Wrede's own summary (1971, 11f); also Räisänen, 1976, 19.

9 Thus Wrede is probably more important than Schweitzer in bringing to an end the "old quest" for the historical Jesus: see J. M. Robinson, 1959, 32ff.

10 See, however, Robinson's article here for doubts about how far Wrede was true to his own principles in this respect.

11 Wrede rejected the view that "Son of Man" here might be a roundabout way of saying "I" or "man" by claiming that for *Mark* it must be a messianic designation. (Wrede tended to use the term "messianic" somewhat loosely to refer to anything which suggested that Jesus had supernatural power and authority.)

12 See Wrede's own summary of the views of his predecessors (1971, 255ff).

13 Wrede referred to 4:13; 4:40–1; 6:50–2; 7:18; 8:16–21; 9:5f; 9:19; 10:24; 14:37–41 (1971, 101f).

14 Wrede has frequently been misread as claiming that the secret is due to Mark himself (cf. Räisänen, 24, for a list of authors). But see also Robinson's article here, where he shows how, in most of his book, Wrede appears to assume that the secret is the work of Mark himself, and only introduces the theory of a pre-Marcan stage at the end of his analysis.

15 Robinson says that Wrede appealed to "inconsistencies" (pp. 98f here); however, Wrede only spoke of elements that were unresolved or unharmonized (*unausgeglichenes*), which is perhaps rather weaker than "inconsistent".

16 Cf. Schweitzer's criticism of Wrede, noted below; also Taylor, 1948; Aune, 1969; see too Dunn's essay reprinted here.

17 Cf. the comment of Barbour, 1968, 327: "Much of Wrede's theory about Mark could still be true even if Jesus had as a matter of history only forborne to make Messianic claims because they would be misunderstood."

18 See Jülicher, 1906, 23; Bousset, 1906, 168f (Bousset later changed his mind about the secret: see n. 46 below). In England the same argument was used by Sanday, 1907, 75f; Peake, 1924, 56; Rawlinson, 1925, 260; Taylor, 1948, 147. The argument has some validity, but it is by no means clear that the only alternative is that the title stems from Jesus' own claims for himself during his ministry. Cf. N. A. Dahl, "The Crucified Messiah", in *The Crucified Messiah and Other Essays* (ET Minneapolis: Augsburg, 1974) 10–36, who argues that the title Messiah may derive primarily from the charges made against Jesus at his trial: Jesus' silence in the face of the charge meant that he was crucified as Messiah. The early Church then turned this into a positive confession of faith in the light of the resurrection, seen as God's vindication of the crucified Messiah.

19 See n. 46 below.

20 Wrede replied to Weiss in his later article of 1904, this being virtually the only answer made by Wrede to his critics (he died in 1906). Wrede still defended his thesis by referring to the stereotyped nature of these commands as implying a common origin for them all. (For a similar modern view, see Horstmann, 1969, 125.) In fact Wrede was probably on weak ground here: many would now see the command in 1:25 as traditional in Mark, the silencing of the demon being the standard means whereby the power of the demon is overcome – cf. O. Bauernfeind's programmatic study, *Die Worte der Dämonen im Markusevangelium* (Stuttgart, 1927). See too Bultmann, 1963, 209f; Kee, 1977, 169; and several others including Luz, p. 81 here, and Strecker, p. 51 here.

21 Weiss, 1903, 236f; Bousset, 1906, 172ff; Wernle, 1917, 339.

22 For the generally negative reaction of English scholarship to German "scepticism" in the earlier part of this century, see Robert Morgan, "Non Angli sed Angeli: Some Anglican Reactions to German Gospel Criticism", in S. W. Sykes, D. Holmes (ed.), *New Studies in Theology I* (London: Duckworth, 1980) 1–30. Cf. Peake's comment: "Wrede's solution has met with little or any acceptance. And rightly so, for it involves a scepticism as to the trustworthiness of our narratives so radical that, if it could be justified, we could hardly trust them for anything" (1924, 56). This can scarcely be called a scientific argument!

23 He said that Wrede wrote "in the style of a Prussian official" with "all the arrogance of a certain sort of common sense" (70). He accused Wrede of a lack of imagination (70) and called his theory "utterly artificial and impossible" (74).

24 S. Neill, *The Interpretation of the New Testament 1861–1961* (Oxford: OUP, 1966) 248.

25 The secrecy must be "connected with the recasting of the Messianic idea which our Lord certainly carried out, divesting it of its associations with political action and transforming it from a kingdom of this world to a Kingdom of God and of the Spirit" (1904, 324).

26 Cf. Taylor, 1948, 151: "In truth the Messiah, He would not be the Messiah until His task was accomplished." Cf. too Longenecker, 1969, noting possible parallels with the Teacher of Righteousness at Qumran and Bar Kochbah, claims that "no man can be defined as a messiah in Judaism before he has accomplished the task of the anointed" (213, quoting Flusser). See too Dunn, p. 129 here. Sanday revised his views about the apocalyptic element in Jesus' teaching in a later article (1911), where he rather backtracked on his earlier enthusiasm for Schweitzer's views. He did not discuss the secrecy elements explicitly here, but the logic of his view would suggest a return to the position of his 1904 article.

27 Cf. Sanday's earlier view (n. 25 above); J. Weiss, Bousset and Wernle as in n. 21 above; Peake, 1924, 66f; Rawlinson, 1925, 262; Taylor, 1952, 377 (though he appears to criticize this view on p. 123); O. Cullmann, *The Christology of the New Testament* (ET London: SCM/Philadelphia: Westminster, 1959) 124f; Moule, 1975, 241; Dunn, pp. 127f here; cf. too Manson's claim: "The messianic secret ... is not concerned with the identity of the Messiah but with the nature of his task" (1955, 220).

28 Wrede, 1971, 41f; see too Percy, 1953, 272; Minette de Tillesse, 1968, 19; Räisänen, 1976, 30. Dunn infers this from a number of different passages.

29 But if so, why does the secrecy charge come *before* Peter has rejected Jesus' teaching about the necessity of suffering? By v. 30 Peter has given no hint that he has a false idea of messiahship. Thus, contra Manson (n. 27 above), 8:30 does appear to be about the identity of the Messiah, rather than simply about the nature of his task. (8:30 is not discussed by Manson.)

30 As indeed is done by Rawlinson, Moule and Dunn (e.g. Jesus might have wished for privacy). Cullmann does not deal with the rest of Wrede's evidence. Taylor's explanation of other texts appears to be somewhat confused: see Powley, 1980. Cf. too Barbour's comment about the theory that Jesus was avoiding political ideas of messiahship: "This does not cover all the passages concerned

very effectively, and there is a remarkable lack of passages in which Jesus is reported as trying to counter possible misunderstandings" (1968, 327).

31 Cf. Bultmann's famous sentence: "Jesus' call to decision implies a Christology" (1951, 43).

32 Cf. Räisänen, 1976, 32. See too Bultmann's critique (1951, 32) and also Strecker, pp. 51–3 here, where this claim is given further backing. If this claim can be established, then it renders questionable all attempts to see the secrecy texts as basically historical: cf. Fuller, 1963, 94f. There is, however, a danger of circularity in the argument: a secrecy text is said to be redactional because the secrecy motif is Marcan, but the secret is only said to be Marcan because all the secrecy texts are redactional. Vocabulary statistics are perhaps a better guide (cf. Luz's article here).

33 Cf. Lohmeyer, 1963, 41. E.g. 1:44; 5:43; 8:26 are taken as pre-Marcan, whilst 1:34; 7:36; 9:9 are taken as redactional.

34 1963, 25 (on 1:11), 28 (on 1:12f), etc.

35 Ibid., 5–7.

36 See Percy, 1953, 282–6; Burkill, 1961, 206–13; Minette de Tillesse, 1968, 30f; Horstmann, 1969, 111f.

37 First in Justin's *Dialogue with Trypho*, 8.

38 4 Ezra is to be dated *c.*100 A.D. The date of the Similitudes of Enoch (i.e. chaps. 37–71, which is the part containing the references to the "Son of Man") is uncertain. So far, however, no parts of this section of 1 Enoch have been found at Qumran, although fragments from elsewhere in the book have been discovered. This must, therefore, cast some doubt on whether the Similitudes are pre-Christian.

39 The parallelism would be better if in 1 Enoch, Enoch could be identified as the Son of Man whilst on earth. However, Sjöberg rejected this interpretation, claiming that in chap. 71, Enoch *becomes* the Son of Man only after leaving the earth (Sjöberg, 1955, 125 n. 1).

40 Cf. n. 32 above.

41 See p. 130 here; cf. Moule, 1975, 242f.

42 Cf. Räisänen, 1976, 32f. The issues of historicity and Mark's theology are logically separable: what is theologically important for Mark is not *ipso facto* unhistorical. Cf. Barbour's comment quoted in n. 17 above.

43 Bultmann, 1951, 32; 1963, 347; 1964, 41.

44 See Strecker, pp. 50f here.

45 Manson, 1955, 212, is somewhat misleading when he appeals to Dibelius and claims that a distinction must be drawn between the manner and the fact of the cure, and that 5:43 etc. apply to only the former. In fact, Dibelius does make this distinction, but claims that texts like 5:43 are about the fact, and *not* just about the manner, of the cure; Dibelius thought that they were patently unhistorical and therefore part of Mark's messianic secret.

46 See pp. 44–8 here. Also Weiss, 1903, 58 (for those parts of the text which are not historical); Wernle, 1907, 115; Bousset's later view, 1970, 107f; Lightfoot, 1935, 66–76; Grant, 1943, 161f; Nineham, 1963, 31f; Haenchen, 1968, 133f; also, in

part, Minette de Tillesse, 1968, 323f. Cf. too Boobyer, 1960, who says that the secret sets out to explain not the Jews' rejection of Jesus, but God's rejection of the Jews. In Burkill's view Mark also has a tendency to portray the earthly Jesus in the full glare of a divine epiphany, as in the Fourth Gospel, and this leads to some "strain" on the secret. (Cf. Burkill, 1961, 196f; 1963, 188–209). This tension in Mark is similar to that postulated by Wrede; but whereas for the latter the two views were ascribed to distinct streams of tradition, Burkill appears to postulate two radically different views in Mark's own redaction.

47 Hence one must not confuse Wrede's view with the apologetic theory, as is done by, for example, Cullmann, 1959 (n. 27), 124f; Vielhauer, 1965, 201; Kee, 1977, 168.

48 For this standard critique of the apologetic theory, see Percy, 1953, 281; Sjöberg, 1955, 117f; Räisänen, 1976, 35f; see further, Dahl's essay here, p. 29f.

49 But see Theissen, 1974, 220.

50 See Luz's essay here; also Tagawa, 1966, and Roloff, 1969 (see n. 79 below); Minette de Tillesse, 1968, 51, 111, 180, 251, etc.; also Percy, 1953, 289, referring to 4:40f; 8:32f; 9:32.

51 See Powley, 1969, 309.

52 Ebeling, 1939, 133; cf. the comment of Koch, 1975, 66.

53 See Strecker, p. 58 here; also Räisänen, 1976, 115.

54 Percy, 1953, 299.

55 Cf. Kertelge, 1970, 191ff; also those listed in n. 61 below.

56 As recognized by Percy himself (1953, 298); also Räisänen, 1976, 44.

57 See Ambrozic, 1972, 28f.

58 See Vielhauer, 1965, 200; Strecker, p. 55 here; for a fuller discussion of Schreiber's views, see E. Best, *The Temptation and the Passion – The Marcan Soteriology* (Cambridge: CUP, 1965) 125–32.

59 Cf. Marxsen, 1968, 137; also Glasswell, 1965b, 157: "The theme of the messianic secret stands over against false approaches to history or miracle which would preclude the choice of faith and forget that this is based on the Gospel and not on anything to do with the history itself."

60 Cf. also Glasswell, 1980. For Glasswell, the secret's significance is that it brings out the true relationship between history and the gospel as one of constant tension: neither can be dissolved into the other, but the two cannot be separated. The historical Jesus is the basis and presupposition of the gospel, but the preaching of the gospel and the corresponding commitment of faith are not dispensable.

61 See also Vielhauer, 1965, 213f; Luz p. 87 here; Schreiber, 1961, 158f; J. M. Robinson, 1962, 203f; Koester, 1971, 189; Keck, 1966, 368; Fuller, 1965, 228; Betz, 1968, 124; Minette de Tillesse, 1968, 321ff; Ambrozic, 1972, 99; Lambrecht, 1973, 273; Koch, 1975, 186; Anderson, 1976, 94f, 216.

62 See, for example, Keck, 1966; Minette de Tillesse, 1968, 278, 319ff; Lambrecht, 1973; also the essays here by W. C. Robinson and Dahl.

63 For the importance of the "ending" of any literary work as giving meaning and coherence to the whole, see Kermode, 1967. However, it should be noted that this claim about the literary function of the secret within Mark is quite indepen-

dent of the question of the historicity of the secret: cf. nn. 17, 42 above. Also the possibility that the cross constitutes the literary "ending" of the story does not necessarily mean that the secret itself is thought of as ended: cf. the difference between Conzelmann and Strecker noted above.

64 So, for example, Schreiber, Vielhauer, Fuller, Koester, Keck, Luz, Schweizer; also Weeden, 1971.

65 See p. 88 here. Luz has recently attempted to reconstruct more precisely the views of the pre-Marcan tradition in "Das Jesusbild der vormarkinischen Tradition", in G. Strecker (ed.), *Jesus Christus in Historie und Theologie* (Festschrift for H. Conzelmann. Tübingen: Mohr, 1975) 347–74.

66 For attempts to isolate pre-Marcan traditions, especially in the miracle stories, which present the view which Mark may be trying to correct, see L. E. Keck, "Mk 3,7–12 and Mark's Christology", *JBL* 84 (1965) 341–58; P. J. Achtemeier, "Toward the Isolation of Pre-Markan Miracle Catenae", *JBL* 89 (1970) 265–91, and "The Origin and Function of the Pre-Marcan Miracle Catenae", *JBL* 91 (1972) 198–221; Kuhn, 1971, 191ff.

67 See especially Conzelmann and Glasswell.

68 See Räisänen, 1976, 42; also W. C. Robinson's article here.

69 See the articles of Moule and Dunn; also Manson, 1955, 212: "No voice from Heaven has declared that all the injunctions to secrecy in Mark spring from the same motive, and there is no reason on earth why we should suppose that they do."

70 See Tyson, p. 36 here; cf. too Kuby, 1958.

71 See Bultmann, 1963, 258; Schreiber, 1961, 177–9; Tagawa, 1966, 174ff; Trocmé, 1975, 120ff; J. D. Crossan, "Mark and the Relatives of Jesus", *NovT* 15 (1973) 81–113; Kelber, 1974.

72 A similar theory, i.e. that Mark's presentation of the disciples is wholly negative, is given by Kelber, 1974. However, according to Kelber, the opponents of Mark (represented by the disciples in the story) err not so much in their Christology as in their eschatological beliefs.

73 Wrede, 1971, 106; see too Catchpole's review of Wrede (n. 3), 56f.

74 Cf. D. R. Catchpole, "The Fearful Silence of the Women at the Tomb", *Journal of Theology for Southern Africa* 18 (1977) 3–10.

75 See Meye, 1967, and Räisänen, 1976, 136, who refer to texts such as Mark 1:17; 3:14f; 6:7–13. Weeden, 1971, 168, thinks that these give the opponents' views of the disciples.

76 Best, 1977, 393f, points out that where the disciples do oppose Jesus, it is by no means exclusively with reference to the question of Christology. For further discussion of Weeden, see Schweizer, 1973; C. J. A. Hickling, "A Problem of Method in Gospel Research", *Religious Studies* 10 (1974) 339–46.

77 E.g. as guarantors of the Church's tradition of Jesus' words (Meye, 1967); as representatives of the later Church and examples for later Christians, partly to be followed (Peter's confession), partly to take warning from (Peter's rejection of Jesus' way of the cross) (Hawkin, 1972); as examples for the community to show God's love as refusing to give up even after human failure (Best, 1977).

78   See Focant, 1975; also Räisänen, 1976, 136.

79   See pp. 75ff here. Similarly Roloff, 1969, distinguishes three motifs: the silencing of the demons is taken over from the tradition and should be seen as no more than a standard feature of exorcism stories (cf. n. 20 above); the commands to silence after the miracles are to be interpreted in the light of their being disobeyed (hence as Luz); only the commands to silence addressed to the disciples are really part of the messianic secret, and this shows an historical awareness that the disciples receive instruction from the earthly Jesus, but they can only understand it after Easter. (Hence Roloff is close here to the interpretation of Percy and Strecker.) Roloff's threefold division of the texts is also that of Tagawa, 1966. Tagawa interprets the first two groups (commands to the demons and to those who have been healed) as Roloff does. However, he sees the motif of the disciples' incomprehension as part of a polemic against the Jerusalem church.

80   Pesch, 1977, 36–45.

81   Cf. the recent study by Kermode, 1979. However, despite its title, Kermode's book does not set out to deal with the texts in Mark usually associated with the messianic secret, apart from Mark 4:11f. Kermode deals more with the general opaqueness of all narrative, rather than with the secrecy elements in Mark's Gospel. His book is suggestive rather than definitive, and there are clearly further insights to be gained from considering Mark from a literary-critical point of view. See review article by H. D. Betz, *Journal of Religion* (1982).

82   Cf. the recent study of Mark's Gospel by Kee, 1977. According to Kee, the secret is related to the confidence of Mark's community that its hopes will be realized (1977, 174f).

1

*The Purpose of Mark's Gospel**

NILS ALSTRUP DAHL

The so-called messianic secret (better: the Christ-mystery) is not a literary device intended to maintain suspense by keeping something hidden from the reader until he learns the solution of the enigma. The Christ-mystery is a secret only for those persons who appear in the book. The readers know the point of the story from the very beginning: it is the gospel of Jesus Christ. They know that Jesus was the stronger one who would come after John and baptize with the Holy Spirit, the one in whose name they themselves have been baptized. It has never been concealed from them that during his entire earthly life Jesus was the beloved Son in whom God was well pleased. They know the answer to the disciples' astonished question: "Who can this be?" They know that when Jesus died, forsaken by men and by God, it happened in order that the Scriptures should be fulfilled: the Son of man gave his life as a ransom for many. Mark is not presenting the solution to something which has been an unanswered riddle; he is emphasizing the mysterious character of something with which his readers are familiar.

Wrede claimed that the messianic secret was an attempt to harmonize the earlier view that Jesus became Messiah only at the resurrection with the later view that Jesus' earthly life had a messianic character. This understanding of the messianic secret as a transitional device hardly explains the origin of the motif and certainly does not explain its function in Mark.[1] More widespread than Wrede's explanation of the messianic secret is the view that it is apologetic in character.[2] According to this interpretation, the injunctions to silence and the theme of divine hardening of hearts explain Jesus' rejection by his own people though he was the Messiah and a great worker of miracles. But if the concern had been apologetic, one would have expected Matthew and Luke to have made greater use

* First published in English in *Jesus in the Memory of the Early Church* by N. A. Dahl (1976) 55–60. Original publication in Swedish (1958).

of the idea. In fact, the other two synoptics do have an apologetic tendency, each in its own way, which it is difficult to find in Mark. Further, Israel's unbelief does not play the role in the second Gospel that the theory presupposes. Matthew shows how Jesus' life and passion are the foundation of the Church's existence in its opposition to the synagogue, and at the same time he emphasizes that the new people stand under the command of Jesus and will appear before his judgement seat. Luke–Acts tells how God's promises to Israel were fulfilled in Jesus, and how the salvation promised to Israel was extended to the Gentiles. In Mark, the portrayal of the Jews is more differentiated than in the other Gospels. The relation to the Jewish people is neither a present conflict as in Matthew nor a problem of salvation history as in Luke.

Mark presupposes the Church and the Gentile mission, but his interest is concentrated on Jesus himself. The contrast between "you" and "those outside" in Mark 4:11 cannot be identified with the contrast between the Church and the synagogue. It has to do more generally with the division between believers and non-believers. Together with the injunctions to silence and the messianic secret in general, the distinction between public teaching in parables and esoteric interpretations serves to elucidate the gospel's character as a revealed mystery. Jesus and his word become genuine revelation and salvation only for the chosen circle to whom the secret is given.

The connection between the messianic secret and the crucifixion must be different from that which proponents of the apologetic theory have supposed. Mark's stress on the mystery of Jesus' life must be closely associated with the peculiar character of the Marcan passion story. Mark does not give prominence to Jesus' sovereign power in the midst of suffering as do Matthew and John, nor does he portray Jesus as the exemplary martyr as Luke does. In Mark, the picture of Jesus as the hidden, contradicted and misunderstood Messiah reaches its high point in the passion story. There Jesus is depicted as the rejected one who was betrayed, deserted and denied by his own, slandered, condemned, spat upon and ridiculed, mocked as he hung on the cross, even by those who were crucified with him. Not the physical suffering but the expulsion from human fellowship is stressed again and again. Even his cry in deepest need and loneliness, "My God, my God ... !" elicits only a crude joke. The concealing of Jesus' messiahship is not an apologetic theory intended to explain how Jesus was rejected. The case is just the reverse. In Mark, the historical fact that Jesus was spurned by the majority of Jews serves to illustrate the mysterious character of the revelation and salvation given in him. It has to do with "what no eye has seen, nor ear heard, nor the heart of man conceived, what God has prepared for those who love him".

Partly in line with the interpretation advanced here, H. J. Ebeling has made the evangelist's kerygmatic intention the basis for his explanation of the messianic secret in Mark.[3] He believes the secret to be a literary device which serves to stress the greatness of the revelation in which the readers participate as they hear the Christian message. Against this interpretation it has been rightly maintained that Ebeling has overemphasized the purely literary at the expense of content and religious meaning. It has been further objected that it is not legitimate to place the evangelist's kerygmatic intention in any exclusive contrast to historicity.[4] Ebeling writes in a somewhat inflated style, without sufficient precision, which is shown not least by his use of the fashionable word "kerygmatic". The worthwhile element lies in the emphasis that there must be a close connection between the messianic secret and the evangelist's "message" or purpose. But he misses the mark because his understanding of revelation and proclamation as an always contemporary call to decision is one-sided. Mark writes for those who are already in the Church and have received the secret of God's Kingdom as a gift. His goal is not to persuade readers to believe in the message but to remind them of what is contained in it in order that they might understand what has been given to them. The purpose is not kerygmatic in the word's narrower sense, but rather theological or – to coin a word – anamnetic.[5]

That the evangelist has Christian readers in mind is evident especially from his description of the relation of the disciples to the Christ-mystery. As often pointed out, it is a two-sided relationship. The secret of the Kingdom of God is given to the disciples; they recognize that Jesus is the Messiah and are instructed concerning the necessity of suffering. An inner circle receives special revelations. Nevertheless, we constantly hear that the disciples lack faith and do not understand. There are certain hints that their insight gradually increases; but even so, they fail in the hour of crisis. Contrasted to those outside, the disciples are the recipients of revelation. Despite this fact, they form the dark background against which the figure of Christ appears. Mark does not go as far as the author of the letter of Barnabas, who says that the disciples were sinful beyond measure (5:9). But Mark's picture of the disciples can also serve to illustrate Jesus' words: "I came not to call the righteous, but sinners." Not their own fitness, but Jesus' call and God's gift make them

Jesus' disciples and recipients of the mystery of God's Kingdom. Not because of their fidelity, but despite their failures, they became after the resurrection the bearers of Jesus' message and the kernel of the Church.

Mark's picture of the disciples cannot without qualification be regarded as typical of his view of Christians. He markedly contrasts time prior to the resurrection with time after the resurrection. It was during the time of Jesus' earthly life that the miracles, the messiahship, and the necessity of suffering were to be kept hidden; during this time the disciples lacked understanding and faith. Throughout Mark's Gospel, the messianic secret expresses an understanding of the "history of revelation" (Percy), according to which the decisive and complete revelation of the mystery, the realization of God's saving plan, first occurred with Jesus' death and resurrection. The Easter events place a dividing line between the period when Jesus lived as the hidden and misunderstood Messiah, and the time when he is openly proclaimed as the Crucified and Risen One. But this does not mean that the possibility for failure among Jesus' followers has ceased, that the dark picture of the disciples' behaviour during Jesus' life on earth was only to be a foil for an all the more radiant picture of the Church which lives in faith in the risen Lord. The conclusion of the Gospel shows on the contrary that even when the message that Jesus is risen is proclaimed by angels, those who hear can react in a manner which is no more adequate than that of the disciples when Jesus was among them.

If it were the case that the disciples' misunderstanding only provided contrast to the understanding which is now granted to the Church, the same should apply to the disciples' inability to work miracles.[6] But even if we retain the full force of the sayings concerning the boundless possibilities open to believers, it is unlikely that Mark thought these possibilities were realized in the Church. His emphasis on the disciples' shortcomings cannot be fully explained as stemming from Mark's view of the "history of revelation". The additional feature is paraenetic. This paraenetic concern was already present in tradition, most clearly in the Gethsemane narrative: "Watch and pray that you may not enter into temptation." Mark makes it something of a continuing theme. The members of the Church who have partaken of the full revelation and salvation must see to it that they do not fall short, misunderstand and fail as the disciples did in the time before the resurrection. Ferdinand Kattenbusch once wrote: "The Twelve are 'authorities' for the learning church, *types* for the celebrating 'church'."[7] With reference to Mark one might add: they are examples intended to serve as a warning to a complacent Church lacking in faith.

What is said here about the Christ-mystery in Mark can be illuminated by analogous conceptions in the epistles. Ephesians and Colossians, and texts like 1 Cor. 2:6–16 and 1 Pet. 1:1–12 imply that the presentation of the gospel's content as a mystery had its setting in preaching to the community rather than in missionary proclamation. But there is a significant difference. The epistles speak of the mystery which was hidden from angels, powers and principalities. But according to Mark, the demons knew who Jesus was. Especially in the Pauline letters, the Christ-mystery is placed within a cosmic framework which is missing in Mark. But the difference has to do mostly with the forms of perception. If one enquires as to what function the conceptions have, the similarity becomes more pronounced. The ignorance of the angelic powers underlines the hiddenness of God's plan, now revealed in Christ for man's salvation. Mark achieves the same end by stressing that the demons were forbidden to make Christ known though they recognized Jesus to be God's Son, while men did not understand the secret of his person and suffering.

In the epistles too the purpose is practical and paraenetic: Christians are urged to realize the greatness of the revealed mystery and to conform their lives to the pattern provided by the salvation granted them. In 1 Corinthians 2 Paul speaks of God's mysterious wisdom which was hidden from the rulers of this age but is revealed to Christians through the Spirit. Paul's stress on this wisdom contained in the word of the cross, which he was unable to unfold fully in Corinth, is meant to put to shame those Christians who are quarrelling and fighting, who brag about their leaders and want to be great themselves. It is not inconceivable that a similar concern lies behind Mark's emphasis on the messianic secret and related concepts.

NOTES

1   Cf. the critical objections of Ebeling, Percy and Sjöberg.
2   The explanation offered by T. A. Burkill in a series of articles and in his book, *Mysterious Revelation*, is a variant of this theory. It has been criticized by Ebeling, Percy and Sjöberg.
3   Ebeling, 1939.
4   Percy, 288ff; Sjöberg, 118ff.
5   Cf. my essay, "Anamnesis", *Jesus in the Memory of the Early Church* (Minneapolis: Augsburg, 1976) 11–29.

6 J. Coutts, "The Authority of Jesus and of the Twelve in St Mark's Gospel", *JTS* 8 (1957) 111–18, has observed that the disciples' inability to perform miracles should be added to the features noted by Wrede.

7 *Festgabe für Karl Müller* (1922) 347, n. 1. Cf. O. Linton, "Das Problem der Urkirche", Uppsala univeritets årsskrift (1932) 96–100.

2

*The Blindness of the Disciples in Mark**

JOSEPH B. TYSON

I

The blindness of the disciples is usually regarded as a device of Mark and as part of his messianic secret motif. William Wrede, in 1901, said that the motif of the messianic secret in Mark was the evangelist's explanation of the fact that Jesus was not accepted as Messiah during his lifetime but was proclaimed as Messiah after the death and resurrection. Wrede felt that the facts of history demanded the conclusion that Jesus did not proclaim himself as Messiah, but that the disciples did; Mark could not, of course, say this directly; so he explained the phenomenon of silence as an intentional secret. The explanation of the purpose of parables in chap. 4 is one clue to this, as Mark 9:9 is perhaps the keystone. The very purpose of Jesus' parables is to hide the secret of his nature. The demons recognize the nature of Jesus, but Jesus commands them to be silent. The disciples partially understand who Jesus is, but they, too, are commanded to keep silence. The hostility and opposition of the Jewish authorities to Jesus is easily explained by the supposition that God had intentionally blinded them to the reality of Jesus.

Mark seems to work out this theory on three levels:

1 The demons recognize Jesus, but they are commanded to be silent.[1]
2 The disciples partially recognize Jesus, but they are commanded to be silent.[2]
3 The Jewish authorities fail to recognize Jesus because they have been blinded.[3]

It is the second level that engages our attention at this point. The disciples are commanded to be silent, but their recognition of Jesus

*First published in *JBL* 80 (1961) 261–8.

35

is only partial, due to their blindness and their hardness of heart.[4] Moreover, their incomplete understanding is actually a misunderstanding of the nature of Jesus. When we look at the incidents related by Mark in which the disciples fail to understand, then it will appear that this element is not properly a part of the messianic secret motif. It is not as if the disciples had discerned the nature of Jesus but are prohibited from broadcasting it, but it is that the disciples have a wrong conception about his nature.

There are many instances of the disciples' blindness – they do not understand the stilling of the sea (4:41), the feeding of the five thousand (6:52), Jesus' attitude towards children (10:13ff), the saying about the rich entering the Kingdom (10:23); they are characteristically unable to understand parables (4:1–20, 33f).

Above all, however, the misunderstanding of the disciples is connected with Jesus' threefold prediction of suffering. It is profitable at this point to look briefly at the actual contents of these three predictions.

The first prediction (Mark 8:31–3) is intimately connected with the confession of Peter in 8:27–30. This is the first indication we have that the disciples suspect Jesus to be the Messiah. Throughout the narrative, Peter is the spokesman, but he clearly seems to be speaking for the group. Although it is not crystal-clear that Jesus accepts the confession of Peter at this point, he moves quickly into an introduction of the necessity of his own suffering. To this Peter expresses not only surprise but some indignation. Jesus rebukes Peter in very harsh words, equating his point of view with that of Satan.

The second prediction of suffering in 9:30–2 is substantially the same as that of 8:31–3. The prediction is followed by the words, "But they (the disciples) did not understand the saying, and they were afraid to ask him." The following pericope in Mark tells us that the disciples had been discussing their relative greatness, giving Jesus a chance to discourse on true greatness.

In the third prediction in 10:32–4 we have much the same pattern, except that the prediction of suffering is much more detailed. Nothing is said in this paragraph about the misunderstanding of the disciples, but the following paragraph tells the story of the request of James and John for places of authority when Jesus comes into his Kingdom.[5]

In these three predictions of suffering, not only does Mark indicate that the disciples misunderstood the nature of Jesus, but he also sees this misunderstanding as of two specific kinds: (1) No understanding of the necessity of Jesus' sufferings; and (2) no understanding of their own position in the community. The point is this: Mark is not here saying that the disciples understood that Jesus was Messiah and were commanded not to broadcast it; rather he is saying that they completely misunderstood the nature of Jesus' messiahship, not understanding it as a suffering messiahship but as a royal messiahship which would issue in benefits for themselves.

II

Now it will be our intention to examine both of these "misunderstood elements" to see exactly what Mark would seem to be driving at. If the case is simply that Mark is trying to explain the fact that Jesus was not understood to be the Messiah during his lifetime, that is one thing. But this does not seem to be the case. Rather Mark seems to be trying to indicate that the disciples really misunderstood the position of Jesus. Why would Mark say this? The most obvious answer is that Mark is aware of a significant difference between his own point of view and that of the disciples.[6] To Mark the disciples' understanding of Jesus' messiahship is a misunderstanding. If Mark 9:9 indicates that it was only after the resurrection that the disciples began preaching the messiahship of Jesus, then the predictions of suffering indicate just what kind of messiahship they understood and preached.

There would be two important elements in their preaching:

1   It would be a preaching which (to Mark) did not take full account of the *necessity* of suffering. Mark's portrayal of the events makes it clear that the disciples did not really anticipate the suffering and death of Jesus. They fled the scene. Peter denied his relationship to Jesus. All indications in Mark point to the probability that they had not been warned about the death of Jesus.[7] They, in fact, did not expect the death of Jesus because they had not been warned of it. This probably means that the predictions of suffering in Mark are quite artificial and bear no resemblance to authentic history. But does it mean any more than that? Does it mean that even after the death/resurrection the disciples did not understand the profound meaning of the suffering?

It has been a most difficult position to maintain that the disciples did not understand the necessity of Jesus' sufferings, because it is difficult to see how the disciples could have preached the messiahship of Jesus without making some sense out of his death. How could a crucified criminal be the saviour of the world? This, it is said, would be a considerable stumbling block to Christian proclamation. The Christian preacher would meet this stumbling block from the very first and would find it necessary to explain the relation of death to messiahship as a first step in gaining acceptance for this new message. But this is not quite the problem it might at first seem; for the disciples were, from the beginning, preaching, not simply a death, but a death/resurrection. The resurrection is the only answer that is necessary. If the speech of Peter in Acts 2 can be regarded as, in any way, authentic, it represents precisely this point of view. "This Jesus whom you crucified, God has raised up and has made both Lord and Christ." Here is no attempt to explain the necessity of the death of Jesus. It is simply treated as an historical fact which illustrates the cruelty and stupidity of the Jewish authorities. But there is no hint that the death is necessary for the messiahship. The very opposite is the more nearly true. Jesus is the Christ in spite of, not because of, the death. The resurrection answers all questions.[8]

By calling attention to this deficiency on the part of the disciples, Mark is, to some extent, condemning them. He sees quite clearly the necessity of Jesus' suffering and death, but the disciples did not. Mark seems to have been quite aware that he is introducing something into the Christian tradition that was not a part of the preaching of the disciples. Nor do we have to look far for the basis of Mark's point of view. Whether or not Mark and Paul represent identical points of view, they both place great importance on the necessity of Jesus' death.

2   When we come to the second element in the disciples' misunderstanding, it becomes quite clear that Mark thinks of himself as holding a different view of messiahship from that of the disciples. Hence Mark calls attention to the fact that the disciples did not understand what was to be their own relationship to the community. This, in Mark, forms a part of the second and third predictions of suffering. The second prediction is followed by a report that the disciples had been conversing with one another about their relative importance in the Kingdom of God (9:33–7). This seems to amplify the statement in 9:32 that the disciples did not understand. No, says Mark, the disciples did not understand about Jesus' coming death, and this illustrates it. Likewise, although there is no direct statement in the third prediction of suffering, the saying is followed by the request of James and John for the chief seats when Jesus comes into his Kingdom (10:35–45). The third prediction of suffering is exactly

parallel to the second in idea, though not in specific content. Both are followed by a story in which the disciples discuss their own importance.

Whatever historical episode may lie behind the narrative, the important thing is to discover the reason for its presence in Mark. That reason seems to be Mark's feeling that the disciples understood Jesus in terms of a royal messiahship, and that this is simply a misunderstanding. The question of rank can only come up among the disciples if the disciples accept Jesus as a royal Messiah. Mark is saying that this is the way the disciples conceived of Jesus.[9]

Now, one can admit that this was the thinking of the disciples before the death of Jesus, but would this have been the case afterward? The first thing that can be said is that there is nothing to show that the early disciples did not have such an idea. It is true that Jesus did not exercise messianic functions during his lifetime, but he was now the Christ, and he would return soon to establish his Kingdom.[10] On the positive side must be noted the fact that there was in the Jerusalem church a kind of family dynasty set up which began with James, the brother of Jesus, and, according to Hegesippus as reported in Eusebius, passed to James' cousin, Simeon bar Clopas,[11] who was executed for being of the house of David.[12] Eusebius records a total of fifteen members of this family who held the position of "bishop" of Jerusalem.[13]

There is every indication that the Christianity of this church, which probably included most of the original disciples, took the form of a mildly modified Judaism, Paul's controversies with the church reveal a great deal about Jerusalem Christianity, but two things in particular: (1) that there was something of a struggle for power which attempted to keep Paul within bounds on the basis that he was not an apostle of Jesus during Jesus' lifetime; and (2) that the leaders of the church really wished to require circumcision and obedience to the kosher food laws for incoming Christians.[14] The distinctive element in the thinking of this group is belief in the future messiahship of Jesus. We must recognize that, if it were not for Mark and Paul, we would have to assume that the messiahship in which the disciples believed was a royal messiahship. That is to say, if there were no specific indications one way or the other, we would have no alternative but to assume that by Messiah the disciples meant a new Davidic king. But the fact is that we do have evidence: (1) the family of Jesus is in control of the church at Jerusalem from the very earliest period. The attempt is made to establish a dynasty of the family of Jesus, a royal family waiting for the return of the king.[15] (2) Other disciples seem to have high-ranking offices in the Jerusalem church. Those "reputed to be pillars" make it very difficult for a free lance like Paul to gain any kind of authority in the church. (3) The Jerusalem church seems to have no desire to initiate a mission to Gentiles. What does messiahship mean to Gentiles? Jesus is to be the new king of Judah, and this will have only an indirect bearing on the gentile world. Basically, the messiahship of Jesus is meaningful only for the Jewish people. (4) Therefore, there seems also to be no question in the Jerusalem church about the abandonment of long-established Jewish practices. The future messiahship of Jesus only makes it all the more necessary to carry on the best religious principles one knows in as pure a fashion as possible until his return. It cannot be imagined, of course, that the teaching of Jesus would not have been remembered and would have had no real influence over the practices of the church. But over against this are the facts which necessitate the view that Jerusalem Christianity entailed only a mildly modified Judaism. The major modification was the vivid expectation of the return of Jesus as a royal Messiah.

III

Now we are in a position to see where Mark stands in relation to the Jerusalem church, whose point of view seems to be represented in the Gospel by the disciples. Mark is aware of two things: (1) He is aware that the death of Jesus is much more than an historical fact. He feels that it has redemptive significance. Jesus gives his life as "a ransom for many".[16] (2) Mark is also aware that Jesus' messiahship is not simply a nationalistic royal messiahship. For this reason he makes relatively little of the "Son of David" theology.[17] Accordingly he calls attention to the fact that Jesus' family had no understanding of him and no little hostility towards him.[18] For this reason he twice tells of incidents in which the disciples foolishly vie with one another for some kind of reflected or delegated authority. Mark is aware, then, of a view of messiahship quite different from that of the original disciples and family of Jesus, and is aware that his own viewpoint is in some conflict with that of these original witnesses. He seems also to know that his readers recognize this conflict; therefore, he must give some explanation for it. His explanation is that the disciples did not understand, even though Jesus many times tried to explain it to them.

If it is correct that Mark's view of messiahship is different from that of the early disciples, it is necessary to ask where this later view came from. There are several possibilities:

1   It is quite possible that Mark has been influenced by Paul. We do not wish to dredge up all the old arguments for and against Pauline influence on Mark. But what we seem to have arrived at is this. In the first place, Mark seems to appreciate the significance of the death of Jesus in a much more profound way than did the disciples. Although we do not have, by any means, a complete picture of the history of early Christianity, what we do know is that Paul had a very deep appreciation of the necessity of Jesus' death. There may have been others, but there is certainly Paul. In the second place, we know that Mark does not think much of apostolic authority; that is, he does not think very highly of those who held the point of view of the Jerusalem church. Again, we do not have a complete picture of primitive church history, but we do know that if ever anyone came into conflict with the Jerusalem church it was Paul. Whether there is any historical connection between Paul and Mark or not, Mark lands on Paul's side in questioning the authority of the pillars in Jerusalem. There is enough here that we can entertain the possibility, if not the probability, that it was under the influence of Paul that Mark (and the group which Mark represents) was led to see the death of Jesus as of redemptive significance and to question the authority of the apostles.

2   It is possible that Mark represents Galilean Christianity rather than Jerusalem Christianity. Here we are obviously drawing on Ernst Lohmeyer, who maintained that the basic Christology of the Galilean church was a "Son of Man" Christology and that of the Jerusalem church was a "Son of David" Christology. Lohmeyer quite convincingly argues that Mark stands within the Galilean tradition.[19]

3   It is more than likely that it is Mark's appreciation for the gentile mission which has brought about this difference in point of view. Obviously, appreciation for the gentile mission would involve appreciation for Paul, the apostle to the Gentiles par excellence. But Mark is not limited to this. To him, Jesus is much more than a nationalistic Messiah to the Jews. He has significance for all the world, and this significance cannot involve the strait-jacket limitations imposed by a hierarchy of relatives and friends of Jesus. Mark is apparently writing from and representing the point of view of the church which is soon to become the leading church of Christendom. As a matter of fact, it is not long after the time of Mark that Rome begins to rise to a leading position among the Christian churches. In a sense, Mark's Gospel represents a challenge to the power of the Jerusalem church, which, at least in the time of Paul and probably

for a few years afterward, exercised almost unquestioned authority over the other churches. Mark is a challenge to this church and its leaders, a challenge not only of authority, but of theology. The fact that Mark feels it necessary to make this challenge indicates that even in his time the disciples enjoyed considerable prestige if not authority.[20]

In summary, Mark consciously differs from the original disciples along two lines: (1) He feels that they have a narrow view of the messiahship of Jesus which involves an inflated understanding of their own position; (2) He feels that they do not have a profound enough understanding of the significance of the death of Jesus. In this light, it is possible to maintain that the Gospel of Mark ended exactly as we now have it. Even the resurrection is not understood by Jesus' associates. They were in a position to see and to proclaim, but they told no one, for they were afraid. Although only three women are mentioned as seeing the empty tomb, surely the disciples are in Mark's mind, as 16:7 indicates. Moreover, it may be significant that Mark does not describe an appearance of the risen Jesus to the disciples. Here is the climax of the Gospel, and, although Mark looks forward to some kind of experience on the part of the "disciples and Peter", these are not the first to hear the news of Jesus' resurrection. What a strange ending for our earliest Gospel, and yet what an appropriate and significant one if one of Mark's chief purposes was to call attention to the ways in which the disciples fell short in their understanding and proclamation of the Chritian gospel.

NOTES

1 Cf. Mark 1:23–5, 34; 3:11–12; 5:6, 7; 9:20.

2 Mark 7:36; 8:30; 9:9.

3 Cf. especially Mark 4:12.

4 Mark 6:52; 8:17.

5 Cf. Taylor, 1952, 436f. Although Taylor can find no reason to doubt the substantial historicity of the first two predictions, he does believe that, in its precision and close relationship to the passion narrative in Mark, the third is a *"vaticinium ex eventu"*.

6 Cf. Kuby, 1958, who maintains that the Gospel of Mark falls into two main divisions. The first, 1:16—8:21, deals with the failure of the disciples to understand who Jesus is. The second half, 8:22—14:72, deals with the misunderstanding of the disciples, i.e., their unwillingness to grasp the fact that the Messiah must suffer.

7 Especially the notice in Mark that prior to the arrest the leading disciples were

sleeping (14:32–42) and that upon the arrest of Jesus they fled the scene (14:50).

8 The fact that Luke also gives us a story of Philip, in which the death of Jesus is explained by the help of 2 Isaiah, need not cause us to detour from this position. The question is simply – is it possible that the disciples could have preached the messiahship of Jesus without explaining the death? The answer is that in the early chapters of Acts this possibility is opened up: that is to say, the disciples could have been preaching in just the way Mark seems to think they were preaching. In addition, Paul represents this thinking, at least in part, where he says that Jesus was "designated Son of God in power according to the Spirit of holiness by his resurrection from the dead" (Rom. 1:4).

9 Taylor, 1952, 438f, defends the historicity of Mark 10:35–40, on the grounds that the community would not create a story which discredits these disciples. Be that as it may, the point being made here is that Mark is aware that, not only in the life of Jesus, but in the life of the early Church, certain disciples felt themselves called to positions of great authority. This feeling, to Mark, must rest on their misunderstanding of the messiahship of Jesus.

10 Luke certainly is aware of this when, in Acts 1:6–7, he has the risen Christ correct the disciples who expect him at that time to "restore the kingdom to Israel".

11 Eusebius, *Eccl. hist.* 3, 11, 1.

12 Ibid., 3, 32, 3.

13 Ibid., 4, 5, 3–4.

14 Gal.1—2.

15 Cf. S. G. F. Brandon, *The Fall of Jerusalem and the Christian Church* (London, 1951). In chap. 10 of this book Brandon states his belief that it was actually the fall of Jerusalem and the end of the Jerusalem leadership in the church which called forth the writing of the Gospel of Mark. In this light, Mark feels it necessary to make clear his own differences with the Jerusalem Christianity. Brandon here says that Mark's rejection of the "Son of David" motif is a definitive attempt to repudiate an interpretation of the status of Jesus which would connect him with the nationalistic aspiration of the Jews.

16 Mark 10:45.

17 As a matter of fact, he directly repudiates the "Son of David" theology in 12:35–7.

18 Mark 3:21, 31–5; 6:2–3.

19 *Galiläa und Jerusalem*, 26–35.

20 This point of view need not involve the question of the date of Mark, although these matters should be considered in establishing such a date. On the other hand, although the Jerusalem church did, in all probability, cease to exist after A.D. 70, it prestige would not die immediately. Brandon seems to feel that Mark's Gospel is an attempt to say what the Christian Church will now do without the Jerusalem leadership.

3

*Mysterious Revelation**

T. A. BURKILL

Mark's Gospel is not an essay in scientific biography, but a religious document which was written for the edification of believers. As we gather from its superscription, the evangelist is concerned to depict the life of Jesus as the earthly career of the Messiah, the Son of God, and it is interesting to find that the declarations of the heavenly voice and the confessions of the demons are supplemented in the later part of the Gospel by a Jew's testimony to the messiahship at 8:29 and by a Gentile's testimony to the divine Sonship at 15:39. Despite the fundamentally divine character of its central figure, however, the gospel story is not an epic of unrelieved triumph and continuous success, for it relates how Jesus was rejected by his own people and crucified by the Gentiles, and Mark evidently seeks to overcome the difficulty thus raised by holding that the true status of Jesus was a predetermined secret. The Master was not accepted as the Messiah, and the evangelist maintains that it was an integral part of the divine purpose that he should not have been so accepted. Hence in the second Gospel Jesus is represented as deliberately concealing the truth from the public by the injunctions to silence and by the cryptology of parabolical teaching.

Accordingly, Christianity was (as it remains) essentially a paradoxical religion which had to make room in its total interpretation of messiahship for the shame of the crucifixion. The situation demanded that the Church should reconcile the indubitable fact of the humiliation of Jesus with its ardent faith in his ultimate supremacy as the plenipotentiary of God. Indeed, it was precisely the task of synthesizing such opposing conceptions in a coherent scheme of thought that constituted the main problem of apostolic Christology. The earliest solution, which finds characteristic expression in the writings of Paul, appears to have been that the Messiah's sufferings were a necessary prelude to his final manifestation in

* First published in *Mysterious Revelation* by T. A. Burkill (1963) 319–24.

44

glory. Mark, however, refuses to regard the messianic glory purely as an object of anticipation to be realized in the future and, in some measure, he considers that it is already evident amid all the lowliness and shame of the Master's life on earth. But in so far as the Church's historical traditions concerning the career of its founder are evaluated from such a standpoint, the difficulty raised by the rejection of Jesus becomes all the more acute; and this helps us to understand why the evangelist emphasizes the secret character of the messiahship.

Broadly speaking, Mark seems to distinguish four principal stages or periods in the historical realization of God's plan of salvation: the period of preparation, which comes to an end with the imprisonment of the appointed forerunner; the period of the incarnate life, which is characterized by suffering and obscurity; the post-resurrection period of enlightenment, in which the gospel of the crucified Messiah is publicly proclaimed by the Church; and the period of eschatological fulfilment, which will be gloriously inaugurated by the Son of Man at his awaited parousia. It is not to be supposed, however, that the evangelist presents us with a systematic body of doctrine concerning these periods and the manner of their interconnection. He is much less a master of his material than the fourth evangelist, for example, and this is not surprising seeing that he was apparently the first writer to respond to the Church's increasing need for a connected account of the ministry.

But there can be little doubt regarding Mark's fundamental attitude. Convinced that Jesus is the Messiah, he takes the view that the Lord's humiliation represents the pledge or guarantee of his triumph in glory which is subsequently to be made manifest. It is as though the soteriological process were governed by a principle of divine retribution which ultimately effects a reversal of the situation existing during the period of the earthly ministry. Heavenly exaltation is the reward of self-abnegation. The evangelist therefore contemplates the sufferings of Jesus and the tribulations of the Church in the light of a revelation in glory, and yet, since the reward always comes after the humiliation, there is a break or rift in the soteriological process. Thus, in an important sense, Mark's thought is basically bipolar. The sufferings and the glory belong to different epochs, and the relationship between them has the appearance of being no more intimate than that which obtains between means and end. They are not brought together in the unity of a single conception as they are, for example, in the Fourth Gospel, where the notion of the cost of the passion has almost disappeared.

On the other hand, there is a counter-tendency at work which militates against the bipolarity of the evangelist's fundamental position and induces him to represent the life of Jesus as the locus of secret revelation. Apparently, he is not completely satisfied with the doctrine that the humiliation of the Messiah is the appointed means to his future triumph, and thus he comes to attach a greater degree of intrinsic importance to the incarnate life than seems to be allowed in the epistles of Paul, who betrays little or no interest in the actual details of the Lord's earthly ministry. Probably the delay in the arrival of the parousia helped to bring about the new emphasis. But in whatever manner the change is to be accounted for, Mark undoubtedly goes some way towards closing the gap, as it were, between the notion of the Messiah's humiliation and that of his supremacy, or towards overcoming the bipolarity of what appears to be his primary philosophical position. In the story of the transfiguration, for instance, the veil of the flesh is temporarily withdrawn, and the three most intimate disciples are privileged to behold their Master as he really is and in the form in which he will be made manifest to the world when he comes again finally to establish the Kingdom of God with great power and glory.

But the counter-tendency in question is more pronounced in some passages than in others, and, whenever it becomes particularly strong, Mark is inclined to overstep the limits prescribed by his doctrine of the secret and to delineate the incarnate life openly in terms of the apostolic faith. Hence certain passages convey the impression that the true nature of Jesus is reaching out for some definite form of articulate expression which, however, it cannot yet receive; in the stories of the triumphal entry and of the anointing at Bethany, for example, the evangelist's belief in the reality of the messiahship is apparently pressing for overt recognition in the narrative, thereby putting great strain on the requirement of secrecy. And, notably, in the account of the nocturnal trial the pressure exerted by the evangelist's conviction subjects his doctrine of the secret to a strain which it cannot withstand, the result being that in 14:62 there is actually a disclosure of the fact of the messiahship outside the circle of the initiated. Forsaken by his followers and confronted by his enemies in all their worldly might, Jesus gives open confession to his messianic status and confidently declares that his judges shall see the Son of Man coming with the clouds of heaven. Thus something of the supernatural glory of the parousia lights up the darkest depths of the humiliation to which the passion narrative bears witness; and we are presented with what is, from one point of view, the most striking exemplification in the entire Gospel of Mark's inclination to move away from the conception of the incarnate life as the period of obscurity towards a characteristically Johannine mode of representation.

In the last-mentioned passage, however, the urge to set forth the earthly ministry directly in terms of the apostolic faith seems to be reinforced by the motive to ascribe responsibility for the crucifixion to the Jews as represented by their leaders. For, although Mark believes that the passion was provided for in God's sovereign purpose, he none the less wishes to show that the crucifixion really took place through the unwarranted hostility of the Lord's own countrymen and hence that the burden of guilt for that most terrible crime is borne by a people whose God-given privileges only serve to make their conduct the more reprehensible. The operation of such a motive naturally makes for a certain inconsistency in the evangelist's treatment of his material. As we should expect, in so far as he is concerned to emphasize the culpability of the Jews, he tends to contravene the requirement of secrecy by allowing the true nature of Jesus to come out, so to speak, into the light of day. Consequently, in Mark's representation Jesus does not always address the public in the cryptology of parables, as he is said to do in 4:34, and he does not always seek to perform his miracles in private, as he does, for example, in 5:40. On the contrary, in certain passages the fact of the messiahship is to a greater or less extent exposed to public view, and so it could be maintained that the Jews were in an inexcusable position, since they had perpetrated their crime not in ignorance but with a cognizance of that for which Jesus stood.

In Mark's interpretation, then, the life of Jesus, despite its outward show of tragic frustration, is really a continuous fulfilment of God's plan of salvation. The failure of the public to recognize the fact of the messiahship and the failure of the disciples to understand its meaning are alike provisions of the divine purpose for the redemption of humanity. But it is important to notice that the two instances of failure do not make their historical appearance in the same way. For, while the fact of the messiahship is concealed from the public by the injunctions to silence and by the teaching in parables, it is discovered by Peter at Caesarea Philippi, whereupon its implications are expounded to the twelve and something of its essential glory is made manifest to the privileged three on the occasion of the transfiguration. The veil is withdrawn in the presence of the chosen few, but they are not yet in a position to grasp the significance of the *mysterium* revealed to them. Their spiritual sight is dim, and so it must remain until the time of the Messiah's resurrection, which marks the end of the period of obscurity and the beginning of the period of enlightenment. Thus the confession at Caesarea Philippi is of importance in the evangelist's thought because it serves as a basis for further instruction which, besides preparing the mind of the reader for a right appreciation of the passion narrative, enables the disciples to receive the saving truth of the gospel from the Lord himself. For, although they cannot understand the divine word when it is communicated to them, they can retain it as authentic tradition and can thus equip themselves for their future role as apostles and pillars of the Church.

4

*The Theory of the Messianic Secret in Mark's Gospel**

GEORG STRECKER

The problem of the theory of the messianic secret in Mark's Gospel is still defined in exegetical research in the terms of William Wrede's epoch-making study *The Messianic Secret*, which was first published more than sixty years ago.[1] In this book Wrede directed his attack against historicist life of Jesus research which sought to reconstruct a messianic life of Jesus on the basis of Mark's Gospel. He showed that what the evangelist was actually saying could not be interpreted psychologically, and therefore could not be verified historically: rather, it was "supernaturally" coloured. As the supernatural view of the life of Jesus went back to the faith of the community, so too, according to Wrede, the concept of the secret revelations of Jesus the Messiah was pre-Marcan. It appears in Mark unharmonized, in a multiplicity of variations, so could scarcely be the work of an individual. The same conclusion seems to emerge when the contents are considered:

> How would Mark come to introduce such an idea into a tradition that knew nothing of it? There is no discernible reason for his doing so. Historically speaking, the idea cannot be fully understood just from Mark directly. We find it there ready-made, and Mark is under its sway, so that we cannot even speak of a *Tendenz* (Wrede, 1971, 145).

The problem for Wrede is thus basically one of tradition-history: what gave rise to the concept of the messianic secret?

Wrede's answer starts with the obvious importance which the resurrection had for the community's faith: belief in the messiahship of Jesus as the future Judge of the world dates from this point. The idea does not necessarily presuppose that the life of Jesus was messianic; but secret messiahship does presuppose a belief in the

* First published in *SE* 3, TU 88 (1964) 87–104. Translated by C. M. Tuckett.

future Messiah. How could the theory have arisen "if everyone already knew and reported that Jesus had openly given himself out as messiah on earth ... What would have prompted making the messiahship of Jesus a matter of secrecy in contradiction to the original idea, in other words simply denying in retrospect Jesus' messianic claims on earth" (227)? There is scarcely any other possibility than "that the idea of the secret arose at a time when as yet there was no knowledge of any messianic claim on the part of Jesus; which is as much as to say at a time when the resurrection was regarded as the beginning of the messiahship" (228). The original idea must have already been losing ground, and already in the life of Jesus "hints about his future standing, characteristics and utterances were being found" (ibid.). So, as a consequence of resurrection faith, messiahship was read back into the life of Jesus. The messianic secret is thus "a transitional idea and it can be characterised as the after-effect of the view that the resurrection is the beginning of the messiahship at a time when the life of Jesus was already being filled materially with messianic content" (229). This has implications for the historical life of Jesus: for the secrecy idea could only have arisen at a time when nothing was known of any messianic claim by Jesus. This therefore seems to be a positive indication "that Jesus actually did not give himself out as messiah" (230).

Although not central to the whole study, this final claim provoked critical reaction which almost universally took the form of vehement rejection of Wrede's theory. The result was that the starting-point which had been carefully established, i.e. the consideration of the problem of the tradition–history involved, remained virtually ignored. It was only with the work of the form critics that this aspect of Wrede's work was taken up again and used to clarify the pre-synoptic material in the tradition. Thus R. Bultmann, in *The History of the Synoptic Tradition*, took up again the question of the tradition–history of the messianic secrecy concept, though in another connection. On the basis of form-critical analysis, he came to the conclusion, in contrast to Wrede, that the elements which make up the messianic secret all occur in Mark's redactional material. But he thought that in other respects Wrede's proposed solution could be maintained. Thus for Bultmann too, the theory of the messianic secret was "a veiling of the fact that faith in Jesus' Messiahship begins from belief in his resurrection".[2] Bultmann's literary–critical analysis is, in my view, convincing; but his interpretation of the secrecy theory is open to question. Is it possible to retain Wrede's explanation of the tradition–history involved when its basis, i.e. the pre-Marcan origin of the secrecy theory, is rejected? Can it be shown that the evangelist consciously adapted a tradition which presented the life of Jesus as unmessianic? In what follows, the sayings about the secrecy concept will be briefly examined first with this in mind. Part two will consider the origin of the secrecy motif in the history of the tradition; and in part three, the interpretation of the secret in the context of Mark's Gospel will be discussed.

I

As far as Jesus' secrecy commands are concerned, there is no question that the exorcisms reported in the summary sections are secondary, i.e. they have been formulated by the redactor. These commands of Jesus to the demons to be silent (1:34; 3:11f) stem from the evangelist. The pre-Marcan pericope 1:21–8 is different. Here the command to silence is connected with the exorcism. It is thus an original part of the story. However, this proves nothing about a pre-Marcan origin of the secrecy theory, for, as Bultmann has shown, recognition by the demons and commands to silence are a part of exorcism stories in general.[3] But Mark himself will have understood it in terms of the theory of the messianic secret.

The redactor's hand can easily be traced in the way that other miracle stories are presented. Their statements about secret messiahship can be removed as secondary without disrupting their logic. Where these statements are part of the pre-Marcan tradition (e.g. the withdrawal from the crowds in 5:40, or the separation of the patient in 8:23), they have parallels in secular miracle stories.[4] This has been established in detail by Bultmann. But this means that the evangelist's tradition was already completely coloured by the belief that the earthly Jesus was the Messiah; for if the exorcism in 1:21–8, with its demon's confession, comes from the pre-Marcan tradition, the community prior to Mark which preserved this tradition about Jesus is unlikely to have understood the cry *ho hagios tou theou* ("the holy one of God") (1:24) in an unmessianic way. The same applies in the other miracle stories. The cultic worship of the *Kyrios* has affected the words and actions of those seeking help no less than the way in which the majesty of the miracle-worker himself is presented. There are thus no grounds for concluding that the evangelist knew of any discrepancy between messianic and unmessianic traditions about Jesus. This is confirmed by the fact that Mark's tradition already contained stories of confession and revelation, e.g. Peter's confession (8:27b–29) and the appended passion prediction (8:31), as well as the transfiguration story (9:2–8). The evangelist incorporated these elements into his theory of secret epiphanies by adding secondary commands to silence (8:30; 9:9–10).

The second basic motif of the secrecy concept, i.e. the lack of understanding by the disciples, can be seen more frequently in the pre-Marcan tradition.[5] Originally, it was perhaps simply a typically human reaction to divine revelation.[6] The evangelist not only repeats the motif, but also inserts it into his source (e.g. 14:40b) and independently creates it (9:10 and elsewhere), which indicates a change of meaning at the level of Mark's redaction: for it occurs explicitly in connection with the idea of Jesus' secret messiahship, when it refers back to some esoteric instruction (e.g. at the end of the transfiguration story) or when it points forward, as in other instances. It follows that the motif of lack of understanding, like the secrecy commands, presupposes an epiphany. The basis for Mark's redactional work is thus not the tradition of an unmessianic life of Jesus. Rather it is the idea, already present in the tradition, of the messiahship of the earthly Jesus.

Finally in this connection, there is the peculiar and often over-looked motif of the topological statements. Their significance can be made clear from the example of *ploiarion* ("little boat") or *ploion* ("ship"). The idea comes from the pre-Marcan tradition (1:19f; 4:36ff; 6:47ff) and is sometimes used quite generally (5:2ff; 6:53f; 8:10). But in Mark's redactional material it has special significance. It is used in contexts which show that the disciples, in contrast to the crowds, are especially close to Jesus. Mark has the *ochlos* ("crowd") remain behind on the sea-shore, while the Messiah reveals himself *en tǭ ploiǭ* ("in the boat") to his trusted friends by means of a miracle (4:36ff) or teaching (8:14ff). But this means that, in the redactional context of the secrecy theory, the motif signifies the place where revelatory events occur in secret.

Topological expressions have far more importance within Mark's redaction than can be dealt with here. But the idea of the *oikos* ("house") must be mentioned. It is not geographically fixed, and it appears where the revelation needs its own space, separate from the crowds.[7] The "mountain", to which Jesus withdraws either alone or with his disciples, is another example. There is too the typically Marcan *en tę̄ hodǭ* ("in the way"), as well the term *topos erēmos* ("desert place"): the latter is the place where Jesus prays and to which he retreats, and is thus again characteristic of the desire for concealment. All these are similar expressions which, insofar as they occur originally within the context of the secrecy theory, come from the redactor.

Though not part of the spatial background, what Mark says about those who accompany Jesus also has topological significance. The constant companions of Jesus are the "twelve", and it is they who first receive the revelations of the Messiah. The number can be varied. Sometimes only the four disciples who were called at the Sea of Galilee are mentioned. The motif comes from the call pericope (1:16–20), and Mark can use it, for example, in the introduction to Jesus' apocalyptic discourse (13:3). It is only in redactional material that the three disciples Peter, James and John are mentioned; these act as witnesses to characteristic manifestations of the revealer. Here, therefore, revelations take place amongst a narrower circle of the disciples. On the other hand, it almost seems to contradict this when, in the passage about the interpretation of the parables at 4:10, we hear of *hoi peri auton* ("those who were around him") as well as the twelve; and they, like the disciples, appear to have been granted the "secret of the Kingdom of God". Similarly, in the pericope about the relatives of Jesus, even the *ochlos* ("crowd") are said to be Jesus' confidants. However, the number of Jesus' disciples makes no material difference, and in the texts just mentioned the principle of secret epiphanies is not broken either. What really matters is the context of what is said, and this is quite clear in each instance: the wider circle of the disciples is set over against those who "stand outside". This means that the topological idea is not bound to any one expression of it; even the *ochlos* ("crowd") can be included in the inner circle if the situation demands it. All that matters is that the idea of messianic hiddenness, that any revelatory event occurs in isolation, is maintained.

We can now summarize what has been established so far and what follows from it:

1 The motif of the messianic secret appears very frequently in a variety of ways. This indicates that we should acknowledge the fundamental significance of the motif for the interpretation of the whole Gospel.
2 Bultmann's analysis has been confirmed. The motif is basically redactional.
3 We have seen that the pre-Marcan tradition was itself already christologically coloured. Since this can be shown to be the case in individual pericopes, there is no need to prove that Mark has not used an unmessianic Jesus–tradition; Mark uses the traditions

of the community which have all been coloured by the community's confession of faith.

This means that the attempt to apply Wrede's history of traditions explanation of the secrecy concept to Mark's redactional work (as is still done by Bultmann) must be dropped. Since Mark probably did not know any unmessianic traditions about Jesus, his use of the secrecy theory cannot be seen as an attempt to reconcile messianic and unmessianic traditions about Jesus. (A corollary of this is that the Marcan secrecy motif cannot be used as even an indirect argument against the historical Jesus' having a messianic self-consciousness.)

Whether Wrede's view can be maintained at the level of the pre-Marcan tradition, i.e. whether the secrecy idea in the pre-Marcan tradition presupposes the coming together of messianic and unmessianic traditions about Jesus, is another matter. This raises the question of the origin and tradition history of the motif in Mark's Gospel.

II

The essence of the messianic secrecy motif is the paradoxical unity of hiddenness and revelation. Even though the hiddenness is not infrequently ruptured, e.g. when the commands to silence are disobeyed, the stress at the level of Mark's redaction still lies on the motif of hiddenness. This is clear (i) from the importance of the epiphany of the *Kyrios* in the pre-Marcan tradition; and (ii) above all from our conclusion that the lack of understanding and the commands to silence are redactional motifs.

The revealer's intention to remain hidden is also part of the redactional motif of hiddenness, as is the limitation of this hiddenness to a given time limit, i.e. Jesus' resurrection. (This anticipates what will be said about 9:9 later.)

This provides the starting-point for asking about the origin and tradition history of the motif in Mark's Gospel. There is no need here to go any further into the question of the universal correspondence between revelation and hiddenness, which is widespread both inside and outside the NT (e.g. Matt. 11:25ff; 28:17; Jewish wisdom teaching, etc.): it is a motif which is widely linked with the idea of revelation, but it does not clarify the special characteristics of Mark's messianic secrecy theory.

More important is the recent hypothesis that the messianic secret in Mark might derive from the christological tradition of gentile

Christianity, namely the tradition found in Phil. 2:6ff. According to this view, the messianic secret in Mark is modelled on the pattern of the gnostic myth, with its ideas of the cosmic descent of the pre-existent redeemer, his earthly presence in hidden form under the powers of the world, and his final exaltation to be the Cosmocrator.[8] This kind of derivation might explain the hiddenness motif in the messianic secrecy concept. However, a comparison between the "gnostic", or "pre-gnostic", redeemer myth and Mark's Christology shows that in other respects there are important differences. There is no "descent" idea in Mark's Gospel; that alone makes it unlikely that Mark's Christology includes the idea of pre-existence; this idea can scarcely be deduced from the fact that the verb *apostellein* ("send") is applied to the "Son", nor from the fact that Jesus' baptism is presented as an epiphany. Epiphany and adoption are not mutually exclusive; Jesus' baptism is understood as his adoption to be *huios tou theou* ("Son of God"), as can probably be deduced from the words of address in Mark 1:11 when compared with the parallel versions, and above all from the different form of expression used in Mark 9:7.[9] But it is not only this which tells against the connection with gnostic ideas. It is also notable that Mark's Gospel lacks any cosmological ideas which might be compared to the gnostic myth; above all, the intention of the revealer to remain hidden does not correspond with any parallel idea in genuine gnostic thought, where the hiddenness motif is connected more with what happens in the myth itself.

The result of all this is that Mark's motif of the messianic secret is not prefigured by the christological ideas found in Philippians 2; and we shall have to go further and reject even the possibility of any such genetic derivation, even in the sense of individual details being taken over from this idea.

W. Wrede gave other reasons for his view that the motif of the messianic secret was a pre-Marcan idea. He supported it by parallel texts in the Gospel of John. The relevant evidence can be divided into three groups:

1 Sayings about the Spirit, or Paraclete (e.g. 7:39; 14:19f, 26; 15:26f; 16:7, 12ff; 20:22). Here the revealer promises to his own followers perfect instruction through the Spirit who will be sent by the Father. There is a close relationship to what is said in Mark, in that the resurrection (or exaltation) of Jesus seems to be a temporal turning-point, and that a time of perfect revelation appears to follow a time when illumination is lacking. But it is clear that in John's understanding, the eschatological gift of salvation has

already been fully given with the arrival of the Son (11:24ff; 4.23f; 6:63). This means that the parallelism between John and the Marcan secrecy concept disappears. Certainly one could enquire whether the pre-Johannine tradition distinguished between a time of more limited illumination and a future time of complete instruction. The question can be focused on the problem of the Paraclete in the pre-Johannine tradition. But there is no need to show in detail that the points of contact with the Marcan secrecy motif would then be minimal.

2   A second group contains sayings about parabolic speech (10:6; 16:25, 29); these speak of failure to understand speaking in parables, which brings to mind the parallels in Mark 4:10ff and 7:17. This comparison shows that both the pre-Marcan and pre-Johannine traditions already presuppose a connection between speaking in parables and the motif of the failure to understand. The idea that the parables are incomprehensible may be suggested by the Hebrew term *mašal* (see R. Otto, J. Jeremias); it is also tied up with the fact that the community added secondary interpretations to parables which were in the tradition. But this then means that this idea was originally linked with speaking in parables, and not with a messianic secrecy motif. It is probably Mark who took the motif of the lack of understanding from the context of parabolic discourse and incorporated it into the wider context of the messianic secret. This is supported by the motif of lack of understanding being interpreted differently in John's Gospel. (See 16:25, 29: the dialectic of revelatory discourse involves hiddenness and frankness.)

3   Thirdly, and finally, there are the sayings about the disciples' insufficient understanding of Scripture, and these include a reference to the resurrection as the moment when more complete knowledge will ensue (2:22; 12:16; 20:9). In Mark one is reminded, as in the first group of sayings, of the mention of a point in time when misunderstanding will be removed. However, the differences should not be overlooked. Mark does not relate the misunderstanding of the disciples to any failure in their understanding of Scripture. Conversely, in the examples given from John's Gospel there is no intentionality involved. It is also striking that, in the context of John's Gospel, these sayings express an undialectical understanding of time, in that they appear to be wholly related to the future. Further, the idea of referring to Scripture, and also the fact that in John 2:22 the word of the Lord is set on a par with Scripture, support Bultmann's analysis which ascribed these texts to a post-Johannine ecclesiastical redactor. This can also be argued from a literary-critical point of view: all three passages can be removed from their context without disruption.

The result of all this is that, although John's Gospel may contain individual motifs which are reminiscent of the Marcan messianic secret, these statements are quite varied both in content and tradition–history. This excludes any theory which would derive the motif in question in Mark in this way. A messianic secrecy motif comparable to what we have in Mark is thus to be seen neither in the NT (nor in the traditions within the NT) nor in the contemporary environment. Wrede's attempt to explain the messianic secrecy theory in terms of its tradition–history is probably redundant. Of course, this is not to deny the fact that in shaping the motif, Mark used traditions which were already present. But this applies only to individual elements. It is only in the context of Mark's final redaction that they are linked together to form the comprehensive statement of the messianic secret.

III

Mark writes as a member of his community. Mark's redactional messianic secret must therefore be seen in connection with the kerygma of the evangelist's community, as H. J. Ebeling stressed in his monograph,[10] and as Willi Marxsen subsequently spelled out in his article "Redaktionsgeschichtliche Erklärung der sogenannte Parabeltheorie des Markus".[11] The question arises, however, whether this so-called kerygmatic intention alone determines the gospel, or whether the concept of the messianic secret itself might not disclose a specific understanding of the gospel. We shall try to consider this question on the basis of individual sayings.

Mark 9:9 is part of the conversation which takes place on the way down from the mountain of the transfiguration. Its language and content indicate that, together with v. 10, it is a redactional construction, and in the wider context, it bears all the marks of the messianic secrecy concept. The selection of the three trusted disciples in v. 2 means that the transfiguration is already characterized as an esoteric revelation; the command for silence in our verse, and the typical misunderstanding of the disciples in v. 10, correspond to this. These statements can first be interpreted as direct address to the community – as different ways of referring to the "lofty nature of the divine mystery, which is here revealed to the reader [!]" (Ebeling, 200). But it is difficult to interpret the limitation of the silence command "until the Son of Man is risen from the dead" in the same way; for this appears to be fixing a definite point in time, and is thus directly opposed to a contemporary interpretation which is not bound by time.

Ebeling of course thinks that he can establish the directly kerygmatic reference here: he sees the transfiguration story as a preview of the resurrection, and he refers to parallels in apocalyptic literature. Here, the apocalyptic writer is instructed to keep the revelation which he has received secret, because it applies to later times (Dan. 8:26; 12:4, 9; As. Mos. 10:11f, and elsewhere). As in those texts, the command here too "indicates correspondingly the mysterious, i.e. revelatory, nature of what has happened" (Ebeling, 201). "As in the parallels which have been referred to, the given revelation points to the future, and its fulfilment is now to be awaited. This will confirm what the revelation, given here in advance, has already made certain to the witnesses in the present" (203). However, the interpretation of the transfiguration story as a preview of the resurrection is disputed, so the parallels drawn from the apocalyptic predictions are not necessarily convincing. But quite apart from this, we must note that the apocalyptic command to silence with a time limit aims to include the reader within the time of the keeping of the secret. The fact that the secret revelation has been partly realized then serves to guarantee the reliability of what has been predicted but has not yet happened. For Mark by contrast, the resurrection is an event lying in the past; it is this which is referred to here, without any parallel idea of a prophecy which has not yet been fulfilled. Thus, for this reason too, what is said in v. 9 cannot be taken as just a stylistic device, intended simply to stress the esoteric nature of what has been proclaimed.

Wrede showed that this passage has fundamental significance for the whole idea of the messianic secret. It is unlikely that the silence command refers only to the transfiguration and not to the messiahship of Jesus in general.[12] For, on the one hand, the transfiguration clearly belongs for the evangelist within the context of the messianic revelations of the earthly Jesus; and on the other hand, the command for secrecy is parallel to the other expressions of the messianic secret. These together constitute a unity which runs through the whole Gospel and forms a counterpart to the revelation given. But if then there is a material connection with the other secrecy elements, then the time limit in 9:9 cannot be taken in isolation; rather, it concerns the whole secrecy motif. It points forward to the resurrection as the time when the keeping of the secret, and that means the hiddenness of the Messiah, will come to an end.

The parable about the lamp and the lampstand and the appended sayings in Mark 4:21–3 are of pre-Marcan origin. This is shown by their presence in the sayings tradition, seen in the synoptic parallels. These sayings have been introduced into their present context by the evangelist. This can be seen from the Marcan introductory formula *kai elegen autois* ("and he said to them") (v. 21).[13] The significance of this for Mark's redaction was already stated by Wrede: if Mark introduces sayings material at this point, he does not do so "with some degree of embarrassment or by laboriously holding discrete ideas together, as if impelled not to permit such *logia* to perish, but in order to express an idea which is important in the context" (Wrede, 1971, 70f).

The original significance of the verses within the Jesus-tradition probably lies in the stress on the openness involved in the commission which Jesus claimed for himself and his preaching.[14] However, the specifically Marcan interpretation can only be discovered by considering the context. The natural starting-point for the interpretation seems to lie in the explanation of the parable of the sower which comes just before (vv. 13–20), as Ebeling thought.[15] These verses are then a paraenetical addition, saying that faith should not remain hidden but should lead to action. The contemporary application of this interpretation is obvious: as Ebeling says, it is aimed directly at the reader of the Gospel – it is a "direct application to the heart and mind of the community" (192).

But there are problems about this. The preceding verses comprise an original piece of source material containing the parable of the sower and its explanation; apart from our text, the evangelist added vv. 10–12 as well as the introduction (v. 1) and the conclusion (v. 34). But if it is a matter of a whole thematic unit, then it seems more correct methodologically to consider the redactional additions as a whole. This means that we should not interpret our text on the basis of the fact that it is appended to the immediately preceding explanation of the parable of the sower; rather, it should be interpreted in the context of the evangelist's theory about parables and in the light of the other redactional additions, especially as these statements correspond to one another; for here, as there, there is an echo of the same motif of "hiddenness and revelation".

In this connection we must consider the question of the meaning of the parables in 4:10. Here, in the double reference to the audience, the concept of the "twelve" is Mark's interpretative addition to the original *hoi peri auton* ("those around him"). The term *dōdeka* ("twelve") appears elsewhere in redactional contexts, including secrecy contexts where it has topological significance. It describes the smaller circle of people amongst whom revelation takes place. As we saw, this circle varies in size, i.e. even the traditional *hoi peri auton* is to be understood in a topological sense. But if the whole reference to the audience in v. 10 is part of the secrecy theory, this does not exclude a historical intention. For the topological expressions can clearly be used also as a stylistic means of presenting revelation as an event which, from the point of view of the author, lies in the past. This can be taken as certain, for the motif of the "twelve" refers back to the time of Jesus.

The interpretation of vv. 21–3 is also determined by this. These verses are joined to the explanation of the parables without any transition, and are thus addressed to the same "inner circle".[16] This means that here too the reference is not to the evangelist's community but to the time of Jesus. This shows that Wrede's interpretation of this text was right when he connected it with the idea of the messianic secret: as is explicitly said in 9:9, so too here, the secret revelation is limited in time. What is revealed to the disciples secretly in the time of Jesus is to be proclaimed openly in the future. We may therefore presuppose the same time-limit as in 9:9: after the resurrection what is hidden may be uncovered. Mark has "seen the resurrection as the dividing-line between two periods"[17] and from this he has developed the concept of the messianic secret.

Finally there are the three passion predictions of Jesus handed down by Mark. Linguistic considerations suggest that the last two predictions (9:30–2; 10:32–4) stem from the evangelist.[18] Further, it is unlikely that they were ever handed on in isolation, i.e. as original doublets of Jesus' first passion prediction in 8:31. For they are not complete units, but can only be understood in the total context of the Gospel. Their origin can be explained by the influence of the corresponding events of the passion narrative on the first passion prediction. 8:31 is different. Linguistic details suggest a pre-Marcan origin. The link with Peter's confession becomes clearer when one removes the command to silence (8:30) and v. 32a as Mark's interpretative additions. V. 31 could then have been handed down in the pre-synoptic tradition as a correction of Peter's confession by Jesus. It could have arisen on the basis of the community's faith in Jesus crucified and risen, confirming with a saying of Jesus the Church's Christology which differed from traditional Jewish ideas.

The relationship of this to the messianic secret has hardly ever been noted before,[19] although even a schematic comparison shows how very striking it is. Corresponding to each other are:

the *revelation motif* in the main part of the passion prediction (8:31; 9:31; 10:33f);

the *secrecy motif* in 8:30 (the command), 9:30 (Jesus' attempt to remain hidden), and in 10:32 (the separation of the twelve);

the *misunderstanding motif* in 8:32b (Peter's remonstration), 9:32 (the disciples' lack of understanding) and 10:35ff (the pericope about the request of the sons of Zebedee which has been added here redactionally).

We should therefore count the passion predictions as expressions of the messianic secrecy theory. Corresponding to the revelation of the suffering Messiah, whose majesty comes to expression in the predictions,[20] there is the failure of the disciples to understand and, above all, the hiddenness motif.

Linking the passion predictions with the other parts of the secrecy concept has various consequences. Since the passsion predictions point forward to a specific point in time, i.e. Jesus' death and resurrection, they have validity prior to this, but after their fulfilment they have only historical significance. The hiddenness remains until the fulfilment; but after this it comes to an end, the disciples understand, and open proclamation of Jesus' messiahship is permitted. If the passion predictions are incorporated within the whole pattern of the secrecy concept, this also has implications the other way: the time limit involved in them must be applied to the messianic secret in general. They stand on a par with the texts considered above (4:21f; 9:9f), and together with these, they qualify the Marcan secrecy motif as being something which is limited in time and belongs to past history. As such, it has validity only for the life of Jesus.

What we have tried to show about the concept of the messianic secret from these parts of the data can be confirmed by looking at Mark's redactional work as a whole. Although Mark's Gospel contains a large number of varied, even contradictory, statements, there is no doubt that on the whole the story constitutes a unity with its own temporal order, stretching from the appearance of the Baptist through to the death and resurrection of Jesus. Its contents correspond to this. For even if the author can hardly be credited with a systematic organization, or even any development in his portrayal of Jesus or the twelve, nevertheless the geographical notes show that the story goes along a certain path. After the introduction, the section about Jesus' activity begins in Galilee. This contains a few stories which were located in Galilee in the pre-Marcan tradition, but most of the units included here were not geographically fixed. The setting in Galilee, or its immediate neighbourhood, is maintained until the journey up to Jerusalem, which is indicated by 10:1, the start of the journey from Galilee to Perea. This direction of the Gospel is underlined by the three-fold passion prediction which begins after Peter's confession.

The numerous spatial and temporal links, which Bultmann showed to be part of the redactional material in the second Gospel,[21] have material significance in this context too. Connecting links made by verbs (*exelthein* ("to come out") etc.), the use of adverbs of place (e.g. *ekeithen* ("from there") in 6:1; 7:34 and elsewhere), and the specific redactional comments about the starting-point or goal of Jesus' journey are all characteristic of this. Even the topological expressions such as *oikos* ("house"), *oros* ("mountain"), *hodos* ("way"), *topos erēmos* ("desert place") belong here; despite their dogmatic significance, it is not fortuitous that they are taken from a vocabulary describing place.

Time references indicate the same thing. Adverbs (*euthus* ("immediately"), *palin* ("again"), *tote* ("then") and others), temporal links like *en ekeinais tais hēmerais* ("in those days") etc. all enable us to recognize the linear form of the Gospel. Above all, there is the well-known way the redactor has developed the account of Jesus' final activity in Jerusalem chronologically.[22]

All this shows that Mark is seeking to write the life of Jesus as an event complete in itself. It is not a critical view of history, but it is a historical view, insofar as one can describe an awareness of the distinction between past and present, evident in Mark's chronological and geographical perspectives, as "historical" thought. Eschatological salvation is manifested in the temporal sequence of the life of Jesus. The evangelist makes no distinction: the salvation *event* is presented as salvation *history*.

On the one hand, these temporal aspects of the messianic secrecy theory confirm the basic understanding of the Gospel; on the other hand, the theory itself must be seen against this background. Mark brings out the temporal elements in the theory, and this means that it is influenced by the process in which the gospel tradition is historicized. It becomes an element in the presentation of the life of Jesus as an event of salvation history. So it is not a "historically subsidiary idea"[23] which can be dissolved by reference to the history of the tradition, but rather an essential expression of a theology of salvation history. Its goal is the time after the resurrection; it implies the christological recognition that the story of the earthly Jesus does not remain on its own but points to his enthronement as Lord. Ecclesiologically, this means that Mark's community possesses remarkable self-awareness: it engages in a preaching which was only possible in hidden form during the life of Jesus (4:21ff). But now there are no bounds: that preaching now takes place with no time limit, i.e. until the end of time, and with all people in view (13:10). Above all, however, is the fact that, unlike the "twelve", the post-Easter community understands Jesus' messiahship (in contrast to the lack of understanding shown at the transfiguration or the passion predictions); the concept of the messianic secret thus implicitly expresses the fact that the presuppositions for a genuinely Christian preaching only exist after Easter.

There are still questions to be answered, but that is in the nature of the case. Mark writes a life of Jesus, but does not tell of the period in time after the resurrection; and it is only from this stand-point, in a presentation expounding Mark's ecclesiology, that the solution of the messianic secret could have been made clearer.

In what has been said here, the one important thing noted was the historical aim of the concept. What has already been established in the case of the topological expressions applies to the paradox of the messianic secret *in toto*: it does not contradict the historical orientation, but it needed incorporating into the historicizing presentation of the life of Jesus. It has a kerygmatic character, because it is the expression of the evangelist who is writing as the representative of his community. This means that the kerygmatic aim does not in fact contradict the historicizing tendency: rather, as a kerygmatic expression the messianic secret is to be seen "historically". It is precisely this that characterizes the Gospel. It is not simply "preaching", nor even "preaching and story",[24] but "preaching as story".

NOTES

1 Göttingen, 1901 (ET 1971; all quotations from this).

2 Bultmann, 1963, 347; also 1951, 32. For more on this, see 1963, 348.

3 Bultmann, 1963, 209 n.1, 223.

4 Ibid., 224.

5 8:32f; 9:5f; 14:37ff; (5:31).

6 Cf. Matt 28: 16ff; John 20:25.

7 See G. Strecker, *Der Weg der Gerechtigkeit. Untersuchungen zur Theologie des Matthäus* (Göttingen: Vandenhoek & Ruprecht, 1962) 95.

8 See Schreiber, 1961.

9 The derivation of the idea of pre-existence from Mark 12:1ff (Schreiber, 167) presupposes a corresponding interpretation of the baptism story.

10 Ebeling, 1939.

11 *ZTK* 52 (1955) 255ff.

12 So, for example, A. Hilgenfeld, "Der mysteriöse Marcus und der reactionäre Jacobus", *Zeitschrift für wissenschaftliche Theologie* 46 (1903) 10; Ebeling, 1939, 198 n. 3.

13 Marxsen (n. 11), 259; J. Jeremias, *The Parables of Jesus* (ET London: SCM/ New York: Charles Scribner's Sons, 1963) 14.

14 Jeremias, 121; Percy, 1953, 284.

15 Ebeling, 191 and elsewhere; see also ibid., n. 1.

16 On the other hand, the crowds are thought of as present again in v. 26; this corresponds with the speaking in parables in v. 2, and also vv. 33f, where there is the distinction made between teaching in parables "to them" and explaining the parables "to the disciples".

17 Wrede, 1971, 72.

18 Despite what is said by H. E. Tödt, *The Son of Man in the Synoptic Tradition* (ET London: SCM/Philadelphia: Westminster, 1965) 172ff, 201f [Strecker argues this in detail in his article "The Passion- and Resurrection-predictions in Mark's Gospel", *Interpretation* 22 (1968) 421–43. (German *ZTK* 64 (1967) 16–39).]

19 See, however, Wrede, 1971, 82f (also the two-fold scheme on p. 101). It does not occur in Ebeling's division. For 9:30f, see Percy, 1953, 293.

20 Wrede, 1971, 84.

21 1963, 339f.

22 Bultmann, 1963, 341; Dibelius, 1934, 223.

23 See Marxsen (n. 11), 267 n. 2.

24 So G. Bornkamm, art. Evangelien, formgeschichtlich, *RGG*, 3rd edn, vol. ii, col. 750.

5

The Question of the Messianic Secret in Mark[*][1]

EDUARD SCHWEIZER

I *Presuppositions*

As long ago as 1901 W. Wrede showed that the messianic secret is a redactional construction of Mark, and belongs to the history of dogma, not to the life of Jesus.[2] There is no going back on this insight. On the other hand, E. Sjöberg has correctly called attention to the fact that between the life of Jesus and Mark's redaction there lies a long tradition–history, which Wrede did not deny but which he nevertheless regarded in far too uniform a manner.[3] We must therefore first see which statements were already part of Mark's tradition. The fact that the demons recognize Jesus and are silenced was certainly part of the tradition;[4] so too were the healings in private,[5] and perhaps also the command to tell no one until after the healing had been ratified by the priests.[6] Further, it had no doubt already been said before Mark that parables need interpretation.[7] Sjöberg's most important reference is to Jewish apocalyptic and its influence upon the secrecy motif of 1 Cor. 2:6ff; Rom. 16:25ff; Col. 1:26f; 2:2f; Eph. 3:1ff; 1 Tim. 3:16.[8] This is in fact Mark's background, though he develops his own, essentially different, conception.

This material must be expanded above all by the Qumran writings,[9] where statements about the "secret", or "mystery", refer almost always to God.[10] In contrast to the NT passages mentioned above,[11] the word often occurs here in the plural, and thus denotes a whole series of separate (eschatological) mysteries. Parallel concepts are "miracle" (1QS 11:3f), "truth" (1QH 7:26f) and "holy plan" (1QS 11:18f).[12] In the end, only God himself can understand the depth of his mysteries (1QS 11:18–20; 1QH 10:2f; cf. 13:3f). If chosen men receive a share in them (1QpHab 7:5; 1QH 11:3f, 10; 12:11–13;

---

* First published in *ZNW* 56 (1965) 1–8. Translated by C. M. Tuckett.

cf. 1QS 9:18f), that is a miracle effected by God's revelation.[13]

The NT passages mentioned above differ from these above all in the fact that as early as 1 Cor. 2:6–16 the saving event of the crucifixion of Jesus is the one "mystery" in which everything is included.[14] One can even say that Christ himself is *the* "mystery" of God (Col. 1:26f; 2:2; 1 Tim. 3:16; cf. Col. 4:3; Eph. 3:4), though increasingly the place of the crucified Christ is taken by the triumphant Christ journeying through the world, and finally by the Church itself (see already Eph. 3:4–6, 10; 5:32).

II *The Differences in Mark's Conception*

The first thing that strikes us is the terminology: *mystērion* occurs only in 4:11,[15] where, unlike the synoptic parallels, it is in the singular. It is thus understood as something single and all-embracing, and Mark, like Paul in 1 Cor. 2:6ff, probably understood it to mean the cross. Whether that is also true for the tradition is doubtful. Further, Mark 4:11 shares with the Jewish apocalyptic texts and their NT offshoots the idea that this mystery can only be given (*dedotai*) to the chosen ones (*hymīn*) by grace though God's miracle. There are chosen people to whom the mystery is revealed. This distinguishes them from the world for which it remains incomprehensible folly.

But it is precisely here that questions arise. It is true that Mark joins all the texts mentioned above in asserting the inaccessibility of God, aiming to maintain the deity of God. He knows, like the apocalyptic writers, that only God's own revelation can unveil his mystery to man. He therefore also shows what efforts Jesus must continually make in order to bring God's mystery to men, especially his disciples (4:34; 7:17–23; 8:15–21, 27–33; 9:30–2; 10:32–4; cf. 5:37; 9:2; 13:3f, etc.). But whilst on the one hand it is clear that God's revelation everywhere bursts through irresistibly in Jesus' miracles and in his authority,[16] it is on the other hand vital for Mark that the disciples, who have received special instruction, show themselves despite this to be just as blind as the world (6:6b—8:26, especially 6:52; 7:18; 8:17–21). This is also shown by the failure of the disciples after the "open" teaching of 8:31, 32a (8:33; 9:6, 10, 18, 28, 32, 34; 10:35–7, 41), culminating in their sleeping, their flight and the denial at the climax of the story of Jesus (14:37, 40, 50, 66ff). The fact that God is at no man's disposal is thus understood far more radically than in the parallels. Not even the initiated, the chosen ones, have God at their disposal. He is thus in his essence God *absconditus sub contrario* ("concealed under the opposite"), and this cannot be overcome simply by miraculous communication.[17] We shall have to ask whether the commands silencing the demons and those who have been healed, absent from both the Qumran texts and the NT parallels, are not also connected with this radicalizing of the theology. Above all, however, we must investigate how Mark solves the problem that God is radically incomprehensible, that men are radically blind, but that still the miracle of revelation occurs.

III *The Theory of Parables*

3:23 is a skilful redactional insertion.[18] It makes Jesus' speaking in parables an answer to the blindness of his own family and of the official Jerusalem representatives. It is meant to lead to the acknowledging of Jesus' authority (3:24–30) and to becoming a member of the family of God which consists of those who listen to Jesus and do God's will (3:31–5). For this purpose Jesus calls everyone to him (3:23). 4:1f starts the big parable discourse with a note about the setting which corresponds precisely with the other instances where Jesus wants to address and reach everyone with his "teaching".[19] The boat serves to emphasize how large and pressing the crowd is. 4:21f shows, after the interpretation of the first representative parable, that the lamp belongs on the lampstand, not under the bushel or the bed, and that what is hidden should be revealed.[20] Granted, one must have ears to hear[21] – it always remains a matter of God's gift – nevertheless Jesus' parable discourse is a call to hear in this way, and is a promise for those who do hear.[22] The most important reference for Mark's own understanding is 4:33f, where he himself speaks most clearly.[23] Here the parable discourse is seen as the only possible means of communication appropriate for human beings. It is not meant to conceal; it aims to reveal and reach men. This certainly expressed the fundamental inaccessibility of God: *only* in a parable, only in a picture can we comprehend him at all, not in direct speech. Certainly this inaccessibility is even more underlined by the special instruction given to the disciples. But 4:33b shows that the parable discourse in itself is an attempt to bear witness to God before men in such a way that the one who is fundamentally inaccessible is revealed to them. This programme is simply carried out more consistently in the case of the disciples. It is thus clear from all these instances that the parable discourse is speech which is appropriate for revealing the incomprehensible mystery of God to human beings.

When we turn to 4:10–13, the question arises as to what is tradition and what redaction. It is certain that not only the parable but also its interpretation is pre-Marcan. It is also certain that v. 10 is a seam, in which the question about the parable told by Jesus has been reshaped into a fundamental question about parables in general, and where at the same time the twelve have been introduced.[24] Further, it is certain that behind v. 11f there lies a tradition, whatever its details may have been.[25] Has Mark inserted it here? This is not as certain as might at first sight appear. It is clear that it is a tradition which is relatively unusual in Mark and uses strange terminology. It goes back to an Aramaic basis, perhaps to an Isaiah Targum, and occurs in the community's tradition outside Mark (John 12:40; Acts 28:26f), where it explains the unbelief of the world. It is probable that v. 10 (with the singular *parabolē* and without *syn tois dōdeka*) together with v. 13a constituted the pre-Marcan transition from parable to interpretation, and that this was transformed at a later stage of the tradition by the introduction of v. 11f. But who was responsible for this?

Now we can see the shift from this one parable and its interpretation to a fundamental statement about parables (in the plural) not only in the change assumed in v. 10, but also in the step from v. 13a to v. 13b. Thus at two different places and in two different ways, we find this advance to a statement of principle. They cannot both stem from the same author. But v. 13b is unlikely to have existed at the stage of the tradition where parable and interpretation were linked, i.e. before the inclusion of v. 11f. The picture of Jesus as sighing, and generally expecting no understanding of his parables, scarcely fits with the tendency to make everything clear through a precise interpretation of all the details. But this corresponds precisely with Mark's theology.[26] Even the disciples show themselves to be blind. Because of their lack of understanding, Jesus' wish to reveal is in danger of being frustrated. They are separated from the crowds at best by Jesus' special loving care for them, not by any better understanding on their part. The real elucidation of the parable discourse (8:32a as opposed to 4:33a) follows at 8:31, and even this the disciples do not understand at all (8:33). 4:11 sees things quite differently. Here those "inside" are sharply distinguished from those "outside". Here there is a group of chosen ones, for whom the mystery is no longer incomprehensible and to whom the mystery has been "given", whereas in 4:13b a fundamental blindness with regard to all parables is made clear from the case of this one parable. In 4:11f there is the secrecy idea of Qumran and the other NT passages mentioned above; what is said here is thus also reminiscent of predestination. It all stands much closer theologically to the community which attached the interpretation in 4:14ff and thereby described itself as the possessor of the key to the mystery. But for Mark all, if one can put it this way, are predestined to blindness, and all are called to perception. This is most clearly visible at 8:14 where a very similar prophetic saying is applied not to those "outside" but specifically to the disciples, and where the following story (8:22–6), with its continuation in vv. 27ff and vv. 34ff, shows that only God's miracle can open blind eyes, but that God wishes to perform this miracle.

The expression *en parabolais* is certainly part of the pre-Marcan tradition; the word was probably therefore already connected with the parable tradition prior to Mark. Equally certainly, the interpretation was added to the parable of the sower prior to Mark. It was thus already asserted that a parable without interpretation remains hidden, and that the special teaching which interprets it has been given not to the world, but only to the Church, where the parable is correctly applied to the word of preaching. It is therefore probable that 4:11f had already been placed between the parable and interpretation in the pre-Marcan tradition. The community had thus adopted the Isaiah quotation as in John 12:40 and Acts 28:26f to describe the unbelieving world from whom the following interpretation remained hidden.[27] The first step in the tradition was thus the addition of the interpretation with the original form of v. 10 and perhaps v. 13a; the second step transformed v. 10 and added v. 11f; finally, Mark was able to take over the idea of the special concern of Jesus for the twelve (v. 11a) together with a provisional distinction between them and the people (v. 11b). But at the same time, in a third step, he used v. 13b to establish that in the last resort the twelve also belong to the blind world. He thus points forward to 8:17ff.[28]

IV *Mark's Answer*

The first half of the Gospel shows the blindness of the Pharisees (3:6 as the conclusion of the first section), of Jesus' own fellow-citizens (6:1–4 as the conclusion of the second section) and of the disciples (8:17–21 as the conclusion of the third section). Jesus then speaks in 8:31 for the first time without parables and openly (8:32 is parallel to 4:33) of the suffering of the Son of Man.[29] But even this plain speaking remains incomprehensible to the disciples (8:33). Thereafter, Jesus summons the whole crowd and challenges people

to become disciples (8:34). This means therefore: 1. Only in discipleship, following in the way of the cross, can one understand Jesus'
way to the cross and so Jesus himself.[30] 2. In discipleship the distinction between those "inside" and those "outside" disappears: all
people are called to it, not only the twelve (8:34a). Both these points
are confirmed in the following two passion predictions, where an
immediate misunderstanding by the disciples and a call to discipleship are attached;[31] similarly, in 15:39 it is not a disciple but the
gentile centurion who is the first to understand what has happened
on the cross; and in 15:41 it is not the disciples who are mentioned,
but the women, who will see the empty tomb first and who have
followed Jesus and served him. Finally, in 16:7 a message will be
sent by the angel to the disciples that Jesus will go before them
into Galilee, as he was doing already on the way to the cross
(10:32), and as he was to promise them in 14:28 in the midst of their
failure.[32]

In Qumran the call to follow him in whom God's "mystery" is
revealed is of course lacking. Neither are there any commands to
silence there. The question arises of whether both these things belong
together. Are not the commands to silence to be explained in that
one cannot understand God's revelation in Jesus in any other way
than in the way of discipleship, and so only after the suffering of
the Son of Man? So it is indeed the messianic, rather than the unmessianic material which causes Mark trouble.[33] The juxtaposition
of the *theios anēr* idea and that of the fundamental hiddenness of
the revelation[34] are both pre-Marcan and cause difficulties. They are
resolved by saying that God's revelation breaks through powerfully
and irresistibly – thus the commands to silence are continually
broken[35] – but that it is bound to be misunderstood except where
the disciple learns the real secret, the suffering of the Son of Man,
by following in this way of suffering.[36] But on this the following
article (that of U. Luz) should be considered.[37]

NOTES

1. This and the following essay come from my summer 1964 seminar on the topic.
   A whole series of students have therefore contributed to them. The two authors
   also have their own individual insights and misunderstandings as is shown by
   some, though not too important, differences between the view of my assistant,
   for whose help I am extremely grateful, and my own.
2. Wrede, 1971, 131.
3. Sjöberg, 1955, 150ff.

4 See Mark 4:39; Sjöberg, 150f, and Luz, p. 81 below. On the first motif, the texts cited in n. 36 below seem to me more relevant than the hellenistic ones.

5 See Luz, p. 77.

6 1:43f; Sjöberg, 158f.

7 Sjöberg, 166f; see n. 24.

8 Sjöberg, 1ff. On the other hand, the concept of the hidden Messiah plays no role (against Sjöberg, 125).

9 G. Bornkamm, art. *"mysterion"*, *TDNT* iv, 815, 819.

10 I am grateful to Herr Wiard Popkes for the list of references.

11 But cf. Matt 13:11; Luke 8:10; 1 Cor. 4:1; 13:2; also the substance of Rom. 11:25; 1 Cor. 15:51.

12 This plan applies to all periods of time, but especially the End-time (1QpHab 7:7f, 12–14) and also the time of iniquity (1QS 4:18).

13 There is also talk of the mystery of wickedness (1QH 5:36; 1QM 14:9f; 1QXXVII 1:2). This is also to be understood in apocalyptic terms and remains subordinate to the divine plan.

14 Bornkamm, *TDNT* iv, 829; also E. Schweizer, art. *"pneuma"*, *TDNT* vi, 425f and n. 617.

15 The same is true for other terms. The following are completely absent: *teleios* ("perfect") (1 Cor. 2:6; Col. 1:28), *apokryptein* ("to hide") (1 Cor. 2:7; Col. 1:26; cf. 2:2; Eph. 3:9), *apokalyptein* and *apokalypsis* ("to reveal" and "revelation") (1 Cor. 2:10; Rom. 16:25; Eph. 3:3, 5), *gnōrizein* ("to make known") (Rom. 16:26; Col. 1:27; cf. 2:2; Eph. 3:3, 5, 10). Other terms such as *sophia* ("wisdom") (1 Cor. 2:6; Col. 1:28; 2:3; Eph. 3:10; cf. Rom. 16:27), *phaneroun* ("to manifest") (Rom. 16:26; Col. 1:26; cf. 1 Tim. 3:16), *synesis* ("understanding") (Col. 2:2; Eph. 3:4), *geneai* ("generations") (Col. 1:26; Eph. 3:5) are not redactional and are used in a quite different connection (Mark 6:2; 4:22; 12:33; *genea* only in the singular).

16 See Luz, pp. 76–80.

17 I have wondered whether some polemic against Jewish Christianity can be seen here (so S. Sandmel, *Journal of Bible and Religion* 31 (1963) 294–300). But it seems to me very unlikely. Certainly Mark is very interested in the positive position of the Gentiles (F. Hahn, *Mission in the New Testament* [ET London: SCM, 1965], pp. 111ff; Schweizer, 1964a, 340, 352f; [cf. Schweizer, 1964b, 422, 429f]); but often it is clear that the real opponents are the Jewish authorities alone, i.e. the Pharisees and scribes, and not the Jewish people (see especially 3:6–8; 7:1ff/14; 10:1f; 11:18, 27/32; 12:12, 13, 18/37 [though cf. v. 34]; 14:1f; 15:11). It should rather be noted that Galilee is valued more highly than Jerusalem, and that, despite their denial of Jesus, the disciples who come from there (see also 15:41) are given the promise of an appearance of Jesus in Galilee (14:28; 16:7). For I am convinced (with U. Wilckens, *Der Ursprung der Über-lieferung der Erscheinungen des Auferstandenen, Dogma und Denkstrukturen* [ed. W. Joest, W. Pannenberg, 1963], pp. 78ff, n. 60) that Mark's readers, who certainly knew of Easter appearances, must have interpreted 16:7 in this way, even if Mark did not (as I believe he did not) go on to record them after 16:8.

71

Is there here (as there probably is at Mark. 5:20) a tradition about the start of the mission outside Jerusalem? If so it contradicts the picture of Acts, where everything derives from the gift of the Spirit in Jerusalem. In this case there would possibly be some hidden polemic against a church that was based too much on Jerusalem, with Galilee in some way prefiguring gentile Christianity. However, quite apart from the question of whether Jerusalem played such a role, this is still unlikely in view of the positive way in which the *people* from Jerusalem are presented from 1:5 to 12:37b. *Barn.* 5:9 (cited by Wrede, 1971, 106) is thus not far wrong.

18 Schweizer, 1963, 97f; 1964a, 344f; [cf. 1964b, 425].

19 See 2:13; 6:33; Schweizer, 1963, 95f; 1964a, 340.

20 Naturally there is tradition here, as is shown by the agreement in terminology with the texts collected above (*phaneroun* ("to manifest"), *krypton* ("hidden"), *apokryphon* ("secret")). But it is presumably Mark who has introduced the sayings at this point.

21 Verse 23 takes up v. 9, and therefore shows that, as v. 21f implies, the parable is intended to be heard.

22 Whatever else the meaning of v. 24f may be, this much is clear. Probably vv. 24b, 25a promise that whoever now hears correctly will be given even more insight.

23 Schweizer, 1963, 98f, 100.

24 J. Jeremias, *The Parables of Jesus* (ET London: SCM; New York: Charles Scribner's Sons, 1963) p. 14.

25 Ibid., pp. 15ff.

26 See 7:17f, where the disciples ask about *tēn parabolēn* ("the parable") (!) and Jesus' reproach then follows.

27 However, if it is Mark who has placed the verses here, he has introduced them simply on the basis of link-words at the first place where there is mention of special instruction given with a parable. His own ideas follow in 4:13b and 8:17ff.

28 Ebeling, 1939, 147f, noted something very important when he saw that the primary mystery is the person of Jesus, whereas words which are not understood, but are made clear by interpretation, are only a mystery in a secondary sense. Mark is concerned with that "primary" mystery; but he refers it entirely to Jesus' way of the cross, not to the person of Jesus as in any way separate from this.

29 Wrede, 1971, 67ff, 215ff, confused the discussion in claiming, on the basis of 9:9, that the resurrection is decisive. The Christology of Rom. 1:4; Acts 2:36 (or rather 13:33) has nothing to do with the Marcan Christology. 9:9 is an isolated instance, determined by the relationship between transfiguration and resurrection, and even here it is linked with the suffering of the Son of Man (9:12). Similarly, 8:33, 34 only take up out of 8:31 the idea of suffering. Even the eschatological–apocalyptic sayings 8:38; 9:1 simply underline the importance of discipleship, following in the way of the cross.

30 Ebeling also points to the connection between announcements of suffering and paraenesis (p. 166f).

31 Schweizer, 1964a, 349f; [cf. 1964b, 428f]. Also 9:35–7; 10:43–5 are formulated quite generally (*hos an* ("whoever"), *anti pollōn* ("for many")); 9:38ff is directed against too narrow a view of the twelve; whether the *akolouthountes* ("those who follow") of 10:32 are limited to the twelve alone is at least uncertain; see too 13:37.

32 It is certainly doubtful if this means to "go at your head" (against J. Weiss, *Die Schriften des NT² ad loc.* (since the 2nd edn is missing in Zurich, I have cited it as in Taylor, 1952, *ad loc.*); see R. H. Lightfoot, *In memoriam E. Lohmeyer* (ed. W. Schmauch, 1951) 115. The present tense in 16:7 (whereas 14:28 has the future) counts against this suggestion. The verse is rather to be understood as in 6:45 (cf. Matt. 21:31 Q) in a more general way; but that does not alter the fact that Jesus shows the way in which the disciples are to follow.

33 Conzelmann, 1968, 42f; see Sjöberg, 1955, 115f, against Wrede, 1971, 217ff.

34 Schreiber, 1961, 157f. No doubt the miracle stories of the gospel tradition show the influence of hellenistic *theios anēr* ideas. After reading D. Georgi, *Die Gegner des Paulus im 2.Korintherbrief* (1964), especially pp. 282–92, I am inclined to agree with Luz (p. 89 here and n. 7) that these ideas have not only influenced a series of individual stories, as might be used in preaching, instruction or discussion, but that also, prior to Mark, one may imagine a more or less complete Christology of this kind. Mark starts from this, but he also distances himself from it with his stress on the theology of suffering.

35 Ebeling in particular, pp. 116ff, points to this; but see too Wrede, 1971, 128.

36 This explains the apparent contradiction between Mark 1:34 end; 3:11 and 1 Cor. 2:8. What the powers here too fail to understand is not Jesus' character as a *theios anēr*, but God's plan of salvation which is fulfilled on the cross. Their knowledge is thus that of Jas. 2:19b. See too 1 Pet. 1:12; on the other hand, the Qumran community shares with the heavenly powers in having insight into God's mysteries (1QH 3:19–23; 1QS 4:22).

37 Apart from details where I differ, I would ask whether one should not see the unity of the miracle–secret and the messianic secret as more tightly knit, though the suggestion that only the demons can engage in messianic preaching proper and hence that this should be clearly distinguished from the other healings, seems to me to be very fruitful for the discussion. But where Mark is writing freely (3:11f), the aim of the prohibition is materially the same as in the healings. For even the prohibition against spreading abroad the news of a miracle is still a ban on proclaiming Jesus' divine authority in the present in a way that would be misunderstood. 1:25 belongs to the tradition, and 1:34, connected to it, is expressed rather more cautiously than 3:12, but probably means the same. The difference lies in the fact that in the exorcism of 1:25, the miracle consists precisely of the silencing of the powerful demon, just as in the healings it is in the ending of the illness (see Luke 4:39, Jesus' *epitīmān* ("rebuke") against the fever, as in Mark 1:25 against the demon; Mark 4:39 has the stilling of the sea by Jesus' *epitīmān* and a "silence command" to the storm). Here a breaking of the command is impossible, because Jesus' power over the demons leads to their overthrow. Mark himself interpreted the command, as in the healings, as a ban on making the messianic secret known prematurely (1:34; 3:12). Finally I wonder, though without claiming any certainty, whether it is a coincidence that the three places

where a silence command is not disobeyed (3:11f; 5:43; 8:26?) occur at the transitions between sections 1 and 2, 2 and 3, and 3 and 4. These are followed, respectively, by the choice of the twelve, their sending out and their open special instruction – in the second case admittedly only after the rejection of Jesus (in Nazareth a silence command would naturally be impossible in view of 6:5f) though it has already happened elsewhere. Also the short note in 1:34 leads to the private discussion with the disciples and the reference to Jesus' commission to preach in 1:35–9.

6

*The Secrecy Motif and the Marcan Christology**

ULRICH LUZ

The "messianic secret" is still a mystery. H. Conzelmann called it the "hermeneutical presupposition of the genre 'gospel'",[2] and thus in effect outlined a new "mystery": the question of the Christology which in Mark's day demanded both the messianic secret idea itself and its embodiment in a Gospel. Mark belonged to a hellenistic community which had taken over numerous traditions about Jesus Christ from the vicinity of Palestine: messianic miracles which were proclaimed, material used in polemic or belonging to catechetical tradition, mostly material that was significant for the life of the community, and a collection of oddly isolated eschatological material.[3] There was also the passion narrative which, separated the rest, was perhaps handed down complete as a memorial (anamnēsis) in worship.[4]

What was the relation of the passion narrative to the rest of the Christ tradition? Christ had been made manifest in his miracles, and the proclamation of him was based on miracle[5]; his power and authority for the present day were clear in the controversy dialogues. So what could the passion add to that? Did it not contradict the rest of the Christ proclamation and need to be superseded by the miracle of the resurrection? And how was the community's suffering,[6] which Mark understood differently from his tradition, related to the view of reality that lay behind the miracle stories? Miracle stories and passion narrative, the divine man (*theios anēr*) and the Crucified, needed relating in a new way. Mark's Gospel grew out of this situation.[7]

The secrecy motif is found in Mark's healing miracles, exorcisms and his accounts of Jesus instructing the disciples. Our method will be to consider these three groups separately, since it cannot be

* First published in *ZNW* 56 (1965) 9–30. Translated by R. Morgan.

assumed that the secrecy motif means the same thing in each case. We are really only concerned with the Marcan redaction, and will use form criticism and examine motifs and word statistics[8] in working out what is redactional material.

I

First the healing miracles. The material seems to provide a variegated picture. Some pericopae lack the motif of keeping the healing secret, whereas others have an express command of Jesus to keep it secret, or at least an indication that might be understood in this sense. There is also great variety as regards the origins of the motif. Sometimes it is clearly there in the tradition; often it is Mark's editorial insertion. The data may be classified thus:

In a few cases, notably 2:1–12 and 3:1–6, there is no hint of a secrecy. This is no great problem because in both cases new meanings have in the course of time been superimposed upon the original aim of the stories. The miracle story in Mark 2:1–12 is now intended only to demonstrate the *exousia* ("authority") of the Son of Man to forgive sins. This aim is incompatible with secrecy. The healing on the sabbath of the man with the withered hand (3:1–6) requires an element of publicity for the sake of the controversy dialogue. Secrecy here would also make the redactional decision of the Pharisees and Herodians to kill Jesus (v. 6) hard to understand. In the case of the woman with a flow of blood (5:25–34) the large crowd is a prerequisite of the scene. The passage is only significant in that the connecting verse 24a, "a great multitude followed him", probably stems from Mark himself.[9] The healing miracle in the second main part of the Gospel (8:27–10:52) will be considered below.[10]

The Marcan summaries contain significant data. The passage 6:53–6 is probably entirely redactional, despite a few unmarcan words.[11] The healings take place in public, in villages, towns and country, at times in the market-place. The whole neighbourhood is present. The meaning of the scene is clear; it shows the extraordinary success of Jesus' healing activity and its enormous scope and impact. Jesus is the wonder-worker or thaumaturge; wherever he appears it is an event. A command to silence is not only absent; the whole design and meaning of the scene make it impossible. Jesus' success is neither evaluated nor interpreted here; the scene is simply intended to show how well known Jesus became through his public healing.

In the two other summaries (1:32–4; 3:7–12) the situation seems to be rather different on account of their silence commands. But that is only apparently the case. In both instances the command to silence is directed at the demons alone. This is "because they knew him" (1:34), or after they had recognized him as God's Son (3:11). However we are to interpret the silence commands, the roots of the conception are not to be found here in the healings. Taking on their own the parts of the summaries concerned with healings, the picture is in full agreement with 6:53–6: Because Jesus healed people, many flocked to him (1:33; 3:8). It is clear, especially in the second summary, that Mark's real aim is to describe Jesus' great impact, seen in the people flocking to him. The healings are only the occasion for that (3:10). 1:32ff is also concerned mainly with the people coming to him.[12] Jesus' work takes place in a house (Peter's) only on account of the preceding pericope (vv. 29–31). We should thus note that in both summaries, the healings and the exorcisms are treated differently. Only the latter come under the silence command. We shall have to keep this difference in mind. The aspect we consider here is the question – at present it is no more than a question – whether the secrecy motif in the miracle stories may not have had a different significance from the messianic secret in the exorcisms.

In a whole series of pericopae the setting of the miracle itself provides a degree of hiddenness.[13] Healings take place in a house (1:29–31; 2:1–12; 5:21–43; cf. 7:24–30), in the synagogue (3:1–6; cf. 1:21–8) or apart from the people (7:31–7).[14] In these cases Mark has normally taken the setting from the tradition. It corresponds to a generally observable tendency in miracle stories to have the actual miracle happening not in public view but in private, just as the actual miracle is not described but indicated only through its impact.[15] One must of course ask how far this traditional feature has significance for Mark in the context of his secrecy theory, all the more since it is elsewhere probable that Mark has made traditional motifs the occasion and starting-point for his secrecy theory.[16] But it is worth noting that the redactional interpretation of all these stories which did not basically take place in public, stresses the public significance of these miracles: 1:29–31 gives an opening for the summary which follows; the healing in 2:1–12 which in itself takes place in the presence of a large audience (2:4) is made the occasion for a disputation with the scribes, and following that the redactor has Jesus for the first time accompanied by "all the crowd" (2:13); the healing of the deaf-mute ends with the silence command being broken (7:36f). 7:24–30, which has the form of a healing rather than an exorcism[17] stresses in its redactional introduction that contrary to his wishes Jesus could not remain hidden (7:24). When 3:1–6 is made the occasion of the (redactional) decision by the Pharisees and Herodians to destroy Jesus, this can only be understood as a response to his public activity. Only 5:43 provides an exception to this rule.[18]

(8:22–6 is a special case. Jesus' command to the blind man, "Go not into the village", was very early on interpreted as a silence command,[19] but probably wrongly since the shorter text represented by B (Vaticanus) is probably the oldest. The question is whether the short command of Jesus is redactional. Vocabulary statistics cannot settle the issue. *Kōmē* ("village") (6:6, 56; 8:27) and *eiserchesthai* ("to enter") (1:21, 45; 2:1; 3:1; 7:17, 24) could well be redactional, whereas a prohibition beginning with *mēde* ("but not") would be odd. One should note that v. 26b refers back to v. 23a, a verse that is certainly traditional since both *epilambanesthai* ("to take hold") and *ekpherein* ("to carry out") occur only once in Mark. So 8:26b is also most likely to be tradition. But how did Mark understand this tradition? There are various reasons for supposing that he understood this pericope, unlike other stories of healings, symbolically. Just as 10:46–52 (the healing of the blind Bartimaeus, who becomes a follower of Jesus) is the close of the second main division, so this story (8:22–6) marks the end of the first. That other pericope is certainly to be understood symbolically.[20] Further, in 8:16 the disciples are reproached for their literal understanding of the feeding story, whereas 8:22–6 connects extremely well with the blindness of the disciples (8:18). So the story is probably not a miracle story but a symbolic presentation of the healing of humanity's blindness by Jesus.[21] Jesus' prohibition against entering the village is perhaps for Mark an indication of the significance of Jesus' saving action which draws the people to whom he grants sight out of their world. But this remains uncertain.)

We come now to the passages where Mark himself introduces a command to silence into a healing story.[22] Firstly, Mark 1:40–5. How much the evangelist himself has contributed to this story is disputed. Verse 45 certainly stems from Mark himself: *Kērussein* ("to proclaim"), *erēmos topos* ("desert place"), is clearly redactional material;[23] the adverbial *polla* ("much"), *exerchesthai* ("to come out"), *archesthai* ("to begin"), *ho logos* ("the word"), *hōste* with the infinitive ("so that"), *dynasthai* ("to be able"), *polis* ("city"), *eiserchesthai pros auton* ("to approach him") are at least frequently redactional.[24] The decision on what is tradition and what redaction is more difficult in vv. 43f. The vocabulary seems to belong to the tradition. This is the case with *embrimasthai* ("to be indignant"), *horān* ("to see"), *kai legei* ("and he says"),[25] and also of *ekballein* ("to cast out"), which is admittedly used frequently by the evangelist, but not with the meaning "to send someone away, dismiss".[26] Verse 44b may well belong to the tradition; it is quite unthinkable that Mark should have had a positive interest in the fulfilment of the OT purity laws. That leaves only the actual silence command in v. 44a which remains doubtful. *Horā* ("see") with the conjunctive is unusual in Mark, and so is the double negative,[27] whereas in the silence commands a preceding *mēdeis* ("nobody") is relatively frequent.[28] The total lack of explicit silence commands in the pre-Marcan tradition makes it at least possible that Mark himself formulated v. 44a redactionally. The parallel in the Egerton papyrus supports this.[29] Its meaning would then be interpreted through the tradition in which it is inserted, i.e. the healed man should be silent because it is Jesus' will that the representatives of official Judaism, the priests, learn of the healing so that in this way a *martyria* ("testimony") to Jews may be given. Be this as it may, it was at any rate Mark's intention to stress by v. 45 the quite different outcome of the scene: the healed man cannot contain himself but begins to proclaim. It is worth noting that Mark does not use some neutral word for the healed man's speaking, but the positive *kērussein* ("to proclaim"). *Ho logos* ("the word") is also a very positive expression, meaning the sum total of Christian proclamation; Mark takes the term over from the Church's tradition.[30] So according to Mark the miracle cannot remain secret, even when Jesus does not want it to be made known. By its very nature it breaks through the silence and leads into proclamation. This is to be seen primarily as Mark's positive message.

We turn now to the other passage which we still have to interpret: 7:36f. Verse 36 is certainly redactional, as is shown by the vocabulary *diastellesthai* ("to command") *mēdeni* ("to no one"), *hosos* ("whoever") *kērussein* ("the proclaim").[31] Verse 37 on the other hand is likely to stem from the tradition, since this probably contained the original "chorus conclusion"[32] of the healing miracle. The vocabulary also supports this view.[33] The parallelism with the passage considered earlier is striking. In both cases the event of the miracle is handed on by *kērussein* ("proclaiming"); so in both cases the breaking of the silence command is interpreted positively. The motif of the public success of this preaching, which we found at 1:45, is missing here because it was made superfluous by the tradition's chorus conclusion being used, and by 8:1. It is striking that the making public of the miracle is stressed precisely in gentile territory[34] (cf. earlier, at 7:24!). That may contain a conscious Marcan intention, like 15:39.

Looking back, the analysis of the three summaries 1:32ff, 3:7ff, and 6:53ff leads us to suppose that the silence command in the exorcisms and the silence motif in the healing narratives might be two fundamentally different things. We can now supplement this observation by another: these passages which we have discussed contain nothing about a "messianic secret". It is not the messiahship of Jesus, or his divine sonship which is to be kept secret but the event of healing, the miracle. It will therefore be better to call the secrecy motif in the healing narratives a "miracle secret".

A survey of all Mark's reports of healings showed that his interpretation of these pericopae is completely uniform,[35] regardless of whether or not they contained a silence command. In Mark's view the miracle is testimony intended for the public. Even where Jesus does not want this to happen it forces its way into the proclamation and is successful. So the silence just underlines this fact that the miracle cannot be kept hidden.[36] The miracle is evident in its own right. This interpretation was confirmed for us by the Marcan summaries.

There is now the question how this conception fits into the Christology of Mark; more specifically, how this type of silence command is related to the others.[37]

II

The exorcisms which Mark includes in his Gospel give at first sight the same picture. Here, too, the miracle itself serves to make Jesus known in the whole region. The exorcism in 1:21–8 ends with a redactional note[38] that the news about Jesus spread through the whole region. In 5:19 the Gerasene demoniac is commissioned by Jesus to remain in his own territory and to tell his fellow-countrymen what a great thing God has done for him. Thus far the scene is certainly tradition, perhaps a founding legend of the church in the Decapolis.[39] But then it is probably Mark himself who goes further, consciously taking up and making minor corrections to what has preceded:[40] "And he went away and began to proclaim in the Decapolis[41] what Jesus[42] had done for him."[43] So here too we find again the same tendency of Mark which we found in the healing miracles, a tendency which there and elsewhere was accentuated by Jesus' silence commands and their being broken: miracles lead to the preaching of Jesus' power being extended; they proclaim it publicly and irresistibly.

There are, however, in the two Marcan summaries, silence

commands to demons. These clearly require a special interpretation, in particular because in contrast to the normal tendency, noted in the summaries and the two exorcisms mentioned above, to understand miracles as the occasion and empowering to preaching, these commands seem to stand on their own. So they must be interpreted as special cases and not too quickly harmonized with the silence commands discussed in the preceding section. The two passages are similar. In both cases the command is related to the person of Jesus: the demons are not to speak, because they know him (1:34b); they are not to reveal him after they have made him known as Son of God (3:11f). The differences between the two passages stem from the different contexts of the two summaries. The first puts the activity of Jesus more in the foreground whereas the second is mainly concerned with the reverence paid by the people and the demons; the exorcizing of the demons is totally absent in this case.

To interpret both these passages we must first ask what traditional motifs Mark might have used in forming his silence commands. We know from elsewhere of (a) the demon's address to the exorcist where the demon naturally recognizes the exorcist, even when the latter is a heavenly being.[44] Even closer linguistic parallels can be found in magical prayers.[45] (b) The command to the demon, "Be silent", is common,[46] but is always found in connection with the actual exorcism, as in Mark 1:25.[47] But this is at best an analogous motif to the silence command.[48]

This material shows that Jesus' being addressed by the demons in Mark is perfectly normal in exorcisms. The "confession" of the demons (1:24; 5:7; cf. 9:20)[49] turns out to be pre-Marcan, since it belongs to their nature for demons to be able to "sniff out" even a heavenly exorcist.[50] This is supported by the curious title *ho hagios tou theou* ("the holy one of God") at 1:24. One must consider carefully whether the Son of God title at 5:7 (cf. 3:11) is original or a Marcan replacement for an older title.[51]

But it is also apparent that Jesus' prohibition to the demons against making his nature known is without analogy in the tradition. This is where we must begin our interpretation. Why does Jesus lay this silence command upon the demons? The following possibilities require consideration:

(a) Because the demons are not the right proclaimers of Jesus' true nature. They recognize him to be unique, but are not appropriate proclaimers because although they are overpowered by Jesus, they are not his disciples.

(b) Because according to Mark Jesus did not yet wish to be revealed. The demons are silenced precisely because they alone are the ones who recognize Jesus' true nature. Why? Clearly because it is not now possible or not the right time to proclaim or understand Jesus as Son of God. In that case the prohibition to the demons must be interpreted as a pointer to understanding Mark's Christology. [52]

A further observation allows us to exclude the first possibility for the moment. Mark's making Jesus forbid the demons to proclaim him has nothing to do with their demonic nature. They only happen to receive this prohibition because they are as supernatural beings able to understand Jesus' divine nature. For the features noted as characteristic of the prohibition to the demons, namely knowledge (the demons' confession) and the relation of the prohibition to the person of Jesus himself, are found also in another passage to which we must now turn: Jesus' silencing his disciples after the confession at Caesarea Philippi at 8:30.

III

The composition of Mark 8:27–33 is difficult and the history of tradition behind it not easy to determine. [53] We are concerned with it only insofar as it is significant for the analysis of the silence command. The first task is to dig out the redactional parts. These are v. 27a;[54] v. 30;[55] v. 31aα;[56] v. 32a. [57] That leaves three pieces of tradition: Peter's confession, the announcement of suffering, and the Satan saying. The first two are each independent pieces of tradition. [58] When and how they came together is difficult to say with precision, but Peter's confession seems to have required very early on some climactic continuation in a reply by Jesus which heightened it. [59] (This does not necessarily mean that Mark drew upon an already existing connection between Peter's confession and a prophecy of the passion.)[60]

What is the meaning of the messianic confession and silence command? Lohmeyer[61] proposed that the silence command applied to the following announcement of the passion of the Son of Man which developed the messianic confession. On this view Jesus neither accepted nor rejected the messianic confession but let it stand as he had previously allowed the opinions of the people to stand. It is true that Mark relatively seldom uses the Christ title in key passages but only takes it over on occasion from the tradition. [62] However, Lohmeyer overlooks the fact that *kai ērxato didaskein* ("and he began to teach") is a common Marcan introductory formula. [63] So

v. 31 begins a new section and the silence command belongs with
what precedes it, i.e. to the confession. This corresponds also to the
previously noted position of the silence commands after the description of what is to be kept silent. But the parallels at 1:34 and 3:11f
clearly imply that a silence command is an indirect affirmation of
what has preceded. What must be kept quiet is true rather than not
yet fully valid.[64] So Mark here understood the Christ title as a valid
definition of Jesus' nature. This corresponds also to 14:61.[65] We can
only surmise why he here uses the title Christ rather than Son of
God. It was probably there in the tradition, fitting well as an anti-
thesis to the belief of the crowd in Jesus as Elijah, or John the Baptist,
i.e. as a forerunner.

So 8:30 is a complete parallel to 1:34 and 3:11f and shows us that
the silence command in those passages cannot be explained by
reference to the special nature of the demons.[66] It is, however, of
course very significant that in 8:30 and from there on the disciples
are initiated into the secret. The special knowledge that from now
on the disciples have over other people consists in their hearing that
the Son of God–Messiah must suffer as Son of Man.[67] This knowledge now distinguishes them from other people even though they
do not yet understand it. It is this proclamation of the suffering of
the Son of Man which Mark designates as "public" in contrast to
"puzzling" talk. So the secret remains a secret. But after Caesarea
Philippi it is one secret for the disciples and another for the rest.
The people grope in the dark over the nature of Jesus; to them the
Kingdom of God is a puzzle and they are amazed. The disciples
by contrast know about Jesus' messiahship, and must now try to
understand what it means that the Messiah must be a suffering
Messiah.

It is plain, too, from other observations that after 8:27 the position
of the disciples has changed.[68]

1 The next main section, 8:27—10:52, contains more explicit
teaching to the disciples.[69] This includes especially all the passion
predictions (8:27; 9:30f; 10:32b), the transfiguration (9:2, 9ff), the
comment on the healing of the epileptic (9:28f), the discussions on
rank (9:33; 10:35: cf. v. 41), the comment on the meeting with the
young man (10:23f).

2 The reaction of the disciples to the deeds and words of Jesus
becomes different. Whereas previously the reactions of both the
disciples and the crowd are described by expressions of astonishment
or fear,[70] this changes after 8:27. The same words continue to

predominate for the crowd,[71] but the disciples are distinguished from the crowd: they (the crowd) were astonished, whereas those who followed were afraid (10:32). Fear is the response of the disciples to the passion predictions (9:6, 32).[72] Whereas the crowd's attitude hardens into unbelieving astonishment – for Mark astonishment is an expression of unbelief which admittedly perceives the event of the miracle but does not understand, because it is hardened[73] – the disciples begin to fear, although they have not yet been granted any real understanding.

3 The observations which E. Schweizer collected on the significance of the "discipleship" motif in the major section 8:27—10:52 are also relevant.[74] To expand them slightly, the verb *akolouthein* ("to follow") is hardly ever in this section used in the simple sense of "go after someone" but always in the pregnant sense of "be a disciple of" (8:34; 9:38(?); 10:21, 28, 32, 52), whereas previously this was never the case (3:7; 5:24; 6:1(?), cf. 11:9; 14:13, 54) – except for the actual "sayings about discipleship". Correspondingly, Jesus appears as the "one who goes on ahead" (10:32; cf. 16:7). Mark seems to have chosen the material available to him with a quite definite viewpoint, namely the theme "discipleship".[75] Further, corresponding to the discipleship motif there is the motif *en tē hodō* ("in the way") which emerges throughout the section in redactional contexts (8:27; 9:33f;[76] 10:32, 52). In view of this, the remaining occurrences of *hodos* ("way") in this section can be said to gain a similar resonance (10:17, 46; cf.11:8), since *hodos* is at the same time both the way up to Jerusalem (10:32), and the way of suffering (8:27; 9:33; 10:32, always in connection with the passion predictions). There is also a question whether Mark understood the citation which introduces his Gospel (1:2f) in terms of the way of suffering. The placing of the destiny of the Baptist in parallel with that of Jesus would count in favour of the suggestion.[77] In all other passages in the Gospel the word *hodos* comes from the tradition and is not used with reference to the way of Jesus. Further, in the section 8:27— 10:52 there are no miracle stories although these have dominated the first main section. 9:14–29 and 10:46–52 are only apparently counter-evidence. Mark has reshaped 9:14–29 on the basis of a motif already there (9:18b) into an instruction of the disciples about the relationship between the authority of Jesus and that of the disciples (9:28f redactional). And the healing of blind Bartimaeus is made into a discipleship story by its redactional framework (vv. 46, 52d).

4 Finally we must touch on the motif of the disciples' lack of under-

standing which Wrede himself brought into his study on the messianic secret.[78] It is found throughout the entire first and second parts of the Gospel,[79] but apparently with characteristic differences. 4:13b (I take the second part of the verse to be redactional)[80] relates the disciples' lack of understanding to "all parables"; 6:52[81] relates it to the feeding miracles; 7:18 to the saying of Jesus in v. 15; 8:17ff again to the feeding miracle. On the other hand, the second part focuses the disciples' lack of understanding christologically.[82] Twice it is related to the suffering of the Son of Man: in 8:32b taking up a fragment of tradition, and also at 9:32. If we include 9:10 here too that gives us another case of concentration on Christology, this time on the resurrection. There is no need to interpret 9:6 here; it is simply a redactional note on v. 5, a verse which does not fit Mark's conception.[83]

So what does the messianic secret consist of for Mark? We can now formulate it more exactly. It is indeed Jesus' messiahship, or as Mark would say in his own terms, Jesus' divine sonship, which remains hidden from the world and is known only to the demons – due to their supernatural knowledge – and since Caesarea Philippi to the disciples – through the miracle of Jesus' authority which they repeatedly experienced. But the disciples can only experience Jesus' messiahship in connection with his suffering. Mark therefore attaches the first passion prediction to Peter's confession and works both up into a single pericope. This suffering remains incomprehensible to the disciples until the cross. Only there, in the light of Jesus' death, is full understanding and genuine confession of Jesus' divine sonship possible, as Mark shows by way of example through the gentile centurion's confession at the cross.[84]

If we try now to verify this interpretation by reference to the one remaining passage, Mark 9:9, it does not seem at once all to come undone. At first sight it seems very different from Mark 8:30, even though both passages are redactional creations of the evangelist.[85] In 8:30 the silence command concerns the messiahship of Jesus, as Peter has formulated it in his confession. 9:9 gives the content of what is to be kept silent in quite general terms with *ha eidon* ("what they had seen"). In 8:31ff the messiahship is described by the passion prediction. In 9:9 by contrast the resurrection is singled out and a temporal limit set to the messianic secret.

However, the differences are really not so significant as might at first sight appear. Even though the difficult problems about the history of the tradition in 9:2–8 are far from solved it seems to me probable that by his additions Mark revised a hellenistic version of an originally Palestinian legend.[86] It seems to me certain that for Mark the point of this worked-over legend lay in the heavenly proclamation of Jesus' divine sonship, i.e. in v. 7, and not for example in the appearance of Moses and Elijah. This seems clear on various grounds. Mark interprets divine sonship as a metamorphosis of a human figure; he weakens v. 5 by his redactional v. 6; finally there is the parallel with Mark 1:9–11, the baptism narrative, which occupies roughly the same position in the first part of the Gospel as this does in the second. *ha eidon* ("what they had seen") therefore probably refers to the proclamation of Jesus' divine sonship itself, to which everything which the disciples "saw" points. On the other hand, crucifixion and resurrection belong so closely together for Mark that in his understanding the resurrection is virtually included in the crucifixion. Unfortunately this hypothesis cannot here be supported in the necessary detail; it would need an interpretation of Mark's crucifixion narrative. We can only mention a few points out of our section: it is no coincidence that Mark interprets the tradition's prophecies of the passion and resurrection only as passion prophecies. For that is all the repudiation of Peter at 8:32f and the first discipleship saying at 8:34 can refer to. And only then is the saying about greatest and least (9:33–5), and the corresponding passage, 10:35–45, explicable in terms of the kerygma. It is also notable that at 9:12b Mark takes up the Son of Man announcement again with a passion prophecy and also understands Elijah as a suffering figure (v. 12a, 13).[87] Finally, the confession of the centurion at the cross (15:39)[88] can only be connected with 9:9 if Mark saw crucifixion and resurrection as a basic unity.

So Mark 9:9 does not contradict Mark 8:30, but interprets it.[89] That the silence command is lifted and abolished only by the resurrection means that Jesus' majesty can only be understood in the light of the cross which is united with the resurrection. That this is so is shown by the way Mark's Gospel continues, especially in the passion narrative, where the disciples are shown as lacking understanding and without courage.[90] Then the divine answer to the cross finally grants understanding to a bystander.

IV

To conclude: a look at what is usually called the "messianic secret" in Mark has shown that there are really two phenomena: the messianic secret, under the constraint of which the demons and after

Caesarea Philippi the disciples stand; and the miracle secret which cannot be kept and shows that Jesus' miracles press onward into the public realm of proclamation. Both motifs have starting-points in the tradition, but in their present form they are both redactional. Both have at first a quite different meaning, even though they are not wholly unrelated. For the messianic secret also is broken during Jesus' lifetime (cf. 10:46ff; 11:1ff; 12:1ff, especially v. 12b), and the miracle secret also may echo the motif that Jesus' miracles can be understood only from the perspective of the cross and resurrection. Admittedly this cannot be demonstrated, but the similar formulation of both types of command,[91] suggests that they should not be too sharply differentiated. There is, however, a fundamental theological difference, because regardless of all kinds of converging motifs, the secrecy motif embraces different contents and indicates theologically two different things: the miracle secret points to the power of Jesus' miracles which cannot remain hidden because it is the sign of the messianic age; the messianic secret qualifies the nature of Jesus' messiahship which must be understood kerygmatically, i.e. from the perspective of the cross and resurrection, if it is to be really understood. Or to put it in another way, the messianic secret warns against interpreting the historical Jesus independently of the cross and resurrection because any such understanding of Jesus' authority can only have the character of a satanic temptation. The miracle secret on the other hand leads back to the historical Jesus, because his authority and action simply press upon the onlooker, whether he wants this or not – and even if he does not understand it. Or to put it in yet another way: Jesus' authority and deed admittedly lead only to unbelieving astonishment; but in Mark's conception this astonishment is for the confessing believer a pointer to Jesus' messiahship.

So Mark seems to harness two christological ideas. One could be seen as tending in the direction of the hellenistic *theios anēr* ("divine man") conception, the other as attempting to make theological sense of the messianic material from the perspective of the cross. The difficulty is that both, although present in differing degrees in the tradition, are Marcan. They cannot be put aside as mere tradition. This raises again the question of their theological unity and the relationship between these two ideas. That can be made more exact by asking whether Mark provides any help towards interpreting their dialectical relationship more precisely.

The kerygmatic summary of Jesus' preaching at 1:15, by which Mark with the help of traditional formulations [92] prefaces his Gospel,

seems to have a related structure. It is put together out of the indications of the new time, the time grasped by the Kingdom of God – "The time is fulfilled and the kingdom of God has drawn near!" – and the challenge to seize this time: "Repent and believe in the gospel." "Gospel", an expression which characteristically occurs mainly in the second half of Mark, designates the presence of Jesus with his community.[93] Mark knows very well that this presence always leads to suffering.[94] The first part of this kerygmatic statement of the preaching proclaims the new age when the Kingdom of God is near; the second part calls for a correct attitude to this new time, for faith in the gospel. The first (1:16—8:26) and the second (8:27—10:52 [13:37]) parts of Mark's Gospel stand in a similar relationship. The first part describes the new time breaking into the world, with the main emphasis on the miracles and the parables of the Kingdom. The second part bears witness that the new time can only be grasped and understood in discipleship leading to suffering.

This structural combination of miracle secret and messianic secret is thus not without analogy elsewhere in Mark's Gospel. The combination of glory which cannot remain hidden, but which is for that very reason not understood, and suffering through following in the way of the cross, which alone can reveal the majesty of Jesus – this combination of miracle secret which cannot remain secret because it really is miracle, and messianic secret which must remain a mystery to the world – this combination is necessary, and finds in Mark's passion its most condensed form. There the majesty of Jesus is first made recognizable (14:61f, 15:39) through its deepest concealment, through his trial and cross. The Marcan Christology is thus to be understood as an attempt not to remove the *theios anēr* ("divine man") Christology and the manifestation idea of the hellenistic community, but to make it comprehensible from the perspective of the kerygma of the cross. There it is precisely the combination of the miracle whose reality cannot remain hidden, and the uncomprehending astonishment of an unbelieving world in the face of this miracle, which becomes a witness for faith.

NOTES

1 Cf. n.1 of the previous essay (by E. Schweizer).

2 Conzelmann, 1968, 43.

3 The eschatological material is almost exclusively limited to the synoptic apocalypse of Mark 13 which Mark found available to him in essentially its present form. In addition cf. 8:38f (on this see Schweizer, above, p. 72, n.29);

12:9; 14:62. The synoptic apocalypse in Mark is quite isolated and Mark never gives advance references to it in the course of his Gospel as he does for the passion. These are the main reasons, along with the minimal redactional activity in Mark 13 and the "eschatological" interpretation of the cross at 15:33ff, why I am sceptical about the thesis of E. Trocmé, 1975, 215ff, who sees in Mark 13 the climax and end of the original Gospel.

4 This can perhaps be assumed from individual pericopae, such as the last supper reports, and the crucifixion narrative in Mark 15:20ff. On this cf. U. Wilckens, "Hellenistisch-christliche Missionsüberlieferung und Jesustradition", *TLZ* 89 (1964) 519. Also E. Trocmé, 1975, 61ff.

5 Do the numerous, mostly redactional – cf. above, pp. 78ff – notes after the miracle stories, that they spread abroad the news about Jesus, contain a pointer back to the original *Sitz im Leben* of the miracle stories, namely proclamation itself?

6 Cf. Mark 8:34ff; 10:39; 13:11ff; 15:16ff, 21.

7 I would thus see the origin of Mark rather differently from E. Schweizer 1964a, 1964b; cf. also Schweizer "Die Frage nach dem historischen Jesus", *EvT* 24 (1964) 403–8. The alternatives which Mark has to choose between are not a hellenistic kerygma theology whose kerygma has largely cut loose from Jesus Christ and become a kerygmatic counter, and a Jewish–Christian theology which, like Q, understands Jesus as *the* teacher. There probably were, as the structure of the pre-Pauline communities clearly shows (on this, W. Schmithals, "Paulus und der historische Jesus", *ZNW* 53 (1962) 156f), some hellenistic communities which knew only a little about the historical Jesus. But Mark comes from a different (Galilean?) hellenistic community which has and uses traditions about Jesus Christ. This community is described by D. Georgi, *Die Gegner des Paulus im 2 Korintherbrief* (1964) 210ff, especially 213f, in my opinion on the whole convincingly, even if the evangelist Mark must be distinguished from it. The materials taken up by Mark into his Gospel have in my opinion almost all been revised in a hellenistic milieu. They do not come to the evangelist direct from Jewish Christian tradition. So the theological achievement of Mark consists not in the fact of taking up pre-Easter Jesus tradition, nor in the selection of this material (Mark probably used everything he knew, as his use of chapter 13 and also 11:27ff shows), but in the manner of his total composition. That means that if the messianic secret should turn out to be a significant piece of Marcan theology it must at the same time also be significant for the total conception of the Gospel. In putting the question this way E. Bickermann (1923) is right.

8 On the method of vocabulary statistics cf. J. Schreiber, "Der Kreuzigungsbericht des Markusevangeliums" (Bonn Dissertation, 1958, 97ff). Also E. Schweizer, 1963, 93ff. Naturally this kind of investigation makes sense only within certain limits. For example, it is likely that Mark received some traditions only orally and then formulated them using his "own" words. But in combination with other methods it gives criteria for ascertaining more precisely the nature of the pre-Marcan tradition.

9 *Akolouthein* ("to follow") is frequent in Mark (19 occurrences; 25 in Matt.; 17 in Luke). Of these passages 3:7; 6:1; 10:52 and probably also 2:15; 10:32 are redactional. *ochlos polys* ("a great crowd") is redactional at 5:21; 6:34; 8:1; 9:14;

12:37. Cf. also 2:13; 3:9, 20; 4:1; 7:14, 17; 8:34; 10:1; 11:18; 12:12. v. 24b is more difficult to judge: *synthlibein* ("to throng") occurs again in the tradition at v. 31, but cf. also 3:9. But other linguistic peculiarities of Mark also make it improbable that the passage 5:25–34 was available to Mark in written form: *euthus* ("immediately"); *mastix* ("plague", cf. 3:10); *haptomai* ("I touch") (cf. 3:10; 6:56); *sōzomai* ("I save", cf. 6:56 and Lohmeyer's *Commentary*, 104). On all this cf. similarly A. Meyer, *Die Entstehung des Markusevangeliums*, Festgabe for A. Jülicher, 1927, 40.

10 See below, p. 84.

11 *Prosormizomai* ("I moor"), Gennesaret, *peritrechein* ("to run around"), *asthenein* ("to be sick") do not occur elsewhere in Mark and some of them do not occur elsewhere in the whole NT. *agros* ("country") *krabbatos* ("bed") occur only in Mark's tradition. Otherwise the vocabulary statistics support the view that it is redactional.

12 The typically redactional phrases, "all those who were sick", "all the city", are worth noting.

13 Cf. R. Bultmann, 1963, 224 and especially 422 in the supplement. Also M. Dibelius, 1934, 94. And E. Sjöberg, 1955, 112 n.1.

14 7.33aα could be redactional. *Ochlos* ("crowd") (cf. n.9 above) and *kat' idiān* ("privately"; see 4:34; 6:31f; 9:2, 8; 13:3) support this suggestion.

15 Cf. Bultmann, 1963, 221.

16 After conservative research had always searched behind the messianic secret for as much tradition as possible to go back to Jesus (cf. for example V. Taylor, 1948, 148ff, and 1952 throughout), it is above all the merit of E. Sjöberg, 1955, to have drawn attention to the question of the tradition standing behind Mark's redactional understanding of the messianic secret. Admittedly he defined the messianic secret concept far too widely and this prevented his investigation of the pre-Marcan tradition from achieving any precision.

17 By the demon remaining completely passive and only the mother, the Syro-Phoenician woman, emerging in an active role, all the typical traits of an exorcism disappear.

18 Verse 43a is certainly redactional (cf. nn. 24, 28, 31), whereas v. 43b contains the original "demonstration" of the miracle. So we have a silence command without any reference to the subsequent spreading of the news of the miracle. This is the only visible exception in Mark's treatment of the miracle stories. How should it be understood? We may point out that a breaking of the silence command here would have made the heavily redacted rejection at Nazareth scene which follows almost impossible. It seems to me most probable that a raising from the dead was so strong a testimony to Jesus' messiahship that a veiling was necessary here if the dialectic between revelation and hiddenness described on p. 87 was to be preserved.

19 Cf. the readings provided by D q Θ φ C K, which apart from their differences from one another also betray their dependence on the text represented by B (Vaticanus) by the *eis tēn kōmēn* ("into the village") which is generally retained.

20 Cf. Schniewind, *Commentary*, 1963, 145; Grundmann, *Commentary*, 1973, 220f; Schweizer, 1964a, 351 [cf. 1964b, 428].

21 Cf. also A. Kuby, 1958, 58; T. A. Burkill, 1963, 149f.

22 On Mark 5:43 see above n. 18.

23 *Kērussein* ("to preach") is in my opinion redactional in all 12 Marcan instances, the only debatable cases being 1:4, 7; *erēmos topos* ("desert place") occurs apart from 4 redactional passages only at 6:35 in the tradition (formulated by Mark?). Elsewhere the tradition speaks only of *erēmos* ("desert"). Mark uses this noun alone only once, following up an OT quotation (1:4).

24 Adverbial *polla* ("many things") 4:2; 6:34; cf. 3:12; 5:43. Also probably a further 6 times in the tradition. *exerchesthai* ("to come out") 1:28, 29, 35, 38; 2:13; 3:6; 6:1, 12, 34(?), 54; 7:31; 8:11, 27; 9:30; 11:11f(?); the remaining 23 instances are more likely to belong to the tradition, many of them referring to demons. *archesthai* ("to begin"): 4:1; 5:20; 6:2, 34(?), 55; 8:31; 10:28(?), 32, 41(?); 12:1; in the remaining 16 passages more likely tradition. *ho logos* ("the word") used absolutely: 2:2; 4:33; 8:32. It stems from tradition in the interpretation of the parable of the sower. *hōste* ("so that") with infinitive: 3:10, 20; 4:1. Also 7 times in passages coming from the tradition. *dynasthai* ("to be able"): 3:20; 4:33; 7:24; 9:28; 10:26(?), and 27 times probably from the tradition. On *eiserchesthai* ("to enter"), see above, p. 78; *pros auton* ("to him") i.e. Jesus: 1:32; 2:13; 3:8, 13; 4:1; 7:1; 10:1; 11:27; 12:18, and also 8 times from the tradition.

25 *Embrimasthai* ("to be angry"), twice, and *horān* ("to see"), three times, are rare in Mark and always come from the tradition. *kai legei* ("and he says") is redactional at 1:38 and otherwise probably from the tradition.

26 Redactional, referring to exorcisms: 1:34, 39; 3:15; 9:28.

27 Double negative with *mē* ("not") otherwise only at 11:14.

28 5:43; 7:36; 8:26, 30; 9:9. Four of these are in the dative.

29 Egerton papyrus 2f. I^r (in Hennecke–Wilson, *New Testament Apocrypha* i, 96f). According to Jeremias (p. 95 in that volume) the author knew all the canonical Gospels but reproduced them from memory so that oral tradition may well also have had some influence.

30 See above, n. 24.

31 On *kērussein* ("to proclaim") see above, n. 23; on *mēdeni* ("to no one") n. 28; *diastellesthai* ("to charge") 5:43; 9:9; 8:15 is questionable; *hosos* ("how great, many") 3:8, 10; 5:20; 6:30, 56; 9:13. The other seven occurrences are tradition.

32 Cf. Dibelius, 1934, 57f.

33 *Hyperperissōs* ("beyond measure") occurs only here in the NT. The perfect tense of *poiein* ("to do") is tradition; Mark prefers the aorist – see below, n. 43. *poiein* ("to do") with accusative and infinitive is found elsewhere only at 1:17. *kōphos* ("deaf") and *alalos* ("dumb") are found elsewhere only in the healing of the epileptic boy, at 9:17, 25. Cf. Isa. 35:5; Wis. 10:21.

34 On the place names see below, n. 54.

35 Against Bickermann, 1923, 132f, who wants to divide Mark's miracles into "easy" (public) and impossible (secret) ones. At best the interpretation of 5:21–4, 35–43 might contain a starting-point for this idea.

36 This tells against the thesis of Bousset, 1970, 107, and Dibelius 1934, 223f, that the messianic secret provides an explanation for Jesus' lack of success.

37 It is perhaps clear that this interpretation of the miracle secret is quite close to the interpretation of the messianic secret by H. J. Ebeling, 1939. As a matter of fact I believe that Ebeling was in many respects correct, especially in trying to understand the miracle stories which carried a silence command, in the light of the miracle stories as such. But he did not see the difference in content between the miracle secret and the actual messianic secret idea, and so generalized his thesis in a way which did violence to the evidence.

38 There is also redactional activity as early as v. 27. At any rate up to v. 27a the narrative contains all the motifs required for an exorcism. The vocabulary of v. 28 is redactional. On *exerchesthai* ("to come out") see above, n. 24. On *euthus* ("immediately") see Schmidt, 1919, 50f. *akoē* ("report") and *pantachou* ("everywhere") admittedly occur nowhere else in Mark's redaction, but *holos ho* ("all the") is a typical redactional phrase. Cf. Schweizer 1963, 97, and 1:33, 39 (!); 6:55; 14:9, which all tell the extent of the proclamation. Galilee is perhaps added redactionally at 1:16 too (Lohmeyer, 1963, 31; Grundmann, 1973, 39). Cf. 1:14, 39; 3:7; 7:31; 9:30; 14:28 (?); 15:41; 16:7. It is undoubtedly a word which expresses a Marcan motif.

39 Cf. Lohmeyer, 1963, 99; on the various attempts to demarcate the redactional material, cf. Bultmann, 1963, 419 (supplement to 210). Burkill, 1963, 94f considers vv. 18–20 to be tradition. Wrede, 1971, 140f, interprets it in terms of the secret.

40 Apart from the words already discussed – *kērussein* ("to proclaim") n. 23; *archesthai* ("to begin") n. 24; *hosos* ("how great, many") n. 31; – Decapolis is also probably redactional at 7:31. *thaumazein* ("to wonder") is certainly redactional again at 6:6 and probably also at 15:44. But the decisive argument for the redactional character of v. 20 concerns the corrections (see below, nn. 41–3) which make it virtually impossible to follow R. H. Lightfoot, 1935, 88ff, Dibelius, 1934, 74, Taylor, 1952, *ad loc.* in taking all three verses as Marcan.

41 *Kērussein* ("to proclaim") instead of apangellein ("to announce").

42 Jesus instead of God.

43 *Poiein* ("to do") never occurs in the perfect tense in the redaction, but does in the tradition. Cf. 5:33; 7:37; 11:17, etc. The aorist is very frequently redactional, cf. only e.g. 3:14, 16; 6:30; 9:13; 14:9. It is rare in the tradition: 2:25; 14:8. In the passage under consideration Mark has changed the tradition's perfect tense into an aorist.

44 For a hellenistic example, compare the story of Chonsu, the God who drives out demons, in R. Reitzenstein, *Hellenistische Wundererzählungen*, 1963², 124. For a Jewish example, the story of Rabbi Schimeon ben Jochai in Billerbeck, *Kommentar zum NT aus Talmud und Midrasch*, 1922–, vol. iv, 535, or the story of Rabbi Hanina ben Dosa and the female demon Agrath in P. Fiebig, *Rabbinische Wundergeschichten*, 1933, 7.

45 Cf. the evidence assembled by R. Reitzenstein, *Poimandres*, 1904, 20f, especially the magical prayer of Astrampsychos. On this see O. Bauernfeind, *Die Worte der Dämonen im Markusevangelium*, 1927, 14.

46 Evidence in Blass-Debrunner-Funk, *A Greek Grammar of the NT* (Chicago, 1961), § 346; Klostermann, *Commentary*, 1950, on Mark 1:25, *Papyri Osloenses* I, ed. S. Eitrem, 1925, 76f at 164. Mark perhaps understood *phīmousthai* ("to be muzzled") in terms of the messianic secret, in contrast to its meaning in the earlier tradition.

47 Cf. Mark 4:39.

48 On the significance of *phīmoun* ("to muzzle"), cf. Burkill, 1963, 72.

49 The demons' self-mutilation means that they have recognized Jesus; since it is *alalon* ("dumb") (v. 17), it cannot of course make confession.

50 Cf. Bultmann, 1963, 223.

51 Cf. on this E. Schweizer, article *"Huios theou"* ("Son of God") in *TDNT*, vol. viii, on Mark 5.7.

52 The secrecy theory would then be the hermeneutical presupposition of Mark's Christology, not of the gospel genre (cf. Conzelmann, above n. 2). Matthew and Luke also belong to the gospel genre.

53 On this see now F. Hahn, *The Titles of Jesus in Christology* (1963, ET London: Lutterworth, 1969) 223–8; E. Haenchen, "Die Komposition von Mk 8.27–9.1 und Par", *Nov T* 6 (1963) 81–109; E. Dinkler, "Peter's Confession and the 'Satan' Saying: The Problem of Jesus' Messiahship", in *The Future of our Religious Past*, ed. J. M. Robinson, 1971, 169–202.

54 On *exerchesthai* ("to come out") cf. n. 24. On *en tę̄ hodǭ* ("in the way"), below, p. 84. *Mathētai* ("disciples") does not necessarily tell against the verse being redaction, although Mark frequently uses *hoi dōdeka* ("the twelve") for the disciples. The word is found in both tradition and redaction. On *kōmē* ("village") cf. above, p. 78. Where the place-name Caesarea Philippi comes from is hard to say. But it certainly cannot be used as an argument for the historicity of the scene. On that basis many passages with even less common place-names could be judged historical, for example the marriage at Cana! It is worth pondering that in the preceding section Mark occasionally introduces unusual place-names in redactional sections (7:24, 31; 8:10, 22). It is doubtful whether a "journey" into Gentile territory can be reconstructed. In 7:24–30 the scene is laid by the tradition too (v. 26!). Nevertheless the trip to Phoenicia is surely meant to be programmatic in view of the significance for Mark of the proclamation to the Gentiles (one has only to consider 13:10 and 15:39). In itself Caesarea Philippi is a quite well known area which Mark might have chosen because he wanted to have Peter's confession taken place on the border of Gentile territory (cf. A. Schlatter, *Der Evangelist Matthäus*, 1929, 502).

55 Cf. 3:12; 7:36.

56 On *archesthai* ("to begin"), n. 24. On *didaskein* ("to teach"), Schweizer, 1963, 95f, cf. esp. 4:1; 6:2, 34.

57 Cf. especially 2:2; 4:33, further for *lalein* ("to speak") 1:34; 4:34; 12:1; 14:9, 43 (?). On *parrēsia* ("openly") cf. Schweizer, above, p. 69. Hahn (n. 53), 224 considers 32b redactional too. But in my opinion that cannot be demonstrated.

58 Against Bultmann, 1963, 258, cf. Hahn (n. 53) 223.

59 John 6:66–71 and *Gos. Thomas* 13 each show one answer by Jesus. The same is true of Matt. 16:13ff, since Matthew's special material in vv. 17ff must surely have been preceded by some such scene as Peter's confession, which is perhaps still echoed in the full title "Son of the living God" in v. 16. It is, however, important that this answer is in each case different. If Mark found in the tradition available to him an answer by Jesus also, and that remains possible, he has replaced it with the silence command. Cf. Dinkler (n. 53) 184ff.

60 Against Schweizer, 1963, 68, there seem to me to be in 8:27–33 at least two
pericopae which did not originally belong together. The following reasons seem
to me to argue for this: (1) If the redactional link phrases between the pieces
of tradition are cut out there is at any rate between 8:29 and 31aβ no further
connection. And only if v. 32b is original (cf. n. 57) is there any between v. 31
and v. 33. It is not very likely that Mark would have replaced an existing connection between v. 29 and v. 31aβ with his own redactional introduction 31aα, since
Mark prefers to use the word *didaskein* ("to teach") at the start of a new piece
of tradition: 1:21f; 2:13; 4:1f; 6:2, 6, 34; 9:31; 10:1; 12:35. (2) It seems to me
more probable that the three pieces of tradition do not have the same origin.
Verses 27b–29 (cf. Mark 6:14ff) come from the Palestinian Aramaic-speaking
area. This is supported by the expectations of a forerunner, the phrase *eipan*
... *legontes* ("they said ... saying") which is so difficult that in my opinion it
can only be explained in terms of the Aramaic (elsewhere only at 12:26), the
semitic predication *su ei* ("you are") (E. Norden, *Agnostos Theos*, 1956⁴, 177ff).
H. E. Tödt, *The Son of Man in the Synoptic Tradition* (ET London: SCM;
Philadelphia: Westminster, 1965), especially 201f, has considered the origin of the
passion prophecies. The connection of the Messiah with the future Son of Man in
Mark 14:61f seems to be earlier in the history of the tradition than this connection
with the suffering one (E. Dinkler, 1971, 185). The Satan word to Peter seems
to me as to Bultmann, 1963, 258, n. 2, to be a hellenistic construction, since
the linguistic counter-arguments adduced in M. Black, *An Aramaic Approach
to the Gospels and Acts* (1954²) 263f do not stand up: *hypage* ("go!") is vulgar
Greek, cf. Liddell-Scott, *Lexicon*, BII; *Satanas* ("Satan") can be adequately
explained from a familiarity with the LXX; *phronein ta tou theou*, etc. ("to mind
the things of God") is in my opinion scarcely conceivable in Aramaic; *phronein*
with accusative plural neuter is typical vulgar Greek, whereas the Aramaic *dî*
("that") for *ta tou* ("the things of") as in the Peshitta, is uncommon, as the
parallels adduced in Billerbeck i 748 show, against Dinkler, 1971, 186: polemic
against Peter was at least possible in hellenistic Christian circles, as is shown by
Gal. 2; Mark 14:66f; John 20:1ff. Cf. Bultmann (as above) and J. Schreiber, 1961,
177, esp. n. 1; rather differently, G. Klein, "Die Verleugnung des Petrus", *ZTK*
58 (1961) 325. These considerations also place question-marks against the reconstruction of Dinkler, 1971, 185ff, where v. 33b is attached to the messianic confession. Dinkler's analysis has not yet fully convinced me here, attractive though it
is, and in my opinion preferable, on account of its greater simplicity and compact-
ness, to the reconstruction of Hahn (n. 53) 224f.

Be that as it may, if Mark was the first to combine at least 27b–29 and 31
– and this is supported also by the parallels in Mark's special material, John
and Gos. Thomas, which clearly knew nothing of a link like Matthew's – then
the sequence "messianic secret – passion prophecy" gains very great theological
weight, because the statement that Jesus' messiahship can only be understood
together with the suffering of the Son of Man becomes Mark's most characteristic
theological achievement.

61 *Commentary*, 1963, 165.

62 Redactional only at 1:1 (?) and 14:61 (?).

63 See above, n. 60.

64 So too Haenchen (n. 53), 87.

65 Against O. Cullmann, *The Christology of the New Testament*, 1959, 122ff.

66 This counts against the thesis of Bauernfeind (n. 45 above).

67 The significance of the title "Son of Man" for the evangelist Mark can only be determined with difficulty, since Mark has only used it in traditional contexts. Did he still understand it at all? For the Son of Man title seems not to come under the messianic secret (2:10, 28). The suffering Son of Man occurs simply in the context of instruction to the disciples. Mark probably thought of a side of the Son of Man comprehensible only to the disciples.

68 Against Wrede, 1971, 115ff, Sjöberg, 1955, 103, emphasizes the central position of Caesarea Philippi.

69 Cf. Lohmeyer, 1963, 161.

70 Referring to the crowd: 5:20 *thaumazein* ("to marvel"); 7:37 *ekplēssesthai* ("to be astonished"); (referring to the disciples: 6:51 *existasthai* ("to be amazed") is tradition, but is interpreted by Mark; cf. in addition the passages from the tradition: 1:27 (*thambeisthai*, "to be amazed"); 2:15; 5:42 (*existasthai*); 4:41; 5:15 (*phobeisthai*, "to fear").

71 9:15 *ekthambeisthai*, "to be greatly amazed"; 10:32 *thambeisthai*. Cf. 11:18; 12:17.

72 *thambeisthai* is used of the disciples only at 10:24, but there relates to a special proclamation of Jesus.

73 In a redactional note at 6:52 Mark explains what he means by *existasthai*.

74 Schweizer, 1964a, 349ff [cf. 1964b, 427ff].

75 I can scarcely believe that Mark 8:27—10:52 simply puts together unsorted material. Rather, every pericope is related to the theme of "discipleship". But on this cf. Schweizer, 1964a, 351.

76 K. L. Schmidt, 1919, 230, rightly observes that v. 35 constitutes a second more original beginning to the following pericope. But the history of the tradition is not clear. Verse 34b seems to depend on something which should really have been related before. The vocabulary provides no clear guidance. The parallel in 8:16 suggests a redactor at work, but the poor construction of these two verses is not explained by the supposition of a purely redactional formation.

77 Consider *paradothēnai* ("to be delivered up") at 1:14; *metanoia* ("repentance") at 1:4, 15; *kērussein* ("to proclaim") at 1:4, 14.

78 Wrede, 1971, 92ff.

79 On its special frequency in chaps. 6–8 cf. Schweizer, 1963, 100 n. 32.

80 Cf. Schweizer, above, p. 68.

81 Cf. above n. 73. Cf. further on *sunienai* ("to understand") 7:14; 8:17(!), 21.

82 Cf. on this Kuby, 1958, 54.

83 Mark 9:5, 18f; 10:35ff, 41ff are from the tradition and should not be used automatically to show Mark's understanding of the disciples. Cf. Sjöberg, 1955, 106.

85 I should note here that the women's reaction at Mark 16:8 remains a puzzle to me. Not even the origin of the half-verse (is 8c redaction?) is clear. There is at any rate a contradiction with 9:9. To assume that Mark is polemicizing

against a theology which ascribes to the resurrection – cut loose from the cross – power to proclaim with understanding, is difficult after 9:9, despite 15:39. It is unlikely that he intends playing off the gentile centurion against the women, since he inserted them redactionally at 15:40f, 47 and characterizes them positively (*ēkolouthoun*, "they used to follow"; *diēkonoun*, "they used to serve"; though *apo makrothen*, "from afar". Cf. on that 14:54!). It remains possible that Mark is using the women's fear, without direct polemic, to point back to the main thing, namely away from the story of the tomb and to the cross, 15:33–9. Or would a once existing old ending to Mark containing further appearances have clarified the passage? We do not know.

85　On the vocabulary, cf. above, n. 28 (on *mēdeis*, "no one") and n. 31 (on *diastellesthai*, "to charge"). 9b seems to point back to 8:31, though the addition of *ek nekrōn* ("from dead") admittedly remains unclear.

86　For analysis cf. Hahn, 1969, 334ff.

87　A hint from E. Schweizer. For the congruence of our view at this point, cf. Schweizer, above, p. 72, n. 29.

88　On the redactional character of this passage, see J. Schreiber (n. 8), 76, 114f.

89　Thus 9:9 does not have the central place that Wrede, 1971, 76f, and Conzelmann, 1968, 43, thought. Similarly Sjöberg, 1955, 105f.

90　Cf. Gethsemane, Peter's denial (which was perhaps placed here by Mark to accentuate the contrast between Jesus and his disciples; cf. P. Winter, *On the Trial of Jesus* (1961) 23f), and the total absence of the disciples in chap. 15 (cf. v. 40f).

91　And 5:43!

92　*Metanoein* ("to repent") cf. 1:4, the nearness of the *basileia* ("kingdom") and the fulfilment of time are motifs in the tradition.

93　Cf. W. Marxsen, *The Evangelist Mark* (1969), 117.

94　8:35; 10:29; cf. 13:10 with 11ff.

7

*The Quest for Wrede's Secret Messiah**

WILLIAM C. ROBINSON Jr

William Wrede wanted to understand the secrecy motifs in the Gospel of Mark, Jesus' commands to the demons to be silent after they had addressed him with christological titles, his orders to disciples and others not to tell of his miracles, indications that he sought privacy, that he taught in parables to disclose the mystery of the Kingdom of God to insiders and conceal it from others, and that even the disciples – despite repeated private instruction – failed to understand. What Wrede accomplished is of importance sufficient to insure his book its place as a classic in NT research, and yet the inadequacies of his argument are such that it does not deserve the influence it still exerts on current efforts to interpret the Gospel of Mark. Wrede was remarkably perceptive as to the principles which should govern historical research into earliest Christianity, but by abandoning his first principle he failed to understand how the data he studied function in the Gospel of Mark. That task therefore remains to be done.

He saw that the gospel writers had to be understood in the social matrix of the communities of faith in which they lived and wrote, that the materials they used had not only survived in the Christian common life but also had been moulded and modified by their *Sitz im Leben* of the Church. He recognized that the evangelists were other than just recorders; they were spokesmen for their faith, so that understanding of the Gospels requires attention to their intentions in writing. That meant the Gospels are primary sources for the evangelists' views but only secondary sources for what they tell of Jesus' life. Even these few items indicate Wrede was operating with the principles which later guided both form criticism and redac-

* A review of *The Messianic Secret* by William Wrede. First published in *Int* 27 (1973) 10–30.

tion criticism. Not only did these insights give his work a future, to that extent ensuring its stature as a classic, but Wrede applied them consistently enough to put an end to the then dominant phase of gospel research, the nineteenth century's quest of the historical Jesus (the *Leben-Jesu Bewegung*), so that the book marks the close of an epoch in the history of the discipline and provided stimuli (along with the work of Wellhausen and others) for new directions.

Put in emotive terms the main effect of his book was to shock its readers with its implicit denial of Jesus' messianic self-consciousness (the sensitive issue in gospel research at the time); in methodological terms, it undermined the foundations on which the liberal lives of Jesus had been constructed. Wrede accused his colleagues of failing their first task, the historical assessment of the sources (4). To specify this charge he asserted three points (5–7): (1) An obvious rule of all critical historiography – too little observed in this case – is that what we actually possess is only a later narrator's view of Jesus' life, a view which is not identical with the thing itself. (2) One too quickly abandons the gospel account, substituting for it – by excising the incredible and arranging the residue – something the gospel writer never thought of and presenting this surrogate as if it were the historical substance of the gospel narratives. "The first task must always be the thorough illumination of the accounts in the spirit of those accounts themselves, to ask what the narrator in his own time wanted to say to his readers, and this task must be *carried to its conclusion* and made the foundation of critical historiography." (3) Third is the problem of psychological interpretation. Not that the use of psychology is in itself inappropriate, but it can be properly employed to help explain the development from one fact to another only when the facts are established *as* facts. Jesus research suffers from psychologizing guesswork.

Wrede presumably thought he was avoiding those errors by seeking first to understand what Mark wanted to say to his own readers (5f), but what Wrede actually did was formally very like the error of the old questers: before completing his analysis of Mark's intention he jumped over the Marcan text and landed in his own reconstruction of earliest Christianity. This is apparent from an analysis of his argument that Mark could not himself have invented the secrecy motif, even though it is rather widespread in his Gospel. Wrede claimed this conclusion is evident from the Gospel itself. In the Gospel of Mark secrecy motifs are presented in various ways and among them there is considerable inconsistency. Such inconsistency, Wrede maintained, could not be the work of a single individual (145).

Wrede's assertion is unambiguous, but when one searches his book for those inconsistencies which rule out Mark as originator of the secrecy motif, the results are initially puzzling, for instead of pointing out inconsistencies which are inconceivable for Mark, Wrede justified them: "Whether the idea existed is one thing; whether Mark carried it out with utter consistency is another. What would be incompatible in actual history might exist side by side in thought" (70; cf. 55f). Furthermore he pressed the point that contradictions are a necessary consequence of introducing the messianic secret into a Gospel: "For if the Evangelist had carried out this view strictly, if his Jesus had really kept himself utterly concealed, Mark would hardly have considered his life worth the telling" (125f). Nor can Wrede have meant the apparent inconsistency that Jesus' wish to remain unknown clashes with the statements that people disregarded his wishes and spread his fame anyway (1:45; 7:36f; 7:24); Wrede took these statements to be from Mark himself, so this inconsistency *is* due to a single person, Mark (127). Then, in a discussion of Mark as an author, Wrede concluded that Mark "did not really think from one point of his account to another" (132), that he had "little ability to put himself into the historical situation he presents.... Otherwise the scenes he presents could not contain such strange and – realistically viewed – such inconceivable things" (133). There is more (e.g., 111f, 237f), but it is of the same sort: Wrede has not really tried to show that a single individual was incapable of such variety of presentation; rather, in the case of Mark, he has shown the reverse.

One's initial perplexity at Wrede's claim that analysis of the Gospel of Mark shows Mark could not have originated the secrecy concept is resolved, I think, when one reaches the third section of his book (209ff), where Wrede presented his reconstruction of the historical origins of the messianic secret, a presentation prefaced (210) with a reference to his earlier claim to have shown that Mark did not invent the concept himself.

Wrede marshalled indications of the view in early Christianity that Jesus became the Messiah at the resurrection,[1] which he claims is the oldest view of which we have any knowledge (218), which arose not as Jesus' own view but as that of the Christian congregation on the basis of the appearances of the risen Christ (220). This earliest view gradually shifted as Jesus' past life received from it a new importance and dignity (218). The growing significance of Jesus' earthly life was to some extent paralleled by a decline in belief in the nearness of the parousia. From these lines of development the view that Jesus had been the Messiah gained substance, giving rise to a new, specifically Christian, messianic concept (219). The gospel writers are not at the end of this development but they are near its culmination: they, in contrast to Paul, narrate the life of the Messiah (223f).

Although Wrede might seem to have hedged somewhat in saying that when the secrecy concept arose, the original view of Jesus' life (by which Wrede meant a non-messianic view) was beginning to change, that hints of Jesus' future status were appearing in the stories of his life,[2] it was nonetheless his opinion that the secrecy concept arose when the traditions of Jesus were essentially non-christological.[3] Wrede's actual line of thought was, I think, as follows: hypothesis – the messianic secret arose at a point in the history of dogma when the tradition was practically void of Christology. Observation – by the time Mark wrote his Gospel the tradition contained obviously christological elements.[4] Inference – Mark did not originate the concept of the messianic secret.

It is not the case that analysis of Mark required Wrede's hypothesis. Rather his reconstruction of the history of earliest Christian dogma produced the hypothesis, and the hypothesis dominated his analysis of the Gospel of Mark.

I

Wrede began his analysis of "the Messiah's self-concealment" (24–81) with a list of the Marcan passages indicating that the demons recognized Jesus as the Messiah,[5] from which – Wrede maintained – Mark's own view of the matter is clearly discernible (25). It was the demons, not the demon-possessed humans, who knew Jesus, and the demons' knowledge was supernatural knowledge, knowledge not of the man but of the one filled with the Spirit, the supernatural Son of God. The "unclean spirits" recognized the bearer of the Spirit as their enemy, their superior, whom they must obey. Thus Jesus' identity was, by its very nature, hidden from mere mortals, and the messianic secret was expressed not only by means of Jesus' commands to silence but also – and logically prior thereto – expressed implicitly in that only the demons knew who he really was (25).

Wrede's conclusions are thus also implicit at the outset, both on the nature of Mark's Christology and that the Messiah secret was not a part of the history of Jesus, for the historicality of the secrecy motif is of a piece with that of the demons, since it is they who provide the occasion for introducing the motif.

Having identified Mark's views on the relation of the demons to Jesus, Wrede then turned to the question, What motivated Mark – or one like him – to express this viewpoint and to emphasize it in the story of Jesus (33)? With that question Wrede presented Jesus' commands not to tell (34–6): (1) prohibitions to the demons (1:25, 34; 3:12), (2) prohibitions after (other) miracles (1:43–5; 5:43; 7:36; 8:26), (3) prohibitions after Peter's confession (8:30; 9:9), (4) Jesus' intention to preserve his incognito (7:24; 9:30f), (5) a prohibition not by Jesus himself (10:47f).

Wrede's observations are acute and his critique of explanations from the history of Jesus devastating. He concluded this part of his discussion by saying:

> Thus all accounts of Jesus' commands to silence which are placed before Peter's confession are shown – for more than one reason – to be incredible. That gives rise to the strong suspicion that the same is true of the few other instances. Mark 9:9 would in any case arouse such suspicion.... Furthermore that suspicion becomes certainty when Mark's own viewpoint is disclosed. For the explanation must lie in Mark's viewpoint if the history [of Jesus] fails to furnish it (53).

Wrede then (53–66) considered "related material" (omitted in English subtitle, 53), first asking whether the various expressions of Jesus' efforts towards privacy were part of the same secrecy motif, a question he left unanswered (55). Next he analysed the statements on the use of parables in 4:10–13, 33–4 (56–66). His conclusion here, much as in the case of the commands to silence, is that "The statement that the mystery of the kingdom of God has been given to the disciples ... together with its opposite gives very precise expression to the evangelist's viewpoint. It is incomprehensible that it should then be attributed to a source other than this viewpoint, to which the other material has been ascribed" (63).

The outcome of these discussions was not however to answer the question of what motivated "Mark or one like him", but to refute the false answers to that question which contemporary Jesus research had thought to give from the history of Jesus. Wrede's discussion of the Marcan text and its then current exegesis produced the conclusion that the idea of the messianic secret was not a part of Jesus' history but had its origin in the history of dogma (see 67). Throughout Wrede argued against the view that the Messiah secret had been a part of the actual history of Jesus,[6] and he seemed unaware that such argument is not the same as a pursuit of Mark's intention.

II

The charge that Wrede read back into Mark his own view of the development of early Christology is also supported by his treatment of the command to silence following the transfiguration, Jesus' statement that the disciples were "to tell no one what they had seen, until the Son of man should have risen from the dead" (9:9).

One is struck by how much Wrede made of this command to silence while exerting so little effort at justifying that emphasis. He considered 9:9 the key text for understanding the messianic secret (67) but hardly bothered to try the key in the lock. Here is the place Wrede jumped over Mark into his own reconstruction of earliest Christian history, taking the reference to the resurrection as his springboard. He almost entirely neglected to assess how the statement functioned in its Marcan context. Rarely did he consider whether 9:9 was related to the predictions of the passion, although that is the Marcan setting of the passage (following the first prediction 8:31f and preceding its echo 9:12), and, when he did consider it, it was only in passing (83, 124). And although he noted the significance of Elijah as messianic forerunner (214), he seems to have felt no need to relate 9:9 to the closely following allusions to Elijah in 9:11–13. Nor, in considering the possibility Mark might have taken the transfiguration as a proleptic portrayal of the coming Messiah (225), did Wrede treat the proximity *in Mark* of the transfiguration (9:2–8) and 9:9.[7]

After tabulating the commands to secrecy Wrede noted that they were stereotyped in form and that a peculiarity of the command at 9:9 is its reference to the resurrection (37). It is this peculiarity which he took to express "the point of Mark's entire conception" (68) of the messianic secret (Jesus' messiahship concealed during his life and first disclosed at the resurrection), for "it is no more difficult to assume this idea frequently in Mark than to find it [only] once. And it is necessary to presuppose it everywhere, if the one instance is of the same kind as the others."[8] This is surely the key to Wrede's argument, whether or not it unlocks an understanding of the composition of the Gospel of Mark. Wrede's case requires the assumption that "the one instance is of the same kind as the others", the assumption that the several expressions of secrecy in Mark are articulations of a single unified viewpoint. And since that unity of viewpoint is not apparent in the Gospel of Mark, Wrede had to locate the origin of the concept prior to Mark. Yet despite its absence from the Gospel of Mark, Wrede held that unified viewpoint to be "the point of Mark's entire conception".

Wrede thought his interpretation of 9:9 was confirmed in the statement about the lamp under the bushel, "For there is nothing hid, except to be made manifest; nor is anything secret, except to come to light" (4:21f). This speaks clearly of concealment and disclosure; what it does *not* clearly say is precisely what Wrede's interpretation requires and what he therefore had to read into the Marcan text: "Rather the passage refers back [sc. to Mark 4:11] to the thought that secrets are communicated in the parables. For the time being only the disciples are recipients of this knowledge. But what they received they are later – let me clarify: *after the resurrection* – to disclose and publicize" (71). Wrede even admitted the point himself: "So far as I can see Mark did not really express these ideas in his Gospel. But he *cannot have held* any other viewpoint" (112). Thereafter Wrede referred to these ideas as Mark's view.[9]

It is important to see clearly the great advantages Wrede's historical reconstruction seemed to hold for the dynamics of his argument. He saw the force of this hypothesis in its ability to provide a single explanation of the phenomena: "The most forceful explanation has to be that one which presents a unified thought" (38). And Hans Jürgen Ebeling made the same point against Wrede's critics: "Up to now the force of his evidence defies all attempts to reduce the complex of his proof-texts or by enlarging the complex to generalize it and so to rob it of its force."[10] By locating the unified secrecy concept prior to Mark, Wrede could tolerate the incoherence he found by positing the coherence he required. He could attribute individual expressions of the concept as well as the articulation of the whole to Marcan editing and yet avoid the burden of showing "what the narrator in his own time wanted to say to his readers", for the concept, in Wrede's view, spoke with clarity and coherence at the time of its origin whereas by Mark's time the initial coherence had slackened and some expressions of the concept were but Marcan mannerisms. While the inconsistencies thus appear to be manageable on Wrede's hypothesis, they do not, as he claimed, require it. In fact the whole category, "inconsistency" among "the individual conceptions of the idea", is a product of Wrede's hypothesis, for they are labelled "inconsistencies" by reference to the hypothetical pre-Marcan unified secrecy concept. The intolerable inconsistency was between Wrede's hypothesis and the Marcan data.[11] Unity of concept is necessary to Wrede's hypothesis. When he and Ebeling claimed it as a strength of the hypothesis, they were turning a necessity into a virtue.

III

The main weakness of Wrede's hypothesis, beyond internal structural faults, appeared only four years after the publication of his book. In 1905 Emil Wendling published his *Ur-Marcus*, in which on literary critical grounds[12] he attributed to Mark all the commands to silence except those at 1:25 and 1:44.[13] With that, Mark himself had to be given responsibility not only for articulating the messianic secret in his Gospel (so Wrede, 145) but also, it would seem, for originating the topic, and those "inconsistencies" which Wrede said could not be the work of a single individual would have to be accounted for as the work of that individual we call Mark.

Bultmann continued to treat the various expressions of secrecy in Mark as presenting a unified concept,[14] and he saw Martin Dibelius' characterization of the Gospel as solving the problem of inconsistencies: Mark's Gospel was "a book of secret epiphanies". Furthermore Bultmann held to Wrede's explanation of the messianic secret, that it served to veil the fact that belief in Jesus' messiahship arose first after faith in the resurrection (*idem*). Ebeling and Sjöberg showed the fallacy of that explanation: "Where in the Gospel of Mark are we to find that unmessianic tradition of Jesus' life which Mark, by means of the secrecy theory, wanted to reconcile with the belief that Jesus was Messiah during his lifetime?"[15] Hans Conzelmann is said to have got Bultmann's agreement on this issue by putting the matter in characteristically pointed brevity: If the messianic secret were a means for imposing a Christology on a nonchristological tradition, then we should expect to find the commands to silence attached to non-christological material, whereas in fact their points of attachment are super-christological.

But Conzelmann's formula does not open up the whole truth, as analysis of the position of the commands will show, so that the unifying principle implicit in his dictum – to modify an already existing Christology – must also be classed as probandum, not as premise.

When we turn to the Marcan data, we recall that Wrede listed nine passages where Jesus commands silence: 1:25, 34, 44; 3:12; 5:43; 7:36; (*v.l.* 8:26); 8:30; 9:9 (plus the command at 10:48, which is not from Jesus). To put these data into perspective with the composition of Mark's Gospel as a whole, it should be noted that Jesus gave orders not to tell anyone else in only three of the thirteen miracle accounts in Mark and in none of the three exorcisms:

EXORCISMS		MIRACLES			
1	1:21–8		1	1:29–31	Healing Peter's mother-in-law
2	5:1–20	+	2	1:40–5	Cleansing the leper
3	9:14–27		3	2:1–12	Healing the paralytic
			4	3:1–6	Restoring the withered hand
			5	4:35–41	Calming the storm at sea
		+	6	5:21–4, 35–43	Raising Jairus' daughter
			7	5:25–34	Stopping the haemorrhage
			8	6:32–44	Feeding the five thousand
			9	6:45–52	Walking on the water
		+	10	7:31–7	Healing the deaf mute
			11	8:1–10	Feeding the four thousand
			12	8:22–6	The blind man at Bethsaida
			13	10:46–52	Bartimaeus receiving his sight

The first command to silence is at 1:25, the man with the unclean spirit, where the literary form is exorcism. The command fits the form, in which it is the exorcist's potent word by which he overpowers the unclean spirit. "Be silent!" functions here just as does the similar command in the account of the stilling of the storm, 4:39: "Hush! Be silent!" That is, the command at 1:25 is *not* an expression of the messianic secret. It may be said to *become* that only in the Marcan interpretation some verses later, in the editorial statement at 1:34, "He did not permit the demons to speak because they knew him."

In this interpretative comment Mark has pulled the command from the exorcism into another language game, and it is only in that second semantic locus that the command expresses the messianic secret. In this first instance then the messianic secret is due to Mark: It is not in the pre-Marcan tradition. It is also worth noting that here Mark seems not to have altered the tradition.

The Gospel of Mark contains two other exorcism accounts, the Gerasene demoniac (5:1–20) and the son possessed from his childhood (9:14–27). In each case the demon recognized the exorcist. In the story of the Gerasene demoniac recognition is evident from the demon's action (running and kneeling before him, 5:6) and his address to Jesus, "Jesus, Son of the Most High God" (5:7), and in the second instance by action (convulsing the boy, 9:20) which included an outcry (9:26) but without any articulated address to Jesus – the demon was mute (9:17, 25). In both cases Jesus exerted his power over the demon by means of a command, but in neither is it a command to silence. Here again the tradition did not express the messianic secret and again Mark did not insert it into the tradition, even though the Gerasene demoniac addressed Jesus with a christological title, and despite the fact that there is an editorial aside inserted just after this word of address, I think inserted by Mark (5:8): "(For Jesus was already saying to him, 'Out, unclean spirit, come out of this man!')". Here then is a super-christological bit of tradition, where there is ground for thinking Mark inserted something but where he did *not* attach the messianic secret. Nor is there any appended interpretation as at 1:34.

As to exorcisms, therefore, it seems one must conclude that the messianic secret was neither in the traditional material nor inserted into it by Mark but occurs only in the Marcan interpretative summaries at 1:34 and 3:12.

Nor does point of attachment seem to offer greater promise as a unifying consideration when one turns from exorcisms to the other miracles. First of all, commands to silence are attached to so few of the miracles – in only three of 13 instances – that they can hardly have been intended to indicate concealment of all the miracles.[16]

Furthermore, in two of the three instances of commands to silence which are attached to miracles, it is expressly stated that the command was ignored. After the cleansing of the leper (1:45), the man went out and made the whole story public; he spread it far and wide until Jesus could no longer show himself in any town, but stayed outside in the open country. Even so people kept coming to him from all quarters. And at 7:36, after the healing of the deaf mute, Jesus forbade them to tell anyone, but the more he forbade it, the more they published it. In this connection it should also be noted that the exorcism account in chapter one concludes by saying that the news spread rapidly, and he was soon spoken of all over the district of Galilee (1:28).[17]

Are we to conclude then that it was Mark's intention to conceal only the exorcisms?[18] But we have just noted that the first editorial statement of the spread of Jesus' fame followed the first exorcism (at 1:28). At that point Mark made no separate category for exorcism, for what got notoriety was not the demon's knowledge of Jesus' true identity but the reaction of those who witnessed the exorcism. In this respect then Mark treated the exorcism like a healing miracle, as a demonstration of Jesus' power. The case is similar at the conclusion of the second exorcism (5:19f), where it is no longer a question of the demon but of the man of Gerasa, now restored, whom Jesus commanded, "Go home to your own folk and tell them what the Lord in his mercy has done for you." I think that statement is from the tradition and that Mark in the next verse modified the tradition only to say that the man told what *Jesus* had done for him. Thus in the second exorcism account Mark found and emphasized what he himself added to the first, an indication that word of Jesus' power spread. But surely the remaining exorcism (9:14–27) fits the view we have been schooled to accept, for is it not clear that Jesus concealed the exorcism by hastening to perform it before the witnesses arrived? "Jesus saw then that the crowd was closing in upon them, so he rebuked the unclean spirit" (9:25). Against this comforting observation two things need to be said. First, Wrede himself hesitated to claim for his concept the various expressions of a privacy motif (55). Withdrawal from the public belongs in the genre of mighty deeds,[19] so that I think we do better to respect Wrede's hesitation[20] rather than to ascribe the various privacy motifs to a Messiah secret complex.[21] The second difficulty is in the peculiar structure of the account itself, for after the exorcism we are told that the boy looked like a corpse; in fact many said, "He is dead." But Jesus took his hand and raised him to his feet, and he stood up (9:26f). Whether or not this is due to a combination of two originally distinct accounts,[22] the story as it now stands turns out to be a demonstration of power, like a healing miracle, and in the presence of witnesses. In his editing of the exorcisms Mark seems not to have distinguished them from other miracles but to have treated all miracles as demonstrations of Jesus' power, not as betrayals of his christological identity.

Hopes for clarity raised by Conzelmann's statement have so far been disappointed. Up to this point it has not seemed possible to unite the data under the rubric that commands to silence are attached to super-christological material. On the contrary, our analysis of Mark's editorial practice in the case of the first exorcism would seem to hold true generally: he has, in the main, left the tradition intact. Even if we leave out of consideration the four miracles which are not healings (stilling the storm 4:35–41, the two feedings 6:32–44; 8:1–10, and the walking on the water 6:45–52) twelve remain (classing exorcisms with other healings, as Mark seems to have done). Commands to silence occur with only three of them, and small as that proportion is, its force is almost completely neutralized by the same number of instances of editorial statements that Jesus' fame spread.[23]

Mark's concern for secrecy seems therefore to be located only within the new language game which he created out of the vocabulary of exorcism and expressed in his summaries. There the object of concealment is Jesus' christological identity (1:34; 3:11f) not his power. And that agrees with what we have seen of Mark's treatment of the exorcism accounts: he presents them in a class with healing miracles, as demonstrations of Jesus' power. Furthermore, the contrast between general notoriety and concealment of this one point, Jesus' true identity, is present even within the two Marcan summaries, as Kertelge has noted.[24]

Hypotheses heretofore advanced to unify the material have seemed inadequate. Wrede's case for a pre-Marcan unified concept was not convincing in itself, and then it was further undermined by the literary analysis which attributed the commands to silence to Marcan editing. Dibelius' concept of "secret epiphanies" may suffice for the healing miracles but not for the silencing of the demons in the Marcan summaries. And Conzelmann's thesis – attachment to super-christological material – though true as far as it goes, does not account for the bulk of the super-christological material in the tradition, for most of it is not buffered with efforts at concealment.

So far our considerations seem to be leading to the conclusion that the messianic secret concept, in anything like the sense it has borne in the history of the discussion since Wrede, is appropriate only for the two editorial passages in which Jesus forbade the demons to disclose his christological identity. At this point we need to turn to the other passages in Wrede's list.

IV

The remaining instances where Jesus forbade disclosure are two, one after Peter's confession (8:30), the other on leaving the scene of the transfiguration (9:9). Our discussion of the other commands has not produced a basis on which to interpret these two, so we must try to interpret them from within their contexts. That procedure is both methodologically orthodox and intrinsically promising as well, since these two have as their context that part of the Gospel where Mark's intentions are most apparent, the central section (8:27—10:52) which Wellhausen once labelled "the gospel in the Gospel".

The central section begins with Peter's confession and Jesus' first prediction of his death, includes two more predictions of his death, and reaches its thematic conclusion with the statement, "The Son of man also came not to be served but to serve, and to give his life a ransom for many" (10:45). Immediately after Jesus's first prediction of his death there is a section on discipleship: "If any man would come after me, let him deny himself and take up his cross and follow me. For whoever would save his life will lose it; and whoever loses his life for my sake and the gospel's will save it. For what does it profit a man, to gain the whole world and forfeit his life? For what can a man give in return for his life? For whoever is ashamed of me and of my words in this adulterous and sinful generation, of him will the Son of man also be ashamed, when he comes in the glory of his Father with the holy angels" (8:34–8). Thus at the start of the central section is stated the contrapuntal theme which governs it all, Jesus going steadfastly to his death as a ransom for many while the disciples tag along, grasping, anxious, petty, utterly blind to the pastoral obligations of discipleship. The central section contains pre-Marcan material and some pre-Marcan arrangement of material,[25] but is clear that Mark has used the material[26] to create the powerful impression, to show by negation what is required of disciples. Here is where we find the remaining two commands to silence.

In discussing the commands to silence we have been using Wrede's distinction based on the material to which the commands pertained, exorcisms and other healing miracles. Formal analysis produces the same two-fold classification. Commands to demons echo the form of exorcism but commands following other healings do not. Demons are "rebuked" (*epitīmān*) while witnesses to healings are "ordered" (*diastellesthai*) to silence. Demons are forbidden to disclose "him", while witnesses to healings are enjoined against telling what they saw. In the exorcism form rebuke follows a christological title, while in the other form the command follows a healing miracle. Jesus' two commands to silence in the central section (8:30; 9:9) fit one in each of the two forms. At 8:30 rebuke follows a christological title addressed to Jesus, and what "they" are forbidden is "to tell about him". At 9:9 they are "ordered" to tell no one what they saw. However 9:9, in contrast to other instances of command (*diastellesthai*), follows a christological title, the voice from the cloud in the transfiguration scene: "This is my beloved Son …".

After Jesus had predicted his death and resurrection Peter rebuked him, whereupon (8:33) Jesus rebuked Peter, called him Satan, told him to get behind him, and explained this by saying "You think as men think, not as God thinks". Here at 8:33 interpretation manages fairly well: in opposing the crucifixion which is part of God's will (*dei*, 8:31), Peter had set himself against God and for that received the rebuke he was due. But why then are "they" rebuked and silenced at 8:30 following the confession of Jesus as the Christ? At that point neither Peter nor the disciples had voiced any heretical positive thinking. Nor was the Christology in error; on the contrary Peter's confession was orthodox. (The same should be said also about the titles the demons used.) Nor can one say the disciples are here declared to be demonic; the Satan statement a few verses later did not refer to supernatural knowledge the demons had of Jesus' identity, but referred to an attempt to thwart the divine will. The point of contact between the disciples and the demons would seem to be that each knew Jesus' true identity and stated it, whereupon Jesus commanded silence on that topic. The Christology was accurate but it was not to be expressed. (To this extent 8:30 is like the two editorial references to silencing the demons, 1:34; 3:11f).

I think Mark did not consider Peter's confession the high point of the Gospel – in the positive sense that phrase usually has in this connection, but that Mark had Jesus repudiate the disciples' confession of his identity because it was Christology separated from the theology of Jesus' death.[27] Whether Mark added Peter's attempt to persuade Jesus to avoid the cross or found it already in the tradition, it was in reference to this that Mark inserted the command to silence at 8:30. This interpretation explains the present context and agrees with what Mark emphasized throughout the central section of his Gospel: Jesus was going to his divinely ordained death "as a ransom for many" (10:45) while the disciples "followed" with an utter lack of comprehension which mocked the meaning of "following after".

In the central section Mark interpreted Jesus' death, an interpretation moving not in christological abstractions but directed towards concretion in discipleship, the issue of living one's life in a way commensurate with understanding one's reality from the theological interpretation of Jesus' death. Since Wrede, the hermeneutical approach to all these passages has been held to be primarily christological, how to think the thoughts of faith; but taken in its context 8:30 is differently aimed, on discipleship, how to live the life of faith. (In this respect 8:30 differs from 1:34; 3:12.)

This view of 8:30 is implicit in a currently popular interpretation of the secrecy motifs which moves in the tow of Georgi's book on Second Corinthians[28] and affirms Ebeling's and Sjöberg's criticism of Wrede, namely, that the Gospel of Mark furnishes us no evidence for the existence of a non-christological tradition onto which Mark might have wanted to impose a Christology. In this interpretation Mark's historical moment, far from being void of Christology, included a miracle-worker (*theios anēr*) Christology with a complementary Christian self-understanding, and Mark's aim was to correct that Christology – together with the view of discipleship implicit in it – by means of the theology of the cross. Nevertheless, attractive as it is, that *theios anēr* explanation of the Marcan commands to silence has the fundamental weakness that it presupposes what it has not shown (and what has been rejected above), the unity of the several expressions of secrecy in the Gospel of Mark, for only on that assumption can it hope to focus the commands sharply against the miracles. Failing that, one must, I think, seek the meaning of 8:30 within its own context, the central section of Mark's Gospel, and perhaps be content with the more general explanation that Mark was motivated by a concern for living the Christian life on the pattern of Jesus who gave himself for others.

In any case this much, I think, is clear: at 8:30 Mark's primary concern was discipleship, not Christology. Interpretation of 8:30 does not, however, necessarily clarify the other commands to silence, and 9:9 is yet to be considered. I think interpretation of 9:9 should begin – in accord with Wrede's principles – by trying seriously to make sense of the statement within its Marcan context rather than – as Wrede did – by taking one's point of departure outside the Gospel of Mark in a hypothetical reconstruction of the history of earliest Christian thought.

The first half of 9:9 is in form like the commands attached to miracles, but then the command is qualified by the statement, "until the Son of man had risen from the dead". Wrede knew all about this, but after testing his argument I feel more like the disciples, who "discussed among themselves what this 'rising from the dead' could mean" (9:10). The *New English Bible* is right to put "rising from the dead" in quotation marks; that is the force of the article before the words. It is not the concept of resurrection which was perplexing but why Jesus should refer to it in that context.

Even among those who reject Wrede's reconstruction, 9:9 is often taken to mean that Christological understanding of Jesus came with the resurrection faith. That is understandable both as a religious insight and as a critical historian's view of earliest Christianity, but it is by no means apparent that Mark meant it that way.

And if he had, how should one understand what follows the command to silence and the disciples' puzzling over why Jesus spoke of the rising from the dead? Why did Mark put 9:11–13 here? The verses are about the Malachi prophecy of the eschatological coming of Elijah, here an allusion to John the Baptist, but why here?

A connection between verses 11–13 and 9–10 is not obvious; agreed. The passage itself does not move smoothly; agreed. Wernle and Bultmann thought verse 12b was a copyist's insertion from

111

Matthew and so not originally in Mark; I disagree. For all its awkwardness the passage makes sense as it is: it reasserts the theme of Mark's central section, and at verse 12b in the very words of the preceding prediction of the passion: "Yet how is it that the scriptures say of the Son of man that he is to endure great sufferings and be treated with contempt?" According to the Malachi prophecy Elijah's eschatological function was "to set everything right" (Mark 9:12a) "before the great and terrible day of the Lord" (Mal. 4:5f). That prediction, in the present Marcan context, poses a theological problem: how is it that the Son of Man "is to endure great sufferings and be treated with contempt" *after* Elijah has come and "set everything right"? Verse 12b speaks to that problem[29] and is therefore integral to Mark's use of the passage here and thus a part of the original text of Mark, not an interpolation. Here the Malachi prophecy is historicized in the fate of John the Baptist, and John is set in parallel to Jesus in that they both were put to death – in both cases, "as it was written"! Though I see no clear continuity of thought from 9:9f to verses 11–13, the sequence is in Mark, and I think that Mark created it,[30] whether he also constructed verses 11–13[31] or only modified them.[32] If Mark put verses 11–13 after 9–10, then it appears that Mark has related the command to silence at 9:9 to Jesus' death just as he did at 8:30. References to the death of the Son of Man belong in chapters 8—10. But why John the Baptist?

A possible answer is this: the Christians were obviously engaged in a christological apologetic and polemic against those disciples of John the Baptist who maintained that he, as Elijah, was the last herald before the coming of God (Luke 1:16f, 76) and as such the "messianic" figure *par excellence*. This conflict began early enough to have left its mark in Q and must have continued for some time, since it appears in the Fourth Gospel and in material peculiar to Matthew or Luke, that is, not derivative from Mark, and therefore not just a literary topic. The Christian polemic in various ways subjected John to Jesus, showing that though John was first, Jesus was greater. One way to do this was to grant the relation of John to Elijah but to modify that Malachi prophecy to make Elijah/John the forerunner of the Messiah, Jesus, rather than of God himself. But that is not the line taken in Mark 9:11–13. Here the problem posed by the priority of John/Elijah is not that of competing christological identities; the question is rather, "Yet how is it that the scriptures say of the Son of man that he is to endure great sufferings and be treated with contempt?" At 8:30 Mark has silenced

Christology when separated from the crucifixion; here he has repudiated a Christian christological polemic against the Baptist's followers and in its place has tried to take over the significance of the Baptist rather than nullify it with christological superiority.

"The messianic secret" – if that term may properly still be used – is a Marcan motif, not in the pre-Marcan tradition nor even latent within it, for while Mark plundered the traditional exorcism accounts to express concealment of Jesus' identity, he so radically altered the meaning that it was not an extension of the tradition but something new. The traditions also furnished him certain privacy motifs[33] which he may have extended, for example, to private instruction of the disciples,[34] but a privacy motif prior to Mark requires no assumption of a messianic secret, since the motif is sufficiently explained as belonging to the genre of healing miracles.

Furthermore, it is not apparent that Mark combined the several privacy expressions into an articulation of the course of development of christological dogma. I expect this interpretation will be met with opposition, among other things, on the grounds cited above from Ebeling: it seems to atomize the material and so lacks the appealing tidiness of a unified explanation. Wrede clearly saw the difficulty of unifying the several motifs at the point of Mark's composition of the Gospel and so located the unified concept prior to Mark, but although literary criticism showed that move to be without sufficient warrant, the consequences of that criticism have been largely over-looked, with the result that what Wrede rejected – a discernible unity of concept at Mark's level – has been taken as Wrede's probated legacy. I think Mark did correlate some of the topics in this discussion but not under the principle of "the messianic secret", that is, not around the history of dogma issue of the development of Christology nor on a preoccupation with the historical distinction between Jesus' "then" and Mark's "now". I think Mark related the demons' knowledge and the disciples' ignorance as a means for insisting on relating Christology and the theology of the cross in order to emphasize the pastoral aspects of discipleship, that with that he may have correlated the humane exercise of the Son of Man's authority[35] and a reinterpretation of the relation of Jesus and John the Baptist. In these matters, as well as in some others, Mark took a position over against those who quibble over christological technicalities (scribes, Pharisees, and – disciples) to emphasize the point that disciples – those who "follow after" – are to follow him who gave himself for others.

NOTES

1 215–17; Acts 2:36; Rom. 1:4; Phil. 2:6ff; the meaning of parousia: "coming", not "second coming".

2 228f: "Concealment presupposes something to be concealed."

3 E.g., 228–36.

4 Wrede's most frequent examples were Jesus' triumphal entry into Jerusalem and his answer to the high priest, e.g., 70, 239, although he also noted miracles without commands to silence and messianic address without rebuke, 36, 70.

5 Mark 1:23–5, 34; 3:11f, 5:6f; 9:20.

6 See e.g., 227.

7 He did refer to the connection of 9:9 and the transfiguration in arguing against the historicity of 9:9, p. 53.

8 69, cf. 38, 48, 67f.

9 E.g., 72, 165, 176, 178.

10 Ebeling, 1939, 114.

11 See Schweitzer, 1954, 341 on the triumphal entry and Jesus' reply to the high priest: "The real point is that Wrede cannot bring these two passages within the lines of the theory of secrecy...."

12 *Ur-Marcus. Versuch einer Wiederherstellung der ältesten Mitteilungen über das Leben Jesu* (Tübingen: J. C. B. Mohr [Paul Siebeck], 1905). Detailed in his *Die Entstehung des Marcus-Evangeliums* (Tübingen: J. C. B. Mohr [Paul Siebeck], 1908).

13 Rudolf Bultmann then decided that all but 1:25 were Marcan. See *Die Geschichte der synoptischen Tradition* (Göttingen: Vandenhoeck & Ruprecht, 1921, 1957³). The English translation is not reliable.

14 Ibid., 371.

15 Sjöberg, 1955, 115; so already Ebeling, 60: "The tradition is already interpreted, christologically interpreted, tradition." Cf. 16: "Epiphany tradition is thus the primary substance of the tradition."

16 The view that a few commands to silence were intended to conceal a greater number of miracles would seem to gain in force if the few commands were attached one to each of several collections of miracles, thereby indicating the concealment of all the miracles in each collection, or strategically placed within a single collection of miracles with the same effect. Keck, Georgi, Achtemeier, and others have recently defended the view that Mark made use of collections of miracles, and in Achtemeier's reconstruction, two commands to silence are strategically placed. But in this application that line of argument is not pure gain; it introduces its own difficulties. If the commands to silence were in the presumed pre-Marcan collection(s), their inclusive function – to conceal all miracles in the collection – would cease when Mark broke up the collection(s) but did not repeat the commands when he distributed the miracles in his Gospel, so that one would face the same problem which Wrede thought to avoid by positing a unified expression of a unified concept only prior to Mark. And if it was Mark who added the commands to the collection, but then did not carry out the concealment motif when he

114

distributed the miracle collection(s) in composing his Gospel, what Wrede called "Mark's own viewpoint" would apply to notations Mark made in his source document(s) but did not see fit to spread over his Gospel, so that from the time Mark worked over his source(s) to the time he composed his Gospel, his intention in the former case would have become only a mannerism in the latter. Thus even on the assumption that Mark used an earlier miracle source(s), the point of attachment of the commands to silence does not provide a hermeneutical approach to the composition of the Gospel of Mark. See Leander Keck, "Mark 3:7–12 and Mark's Christology", *JBL*, 84 (1965) 341–58; Dieter Georgi, a paper read at the meeting of the Northeastern Section, SBL, 31 March 1971; Paul Achtemeier, "Toward the Isolation of Pre-Markan Miracle Catenae", *JBL*, (1970) 89:265–91.

17. NB: all three statements on the spread of Jesus' fame are widely held to be Mark's own editorial additions.

18 The violation of commands to silence is so pronounced that several – e.g. Ebeling and Luz – have categorized the material under two headings, saying the intent was to conceal in the case of silencing the demons but that in the case of healing miracles Mark wanted to show that Jesus' power was irrepressibly evident – so already Wendling, *Entstehung*, 17, 53, 60, 80. Then Dibelius' dictum on "secret epiphanies" might apply, but only to the healing miracles, not to the silencing of the demons.

19 Bultmann, 227, 229, 239 and n. 4.

20 So Bultmann, 239.

21 As has been done by Luz, Strecker [see the essays here] and Kertelge, 1970.

22 Bultmann, 241.

23 Sjöberg is right that violation of the commands to silence is just as characteristic of Mark's presentation as are the commands themselves, 116.

24 Page 32.

25 Kuhn, 1971.

26 Ibid., 181ff.

27 So Weeden, 1971. See also 1:34; 3:11f.

28 *Die Gegner des Paulus im 2. Korintherbrief* (WMANT, Neukirchen-Vluyn; Neukirchener, 1964).

29 So Weisse, 1838, cited by Wellhausen.

30 So Wendling, *Entstehung*, 211; Dibelius, 1934, 226f.

31 Taylor, 1952, 83; Johannes Schreiber, *Theologie des Vertrauens* (Hamburg: Furche-Verlag, 1967), 28.

32 Sjöberg, 162 n. 2.

33 E.g., the performance of healing miracles apart from the public, 5:40; 7:33; 8:23.

34 See 7:24, 10:10, which Wrede, 136, 146, considered examples of Marcan mannerism.

35 To forgive sins, 2:10: to humanize the sabbath, 2:27f; cf. 10:45.

8

*The Messianic Secret in Mark**¹

JAMES D. G. DUNN

William Wrede's *Das Messiasgeheimnis in den Evangelien* (1901) marked a turning point of considerable importance in the study of the Gospels inasmuch as Wrede was really the first to recognize and appreciate the theological nature of the synoptics. His specific thesis (that the messianic secret motif in Mark has a theological rather than a historical origin) has "mark"edly influenced the researches of those who came after him, to such an extent that it is often taken for granted, a "given" in the investigation of new propositions and theses. His own statement of the thesis has not escaped criticism and refinement, of course, but his main conclusion still stands as proven for the majority of continental scholars.

Wrede points first to the commands with which Jesus silences the messianic confessions of the demons (1:23–5, 34; 3:11f; cf.5:6f; 9:20). Since the various explanations offered for the possessed individual's knowledge are unsatisfactory, we must recognize a legendary development in the tradition. When other commands to silence are also taken into consideration – to those healed miraculously (1:43–5; 5:43; 7:36; 8:26), the disciples after Peter's confession (8:30) and after the transfiguration (9:9) – as also the intention of Jesus to remain hidden (7:24; 9:30f) and the command addressed by the crowd to Bartimaeus to be silent (10:47f), it becomes evident that what is being thus guarded is the messianic secret. He goes on to cite other evidence, the most notable of which are the private instructions which Jesus gives to the disciples (4:34; 7:17–23; 9:28f; 8:31; 9:31; 10:32–4; 13:3ff) and the saying about parabolic teaching (4:10–13). On the basis of this evidence Wrede delivers his judgement – namely that for Mark there is no historical motif in question; rather the idea of the messianic secret is a wholly theological conception. The key is Mark

* First published in *Tyn Bul* 21 (1970) 92–117. The text used here is a slightly abbreviated version first published in the *TSF Bulletin* (1974), in which the footnotes have been considerably reduced.

9:9, when Peter, James and John are commanded not to speak of what they had seen until the Son of Man should have risen from the dead. Jesus' messiahship is and must be a secret. Only the inner circle can be let into the secret. But with the resurrection comes the relevation to all. In short, the whole is a theological construction. Jesus did not in fact claim to be Messiah during his ministry, and it was not until after the resurrection that his messianic status was affirmed by the Christian community. The messianic secret is nothing other than the attempt made by Mark to account for the absence of messianic claims by Jesus himself.

<h1 style="text-align:center">I</h1>

An analysis of Wrede's thesis reveals three principal strands: first, the isolation of a distinct motif in Mark which can be called the "messianic secret"; second, the argument that certain elements of that motif, noticeably the exorcisms, are non-historical, leading to the conclusion that the whole motif is the construction of Christian or Marcan theology (the more recent rise of form criticism has, of course, given more depth and consistency to this argument); third, as the *raison d'être*, the complementary argument that belief in Jesus as Messiah was an Easter faith and that the messianic secret results from an attempt to read back messiahship into the life of Jesus.

(1) If this is a fair representation of Wrede's argument it seems to me to be open to several major criticisms. The first of these is that Wrede has narrowed the scope of the secrecy motif too much. I strongly question whether the silences commanded by Jesus in connection with the healing miracles can adequately be brought under the category of *messianic* secret. What is there about the healings that cannot be understood before the cross and resurrection which is not *publicly* demonstrated in, for example, the healing of the paralytic before the scribes in chap. 2, or the healing of the man with the withered arm in the synagogue in chap. 3? What is there about the healing miracles which particularly marks out Jesus as Messiah? According to Mark not one of the miracles performed publicly led the spectators to conclude that Jesus was the Messiah (though see below, pp. 122ff), while several passages indicate that their reaction was often completely different. The people of Nazareth saw only the carpenter, the member of a well-known local family, despite the public knowledge of his miracles (6:1–6). Herod and others thought he might be John the Baptist resurrected, or Elijah

or another prophet (6:14f; 8:28). The Pharisees judged him to be possessed by Beelzebub (3:22). Moreover, the only recipient of Jesus' healing who hails him in messianic terms (10:46ff) is *not* silenced by Jesus. So just what secret was being safeguarded by those commands to silence?

The attempt to bring all the healing miracle commands to silence under the heading of "messianic secret" fails to carry conviction. Despite Wrede's belief that only one explanation must be applied to the so-called secrecy passages, it is highly probable that in different situations there was a variety of motives operative – and particularly in Jesus' dealings with the sick: e.g. desire for privacy and concern for the well-being of the individual being cured (cf. 1:44; 5:40; 7:33; 8:22, 26; 9:25), as well as the wish to discourage misleading ideas about himself from gaining fresh currency, and perhaps the strong sense that his destiny was completely in the hands of God. In this connection it is worth noting that there are grounds for recognizing 1:21–45 as a pre-Marcan block of material in whose construction one of the determining motifs was the way in which excessive publicity resulted in increasing restriction on Jesus' movement and ministry (Capernaum, country towns, desert areas – 1:21, 38, 45).

I question also whether the saying about the use of parables can be counted as part of the evidence for the messianic secret. In Mark 4:11 what Jesus says is that parables conceal the mystery of the *Kingdom* from *hoi exō* – and while I would agree that the mystery of the Kingdom is closely related to the historical status and ministry of Jesus, it is not to be wholly identified with the messiahship of the earthly Jesus. Besides, both 4:11 ("to those who are outside *everything* comes in parables") and 4:34 ("he would not speak to them except in parables") indicate that it was his *whole* ministry of word and deed which had this parabolic effect – and his whole ministry cannot be contained within the bounds of the messianic secret. In 7:17, for example, the parable whose explanation he gives to the disciples in private is his teaching about inward cleanliness. One should also note that if 4:11 (the illumination of the disciples) is interpreted in terms of the messianic secret it at once comes into conflict with passages like 9:32 (the incomprehension of the disciples).

Turning to this latter theme, the obtuseness of the disciples, which is often cited as an important element in Mark's theology of the messianic secret, even this cannot be contained within its scope. I would be prepared to admit the instance of the disciples' astonishment and hardness of heart at the stilling of the storm as part of the messianic secret (6:51–2). For I certainly see messianic significance in the feeding of the five thousand, although I am not so sure that Mark wished to bring out that significance, and Mark does specifically say that the disciples were dumbfounded "because they had not seen what the miracle of the loaves meant" (Jerusalem Bible – *ou gar sunēkan epi tois artois*). For the same reason I can see the justification for including the disciples' misunderstanding over the saying about the yeast of the Pharisees and of Herod with the messianic secret, although the passage is a difficult one. For once again their obtuseness is underlined by a reference to the feeding of the five thousand and the feeding of the four thousand, and the pericope ends with the words of Jesus *oupō suniete*; but it is impossible to bring 10:10 under the messianic secret – for what the disciples enquire of him in private (*eis tēn oikian*) is the meaning of his saying about divorce and marriage – hardly a distinctively messianic theme.

Bearing in mind this diversity in the situations which demonstrate the disciples' obtuseness, it is more plausible to recognize in the motif a historical reminiscence of the very natural and unexceptional slowness of unlettered men whose rigid and closed system of thought made it difficult for them to adjust to new teaching. It was not simply the difficulty of coping with new information, but the impossibility of trying to assimilate that new information into a system of thought and reference which had no place for such information. The situation which would cause a computer either to admit defeat or to explode, caused only confusion and incomprehension on the part of the disciples. Such a situation can be resolved only by a conversion of mind, something which by all accounts did not happen to the disciples till the gift of the Spirit after Jesus' resurrection. To go to the other extreme and attribute the motif to a Marcan polemic against the disciples is certainly uncalled for.

I rather suspect that Wrede was misled by taking the exorcisms as his starting-point. It was natural that a nineteenth/twentieth-century man should fasten on to these incidents which were to him among the most bizarre and incredible, and which for that very reason gave him immediate access to the theological viewpoint of the primitive Church – that is, to the way the primitive Church had viewed and worked over the historical facts. No psychological argument could explain how, for example, the Gerasene demoniac came to hail Jesus as Son of the Most High God, and recourse to a supernatural explanation was unacceptable. Therefore, Wrede concluded, we are in the presence of a legendary development in the tradition which leads us straight into the heart of the messianic

secret. Leaving aside the issue of demon-possession and the possibility of "supernatural" knowledge, which I personally hold to be
a far more open question than Wrede allowed, it still seems to me
that Wrede's approach was methodologically suspect. For the
exorcism narratives would not stand out so prominently in Mark's
time. The fact is that in their manner of presentation they accord
by and large with the standard pattern of exorcism stories, even to
the extent of the demon using the name of the exorcist and the
exorcist commanding the demon to silence, and the knowledgeable
reader of Mark's Gospel would see nothing out of the ordinary in
Jesus' response to the demon's cry in Mark 1:25 – *phimōthēti kai
exelthe ex autou.* I recognize that there is weight to the counter-
argument that *Mark* understood the injunction to silence in this first
exorcism in terms of 1:34 and 3:11f, which could well be taken to
indicate that demoniacs regularly hailed him as Son of God and that
Jesus' usual response was a strong warning that they should not make
him known. But if Mark was trying to "get over" to his readers
the message of the messianic secret the first exorcism would give
no indication of it to his readers. In fact, the distinctive messianic
secret motif only appears in these two summary statements, and there
are no commands to silence in any of the other exorcisms where
the narrative goes into any detail (5:1–20; 7:24–30; 9:14–29). I
question therefore whether Wrede was right to single out the
exorcisms as the decisive clue to the meaning of the secrecy theme
in Mark.

(2)   If the first criticism puts a question mark against Wrede's isolation of a specifically *messianic* secret, my second puts a question mark
against his calling the motif "messianic *secret*". For it appears to
me that Wrede did not give sufficient weight to what might be called
a counter-balancing publicity-revelation theme which seems frequently to run directly counter to the secrecy motif. After the first
exorcism Mark says "his reputation spread everywhere (*pantachou*)
through all (*holēn*) the surrounding Galilean countryside" (1:28).
After the healing of the leper we are told that the leper started talking
about it freely and telling the story everywhere, so that Jesus could
no longer go openly into any town but had to stay outside in places
where nobody lived. Even so, people from all around came to him
(1:45). On another occasion Mark says "once again such a crowd
collected that they could not even have a meal" (3:20). And far from
commanding him to be silent Jesus orders the Gerasene demoniac,
now cured, to "go home to your people and tell them all that the

Lord in his mercy has done for you" (5:19f). In Nazareth they certainly knew all about his miracles, (6:2–3), and so remarkable and public were they that all sorts of rumours were current about him (6:14ff; 8:28). The feeding of the five thousand was the result of an attempted escape to seclusion on the part of Jesus and his disciples, because "there were so many coming and going that the apostles had no time to eat" (6:31). And in the region of Tyre and Sidon he entered a house (*eis oikian*) and did not want anyone to know it; but it was impossible for him to be concealed (7:24). To cite but one other instance, it is certainly remarkable, if we believe that the messianic secret motif decisively shaped the material, that Bartimaeus should be allowed to be depicted as twice loudly hailing Jesus as Son of David – *and* Jesus neither rebukes him nor tells him to be silent (10:46ff)! In view of the messianic significance of the title Son of David (12:35–7a) it is surely quite inadequate to dismiss this pericope as having nothing to do with the theory of the messianic secret, as Wrede and those who follow him do.

So far as the messianic secret is concerned the publicity theme is most noticeable in the contexts where one would expect withdrawal and silence. In the healing of the paralytic Mark alone says that the proof of the miracle – his rising and walking off – happened "in full view of them all" (2:12 NEB). And in the case of the man with the withered arm, far from performing the miracle privately, Jesus commands him *egeire eis to meson* and there, having first drawn all eyes upon him, effects the healing (3:3ff). It is true that there is a secrecy, or better, privacy motif in some of the healings (5:37ff; 7:31–7; 8:22–6). But the woman with the haemorrhage is healed in the crowd and it is Jesus himself who draws attention to a cure which no one else had noticed. And Bartimaeus is healed in full view of the crowd. Nor surely was Mark naive enough to impose a messianic secret motif on a story like the raising of Jairus' daughter. How could the raising of a dead girl to life be kept silent when the mourning had already begun? And why is it on several occasions after Jesus gives a strict command to silence that Mark immediately goes on to tell how the news was broadcast far and wide (1:25–8, 43–5; 7:36f)? If the messianic secret motif was added to explain why Jesus was not recognized as Messiah, and part of that motif is the command to demons and men not to tell of their cures, I am at a loss to understand what Mark was trying to achieve by adding or at least retaining the publicity sequel. For the whole point of these passages is that the secret commanded was *not* kept. The commands to silence failed, and so the so-called attempt to keep his messiahship secret also failed.

If the messianic secret was a Marcan theory, then these publicity passages are the *reductio ad absurdum* of that theory. This publicity motif shows that at most we can speak of a messianic *misunderstanding*, but hardly of a messianic *secret*.

There is also a very prominent theme of revelation which should not be ignored. I will not enlarge upon it but simply call attention to its various facets – the authoritative claims made by the Marcan Jesus for himself: to forgive sins, no less (2:10); to have a mission to call (*kalesai*) sinners (2:17); to be sovereign (*kurios*) over the sabbath (2:28); to be the one who binds the strong man (Satan) and ransacks his house (3:27); that loyalty to *him* will be the yardstick of judgement in the parousia (8:38). Again there is the teaching Jesus gives to his disciples in private about the true nature of his messiahship (8:31–3; 9:31–2; 10:32–4, 45; 14:22–5). Schweizer justifiably notes the concern with which Jesus brings God's mystery to men, especially the disciples (4:34; 7:17–23; 8:15–21, 27–33; 9:30–2; 10:32–4; cf. 5:37; 9:2; 13:3f).[1] Finally, one might call attention to such passages as the Parable of the Wicked Tenants, where the Marcan Jesus specifically claims a special relation of sonship and where Mark tells us that the priests and lawyers recognized that the parable was aimed at them (12:12); or again to the Bartimaeus episode where Jesus is twice hailed as Son of David (10:47f) and to 15:39 where the centurion confesses that the *dead* Jesus was truly a or the Son of God. A theory of the messianic secret which does not take account of these other themes which are just as prominent will inevitably give a distorted picture both of the Marcan Jesus and of the Marcan theology.

(3) My third criticism of Wrede's thesis is that it does not give sufficient weight to the element of historicity which is firmly attached to the motif of the messianic secret. As I have already indicated, Wrede believed that Jesus did not claim to be Messiah during his life and that all messianic elements were superimposed upon the tradition. But in my opinion there are several incidents whose historicity it is almost impossible to dismiss and whose central significance has definite messianic overtones – a significance which must have been known to and intended by Jesus.

I think first of the feeding of the five thousand. As John O'Neill observes, "we may suppose that some extraordinary event will lie behind such a miraculous narrative ... it remains true that if Jesus did preside at a communal meal in the desert places of Galilee and Judaea, this would have had peculiar significance to his contemporaries. They would perhaps remember that Moses by praying to God was able to feed the people with manna and quail in the desert; they would perhaps be reminded of the promise that the desert would again be fruitful; and they would think of the shepherd King as they were given food in the barren places (cf. *Pss. Sol.* xvii. 45). The Qumran desert community placed great emphasis on communal meals, and looked forward to the time when the Messiah of Aaron would preside and the Messiah of Israel, whom God had begotten among them, would come (IQSa ii. 11–22)."[2]

Even more to the point is the evidence of John 6:15 that the crowd intended to "come and seize Jesus to proclaim him king". C. H. Dodd argues, convincingly I think, for the historicity of John 6:14f. Most noticeable is the otherwise very odd use of *ēnangkasen* in Mark 6:45 – Jesus had to force the disciples to put out into a difficult sea. The two independent traditions interlock and together provide a very coherent picture. The crowd see the messianic significance of Jesus' action and are so carried away on a wave of mass enthusiasm that they attempt to make him king by acclamation. The disciples themselves are caught up in the excitement, and Jesus in order to forestall the move has first to force the disciples to embark by themselves on an uninviting lake. Only then is he able to turn to the crowd and with the voice of authority to dismiss them (*apoluein*). He then goes off immediately by himself into the hills to pray – and it is perhaps significant that Mark only mentions Jesus praying three times, and that on each of the other occasions the implication is that he resorted to prayer because of temptation – temptation at the time of his early success to remain where he was so popular (1:35, 38); temptation in Gethsemane (14:35f). So in 6:46 there is the implication that Jesus was tempted to give way to the crowd's demands – to be the Messiah of popular conception and popular appeal, and that he fled to the silence and loneliness of the hills that quiet communion with his Father might strengthen his conviction concerning the nature of his mission and messiahship. Whether Mark was aware of the messianic significance of the story he recorded it is hard to say; but I would strongly maintain that that significance is inherent in the historical incident he records.

I think secondly of Peter's confession in Mark 8:27ff, a passage which caused Wrede not a little difficulty. Points in favour of the substantial authenticity of the pericope are: the specification and location of the place of confession (none of the traditional resurrection appearances to the twelve took place so far north), the unique appearance of the title *Christos* addressed to Jesus by a disciple, the evidence that Jesus was *Pneumatiker*, and the total improbability of the primitive Church calling Peter "Satan". Nor should we ignore the otherwise surprising insertion *kai idōn tous mathētas autou* in v. 33a, which has the ring of an authentic reminiscence, and the Jewish character of v. 33. Grundmann also calls attention to the thrice repeated *epitimān* and to the *ērxato didaskein* which is not the normal Marcan semitism but indicates a particular point of time at which for the first time the repeated teaching referred to by the *didaskein* received a concrete content.[3]

As for the passage as a whole, and without being able to go into detail, I may say that I am not convinced by the arguments which attribute the connection between 8:27–30 and 8:31ff solely to Marcan theology. It is unquestionable in my opinion that Jesus saw (or at least came to see) his mission in terms of suffering, and entirely probable that he should begin to explain this to his most intimate followers at some stage in his ministry. Nor do I feel it necessary to attribute v. 30 – the command to silence – to the hand of an interpolator. For it is not the Christ of Easter whom Peter confesses, or else why is he rebuked? And if it is the Christ of Jewish hope and popular expectation whom Peter hails – as the rebuke requires – a pre-Easter origin cannot so readily be denied to the confession. Here again then is an account whose historical substance is of irreducible messianic significance.

The third incident in which I believe historicity and messianic significance go together is the entry into Jerusalem. On the score of historicity Vincent Taylor points to "the local expressions at the beginning, the vivid character of the account ... the description of what happened, the restrained nature of the acclamation, and the strange manner in which the account breaks off without any suggestion of a 'triumphal entry' (as in Matt.)".[4] One might also note that the actions and shouts of those with Jesus create an impression of authenticity, because though they conform in a general way to Zech. 9:9 they include details which are neither necessary nor even particularly appropriate – a fact which makes it unlikely that the narrative is a construction of the primitive Church. Specially worthy of comment is the appearance of *hōsanna*, which is firmly embedded in the synoptic tradition, and also in John's account, but which appears nowhere else in the NT – a strong indication of authenticity. I therefore find Taylor's conclusion wholly justified: "These characteristics suggest the eyewitness rather than the artist."[5]

As for messianic significance, we may note in the words of D. E. Nineham, "It is difficult to see why Jesus sent for the colt

and entered the city on it unless he intended to make clear the fact of his Messiahship. Pilgrims normally entered Jerusalem on foot, so, as the story stands, the fact that Jesus deliberately procured and rode an ass makes it impossible to think of him as simply a passive figure in a demonstration which was none of his doing."[6]

The messianic associations of the Mount of Olives should also not go unobserved. The fact is that there is no effort on the part of Jesus to keep his messiahship secret – certainly not in Mark's narrative, for Mark's narrative, and, I would add, the historical event, can only be construed as a clear assertion of a kind of messiahship.

The fourth incident I want to fasten on to is the trial and condemnation of Jesus. That Jesus was found guilty of claiming to be King of the Jews is the testimony of all four Gospels (Mark 15:26; Matt. 27:37; Luke 23:38; John 19:19). The frequent repetition of the title in Mark 15 – vv. 2, 9, 12, 26, 32 – is particularly noticeable. Since it was not a title employed by the early Church there can be little doubt, Bultmann notwithstanding, that we are on sure historical ground here: Jesus was crucified as a messianic pretender, because of the political connotations of the title King of the Jews. But this implies that there was some basis to the charge and the condemnation – that there were substantial grounds for applying it to Jesus – that, indeed, the title was in some sense accepted by him. The historicity of the trial scene in 15:2ff inevitably reflects favourably on the authenticity of the earlier hearing described in 14:55ff, since it can be fairly argued that the question of Pilate (15:2) is simply the Graeco–Roman version of the question of the high priest (14:61) – the blasphemy charge suitably nuanced for a Roman court.

Turning to that earlier hearing, the presumption is strong that Jesus did actually speak the words about building the Temple, in some form at least. Although Lohmeyer is probably correct in classifying *cheiropoiēton* and *acheiropoiēton* as a Marcan or community explanatory addition,[7] nevertheless the fact cannot be ignored that six NT passages testify to the saying (Mark 14:58; 15:29; Matt. 26:61; 27:40; John 2:19; Acts 6:14); and if the saying sometimes seems obscure that speaks rather in favour of than against its authenticity. Incidentally, the saying also attests to the power which was ascribed to Jesus – *katalusō*. It is not without relevance to the question we are studying that such power could be ascribed to Jesus by way of accusation – and it certainly testifies to some claim, by word or action, to messianic activity and power. As attributed to Jesus by the witnesses it can only be intended and understood messianically. The probability is high that it provided the basis of the prosecution's attack on Jesus, and Otto Betz in particular has shown how naturally an examination at that point leads on to the direct question of the high priest: "Are you the Messiah, the Son of the Blessed?"[8] – for the building of the Temple belonged to the messianic age (1 Enoch 90:29; 4 Ezra 9:38—10:27; cf. Ezek. 40—48; Jub. 1:17, 27f) and the saying involves a claim to fulfil the prophecy of Nathan (2 Sam. 7:12–14) and so to be Messiah, Son of David, and Son of God.

If we can find no adequate reason to dispute the authenticity of the course of questioning, what are we to make of Jesus' reply to the high priest's question? It is here that Wrede's thesis breaks down completely. For however affirmative or evasive were his opening words – and we shall return to this point shortly – there is no doubt that the high priest understood the reply as a messianic claim: the high priest's tearing of his clothes was hardly prompted by the *silence* of Jesus. In the words of Montefiore, "We must surely believe that the Messiahship was at least ventilated, and that it was resolved that Jesus was to be denounced to Pilate on that ground."[9]

II

Wrede's thesis that the messianic secret motif had a theological rather than a historical origin was based on his conclusion that certain elements of that motif were clearly *unhistorical*. We are now in a position to stand Wrede's line of reasoning on its head, for our conclusion thus far is that certain elements of that motif are clearly *historical*; that is, that the messianic character of the tradition is not the reflection of post-resurrection Christian theology – it belongs to the incidents themselves. On the basis of *that* conclusion we can now present the thesis that contrary to Wrede the so-called "messianic secret" motif had a historical rather than theological origin. To argue this thesis in depth is beyond the scope of this paper, but the four incidents already examined almost constitute proof enough.

First the feeding of the five thousand. The important points which emerge here are first: that there was abroad, in Galilee at least, a popular conception of the Messiah as a political kingly figure – the sort of King of the Jews that Pilate felt justified in crucifying; that Jesus was a Messiah of this type was the conclusion reached by those whom Jesus miraculously fed in the desert. The second important point is the evidence of how Jesus reacted against this attempt to force a false messianic role on him. He saw all too clearly how politically inflammable the Galilean crowd was. The lesson learned, or confirmed, by this effect of his display of authority would go a long way towards explaining his reticence in other situations.

With regard to Peter's confession, the interesting thing is again Jesus' reaction. Peter hails him as Messiah; and how does Jesus respond? There is certainly no question of his denying the title – but there is also no indication of his accepting it beyond the impersonal *peri autou* of 8:30. 8:30 is a word neither of rebuke nor of congratulation. It is a command to silence followed immediately by explicit and very pointed teaching about the nature of his messiahship. The implication is strong that Peter was little further forward than the Galilean crowd in his understanding of Jesus' messiahship. The command to silence is given not so much because Jesus' messiahship is secret, but because it is misunderstood.

In the entry into Jerusalem three points call for attention. The first is that Mark carefully avoids making the messianic character of the event fully explicit. The Zechariah prophecy is not referred to; the ovation seems to come from the disciples rather than the crowd, and the cries of welcome fall short of complete messianic recognition and homage. The second is the manner of Jesus' entry: he comes as the humble king who speaks peace, not as the political King of the Jews. The third is the fact that the authorities did not immediately pull Jesus in and that no reference seems to have been made to the entry at the trial – which suggests that no political significance was seen or could easily be read into the entry. In short, Jesus' entry into Jerusalem was an enacted parable about the nature of his messiahship. Those whose ears were attuned to catch political overtones heard nothing. Those who looked and listened for the coming of the Kingdom saw something of eschatological and messianic significance, but fell short of full understanding.

In the trial of Jesus once again interest centres on Jesus' response to the questions put to him by the high priest and by Pilate. I am much impressed by the arguments in favour of the longer reading in 14:62. What scribe faced by the triumphant and unequivocal *egō eimi* would dilute it to the colourless and equivocal *su eipas hoti egō eimi*? And the longer reading certainly accounts for the texts of Matthew and Luke. In that case Jesus' reply to the high priest is very similar to his reply to Pilate. To both questions – "Are you the Christ?" and "Are you the King of the Jews?" – Jesus answers in effect, "You could put it that way." He accepts the titles, but at the same time makes it clear that he does not attach the same significance to them as do his questioners (cf. John 18:33–7). These exchanges are important in that they exemplify the dilemma which must constantly have confronted Jesus – could he accept or use *simpliciter* titles which meant one thing to himself and something very different to his hearers?

The conclusions I draw from studying these passages are that Jesus believed himself to be Messiah, but that his conception of the messianic role was an unexpected and unpopular one. Because the title Messiah had such different connotations to Jesus and to those who heard him he never used it of himself or unequivocally welcomed its application to him by others; and when his actions or words seemed to encourage the to him false conception of messiahship he tried to prevent it by commands to silence. Nevertheless he did not deny his right to the title, but attempted to re-educate his hearers in the significance of it for him. And the claims he made to messiah-ship and messianic authority were of a parabolic sort whose signifi-cance was there, plain for all to see whose eyes were not blinded and whose ears were not clogged by misconceptions (8:17–21).

These conclusions follow directly from the four passages we examined. But I believe that they hold true for the whole of the Marcan tradition, and to round off the argument I will merely illus-trate the force of this contention by drawing attention to three other motifs which shed light over the whole Gospel. First of all, the motif of authoritative teaching and action. I refer in particular to the section 2:1—3:6. We have four very definite claims made by Jesus to very considerable status and authority – authority to forgive sins (2:10), authority to command and call (*kalesai*) people (2:14, 17), status as bridegroom (2:19 – in the context of OT thought a very pointed and meaningful metaphor) and status and authority as Lord over the sabbath (2:27; 3:4–6). In none of these incidents could it be said that Jesus was explicitly claiming to be Messiah, but in each case there were messianic overtones – overtones which the individual seeking the truth would be able to recognize.

Secondly, there is the parabolic nature of Jesus' teaching to which attention is drawn in chap. 4. I would draw attention again to the *ta panta* in 4:11: "to you has been given the mystery of the Kingdom, but to those outside all things are in parables", or, as Jeremias translates, "all things are obscure". Bearing in mind 4:33f, I take the parallelism of this verse to signify that *all* Jesus' teaching was in the nature of a parable; that is, to those who had ears to hear (4:9) the parable unfolded its meaning; but to those whose ears were dulled to the note of divine authority the parable gave no light.[10] I have no doubt that this double-edged quality of Jesus' teaching was his own choice. Rather than a straightforward statement of certain truths which would register on most of his hearers' understanding but make no impact on their emotions or their will, Jesus deliberately chose to speak in parables so that the truth thus conveyed might have maximum impact, even if only on a few.

Thirdly, I would point to the phrase "Son of man", the self-designation preferred by Jesus, as I believe it to be. Again we enter a much-ploughed field, and I will not attempt to plough a fresh furrow. Suffice it to say that the work of Geza Vermes on the one hand, and of Morna Hooker on the other, serve to underline how fully that phrase exemplifies the parabolic nature of Jesus' messianic claims. Vermes cites several examples of Aramaic usage which seem to support the view that *bar nash(a)* could have been used by Jesus as a circumlocution for "I", and that the phrase could have been understood by his hearers in that sense.[11] Nor can the link between the Marcan Son of Man and the Danielic Son of Man so well forged by Miss Hooker be easily broken.[12] In the words of Matthew Black: "No term was more fitted both to conceal, yet at the same time to reveal to those who had ears to hear, the Son of Man's real identity."[13]

Finally, attention should also be drawn to the parallel noted by Richard Longenecker between the synoptic Jesus on the one hand and the Qumran Teacher of Righteousness and Simeon ben Kosebah on the other. Common features in each case include (1) external acclamation, (2) reticence on the part of the individual to speak of himself in terms used of him by others, and (3) consciousness on that individual's part of the ultimate validity of the titles employed. The basis of this common pattern Longenecker finds not in any "messianic secret" theology, but in the Jewish view that "no man can be defined as a messiah before he has accomplished the task of the anointed". If this is so it certainly enhances the historicity of the synoptic picture.

In short, I believe that to speak of a messianic *secret* is misleading and unjustified. So far as Jesus' messiahship was concerned there was no secret as such, only a cautious disavowal of false views – those of the Galilean wonder-worker and of the warrior or political King of the Jews – and an equally cautious assertion and explication of his own understanding of messiahship – that of service and suffering in this world and of exaltation only after death. As to the reason for this, all the evangelists agree: Jesus was indeed Messiah during his earthly life, but his messiahship was incomplete and inevitably misunderstood during that phase. Only with the cross, resurrection and exaltation would he enter into the fullness of his messianic office, and only then could its true nature be properly understood by men. The so-called secrecy motif in Mark is nothing other than *Mark's* method of bringing home to his readers *the programmatic nature of Jesus' messiahship*.

Wrede's thesis has been subjected to many criticisms in the course of its life, and the recent attempts to defend and define its *raison d'être* must be pronounced inadequate. Since the "messianic secret" motif is part and parcel of the tradition itself we are at the end of the day more or less shut up to the choice between the mere "that"-ness of complete Bultmannian scepticism and a Jesus who was a secret or rather a misunderstood Messiah.

I do not want to overstate my case. I would not deny, for example, that Mark may have interpreted simple commands to silence demons in terms of the "messianic secret" motif (1:34; 3:11f) or that it is Mark's own opinion about the disciples which is being expressed in passages like 6:51–2; 14:40b. But the question is whether this interpretation and opinion expresses an understanding of the material which is essentially foreign to it, or whether it is merely developing a theme which is already native to the material. When one takes into account the complexity of the secrecy motif (which reflects the complexity of life) the counterbalancing publicity–revelation theme, the inherent messianic character of the pericope we examined, and the very strong probability which emerged from that examination that there were two understandings of messiahship at issue, I cannot but conclude that the so-called "messianic secret" originated in the life-situation of Jesus and is in essence at least wholly historical.

NOTES

1 E. Schweizer, p. 66 here.
2 J. C. O'Neill, "The Silence of Jesus", *NTS* 15 (1968–9) 163f.
3 Grundmann, 1973, 167.
4 Taylor, 1952, 452.
5 Taylor, 1952, 452.
6 Nineham, 1963, 292.
7 Lohmeyer, 1963, 326.
8 O. Betz, "Die Frage nach dem messianischen Bewusstsein Jesu", *NovT* 6 (1963) 24–37.
9 C. G. Montefiore, *The Synoptic Gospels* [2] (London: Macmillan, 1927), i, 357.
10 The saying has to be read together with those of vv. 21–2, as the repetition of

the challenge to hear aright makes clear (4:9, 23). Jesus came to give light, and his teaching shed light enough; nevertheless that light was hidden for many, and would remain so for the time being, till either the resurrection or the parousia.

11 G. Vermes in an appendix to M. Black, *An Aramaic Approach to the Gospels and Acts* (Oxford: Clarendon Press, 1967) 310–28; although see J. A. Fitzmyer's critical review in *CBQ* 30 (1968) 424–8.

12 M. Hooker, *The Son of Man in Mark* (London: SPCK, 1967).

13 Black, 329; see also I. H. Marshall, "The Synoptic Son of Man Sayings in Recent Discussion", *NTS* 12 (1965–6) 350f; cf. Sjöberg, 1955, 126; O'Neill, 161.

9

The "Messianic Secret" in Mark's Gospel*

HEIKKI RÄISÄNEN

1 The question of the unity of the secrecy theology

Wrede's study brought to prominence the basic question of whether the theological viewpoint of Mark's Gospel is based on a *single* secrecy theology. After the analysis undertaken here, the answer must be in the *negative*. Indeed it is not enough to separate from the secrecy theology the "contradictions" which were also identified by Wrede.[1] It has transpired that even the material assembled by Wrede does *not* present the homogeneous unity that he and most exegetes have thought.

(*a*) Of the motifs which were closely linked by Wrede, only *the commands to silence addressed to the demons and those addressed to the disciples* belong closely together. One may say that these two motifs constitute the *real* "messianic secret". The secret concerns Jesus' nature, or identity: the fact that he is the "Son of God" or the "Christ" must be kept secret. These commands to silence are not disobeyed.

(*b*) The motif of the *secret healings* should be distinguished from the real messianic secret. Jesus often (but not always) forbids those who have been healed to make known what has happened. These commands are often disobeyed. In this context, the stress lies on the fact that Jesus' miraculous deeds cannot remain hidden. This aspect within Mark's Gospel was correctly stressed by Ebeling. His mistake was to generalize this aspect, and to believe that the whole secrecy theme could be explained by it. Ulrich Luz deserves credit for having separated the miracle secret from the messianic secret in showing that, on the whole, Ebeling's interpretation explains the

* First published in *Das "Messiasgeheimnis" im Markusevangelium* by H. Räisänen (1976) 159–68. Translated by C. M. Tuckett.

former quite easily. However, the healing-, or miracle-secret does not constitute a completely unified whole. Ebeling's (and Luz's) interpretation does not fit those commands which are obeyed (5:43; 8:26). It is here that another motif (which also appears elsewhere in Mark) comes into play: Jesus seeks to avoid those interruptions which bring with them all too much publicity. (It is quite clear that this motif is somewhat discordant with what has just been said.)

(*c*) The *parable theory* should be clearly separated from the messianic secret. 4:11f remains an alien element in Mark. The idea found in these verses is not repeated elsewhere. Behind it there probably lies the experience of the negative attitude of the Jews to the gospel message. The parable theory has constituted the firmest basis for the apologetic interpretation of the messianic secret (Dibelius, Burkill). But when it is separated from the real messianic secret, then that interpretation loses much of its support.

(*d*) The motif of the *disciples' lack of understanding* clearly has a point of contact with the messianic secret in that the lack of understanding concerns first of all the identity of Jesus. But apart from this it is difficult to link the two themes very closely together. The motif of lack of understanding does not require that of the messianic secret: it can make do very well without it, as can be seen from the Fourth Gospel. The theme of the disciples' lack of understanding in Mark seems to be tied up with a contemporary, paraenetic concern, and there is scarcely any trace of this in other passages connected with the secrecy motif.

(*e*) When the secrecy concept is in this way broken down into parts which are only relatively loosely connected with each other, it becomes less surprising that the secrecy theme is completely absent from some stories. Many parts of the Gospel, e.g. the second chapter, are dominated much more by the motif of *publicity*. Cadbury and Morton Smith were clearly on the right track when they remarked that Mark's Gospel reflects the variety of the oral tradition.[2] Different motifs intersect in Mark's Gospel; individual stories, and perhaps even whole collections (2:1ff!), each have their own aims. Yet the tension between different motifs does not arise solely from the diversity of the traditions. Even within the evangelist's redactional activity there are contradictory tendencies. (E.g. the mystery of Jesus is not hidden from his opponents.)

2 *The question of the relationship between tradition and redaction*
The real messianic secret (in the narrow sense defined above) *is a redactional construction of the evangelist*. The commands to silence

addressed to the demons (1:34; 3:12) as well as the command to the disciples at Caesarea Philippi (8:30) go back to Mark. However, in building up this construction, Mark was able to take up seeds which were already present in the tradition.[3] In the case of the command to silence on the descent from the mountain of the transfiguration (9:9), only three disciples are given a command, and this is for a fixed time and only concerns one special case; in all probability this should be taken as part of the tradition. In 8:30 Mark appears to have *generalized* this command: all the disciples are now bound to secrecy; the secret concerns Jesus' nature and identity as a whole; also, any time limit disappears. The commands to the demons are equally general and without limit. Here too Mark's tradition gave him a starting-point (1:25) in that it related how, in the case of a demon who had addressed Jesus as the "holy one of God", Jesus had spoken sternly and silenced it. Of course, in the tradition, this kind of action did not involve any secrecy about Jesus' identity: rather, it formed part of the exorcism. But Mark interpreted the story with his own point of view in mind, as 1:32–4 and 3:11f show.

Over and above this, other traditional statements, which in various ways placed a veil of mystery about Jesus, were fed into the Marcan view of the secret. The tradition knew how Jesus sometimes withdrew into solitude, how he healed some people in private or in the presence of only a chosen few, etc. The idea of the "miracle secret" (the command not to make the healing known in 8:26, perhaps also 5:43) appears to have been already present in the tradition. All that could have influenced the real Marcan messianic secret. However, the latter clearly presents a reinterpretation of the tradition. On the other hand, Mark developed the idea of the miracle secret in a different direction from that of the messianic secret, so that the stress now lies on the disobeying of the command and the ensuing publicity (7:36). This motif too was at his disposal in the tradition (1:45, cf. Matt. 9:30f).[4]

The tradition also knew of the disciples' lack of understanding and of their improper behaviour on many occasions. Mark brought this idea sharply into focus. The parable theory also stems from the tradition, but Mark did not develop it further. Neither of these two motifs has any direct significance for the real messianic secret.

3 *The question of the interpretation of the real messianic secret*
What has been said above is an attempt to determine *what* Mark has done: *how* he used and interpreted the tradition, and what new features he introduced into the total picture. But now as ever the question remains unanswered as to *why* Mark proceeded in this way.

Why did Mark develop his own special construction of the (real) messianic secret out of various traditional elements?

This question seems to lead to some frustration. For all that Mark's book has been thoroughly examined during the last decade, the statement with which U. Luz started his article ten years ago still seems to be valid: "The messianic secret is still a mystery."[5] Whoever claims to know precisely what Mark was aiming at with his secrecy theory is probably over-reaching himself. Mark gives no direct indication, and the only remaining method, i.e. reading between the lines, carries with it considerable possibilities for error. One can thus do little more here than give a final review of the most important interpretations of the secret in the light of the analysis undertaken above.

(a) *Wrede's* interpretation. With regard to Wrede's four basic tenets we can say this. First, the motifs linked by Wrede cannot be explained as an unbroken whole (against Wrede). From this it follows, secondly, that the key offered by Wrede (9:9) cannot open all the doors. There is still the question of whether this verse might nevertheless provide the solution to the problem of the real messianic secret. But this is difficult to maintain since 9:9 probably stems from the tradition. Whether this verse can then be used as the basis for the interpretation of *Mark's* redactional construction is at least questionable, the more so since 15:39, which rather contradicts it, *might* be Marcan. I shall have to return to this question in discussing the "history of revelation" interpretation.

According to Wrede, the messianic secret was not an idea which was first created by Mark; this was his third tenet. This view has not been supported by our analysis. The real messianic secret is to be ascribed to the evangelist. Consequently, Wrede's fourth tenet, i.e. his view about the origin of the secrecy idea, is also untenable.[6] Thus all Wrede's basic tenets have been shown to need correction. This does not of course alter the fact that the impetus given by Wrede has been, and still is, of decisive importance for the interpretation of Mark.

(b) The *apologetic* interpretation. The breaking up of the secrecy complex into separate parts seems at first sight to remove some of the difficulties associated with this theory. The publicizing of some miracles is not a decisive objection to this theory if the miracle secret is to be separated from the real messianic secret. Further, the apologetic theory no longer completely comes to grief on the fact that the disciples' failure to understand originates in their obduracy, if the lack of understanding motif is no longer intrinsically linked with the real messianic secret. But there are still problems for this interpretation, since the parable theory must also be excluded from the context of the messianic secret. Certainly the parable theory concerns the problem of the Jews, but the messianic secret is not to be interpreted in relation to this. That does not mean that the apologetic theory is absolutely impossible. It is simply that it has lost its most important positive basis. A further weakness is the fact that, according to this interpretation, the messianic secret remains a "subsidiary concept", which the evangelist uses to reply to specific objections from outsiders. It is somewhat difficult to believe that the secrecy theory does not have a positive significance of its own.

(c) The *epiphany* interpretation. The merits of Ebeling's interpretation have been noted in this chapter too. Practically the whole of the miracle secret can be explained in this way without difficulty. On the other hand, this interpretation cannot explain the real messianic secret, unless the commands to silence addressed to the demons and the disciples are interpreted away as purely literary and symbolic references to the reader.

(d) The "*theology of the cross*" interpretation. The breaking up of the secrecy complex removes some obstacles in the way of this interpretation too. There is no longer any need to try to interpret the miracle secret in the light of the theology of the cross in an artificial way. Also 9:9 (where the resurrection, rather than the cross, marks the central point) need not be a stumbling-block if the verse is traditional and does not represent Mark's view completely. It is also undisputed that the theology of the cross does justice to a central feature in Mark's theology.

But it is another matter how the theology of suffering in Mark is connected with the secrecy idea in particular. Even the removal of all the commands to silence from the Gospel would hardly detract significantly from Mark's theology of the cross! Also, the "theology of the cross" interpretation assumes that the commands to silence are to be understood primarily as symbolic references for the reader. Added to this, finally, is the fact that in 3:12 it is the majesty of Jesus which is hidden.

Accordingly, the secrecy idea cannot be seen as correcting a *theios anēr* Christology. That is not the meaning of Mark's cross-centred theology when this is separated from the messianic secret either. Mark's Jesus is a *theios anēr* even at his death.[7] In speaking of his suffering, Jesus' sovereign knowledge about the future is brought clearly into prominence. A theology of suffering and a *theios anēr*

Christology are in no way mutually exclusive for Mark. Their mutual exclusion is due to modern wishful thinking.

(*e*) The *"history of revelation"* interpretation. Again the breaking up of the secrecy motif removes some difficulties. If the miracle secret is a separate motif, then the publicizing of the miracles before Easter is no longer fatal to the theory. The difficulty of the fact that the disciples' total lack of understanding ends long before Easter is perhaps also not too serious, if the lack of understanding motif cannot be linked very closely with the messianic secret. Certain problems arise, however, from the fact that 9:9 constitutes the corner-stone of this theory, an inheritance from Wrede. Here the resurrec-tion is explicitly mentioned as the moment when the secret ends. As was stressed earlier, however, this verse mentions only one individual case and therefore seems to be traditional. On the other hand, one could claim that precisely this saying seems to have pro-vided a starting-point for the redactional secrecy theology; did it perhaps even give rise to the theory? Has Mark then silently general-ized the time limit of 9:9 (the resurrection), so that in his view it applies to the whole of the real messianic secret?

15:39 presents difficulties for this hypothesis. It is a verse which may have been added by Mark. In the light of this saying, it seems that one can only advocate the periodization of history which this interpretation presupposes in a modified way, i.e. so that the resur-rection is not particularly stressed. If Mark has indeed generalized the *terminus ad quem* implied in 9:9, then he has also made it less precise and blurred the line between crucifixion and resurrection. The death and resurrection of Jesus would then *together* constitute the decisive watershed between hiddenness and openness.

It must be conceded that it is difficult to find any really positive point of support for the "history of revelation" interpretation (unless it be 15:39) – that is, after 9:9 is questioned as evidence for Mark's redaction. Nevertheless, it seems to me that *the "history of revelation" interpretation in modified form is least beset with difficulties* as an explanation of the messianic secret. But note that this is as an explanation of the *real* messianic secret (and not of the whole complex which Wrede suggested, as Percy and Strecker suppose).

It seems to have been an important idea for Mark that something fundamental about Jesus was evident only *after* his earthly activity. A real christological confession is only possible in the new situation created by Jesus' death and resurrection – in the situation where Jesus acts as the exalted Lord.[8] In the new circumstances one understands things which were previously beyond one's grasp. Things which were hidden from of old have now been revealed to the saints. These include, above all, Christ, the mystery of God "in whom all the treasures of wisdom and knowledge lie hidden" (Col. 2:2f).[9] We may speculate a little further. Against this background, the fact that the tradition about Jesus contained christological sayings, even in the form of open confessions of faith during Jesus' lifetime, must have been a difficulty for the evangelist. One could not eliminate them. But Mark stressed that the situation was exceptional. The closest companions of Jesus were in a special position. By God's grace they learnt the fundamental truth before it was possible for others. For these others, things *had* to remain hidden. That is how Jesus must have intended it. But he had also (as Mark knew from the tradition) forbidden the transfiguration to be made known. It was similar with the demons who, as spiritual beings, were capable of knowing more than human beings.

Mark therefore intervened in his traditions whenever the community's christological confession was about to be heard "prematurely". He wanted to make clear that this confession was really only possible in the new period of salvation history. Of course the reader could have expected much more consistency from him. Mark seems to have intervened only where Jesus was acclaimed Son of God or something similar in the form of a quite direct "You are" or "I know you". No explanation of the secrecy motif can remove the tension which exists in the Gospel between secrecy and openness. The reader inevitably gets the impression from Mark's work that Jesus in no way kept his identity hidden in every situation, and that some outsiders like Bartimaeus could be clear about it. Mark might have been able to resolve part of this inconsistency by being more skilful in his redactional technique. However, openness plays so great a role in his material that it would not have been possible to remove it completely. The contradictions in the motif thus stem on the one hand from mutually contradictory traditions, but on the other hand from the unsystematic nature of Mark's redactional work. Mark can of his own accord stress the idea of openness redactionally where this fits his own (perhaps polemical) aims. The way the disciples appear in many, somewhat diverse, roles would also be comparable with this phenomenon.[10]

4   Even this modified "history of revelation" interpretation of the commands to silence to the demons and the disciples is not completely satisfactory. It does not matter to me very much whether it is accepted or not. The conclusions about the nature of Mark's

redaction overall, to which the analysis of the secrecy problem has given rise, appear to me far more important. Classic form criticism saw in Mark a bearer and collector of traditions with a few ideas of his own. Modern redaction criticism has made him into an important, original and independent theological thinker. In my view the new picture urgently needs correcting. If the analysis presented in this book is on the right lines, then the pendulum will have to swing back to the older position – perhaps to stop half way. Certainly Mark has his own theological ideas; certainly he presents some new nuances of his own. But a complete, unified picture of his theology which is in any way satisfactory can scarcely be attained without forcing the evidence. One must therefore be content to see the earliest evangelist as more of a bearer of tradition, and less of a theologian or interpreter, than recent research has generally assumed him to be.

NOTES

(Some extra notes have been added to clarify some of the cross-references made by Räisänen to earlier parts of his book. These have been enclosed in square brackets.)

1 [Cf. Räisänen, 1976, 143ff. See also Wrede, 1971, 124ff, and the introduction in this volume, p. 5 above.]

2 [Räisänen earlier (48) cited the remarks of H. J. Cadbury, "Mixed Motives in the Gospels", *Proceedings of the American Philosophical Society* 95 (1951) 119f: "If he [Mark] had any purpose of his own it is either parallel to that of his material or not distinctive enough to be conspicuous amid the medley of motifs and motives in his material ... The material marshalled for the theory [the messianic secret] seems to me to represent several quite different motives instead of a single one." Also M. Smith, "Comments on Taylor's Commentary on Mark", *HTR* 48 (1955), 21–64, on p. 29: "Actually, the early Church had a wide variety of motives for attributing secret doctrine to Jesus ... Every such attribution, therefore, must be judged individually."]

3 This is the answer to Wrede's question of how Mark could have introduced a new secrecy idea into his book [cf. Wrede, 1971, 145]. The idea was only *partly* new.

4 [Räisänen earlier (66ff) argued that Matt. 9:30f may represent an independent tradition, rather than being a Matthean redactional construction, as is usually assumed: despite the Matthean language and style, the presence of the secrecy motif seems somewhat alien to Matthew's own redactional interests (e.g. his stress on the value of faith).]

5 Luz, p. 75 in this volume.

6 Wrede's critics are right in saying that the tradition gives no trace of an "unmessianic" view of the earthly life of Jesus. [Räisänen also refers here to

an earlier point in his book (33 n. 1) where he endorses Strecker's argument against Wrede's theory on this point (see p. 54 in this volume).]

7   [Earlier (157) Räisänen argued this on the grounds that the centurion's confession may be a response to the miracles occurring at the time of Jesus' death (e.g. the darkness).]

8   See Strecker (p. 62 in this volume); the messianic secret "is an essential expression of a theology of salvation history. Its goal is the time after the resurrection; it implies the christological recognition that the story of the earthly Jesus does not remain on its own but points to his enthronement as Lord." On the other hand, Percy, 1953, 294f, places too much stress on the alleged similarity between Mark's viewpoint and Paul's theology, whereby the period prior to the resurrection would be also for Mark "only a period of humility and therefore also of secrecy". This is not the case; openness plays all too great a role in Mark's Gospel. No doubt the earthly life of Jesus only constitutes the prelude to the real "gospel" of the heavenly Lord – but the tone is still the same.

9   Strecker (pp. 62f in this volume) correctly stresses the ecclesiological background of the secrecy theology. Mark's community possesses "remarkable self-awareness".

10 [Räisänen earlier argued that the disciples have various positive roles in Mark, e.g. as mediators of the tradition (cf. 9:28f; 13:3ff) (56), as examples for discipleship (1:16–20) or as representatives of later Christian missionaries (6:7ff) (136).]

Bibliography

Ambrozic, A. M. *The Hidden Kingdom. A Redaction–Critical Study of the References to the Kingdom of God in Mark's Gospel.* Washington, D.C.: Catholic Biblical Association, 1972.

Aune, D. E. "The Problem of the Messianic Secret", *NovT* 11 (1969) 1–31.

Barbour, R. S. "Recent Study of the Gospel according to St Mark", *ExpT* 79 (1968) 324–9.

Best, E. "The Role of the Disciples in Mark", *NTS* 23 (1977) 377–401.

Betz, H. D. "Jesus as Divine Man", in F. T. Trotter (ed.), *Jesus and the Historian* (Festschrift for E. C. Colwell. Philadelphia: Westminster, 1968) 114–33.

Bickermann, E. "Das Messiasgeheimnis und die Komposition des Markusevangeliums", *ZNW* 22 (1923) 122–40.

Blevins, J. L. *The Messianic Secret in Markan Research 1901–1964.* Ph.D. thesis, Southern Baptist Theological Seminary, 1965.

Boobyer, G. H. "The Secrecy Motif in St Mark's Gospel", *NTS* 6 (1960) 225–35.

Bousset, W. *Jesus.* ET London: Williams & Norgate; New York: Putnam's, 1906 (German 1904).

—*Kyrios Christos.* ET of 2nd 1921 edn. New York: Abingdon, 1970.

Brown, S. "The Secret of the Kingdom of God (Mark 4:11)", *JBL* 92 (1973) 60–74.

Bultmann, R. "Die Frage nach dem messianischen Bewusstsein Jesu und das Petrus-Bekenntnis", *ZNW* 19 (1919/20) 165–74 (= *Exegetica* [Tübingen: Mohr, 1967] 1–9).

—*The Theology of the New Testament I.* ET New York: Charles Schribner's Sons, 1951; London: SCM, 1952 (German 1949).

—*The History of the Synoptic Tradition.* ET of 2nd 1931 edn and 1958 supp. Oxford: Blackwell; New York: Harper & Row, 1963, rev. 1968. (First German edn, 1921).

—"The New Approach to the Synoptic Problem", *Existence and Faith* (London: Collins, 1964) 39–62.

Burkill, T. A. "The Hidden Son of Man in St. Mark's Gospel", *ZNW* 52 (1961) 189–213.

—*Mysterious Revelation.* Ithaca, New York: Cornell University, 1963. (See pp. 44–8 in this volume.)

Clark, J. L. *A Re-examination of the Problem of the Messianic Secret in its Relationship to the Synoptic Son of Man Sayings.* Ph.D. thesis, Yale University, 1962.

Conzelmann, H. "Present and Future in the Synoptic Tradition", *Journal for Theology and the Church* 5 (1968) 26–44 (German in *ZTK* 54 (1957) 277–96).

—*An Outline of the Theology of the New Testament.* ET London: SCM; New York: Harper & Row, 1969 (German 1968).

—"History and Theology in the Passion Narratives of the Synoptic Gospels", *Int* 24 (1970) 178–97.

Dahl, N. A. "The Purpose of Mark's Gospel", *Jesus in the Memory of the Early Church* (Minneapolis: Augsburg, 1976) 52–65 (Swedish 1958). (See pp. 29–34 in this volume.)

Dibelius, M. *From Tradition to Gospel.* ET New York: Charles Scribner's Sons; London: Ivor Nicholson & Watson, 1934 (First German edn, 1919).

Dunn, J. D. G. "The Messianic Secret in Mark", *Tyndale Bulletin* 21 (1970) 92–117. (See pp. 116–31 in this volume).

Ebeling, H. J. *Das Messiasgeheimnis und die Botschaft des Marcus-Evangelisten.* Berlin: A. Töpelmann, 1939.

Focant, C. "L'incompréhension des disciples dans le deuxième évangile", *RB* 83 (1975) 161–85.

Fuller, R. H. *The New Testament in Current Study.* London: SCM; New York: Charles Scribner's Sons, 1963.

—*The Foundations of New Testament Christology.* London: Lutterworth; New York: Charles Scribner's Sons, 1965.

Glasswell, M. E. *The Concealed Messiahship in the Synoptic Gospels and the Significance of this for the Study of the Life of Jesus and of the Early Church.* Ph.D. thesis, Durham University, 1965.

—"The Use of Miracles in the Markan Gospel", in C. F. D. Moule (ed.), *Miracles* (London: Mowbrays, 1965) 151–62.

—"St Mark's Attitude to the Relationship between History and the Gospel", in E. A. Livingstone (ed.), *Studia Biblica (1978) II* (Sheffield; *JSOT*, 1980) 115–27.

Grant, F. C. *The Earliest Gospel.* New York: Abingdon, 1943.

Grundmann, W. *Das Evangelium nach Markus.* Berlin: Evangelische Verlagsanstalt, ⁶1973.

Haenchen, E. *Der Weg Jesu.* Berlin: De Gruyter, ²1968.

Hawkin, D. J. "The Incomprehension of the Disciples in the Markan Redaction", *JBL* 91 (1972) 491–500.

Hay, L. S. "Mark's Use of the Messianic Secret", *Journal of the American Academy of Religion* 35 (1967) 16–27.

Horstmann, M. *Studien zur markinischen Christologie.* Münster: Aschendorff, 1969.

Jülicher, A. *Neue Linien in der Kritik der evangelischen Überlieferung.* Giessen: A. Töpelmann, 1906.

Keck, L. E. "The Introduction to Mark's Gospel", *NTS* 12 (1966) 352–70.

Kee, H. C. *Community of the New Age.* London: SCM; Philadelphia: Westminster, 1977.

Kelber, W. H. *The Kingdom in Mark.* Philadelphia: Fortress, 1974.

Kermode, F. *The Sense of an Ending.* New York: Oxford University, 1967.

—*The Genesis of Secrecy*. Cambridge, Mass., and London: Harvard University, 1979.

Kertelge, K. *Die Wunder Jesu im Markusevangelium*. München: Kosel, 1970.

Koch, D. A. *Die Bedeutung der Wundererzählungen für die Christologie des Markusevangeliums*. Berlin: De Gruyter, 1975.

Koester, H. "One Jesus and Four Primitive Gospels", in J. M. Robinson, H. Koester, *Trajectories through Early Christianity* (Philadelphia: Fortress, 1971) 158–204.

Kuby, A. "Zur Konzeption des Marcus-Evangeliums", *ZNW* 49 (1958) 52–64.

Kuhn, H.-W. *Ältere Sammlungen im Markusevangelium*. Göttingen: Vandenhoek & Ruprecht, 1971.

Lambrecht, J. "The Christology of Mark", *Biblical Theology Bulletin* 3 (1973) 256–73.

Lightfoot, R. H. *History and Interpretation in the Gospels*. London: Hodder & Stoughton; New York: Harper & Brothers, 1935.

Lohmeyer, E. *Das Evangelium des Markus*. Göttingen: Vandenhoek & Ruprecht, [16]1963.

Longenecker, R. N. "The Messianic Secret in the Light of Recent Discoveries", *EvQ* 41 (1969) 207–15.

Luz, U. "Das Geheimnismotiv und die markinische Christologie", *ZNW* 56 (1965) 9–30. (See pp. 75–96 in this volume.)

Manson, T. W. "Realised Eschatology and the Messianic Secret", in D. E. Nineham (ed.), *Studies in the Gospels* (Essays in Memory of R. H. Lightfoot. Oxford: Blackwell, 1955), 209–22.

Marxsen, W. *Introduction to the New Testament*. ET Oxford: Blackwell; Philadelphia: Fortress, 1968 (German 1964).

Meye, R. P. "Messianic Secret and Messianic Didache in Mark's Gospel", in F. Christ (ed.), *OIKONOMIA* (Festschrift for O. Cullmann. Hamburg: Herbert Rich, 1967) 57–68.

Moule, C. F. D. "On Defining the Messianic Secret in Mark", in E. E. Ellis and E. Grässer (ed.), *Jesus und Paulus* (Festschrift for W. G. Kümmel. Göttingen: Vandenhoek & Ruprecht, 1975) 239–52.

Minette de Tillesse, G. *Le secret messianique dans L'Evangile de Marc*. Paris: Cerf, 1968.

Nineham, D. E. *Saint Mark*. Harmondsworth & Baltimore: Penguin, 1963.

Peake, A. S. "The Messiah and the Son of Man", *BJRL* 8 (1924) 52–81.

Percy, E. *Die Botschaft Jesu*. Lund: Gleerup, 1953.

Pesch, R. *Das Markusevangelium I & II*. Freiburg: Herder, 1976 and 1977.

Powley, B. G. "The Purpose of the Messianic Secret: A Brief Survey", *ExpTim* 80 (1969) 308–10.

—*The "Messianic Secret" in Mark's Gospel. An Historical Survey*. Ph.D. thesis, Glasgow University, 1979.

—"Vincent Taylor and the Messianic Secret in Mark's Gospel", in E. A. Livingstone (ed.), *Studia Biblica (1978) II* (Sheffield; *JSOT*, 1980) 243–6.

Räisänen, H. *Das "Messiasgeheimnis" im Markusevangelium.* Helsinki: Lansi-Suomi, 1976. (See pp. 132–40 in this volume.)

Rawlinson, A. E. J. *St. Mark.* Westminster Commentary. London: Methuen, 1925.

Robinson, J. M. *A New Quest of the Historical Jesus.* London: SCM, 1959; Missoula: Scholars Press Reprint Series 2, 1979.

—"The Recent Debate on the 'New Quest'", *Journal of Bible and Religion* 30 (1962) 198–208.

—"Gnosticism and the New Testament", in B. Aland (ed.), *Gnosis* (Festschrift for H. Jonas. Göttingen: Vandenhoek & Ruprecht, 1978) 125–43.

Robinson, W. C. "The Quest for Wrede's Secret Messiah", *Int* 27 (1973) 10–30. (See pp. 97–115 in this volume.)

Roloff, J. "Das Markusevangelium als Geschichtsdarstellung", *EvT* 29 (1969) 73–93.

Sanday, W. "The Injunctions to Silence in the Gospels", *JTS* 5 (1904) 321–9.

—*The Life of Christ in Recent Research.* Oxford: Clarendon, 1907.

—"The Apocalyptic Element in the Gospels", *Hibbert Journal* 10 (1911) 83–109.

Schmidt, K. L. *Der Rahmen der Geschichte Jesu.* Berlin: Trowitzsch & Sohn, 1919.

Schniewind, J. "Messiasgeheimnis und Eschatologie", in E. Kähler (ed.), *Nachgelassene Reden und Aufsätze* (Berlin: A. Töpelmann, 1952) 1–13.

—*Das Evangelium nach Markus.* Göttingen: Vandenhoek & Ruprecht, [10]1963.

Schreiber, J. "Die Christologie des Markusevangeliums", *ZTK* 58 (1961) 154–83.

Schweitzer, A. *The Mystery of the Kingdom of God.* ET London: Black, 1925 (German 1901).

—*The Quest of the Historical Jesus.* London: Black, [3]1954, reprinted SCM, 1980; New York: Macmillan, 1961 (First German edn 1906).

Schweizer, E. "Anmerkungen zur Theologie des Markus", *Neotestamentica* (Zurich: Zwingli, 1963) 93–104.

—"Die theologische Leistung des Markus", *EvT* 24 (1964) 337–55.

—"Mark's Contribution to the Quest of the Historical Jesus", *NTS* 10 (1964) 421–32.

—"Zur Messiasgeheimnis bei Markus", *ZNW* 56 (1965) 1–8. (See pp. 65–74 in this volume.)

—*The Good News according to Mark.* Richmond, Va.: John Knox, 1970; London: SPCK, 1971.

—"Neuere Markus-Forschung in USA", *EvT* 33 (1973) 533–7.

—"Towards a Christology of Mark", in J. Jervell and W. A. Meeks (ed.), *God's Christ and His People* (Festschrift for N. A. Dahl. Oslo: Universitetsforlahet, 1977) 29–42.

Sjöberg, E. *Der verborgene Menschensohn in den Evangelien.* Lund: Gleerup, 1955.

Strecker, G. "Zur Messiasgeheimnistheorie im Markusevangelium", *SE* 3 (TU 88. Berlin, 1964) 87–104. (See pp. 49–64 in this volume.)

Tagawa, K. *Miracle et Evangile. La pensée personelle de l'évangeliste Marc.* Paris: Presses Universitaires de France, 1966.

Taylor, V. "The Messianic Secret in Mark", *ExpTim* 59 (1948) 146–51.

—*The Gospel according to St. Mark.* London: Macmillan, 1952.

—"W. Wrede's The Messianic Secret in the Gospels", *ExpTim* 65 (1954) 246–50.

Theissen, G. *Urchristliche Wundergeschichten.* Göttingen: Gerd Mohn, 1974.

Trocmé, E. "Is there a Markan Christology?", in B. Lindars and S. S. Smalley (ed.), *Christ and Spirit in the New Testament* (Festschrift for C. F. D. Moule. Cambridge: Cambridge University, 1973) 3–13.

—*The Formation of the Gospel according to Mark.* London: SPCK; Philadelphia: Westminster, 1975 (French 1963).

Tyson, J. B. "The Blindness of the Disciples in Mark", *JBL* 80 (1961) 261–8. (See pp. 35–43 in this volume.)

Vielhauer, Ph. "Erwägungen zur Christologie des Markusevangeliums", *Aufsätze zum Neuen Testament* (Münich: Kaiser, 1965) 199–214.

Weeden, T. J. *Mark – Traditions in Conflict.* Philadelphia: Fortress, 1971.

Weiss, J. *Das älteste Evangelium.* Göttingen: Vandenhoek & Ruprecht, 1903.

Wernle, P. *The Sources of our Knowledge of the Life of Jesus.* ET London: Green, 1907.

—*Jesus.* Tübingen: Mohr, 1917.

Wrede, W. "Zur Messiaserkenntnis der Dämonen bei Markus", *ZNW* 5 (1904) 169–77.

—*The Messianic Secret.* ET London and Cambridge: James Clarke; Greenwood, S. Carolina: Attic, 1971 (German 1901).

Index of New Testament References